An avid romance reader, ... writing the books that gave h... busy getting married to her .... raising a family. Now a *USA TODAY* bestselling author, she has won several awards—including the Australian Readers' Association most popular category/series romance in 2008, and the prestigious Romance Writers of Australia R*BY award in 2011. She loves to hear from readers!

MelanieMilburne.com.au
Facebook.com/Melanie.Milburne
Twitter: @MelanieMilburn1

Cathy Williams can remember reading Mills & Boon books as a teenager, and now that she is writing them she remains an avid fan. For her, there is nothing like creating romantic stories and engaging plots, and each and every book is a new adventure. Cathy lives in London. Her three daughters—Charlotte, Olivia and Emma—have always been, and continue to be, the greatest inspirations in her life.

Clare Connelly was raised in small-town Australia amongst a family of avid readers. She spent much of her childhood up a tree, Mills & Boon book in hand. Clare is married to her own real-life hero, and they live in a bungalow near the sea with their two children. She is frequently to be found staring into space—a sure-fire sign that she is in the world of her characters. She has a penchant for French food and ice-cold champagne, and Mills & Boon continue to be her favourite ever books. Writing for Modern Romance is a long-held dream. Clare can be contacted via clareconnelly.com or through her Facebook page.

The Rumours
COLLECTION

July 2019

August 2019

September 2019

October 2019

November 2019

December 2019

Rumours: The Legacy of Revenge

MELANIE MILBURNE

CATHY WILLIAMS

CLARE CONNELLY

MILLS & BOON

First Published in Great Britain 2019
By Mills & Boon, an imprint of HarperCollins *Publishers*
1 London Bridge Street, London, SE1 9GF

RUMOURS: THE LEGACY OF REVENGE
© 2019 Harlequin Books S.A.

The Most Scandalous Ravensdale © Melanie Milburne 2016
Legacy of His Revenge © Cathy Williams 2017
Bought for the Billionaire's Revenge © Clare Connelly 2017

ISBN: 978-0-263-27667-1

0819

MIX
Paper from
responsible sources
FSC C007454

This book is produced from independently certified FSC™ paper to ensure responsible forest management.

For more information visit: www.harpercollins.co.uk/green

Printed and bound in Spain
by CPI, Barcelona

THE MOST SCANDALOUS RAVENSDALE

MELANIE MILBURNE

To the *First Sisters of Oz* Immersion Class
held in Melbourne 2015 – Dorothy Adamek,
Natasha Daraio, Wendy Leslie, Nas Dean and
Kristin Meacham and of course, the amazing
Margie Lawson who taught us all so much.
It was such a privilege to spend a week
with such talented writers. xxxxxx

CHAPTER ONE

'I AM *NOT* serving that man on table nine,' Kat Winwood said to her co-worker Meg on her way through to the café kitchen. Aspiring actor she might be, but being polite to that Savile Row–suited, silver-tongued smart ass was way outside Kat's repertoire. She couldn't afford to lose *this* job—not unless she got the dream part in the London stage play. The role that would launch her career so she would never have to wait on another table or do another crappy—no pun intended—toilet-paper advertisement.

Meg glanced at the man before looking back at Kat. 'Isn't that Flynn Carlyon? The hotshot celebrity lawyer to those famous theatre actors Richard and Elisabetta Ravensdale?'

'Yes.' Kat gritted her teeth and unloaded the tray, stabbing the knives into the dishwasher basket as if it were Flynn Carlyon's eye sockets. How had he tracked her down? Again?

Kat didn't want her co-workers or her new boss to know she was Richard Ravensdale's scandalous secret. The secret child of his two-night-stand hotel barmaid.

His love child.

Ack. Thinking about the tacky words was bad enough. Seeing them splashed all over every London tabloid for the last three months had been nothing short of excruciating. Toenails-torn-off-with-pliers excruciating. What had love had to do with her conception? She was the product of lust. The dirty little secret Richard had paid to be removed. Obliterated.

So far no one at work had recognised her. So far. She had styled her hair differently so she didn't look like the photos that had been circulated. She had even modified her name so the press would leave her alone. For the last couple of months Flynn had been doing his level best as Richard's lawyer to get her to play happy families, but she wasn't going to fling her arms around her biological father and say 'I'm so glad I found you' any time soon. Not in this millennium. Or the next. If Flynn thought he could wave big, fat cheques in front of her nose, or wear her down by turning up at her workplaces, then he had better think again.

Meg was looking at Kat with eyes as wide as the plates on the counter. 'Do you know him? Personally, I mean?'

'I know enough about him to know he drinks a double-shot espresso with a glass of water—no ice—on the side,' Kat said.

Meg's eyebrows lifted. 'You sure you don't want to…?'

'No.' Kat slammed the dishwasher shut. 'Absolutely not. You take him.'

Meg walked somewhat timidly towards Flynn's table where he was sitting alone with one of the daily broadsheets spread out in front of him. They exchanged a few words and Meg came back with brightly flushed cheeks and a wincing don't-shoot-me-I'm-the-messenger look. 'He said, if you don't serve him in the next two minutes he's going to speak to the manager.'

Kat glanced at her boss, Joe, who was behind the hissing, steaming and spluttering coffee machine working his way through a list of early morning orders. If this job went kaput, she wondered how long she could couch surf in order to get enough money together to get a place of her own. At least she had the house-sitting job in Notting Hill starting this evening. The money was good, but it was only for the next four weeks. Come the first of February, she would be homeless, unless she could find another dirt-cheap bedsit. Preferably without fleas. Or bedbugs.

Any wildlife.

Kat sucked in a steadying breath, aligned her shoulders and walked to table nine with her best be-polite-to-the-annoying-customer smile stitched in place. 'How may I help you?'

Flynn's molasses-black gaze surveyed her tightly set features and lowered to the name badge pinned above her right breast. 'Kathy is it, now?' His smile was slow. Slow and deliberate. Amusement laced with mockery and a garnish of 'got you.'

Kat tried to ignore the faint prickle in her breast where his gaze had rested. 'Would you like the usual, *sir*?'

His eyes gleamed. 'In a cup, preferably. It doesn't taste quite the same when it's poured in my lap.'

He was baiting her. Goading her. She. Would. Not. Bite. 'Would you like anything with your coffee?' she asked. 'Croissant? Muffin? Sour dough toast? Eggs? Bacon? No, perhaps not bacon. We can't have you being a cannibal, can we?'

Damn it.

She'd bitten.

The corner of his mouth tilted in a smug smile, making him look like he thought he'd won that round. 'What time do you finish work?'

Kat gave him a brace-yourself-for-round-two look. 'I'm here to serve you coffee or a meal or a snack. I'm not here to give you details about my private life.'

Flynn glanced towards the coffee machine. 'Does your boss know your true identity?'

'No, and I'd like to keep it that way.' Kat gripped her pen to stop herself from holding it to his throat to make him promise not to tell. 'Now, if you'll just give me your order…'

'Richard's agent has organised a Sixty Years in Showbiz celebration for him later this month,' he said. 'It's going to be a *This Is Your Life* format. I want you there.'

His tone suggested he was used to getting what he wanted. Every. Single. Time.

But Kat hadn't been cast in her kindergarten nativity play as a donkey for nothing. The most intractable mule had nothing on her. 'Why would I want to go to some ghastly, alcohol-soaked bragging fest about his theatre career when he *paid* my mother to get rid of me before I was born?'

Just like he'd tried to pay Kat to keep away once the news had first broken of her existence. Where had her father been when she'd needed a father? How many times during her childhood had she prayed for a dad? Someone to provide for her. Someone to protect her. Someone to love her.

Someone.

Richard hadn't even had the decency to come to see her face-to-face, but had sent his arrogant, up-himself lawyer Flynn Carlyon.

'You're being unnecessarily stubborn,' Flynn said.

Unnecessarily? Of course it was necessary. Her pride was necessary. It was all she had now her mother was dead. Kat leaned down so the customers at the nearby tables couldn't hear. 'Read my lips. N. O. No.'

His hooded gaze went to her mouth, his face so close to hers she could smell his aftershave, a citrus blend with an undertone of something else, something that reminded her of a cool, dark pine forest where secrets lurked in the shifting shadows. He had recently shaved but she could see every tiny dot of stubble along his lean jaw and around his nose and mouth, the signal of potent male hormones surging through his blood.

His eyes dipped to the open V of her shirt. Only the top two buttons were undone, revealing little more than the base of her neck, but the heat in his gaze made her feel as if she was standing there bare breasted. She straightened as if someone had fisted the back of her shirt and pulled her upright.

Do. Not. Look. At. His. Mouth. Kat chanted it mentally while her eyes continued their traitorous feasting on the contours of his lips. He was smiling again as if he knew exactly the effect he had on her. How could a man she hated so much have such a gorgeous mouth? He had the sort of mouth you could only describe as sinful. Smoking-hot, sex-up-against-the-kitchen-bench sinful. Sex-with-the-curtains-wide-open sinful. The upper lip was straight across the top, but the lower lip more than made up for it. It was full, sensual. The midpoint in perfect alignment with the sexy shallow cleft in his chin.

The only reason she was obsessing about his mouth was because she was doing 'Winter Deep Freeze' with her best friend, Maddie Evans. Their celibacy pact had started in November and, with only a month to go, Kat was determined to win. She had to prove a point, not just to her best friend, but also to herself. No way was she going to play out the script of her mother's life. Bad date after bad date. Sex that scratched an itch but left filthy finger marks on the fabric of her soul.

Who said Kat couldn't go three months without sex?

She *could*. And she damn well *would*.

One of the customers tried to move past, bumping against Kat so she had to suck in her stomach and press herself against Flynn's table. The brush of his trouser leg on her knee sent a lightning zap of heat through her body. Hot. Searing. Scorching. So scorching she expected to look down and see a singed and smoking hole in her thick black tights.

She stepped back once the customer had gone, pen poised pointedly. 'Espresso? Water no ice?'

'He's your only living parent,' Flynn said.

Kat sent him a look that would have frozen mercury. 'So? With relatives like him, lead me to the nearest orphanage. I'm checking in.'

Something moved in his gaze as quickly as a camera-shutter click. But then his lazily slanted smile came back. 'Are you going to get my coffee?'

'Are you going to take no for an answer?'

His eyes beneath those dark, winged brows roved her lips. Did he feel the same flicker of animal attraction deep and low in his belly? Kat could feel it now. The pulse of lust thrumming in her blood every time his dark eyes trapped hers, as if he too were thinking of what it would feel like to have her stripped naked and pinned beneath his body.

Or against the kitchen bench.

Be still her heart, her pulse, her giddy-with-excitement girly bits.

Another customer came past, but this time Kat turned so her back was to Flynn. *Big mistake.* She could sense his gaze on her bottom, burning through the layer of her boring black uniform to the satin and lace secrets beneath. She turned and carefully masked her features, but even so she could feel the warmth glowing in her cheeks.

'What are you doing for dinner this evening?'

Kat put her hands on her hips, anchoring her resolve in case it took it upon itself to quit its shift. 'I suppose this is a rarity for you? A woman actually having the willpower to say no to you?'

The glint in his eye made something in her stomach swoop. 'Nothing I like more than a challenge. The harder, the better.'

Joe came up carrying a tray of coffees. 'Kathy, are you working the floor or flirting with the customers?'

'Sorry, Mr Peruzzi,' Kat said. 'This customer has a…a complicated order.'

'Tables seven and ten are waiting for their bills,' Joe said. 'And tables two and eight need clearing and resetting. I'm running a café, not a freaking dating agency.'

Kat smiled sweetly even though her back teeth were glued together. 'There isn't a man inside this café I would be even *remotely* tempted to date.'

Joe hustled past and Flynn said, 'Would you be remotely tempted to serve them some coffee?'

She held his mocking look with steely intent. 'You won't win this, Mr Carlyon. I don't care how many jobs you make me lose. I will not be told what to do.'

He leaned back in his chair as if he had all the time in this world and the next. 'By the way, you were great in that toilet-paper ad,' he said. 'Very convincing.'

Kat could feel her back molars grinding down to her

mandible. At this rate, her dental hygienist would be charging a search fee. The only thing more humiliating than doing a job like that toilet-paper gig was having your worst enemy see it. 'So, just the coffee, or would you like a full breakfast to clog your arteries?'

He gave a low, deep chuckle that made the backs of her knees shiver. 'I'll have some cake.'

Kat frowned. It was seven thirty in the morning. Who ate cake at that hour? *Cake?*

'Yep.' He winked at her. 'And I'm going to eat it too.'

'What was that all about?' Meg asked when Kat came back to the servery. 'You're so red I could cook table four's buckwheat pancakes on your cheeks.'

'I swear to God I'm going to explode if I have to go anywhere near that man,' Kat said. 'I seriously do not get what women see in him. So what if he's good looking? He's an arrogant jerk.'

'I think he's gorgeous.' Meg's expression had that whole star-struck thing going on. 'He has such dark-brown eyes you can't tell where his pupils begin and end.'

Kat got out a large slice of devil's food cake and liberally coated it with cream. 'There,' she said. 'That should fix him. If that doesn't give him a heart attack, nothing will.'

'I don't think there's anything wrong with his heart,' Meg said. 'He looks like he seriously works out. And he's so tall. Did you see him stoop as he came in?'

'I suppose he has to be that tall to allow room for all that ego,' Kat muttered, picked up the coffee and made her way back to his table.

'Here you go.' She placed the plate, the coffee and the glass of water in front of him.

Flynn cocked an eyebrow. 'Aren't you going to give me a cake fork?'

Kat rounded her eyes in mock surprise. 'Oh, you actually *know* how to eat with cutlery, do you? I would never have guessed.'

His lopsided smile did that swoop and dive thing to her belly. 'You should be onstage.'

'Yeah, well, that's the plan.'

'So how's that going for you?'

Kat wasn't going to tell him anything about her audition in a few days' time in the West End. The AR Gurney play *Sylvia* couldn't have come along at a more opportune time. It was one of her favourite plays and she knew deep in her bones she was right for the part of the dog Sylvia. Audiences worldwide loved the notion of a human playing a dog. If she landed the role and did it well, it could launch her career. She wanted the part on her own merit, not because of whose DNA she shared. She didn't trust Flynn not to leak something to Richard Ravensdale, who might then open doors she wanted to open with her own talent.

'I'll go and get that fork for you.' She gave Flynn a tight smile. 'Or would you like a shovel?'

His eyes held hers with implacable intent. Hinting at an iron will that was energised, excited, exhilarated by the mere whiff of a challenge. 'I'd like to see you tonight.'

'Not going to happen,' Kat said. 'I have an appointment with a cat and a fur ball.'

That glint was back in his eyes. 'I didn't know you had a cat.'

'I don't,' she said. 'I've picked up a new house-sitting job. The agency I work for occasionally rang me this morning. The person they had for the post had to pull out at short notice due to a family crisis. Apparently the cat is one of those ones that are too precious to go to a boarding centre. It has—' she put her fingers into air quotes '—issues.'

'How long will you be house-sitting?'

'A month.'

'Where in London?'

Kat gave him a cynical look. 'Why would I tell you? You'd be on my doorstep day and night pestering me to meet my sperm donor.'

The corner of his mouth tipped up in an enigmatic smile. 'So, I guess I'll see you when I see you.'

Not if I can help it. She swung around and stalked back to the kitchen.

Flynn's gaze followed that deliciously pert behind until it disappeared into the servery. The thrill of the chase had always excited him but *this* chase was something else. Kat Winwood was hot. Flames, flares, and hissing and spitting fireworks hot.

It was amusing to set the bait and sit back and wait for her to take it. She pretended to hate him. To loathe the ground he walked on, the space he occupied. The air he breathed.

But behind the fiery flash of her green-grey gaze he could see something else. Something she was at great pains to conceal. That betraying flicker of attraction. The way her pupils flared like spilled ink. The way she swept the tip of her tongue over her lips. The way her eyes kept tracking to his mouth as if drawn there by an invisible, irresistible force.

He felt the same stirring in his body whenever he was near her. Lust rumbled and rolled through his body like a cannonball. It was taking longer than usual to get her to admit her interest. But that was what made him all the more determined. The challenge made his blood tick and flick with excitement. He was used to having anyone he wanted. Dating had become almost boring. He couldn't remember the last time a woman had said no to him.

Not since Claire had walked out on their engagement.

He ducked back out from under the crime-scene tape in his mind that blocked him from thinking of how desperate he had felt back then. Desperate to be with someone. To have a family. To have a future to make up for the blank space of his past.

He wasn't that commitment-with-a-capital-C man now.

He was a lower-case lover. The chase, the conquest, the 'don't call me I'll call you' was how he played things now.

And he wanted to play with Kat Winwood.

He wanted to feel her sexy little body gripping him like a clamped fist. To feel her mouth breathing fire over his skin. To feel her tongue twisting, twirling and tangling with lust around his. He wanted to hear that cute little Scottish accent screaming out his name as she convulsed around him.

Kat might be playing it cool, but how long could she ignore the heat that flared between them?

Especially when he was going to be a lot closer to her than she'd bargained for.

A whole lot closer.

CHAPTER TWO

OKAY, THERE HAS to be catch. Kat unlocked the door of the Notting Hill Victorian mansion the house-sitting agency had assigned her. Call her a pessimist, but she knew from experience that anything that looked too good to be true usually was. But so far all she could see was luxury. The sort of opulent luxury she had dreamed of since she was a kid growing up on a council estate in Glasgow. Even the air inside the house smelt rich. The grace notes of an exclusive perfume and the base note of some sort of essential oil made her nostrils quiver in sensory delight. She closed the door and the stunning crystal chandeliers overhead tinkled against the bitter early January wind, as if disturbed by the whispery breath of a ghost.

Kat ignored the faint shiver that crept over her scalp. She was being ridiculous. Of course she was. It was her nerves because of the audition next week. She could feel the moths fluttering in her belly even now. Big, winged ones, beating against the walls of her stomach like razor blades. If she got the part in the West End play and her career finally took off she would never have to waitress or house-sit again. She would be able to buy her own luxury mansion, have her own space instead of borrowing a stranger's.

Usually the houses she looked after were a little more modest than this. But she wasn't complaining. Although, four weeks of living with such decadence was going to make it hard to adjust once she went back to a poky little bedsit—if she was lucky enough to secure one.

Someone had kindly left the heating on…or maybe that was because of Monty, the cat Kat was supposed to be minding along with the house. Kat wasn't a great fan of cats. She was more of a dog person. But apparently Monty was a delicate 'inside' cat, which meant there wouldn't be any nasty unmentionable creatures to deal with because he wouldn't be out at night hunting.

Anyway, turning down a job because of a bit of a feline prejudice wasn't an option just now.

Besides, she was an actor, wasn't she? She would *pretend* to like the cat.

Kat wandered through the house looking for the cat…or so she told herself. What she was really looking at were all the photos of the couple that lived there. The Carstairses were both professionals—the wife was a GP and the husband a barrister, and they had two gorgeous kids, a boy and a girl who were both under five. They had taken the kids to Australia to see relatives— or so the agency lady had told her.

It was hard to look at those photos and not feel a little twinge of envy. Well, maybe not just a little twinge. More like a large fist grabbing at her innards and twisting them until the blood supply was cut off.

Kat's childhood hadn't looked anything like these kids' childhoods. Firstly, she hadn't had a father. She had one *now* but that was another story. Secondly, her mother hadn't looked as relaxed and content as the mother in the photos. Her mother had spent most of

Kat's childhood inviting the wolf at the door in for sleepovers. And as for any exotic holidays abroad… the only 'overseas' holidays she'd had with her mother had been to visit her grandparents in the Outer Hebrides on the Isle of Harris. But typically those visits had only lasted a couple of days before her mother had got tired of the I-told-you-so lectures from her strict Presbyterian parents.

Kat found more photos in the gorgeous sitting room that overlooked the even more gorgeous garden. Even though it was back to its bare bones, being the first week in January, it would be the perfect place for a couple of kids to play on long summer afternoons, or for two adults to sit out there with a glass of chilled wine and chat about their day while they watched the children gambolling about.

Funny, but at her last damp and mouldy bedsit the rain had looked every bit as bleak and dismal as winter rain could be. It would drip down the panes of glass…on both sides, unfortunately. But at the Carstairses' house the droplets trickled down—thankfully on the outside only—the triple-glazed windows like strings of glittering diamonds.

Kat shifted her gaze to a photo in a frame on a mahogany drop-sided table next to the window. It was a Christmas photo: she could see a brightly decorated Christmas tree with heaps of beautifully wrapped presents underneath its branches. The same tree was still in situ—it was on her lists of tasks to pack it away before the family returned. There were ten or twelve people in the photo, the children in the front, the shorter adults at the sides and the tallest at the back. But there was one man who stood head and shoulders over everyone else. She picked up the photo with a hand that wasn't quite steady.

What was *he* doing there?

Kat clenched her teeth so hard she could feel the tension turning the muscles in her neck and shoulders into boulders. She put the photo down before she was tempted to smash it against the wall. She swung away from the window, pacing the carpeted floor like a swordfish in a salad bowl.

What was Flynn Carlyon doing in the bosom of the family she was house-sitting for?

The sticky feet of suspicion crawled up her spine and over her scalp. She had thought it a little odd that the people hadn't wanted to speak to her on the phone, especially since there was a pet involved. People were sometimes fussier over who minded their pets than their kids. But her supervisor had said another client had recommended her. Not just the agency, but her. By name.

Which client?

Kat was starting to smell a six-foot-four, Savile Row–suited rat with sooty black hair and eyes the colour of the espresso he drank.

What was Flynn up to?

Kat had told him in no uncertain terms she wanted nothing to do with her father.

No contact. No favours. No money.

She hadn't spoken to the press even though they had hounded her for weeks. She had gone underground to escape them. She kept a low profile when she was out and about. She wore her hair under a beanie or wore sunglasses. It might be considered a little crazy in the dead of winter, but at least she was able to avoid eye contact. She was even auditioning under a false name in order to distance herself from the Ravensdales. She couldn't win either way. If she auditioned under her real name, Katherine Winwood, everyone would know she was Richard Ravensdale's love child, so she might be given the part for all the wrong reasons. Everyone would be crying nepotism. She wanted the part because of her talent, not because of her bloodline. A bloodline she was intent on ignoring, thank you very much, because her father hadn't wanted her in the first place. Why on earth would she want to connect with the man who had not only insisted on her mother having an abortion but *had paid* her to do it?

What was it about the Ravensdales and money? Did they think they could pay her to go away one minute and then lure her back the next?

Why couldn't they accept she wanted nothing to do with them?

Kat had been tempted to meet Miranda, her half-sister. It felt a little weird to think she had half-siblings—twin brothers ten years older, Julius and Jake, and then Miranda who was only two months older than Kat. Two months. Which just showed what a jerk Richard Ravensdale was because he had still been seeing Kat's mother while he'd been reconciling with Elisabetta Albertini, his then ex-wife. His soon-to-be ex-wife again if the tabloids were to be believed.

But, in spite of her longing for a family to belong to, Kat wanted nothing to do with any of them. Not even Jasmine Connolly, the bridal designer who had grown up at Ravensdene with Miranda. Jasmine was the gardener's daughter and had recently become engaged to Jake Ravensdale. She seemed a nice, fun sort of girl, someone Kat would like to be friends with, but hanging out with anyone who had anything to do with the Ravensdales was *not on*.

Kat was used to being an only child. She was used to being without a family. She was still getting used to being without her mother. Not that they'd had the best mother and daughter relationship or anything. Kat always felt a little conflicted when it came to days like Mother's Day. Somehow the pretty pink cards with their flowery and sentimental verses and messages didn't quite suit the relationship she had with her mother. Growing up, she'd felt unspeakably lonely because of it.

If you couldn't talk to your mother, then who could you talk to?

Kat certainly didn't need a rich and famous family to interfere with her life and her career. She was going to make it on her own. She didn't need any favours, leg-ups or red carpet invitations. And she certainly didn't need any hotshot, too-handsome-to-be-trusted London lawyers manipulating things in the background. What was his connection with the Carstairs family? Was Mr Carstairs a work colleague? What did Flynn hope to achieve by having her mind a colleague's house? Did he think it would give him a better chance of 'accidentally' bumping into her so he could flirt and banter with her?

Over her dead and rotting body it would. There was no way she wanted anything to do with Flynn Carlyon. He was exactly the sort of man she avoided. Too good-looking, too sure of himself, too much of a ladies' man.

Too tempting.

There was the sound of a miaow and Kat turned around to see a large Persian cat the colour of charcoal strutting in as if he owned the place. *Which he kind of did.* 'Hello, Monty.' She reached down to pat him. 'I believe we're going to be housemates for a few weeks.' Monty gave her a beady look from eyes as yellow as an owl's and shrank away from her outstretched hand with a hiss and a snarl that sounded scary enough to be in a horror movie. A Stephen King movie.

She straightened. 'So it's going to be like that, is it? Well, you'd better get over yourself quick smart, as I'm the one in charge of feeding you.'

The cat slunk out of the room with its tail twitching like a conductor's baton.

Kat rolled her eyes. 'That's why I prefer dogs. They're not stuck-up snobs.'

The rain was coming down in icy sheets when Kat came back from picking up some shopping an hour later. There was food for the cat and some basic things in the pantry but she preferred to purchase her own food. She would have ordered it online but her credit card was still maxed out after her mother's funeral. The thought of that big, fat cheque Flynn Carlyon had dangled under her nose when he'd come into the café a couple of months back was dismissed by her pride.

No way was she being bought.

No. Way.

If she wanted to speak to the press, she would. If she wanted to connect with her father, she would in her own good time. Not that it was going to happen any time soon, if ever. She couldn't imagine a time when she would feel anything but disdain for a man who had used her mother so callously. Just because she shared some of his DNA didn't mean she was going to strike up a loving, all-is-forgiven father-daughter relationship with him. Where had he been when things had been so dire growing up? He hadn't contributed anything towards her upbringing. Not a brass razoo. He had paid off her mother and then had promptly forgotten about her. The money he had paid had gone before Kat was a year old. She and her mother had lived in hardscrabble poverty for most of her childhood.

The shame of not having enough, of wanting more but never having enough to pay for it, was not something she could easily forget. Her mother had worked a variety of cleaning and bar jobs, none of them lasting very long. Her mother would always have 'an issue' with someone in the workplace. Kat had felt utterly powerless as she'd watched her mother swing from manic enthusiasm for a new job to coming crashing down in a depressed stupor when she lost it and/or walked out. Her black mood would last for weeks, sometimes months, until the cycle would begin all over again.

Kat had decided as a young child she would do everything in her power to make life better for her mother. She'd thought if she could find a way to get her mum some help, to get her some financial stability and support, then her mother might magically turn into the mother she'd dreamed of having.

But in the end she hadn't been able to do it. Her mother had died of cancer, perhaps not in dirt-poor poverty, but close enough to make Kat feel nothing but anger towards her biological father who could at the very least have made their lives decent instead of desperate.

It wasn't just anger she felt. It *hurt* to think Richard Ravensdale hadn't cared anything about her. His own flesh and blood had been nothing to him. Just a problem that had to be removed and then swiped from his memory. Permanently.

The parking space outside the Carstairses' house was tight, especially with the rain obscuring her vision. Kat's car wasn't big by any means but trying to get it into the tiny space between the shiny black BMW and the silver Mercedes was like trying to squeeze an elephant's foot into a ballet slipper.

Not going to happen.

She blew out a breath and tried again. But now a line of cars coming home for the day was banking up behind her. In spite of the biting cold, beads of sweat broke out over her brow. She put her foot on the accelerator and nudged the car backwards, but someone behind her impatiently tooted their horn and put her off her game. She slammed on the brakes and gripped the steering wheel even tighter. She was tempted to roll down the window and give the driver behind the finger, but then a tall figure appeared at her driver's door.

Oh, God. A surge of panic seized Kat's chest. Road rage. Was she to be beaten senseless? Dragged out of the car and kicked and shoved and stomped on and then thrown to the gutter like a bit of trash? She could see the headlines: *Struggling actor beaten to a pulp over traffic incident.* She could see the social media footage. It would go viral. Millions of people would view her demise. She would finally be famous but for all the wrong reasons.

Kat turned to face her opponent with a bravado she was nowhere near feeling. This was the upside of having gone to acting classes. She could do 'affronted driver' down pat. But the man wasn't growling and swearing or shaking his fists at her. He was *smiling.*

She rolled down her window and glowered at Flynn Carlyon's amused expression. 'I would ask you what the hell you're doing here but I'm not sure I want to know the answer.'

He leaned down so his head was on a level with hers. Kat dearly wished he hadn't. This close she could see the bottomless depth of his glinting eyes. The cleanly shaven jaw of this morning was gone; in its place was the dark shadow of late-in-the-day, urgent male stubble peppered all over it. And, if that wasn't enough to make her heart come to a juddering stop, some strands of his ink-black hair fell forward over his forehead, giving him a rakish look. 'Want me to park it for you?'

'No, thank you,' Kat said, doing a prim schoolmistress tone straight out of her actor's handbook. 'I'm perfectly capable of parking my own car.' Not quite true. She had always had trouble with reverse parking, especially in busy traffic. She had failed her driving test three times because of it.

His smile stretched to tilt one corner of his mouth. 'It looks like it.'

Kat clenched her teeth hard enough to crack a walnut. And to add insult to injury two more cars tooted. Flynn straightened and turned, flattening his back against the side of her door as he waved the traffic through. The fabric of his coat—one hundred per cent cashmere, if she was any judge—was close enough for her to touch. She gripped the steering wheel like her hands were stuck there with superglue and wondered why the planets had conspired against her to have Flynn Carlyon witness her humiliation in a busy Notting Hill street.

He turned back and tapped the roof of her car. 'Watch out for the car behind,' he said. 'It's mine.'

She double-blinked. 'Yours?'

'Yeah, didn't I tell you?' That annoying smile again. 'We're neighbours.'

Later, Kat didn't know how she'd parked that car without ramming into his. She wanted to. Oh, how she wanted to. Nothing would have given her more pleasure than to smash up his pride and joy. To reverse her car at full throttle time and time again.

Crash. Bang. Crash. Bang. Crash. Bang.

She got out of her car and pretended she didn't notice how out of place it looked sandwiched between his showroom-perfect BMW and the silver Mercedes. It looked like a donkey at the starting gates at Royal Ascot.

Kat joined him on the footpath. 'Just answer me one question. Did you have something to do with my appointment at the Carstairses' next door?'

'They were looking for a house-sitter. Your name came up.'

Kat narrowed her gaze. 'Why me? You know nothing about me.'

'On the contrary, Miss Winwood,' he said with a slow smile that had a hint of imperiousness, 'I know quite a lot about you.'

'Like what?'

'Your father is Richard—'

'Apart from that.'

'Why don't you want to meet him?' Flynn said.

'The first time we spoke you wanted to *stop* me meeting him. Now you want me to come to his stupid party. How do I know what he'll want tomorrow or the next day?'

He gave a loose shrug of a very broad shoulder. *Did he row for England? Work out? Lift bulldozers in the gym?* 'He's changed his mind since then,' he said. 'He wants to make amends. He feels bad about the way things turned out.'

Kat gave a scoffing laugh. '"Turned out"? Things didn't "turn out." He was the one who tried to get rid me as a baby. He treated my mother appallingly. The only thing he feels bad about is my mother finally telling me of my origin. That's what he's upset about. He thought his dirty little secret had gone away. His agent is probably only doing this as some sort of popularity stunt. I bet Richard couldn't care less about meeting me. He just doesn't want his adoring public to see him as a deadbeat dad.'

'The rest of the family would like to meet you. They haven't done you or your mother any wrong.'

There was a part of Kat that conceded he was right, but she wasn't ready to join them for family get-togethers, because it would pander to Richard Ravensdale—not to mention Flynn, who was acting for him. 'What about his wife, Elisabetta Albertini?' she said. 'I bet she isn't waiting for me with open arms to welcome me to the bosom of the family.'

'No, but she too might change her mind when she sees how sweet and lovable you are.'

Kat shot him a withering look. 'But I thought she was going to divorce him. Who will you represent if she does? Don't you act for both of them?'

'I'm hoping it won't come to that. A divorce would be costly to both of them.'

'Why should you mind?' she said. 'Either way, you'd still get paid bags and bags of money.'

'Contrary to what you might think, money is not my primary motivation in representing my clients,' he said. 'The Ravensdales are people I admire and respect and am deeply fond of. Now, if you'll excuse me, I'd like to get in out of this rain.'

Kat had barely noticed the rain but now that he mentioned it she could feel it dripping down the back of her coat collar in icy shards. God knew what her hair looked like. She could feel it plastered to her scalp and over her shoulders like a Viking helmet. Not that she cared a fig for how she looked in front of Flynn Carlyon. She didn't care for his opinion one way or the other. So what if he only ever surrounded himself with beautiful people?

She. Did. Not. Care.

She balled her hands into fists. 'What do you possibly hope to achieve by having me installed next door?'

His look was inscrutable. 'If you're so uncomfortable with the notion then why not call the agency and be transferred?'

Kate would have done so if it hadn't been for the money. The Carstairs family was paying extra for her to Skype them each day with the cat. Weird, but true. She only hoped Monty would agree to sit on her lap long enough to look at his family on the other side of the globe. 'Once I commit to something, I don't like to let people down,' she said.

'Nor do I,' he said and, giving her another one of those annoying winks, he turned and went inside his house.

Flynn was enjoying a quiet drink in his sitting room, with his little dog Cricket snoring at his feet while he went over a client's brief, but his mind kept drifting to his conversation with Kat Winwood. *Conversation?* More like a verbal fencing match. As soon as he'd met her last October he had felt a compulsive desire to see her again. Even if Richard had told him to forget about making contact with her, Flynn knew he would still have done so, for his own reasons, not his client's.

She was simply unforgettable.

Her sparking green-grey eyes, her beautiful, wild brown hair with its copper highlights, her gorgeous figure, her razor-sharp tongue and acerbic wit were a knockout combination. A sexy, heady cocktail he wanted to get smashed on as soon as he could.

When his neighbours had phoned and asked him if he knew anyone who could house-sit for them at short notice, he had immediately thought of her. Why wouldn't he recommend her? He knew she was well respected at the agency. It suited him to have her close. He was a fully paid-up member of the keep-your-friends-close-and-your-enemies-closer club.

Not that she was really his enemy. She was a challenge he couldn't resist.

As he saw it, Kat had everything to win by making peace with her father. Not that Flynn believed Richard was trying to make up for the way he had handled things. He wasn't so gullible he couldn't see what his client's motives were. He knew it had more to do with Richard wanting everyone to think he was doing the right thing by Kat. He hadn't been a class act in how he had treated Kat's mother, but as for his apology being genuine and heartfelt? Well, Richard hadn't received all those acting awards for nothing.

Kat was being stubborn on principle. Flynn could understand it but he wanted her to put her prejudices aside and form some sort of relationship with the man whose DNA she carried. She was lucky. At least she knew who both her parents were.

He had no idea who his were. And he never would.

For the last couple of months Kat had filled his every waking moment and far too many of his sleeping ones. He wasn't sure what it was about her that intrigued him so much. He'd had his fair share of beautiful women over the years since Claire had left him, but none had made him feel this power surge of attraction. He looked forward to seeing her, to bantering with her. She was smart and funny, and her broad Scottish accent was so darn cute it never failed to make him smile. He liked her energy, the feisty flare of temper that made him wonder what she would be like in bed. All that passion had to have an outlet. He wanted to be the trigger that made her explode.

He *had* to get her to that party. It was his mission. His goal. It wasn't just because Richard had entrusted him with the task of getting her to meet with him. It was because once Flynn set his mind to a task he allowed nothing and no one to get in his way. He had faced down huge challenges all of his life and won.

This was no different.

The party was going to be televised live. His reputation would be on the line. Everyone knew he had been assigned the task of getting Kat into the bosom of the family. He couldn't accept failure. He had to pull this off no matter what. Failure wasn't in his vocabulary. His professional tag line was 'Flynn Equals Win.'

Kat was being pig-headed about meeting Richard out of loyalty to her mother. That wasn't a bad thing. He understood it. Admired it, even. But this wasn't just about her father. The whole family wanted to embrace her because they were decent people who wanted to do the right thing by her. She had no one else. He couldn't see why she wouldn't welcome the chance to be included in one of London's wealthiest and most talented families. Plus they could fast-track her to the fame she was striving for.

Cricket lifted his head off his crossed paws and gave a sharp bark.

'You want a walk at this time of night?' Flynn said.

Cricket bounced up and yapped in excitement, spinning in circles like a dervish on an upper. Flynn put his papers down and smiled. 'You do realise this is why my mother got rid of you? You're seriously high maintenance.'

Cricket ran to pick up his lead, trailing it behind him and getting his stubby little legs tangled up in it in his excitement. Flynn bent down to clip the lead on the dog's collar and ruffled his odd little one-up, one-down ears. 'Come on, you crazy little mutt. But, if it starts snowing, don't say I didn't warn you.'

CHAPTER THREE

KAT WAS ON her way to bed when she realised she hadn't seen Monty since she had given him dinner—or tried to. He had turned up his nose at her and stalked off with his tail twitching as though someone had sent an electric current through him. The Skype attempt hadn't gone well either—she bore the scratches on her hands to prove it. But at least she had met the Carstairs family, who were as lovely as they appeared in their array of photographs. They assured her Monty would soon be purring contentedly in her lap once he established trust. They never once mentioned their handsome neighbour, which seemed a bit suspicious to Kat. If he was smack, bang in the middle of their most recent Christmas photo, then surely they would mention him in passing?

She couldn't stop looking at that photo every time she went into the sitting room. It wasn't just Flynn's smiling face that pulled her gaze, but the way he was so comfortable around those kids. The little boy called Josh was looking up at Flynn in what looked like a state of hero worship. There was another photo in the study, with Flynn and the Carstairses' little girl Bella, who was about three years old, sitting on Flynn's knee. She was sucking her little thumb and leaning contentedly against Flynn's broad chest as he read to her from a children's picture book.

It made Kat wonder if he planned to settle down and have his own family one day. He was known to be a bit of a ladies' man but not as much of a full-on playboy as Jake Ravensdale had been before becoming engaged to Jasmine Connolly. But if Flynn had been seeing anyone on a regular basis lately there hadn't been anything in the press—or not that Kat had been able to find.

The only person he had been seen with, ironically enough, was her.

She looked through each of the rooms but Monty wasn't anywhere to be seen. There was a circular patch of sooty fur where he had been sleeping on the Carstairses' white linen bed but no sign of him in the flesh…or fur, so to speak.

She checked all the windows, even though she hadn't opened any, to make sure he hadn't escaped. But when she checked the laundry window she noticed there was a cat flap on the bottom of the door. She hadn't noticed it there before, but then, why would she? Monty was supposed to be an inside cat. Kat had cleaned his litter tray earlier. He wasn't supposed to go outside and get wet, or snowed on, or run over by a car…or bring in—*gulp*—horrible hunting trophies. The cat flap was unlocked. Should she close it? What if he was outside and couldn't get back in?

Kat decided to do another thorough search of the house before she locked the cat flap. Surely Monty wouldn't go outside on such a foul night? What was that saying about mad dogs and Englishmen? Or was that just a saying about summer?

She was coming through the sitting room when she heard the bump of the cat flap opening and closing.

Then she heard the sound of Monty giving a weird-sounding miaow. Every hair on Kat's scalp fizzed at the roots. Every knob of her spine froze. She knew what *that* was. That was a victory miaow. The sort of miaow a cat makes when it lands its prey and was about to show it off to its owners.

But Kat wasn't his owner. She didn't want to see his handiwork. No way. This was why she didn't own a cat. This was why she didn't even *like* cats. They brought in stuff, horrible stuff, like dead birds and…and…she couldn't even think the word without wanting to jump on a chair and scream. Dread as cold as the snow falling outside chugged through her veins. A hedgehog climbed up her windpipe until she couldn't take a breath. Fear tightened her chest, making her heart go into arrhythmia so bad any decent cardiologist would have rushed for a defibrillator.

Her eyes were glued to the door of the sitting room. It was like a scene in a Friday night fright film. She was frozen with primal fear, unable to move a step forward or a step back. Her feet were nailed to the floor. Monty made that muffled miaow again from just outside the sitting room, the miaow that sounded like he had his mouth full of…something.

No. No. No. Kat chanted manically. This couldn't be happening. Not to her. Not on her first night in this lovely house. Lovely houses like this didn't have dreadful, ghastly, horrid, unmentionable creatures inside them…

It was so quiet she could hear each soft pad of Monty's paws on the carpet as he came round the door into the sitting room. *Puft. Puft. Puft. Puft.* Her eyes widened in horror when she saw what was dangling from his mouth. *'Eeeeeek!'* She screamed so loudly she was vaguely aware she might shatter the chandeliers or windows. Or wake the neighbours. In France.

But then the stupid cat let the thing go. And it wasn't dead! It streaked across the floor right next to Kat's feet and disappeared under one of the sofas.

Kat bolted from the room so fast she could have qualified for the Olympics. She snapped the door shut behind her and fled to the front door, barely stopping long enough to grab her coat from the coat stand. She didn't bother with gloves—she would never have been able to get them on her shaking hands. She had only taken one flying step out of the Carstairses' house when she came face to face with Flynn, who was walking a weird-looking dog.

He frowned and steadied her with a hand on her arm. 'Are you all right? I heard you screaming and—'

Kat pointed back at the house with a quaking finger. 'In—in there… M-Monty brought in a…a…'

'A what?'

'I can't say it,' she said. 'Please will you get rid of it for me? *Please?* I'll never be able to sleep knowing it's in there.'

'What's in there?'

Kat absolutely never cried. Not unless it was written in the script. Then she could do it, no problem. But fear colliding with relief that someone had come to her rescue made her want to throw herself on Flynn's chest and howl like a febrile teething baby. She bit her bottom lip, sure she was going to bite right through before she could stop it trembling. 'I—I have this thing…a phobia… I know it's silly but I—I just can't help it.'

He put his gloved hand on her shoulder. Even though there were layers of fabric between his skin and hers, she felt something warm and electric go right through her body from the top of her shoulder to the balls of her feet. 'Did Monty bring in a mouse?'

Kat squeezed her eyes shut and put her hands over her ears. 'Don't say that word!'

His hand slipped down from her shoulder to take her bare hands in his gloved ones. 'Look at me, Kat.'

Kat looked. But he wasn't laughing at her. His expression was serious and concerned. 'It got away from Monty,' she said, almost wailing like a little kid. *Waa-waa-waa.* 'It—it went under the sofa.'

He gave her freezing hands a warm squeeze. 'I'll deal with it, or at least Cricket and I will.'

'Cricket?'

The little dog at Flynn's feet yapped and spun around on his back legs as if on cue. He was not the sort of dog she was expecting someone like Flynn to own. She had expected some classy, Crufts-standard, purebred Malamute, a regal Great Dane or a velvet-smooth German pointer. Cricket wasn't any bigger than a child's football, was of indeterminate breed and looked like something out of a science fiction movie. His wiry coat was a caramel brown with little flecks of white that stood up at odd angles like they had been stuck on as an afterthought. He had one ear that stood up and one that flopped down, a thin, wiry tail that curled like a question mark over his back and a lower jaw that stuck out a few millimetres like a drawer that hadn't been shut properly.

'My right-hand man,' Flynn said. 'An expert at rodent-ectomies.'

Kat was almost limp with relief. 'I'd be ever so grateful.'

'Do you want to wait at my house while we get the business end of things sorted?'

Another groundswell of relief nearly knocked her off her feet, as if all her bones had been taken out of her body. 'You wouldn't mind?'

He smiled and looped her arm through one of his. 'Come this way.'

Kat was beyond worrying about going all damsel-in-distress with him. She *was* in distress. She would have happily sat in an axe murderer's house rather than face that…that creature under the sofa.

Besides, it was a perfect opportunity to have a look around Flynn's house while he wasn't there.

He unlocked the door and led her inside, telling her to make herself comfortable and that he'd be back soon. Cricket bounced at Flynn's feet as if he knew he was in for some blood sport. *Eeeww.*

Once they were gone Kat had a peep around. It was much the same layout as the Carstairses' house next door but, while the Carstairses' was a family home with loads of photos and family memorabilia, there was nothing to show Flynn's family of origin. There wasn't a single photo anywhere. There were some quite lovely works of art, however. And some rather gorgeous pieces of antique furniture that suggested he was a bit of a traditionalist, rather than a man with strictly modern taste.

Kat found his study next door to the sitting room, which had a beautiful cedar desk and leather Chesterfield chair. There was a black Chesterfield sofa set in front of the floor-to-ceiling bookshelves. The titles went from thick law tomes to the classics and history, with a smattering of modern titles, mostly crime and thrillers.

She went back into the sitting room and sat down at the grand piano that was set to one side of the room near the windows. She put her fingers to the keys, but all she could tinkle out was a nursery rhyme or two—but not

Three Blind Unmentionables. Not exactly Royal Albert Hall standard, she thought with an embittered pang at what she could have had if her father had provided for her during her childhood. No doubt the Ravensdale siblings were all accomplished musicians. They had gone to fabulous schools and been taken on wonderful holidays with no expense spared.

What had she had?

A big, fat nothing. Which was why it was so hard to get established now. She was years behind her peers. She hadn't had acting lessons until recently because she couldn't afford them. She still couldn't afford a voice coach. A Scottish accent was fine if that was what a play called for. But she needed to be versatile, and that came with training, and training was hideously expensive— at least, the good quality stuff was. She could join some amateur group but she didn't want to be stuck as an extra in some unknown play in some way-out suburb's community hall.

She wanted to be at the West End in London.

It had been her goal since she was a kid.

It wasn't about the fame. Kat didn't give a toss for the fame. It was about the acting. It had always been about the acting, of getting into character in real time. About being onstage. About being in that electric atmosphere of being engaged with a live audience, seeing their reactions, hearing them gasp in shock, laugh in amusement or cry with heartfelt emotion. It wasn't the same, acting on a film set. The sequences were shot out of order. The camera had to come to you rather than onstage when you had to project your character to the audience.

That was what she loved. What she lived for, dreamed of, hungered after like a drug.

But there was another side to acting she found therapeutic. Cathartic, even. Stepping into a role was the chance to step away from her background. Her hurt. Her pain. Her shame.

The sound of Flynn's return made Kat scoot away from the piano and sit on one of the plush sofas, hugging a scatter cushion as if she had been there for the last half-hour.

Cricket came in with a panting smile, looking up at his master as if to say, 'Aren't I clever?'

'All sorted,' Flynn said.

Kat glanced at the dog's mouth to see if there was any trace of the murderous act that had gone on next door. 'Is it dead?' she asked, looking back at Flynn.

'Your visitor has gone to the great, big cheese shop in the sky.'

Her shoulders went down in relief. 'I can't thank you enough.'

Flynn looked at her for a beat. 'There is one way.'

Kat sprang to her feet. 'No. No way. You can't blackmail me into seeing my father. Anyway, you said the wretched thing was dead. You can't bring it back to life to twist my arm.'

'It was worth a try, I thought.' He moved over to a drinks cabinet. 'Fancy a drink to settle your nerves?'

She wanted to say no but somehow found herself saying yes. 'Just a wee one.'

He handed her a Scotch whisky. 'From the home country.'

Kat took the glass from him, touching him for the second time that evening, but this time skin to skin. Something tight unfurled in her belly. 'Do you live here alone?' she asked to disguise her reaction to him.

'Yes.'

'No current girlfriend?'

His dark eyes glinted. 'I'm currently in the process of recruiting.'

Kat tried not to look at his mouth but it felt like an industrial-strength magnet was pulling her gaze to that stubble-surrounded sensual curve. 'How's that working out for you?'

'I have high hopes of filling the vacancy soon.'

'What are your criteria?' She gave him a pert look. 'Breathing with a pulse?'

Amusement shone in his gaze. 'I'm a little more selective than that. How about you?'

'What about me?'

'Are you dating anyone?'

Kat raised one of her brows in an arc. 'I thought you knew everything there was to know about me.'

'Not quite everything,' he said. 'But I know you've been single for a couple of months.'

How did he know? Or did he think no one would *want* to date her? Wasn't she up to his well-heeled standards? What was it about her that made him think she had 'single' written all over her? Surely he couldn't tell she hadn't had sex in ages. That was just plain impossible. No one could tell that... *Could they?* Or had he somehow found out about that stupid affair with Charles—the man who had conveniently forgotten to mention he had a wife—which had kicked off her celibacy pact? 'You know?' she said. 'How?'

He gave a light shrug of one of his shoulders. 'Just a feeling.'

'I thought lawyers relied on evidence, not feelings.'

His mouth slanted again. 'Sometimes a bit of gut instinct doesn't go astray.'

Kat moved her gaze out of reach of his assessing one.

'Your place looks like it's much the same layout as next door. Have you lived here long?'

'Seven years,' he said. 'I have another place in the country.'

Kat mentally rolled her eyes. 'Only one?'

He gave a low, deep chuckle that did strange things to the base of her spine, making it go all loose and wobbly. 'I like collecting things. Property is one of them.'

'Does it make you happy, having all that disgusting wealth to throw around?'

Something at the back of his gaze shifted. 'It's satisfying to have something that no one can take away.'

'Did you grow up with money?'

'My parents weren't wealthy by any means but they were comfortable.'

Kat looked at the gorgeous artwork hanging on the walls. None of them were prints. All were originals. One of them was surely a Picasso? 'They must be very proud of what you've achieved.'

He didn't answer for a moment. 'They enjoy the benefits of my success.'

She turned to look at him, wondering what was behind his cryptic response. 'Are you close to them?'

'I live my life. They live theirs.'

His expression had a boxed-up look about it. What was it about his family that made him so guarded? 'Do you have any brothers or sisters?' she asked.

'Two younger brothers.'

'What do they do?'

'Felix is a plumber and Fergus is a builder, like my father in Manchester,' he said. 'My mother stopped work when I came along. But now she does the bookwork and accounts for my father and brothers. She's made quite a career of it.'

Kat was surprised to hear he was originally from Manchester. He had no trace of the regional accent at all. But then, maybe he could afford a voice coach. 'How long have you lived in London?'

'Since I was ten,' he said. 'I won a scholarship to the same school the Ravensdale twins went to. I ended up spending more time at school than with my family.'

'Neither of your brothers got scholarships?'

'No.'

'Were they jealous?'

His mouth twisted. 'They're not the academic type. They both left school as soon as they could get an apprenticeship.'

'You don't sound like you have much in common with them.'

'I don't.'

Kat shifted her lips from side to side, wondering why he was so different from the rest of his family. His father and younger brothers were tradesmen and yet he was one of London's top lawyers, known for his incisive mind and clever wit. Had his stellar career trajectory made him an alien to his family? Had his educational opportunities created a chasm between him and his family that could not be bridged? Or was he just one of those people who didn't have time for family—an unsentimental man who wanted to make his own way in the world without the ties of blood?

There were no photos of his family around that she could see. Unlike the Carstairses' house next door, where just about every surface was covered in sentimental shots of happy family life. Flynn's house was more like a showcase house out of a home and lifestyle magazine. The luxurious decor spoke of unlimited wealth, yet it wasn't overdone. There was a sophisticated element to the placement of every piece of antique furniture, hand-woven carpet and the beautifully crafted soft furnishings.

She wasn't the sort of girl to get her head turned by a good-looking man. But something about Flynn made her senses go a little crazy. She was aware of him in a way she had never been aware of another man. She felt his proximity like a radar signal in her body. Every nerve was registering exactly where he was in relation to her. Even that first day, when he had come to her café and introduced himself, her body had responded with a shockwave of visceral energy. When his gaze met hers that first time she had felt a lightning-bolt reaction, like she was being zapped with a stun gun. She had felt it humming through her blood, an electric buzz that centred deep in her core. He had a sensual power about him way beyond any other man she had encountered before.

The thought of him touching her again was strangely exciting. He had nice hands, broad and square with long fingers and neat nails. He had a sprinkling of dark hair over the back of them that came from beneath the cuffs of his cashmere sweater, which made her imagination go wild, wondering where else it was sprinkled over the rest of his body. Would he be one of those men who man-scaped? Or would he be *au naturel*?

Cricket came and sat in front of her with a beseeching look on his face. Kat bent down and ruffled his funny little ears. 'How long have you had this adorable little guy?'

'I got him at Christmas.'

Kat looked up at Flynn. 'Where did you get him? Is he a rescue dog?'

Again he seemed to hesitate before he answered. 'You could say that.'

Kat frowned. 'What do you mean?'

He put his glass down but she noticed he hadn't drunk more than a sip or two. 'My mother has this habit of collecting cute strays but when they're no longer cute she gets rid of them.'

Kat heard the faint trace of bitterness in his tone. Was there more to the dog story than he was saying? Did it have something to do with his childhood? His relationship with his mother? His family? 'I always wanted a dog but we could never afford one while I was growing up,' she said. 'And we always lived in flats.'

'You could have one now, couldn't you?'

She straightened and glanced at him where he was leaning against the piano. 'I don't have the sort of lifestyle to own a dog. I move around a lot in search of acting work.'

'Anything on the horizon for you?'

Kat wasn't sure she wanted to tell him too much in case he told Richard Ravensdale. She wanted that part in the play on her own acting merit, not because of her famous father's influence. 'Not much.'

'Have you always wanted to be an actor?'

'Ever since I was old enough to know what acting was,' she said. 'I was cast as a donkey in a nativity play in primary school. I'll never forget the feeling I got when I looked out at that sea of faces. I felt like I had come home. They had to drag me off when it was over. I didn't want the play to end. Of course, my mother would've known why it was such a passion in me, but she never told me, not until a couple of days before she died. If anything she tried to discourage me from acting. She didn't even let me take dancing classes. Not that we could've afforded them, of course.'

Flynn was looking at her with a thoughtful expression on his face. 'It must have come as a big shock to find out who your father was. How had she settled your curiosity before then about who had fathered you?'

'She told me she didn't know who he was,' Kat said. 'When I was old enough to understand, she said she'd had a one-night stand with someone and never saw or heard from him again. I believed her because she kind of lived like that while I was growing up. She had men come and go all the time. None of her relationships lasted that long. She married at eighteen soon after she left home but they divorced before she was twenty. She wasn't all that lucky in the men department. She attracted the wrong sort of guy. She wasn't a great judge of character.' *Not that I can talk.*

'Were you close to her?'

Kat liked to think she had been to a point, but with her mother keeping such a secret from her for so long she wondered whether she had imagined their relationship to be something it was not in order to feel more normal. She was nothing like her mother in personality. Her mother had lacked ambition and drive. She hadn't seemed capable of making a better life for herself. She'd had no insight into how she'd kept self-sabotaging her chance to get ahead. Kat was the opposite. She was uncompromising in the setting and achieving of goals. If she put her mind to something, she would let nothing and no one stand in her way.

'I loved her, but she frustrated me because she didn't seem capable of making a better life for herself,' Kat said. 'She didn't even seem to want to. She cleaned hotel rooms or worked in seedy bars ever since she left home after a row with her parents as a teenager. She didn't even try to move up the ranks or try to train for something else.'

What was she doing? She wasn't supposed to be getting all chummy with him. What had made her spill all that baggage out? Was it because he had rescued her from the unwelcome visitor next door? Was it because he hadn't made fun of her about her phobia? Unlike a couple of her mother's dodgy boyfriends, who had found it great sport to see her become hysterical and paralysed with fear.

She rarely spoke to anyone of her background. Even her closest friend Maddie only knew the barest minimum about her childhood. Life had been tough growing up. Kat had always felt like an outsider. She had been the kid with the hand-me-down clothes; the one with the shoes that had come from a charity shop; the one with the home haircut, not the salon one. The kid who'd lived in run-down flats with lots of unwelcome wildlife. Money had always been tight, even though there had been ways her mother could have improved their circumstances. She sometimes wondered if her mother's lack of drive had made *her* all the more rigidly focused and uncompromisingly determined.

Flynn still had that contemplative expression on his face. 'You're so much like your father it's uncanny. He had his first start in theatre at the age of five too. Both he and Elisabetta talk of the buzz of being onstage in front of a live audience. It's like a drug to them. They don't feel truly alive without it.'

Kat wasn't so sure she wanted to be reminded of how like Richard Ravensdale she was. She had his green-grey eyes and dark-brown hair, although her natural copper highlights were from her mother. She used to be quite pleased with her looks, thanking her lucky stars she had a good face and figure for the theatre. But now they felt more like a burden. It was a permanent reminder of how her mother had been exploited by a man who had used her and cast her away once he was done with her.

She didn't fool herself that her mother had loved Richard and his abandonment had set her life on the self-destructive course it had taken. Her mother had already been well on her way down the slippery slope when she'd met Richard. It was more that Richard was one of many men who had used and abused her mother, fulfilling her mother's view of herself as not worthy of being treated with respect and dignity—messages she had heard since childhood. Kat had asked her mother just before she died why she hadn't made contact with Richard in later years to tell him he had a child. Her mother had told her it had never occurred to her. She had taken the money he'd offered and, as far as she was concerned, that was the end of it. It was typical of her mother's lack of drive and purpose. She'd let life happen to her rather than take life by the throat and wring whatever opportunities she could out of it.

'I'm not going to meet him, so you can put that thought right out of your mind,' Kat said.

'But he could help you get established in the theatre,' Flynn said. 'Why wouldn't you want to make the most of your connection to him?'

'It might be the way you lawyers climb the career ladder, by using the old boys' network, but I prefer to get there on my own,' Kat said. 'I don't need or want my father's help. He wasn't around when I needed it most and as far as I'm concerned it's way too late to offer it now.'

'What if it's not help he's offering?' he said. 'What if he just wants to get to know you? To have some sort of relationship with you?'

'I don't want to get to know him,' Kat said. 'I don't need a father. I've never had one before so why would I want one now?'

'Do you have any family now your mother's gone?'

Kat didn't like thinking of how alone in the world she was now. Not that she hadn't always felt alone anyway; but somehow having no living relative now made her feel terribly isolated, as if she had been left on an island in the middle of a vast ocean with no hope of rescue. Her grandparents had died within a couple of years of each other a few years back and, as her mother had been an only child, there were no aunts, uncles or cousins.

The Christmas just gone had been one of the loneliest times in her life. She had sat by herself in a damp and cold bedsit eating tuna out of a can, trying not to think of all the warm, cosy sitting rooms where families were gathered in front of the tree unwrapping gifts, or sitting around the dining table to a sumptuous feast of turkey and Christmas pudding. To have no backup, no sense of a safe home-base to go to if things turned sour, was something she had never really grown up with, but it didn't mean she didn't long for it—that sense of belonging, the family traditions that gave life a sense of security, of being loved and connected to a network of people who would look out for each other.

'There's just me,' she said. 'But I prefer it that way. I don't have to remember any birthdays or buy anyone expensive Christmas presents.'

The edge of Flynn's mouth tipped up in a wry smile. 'Always a silver lining, I guess.'

A small silence ticked past.

His eyes did a slow perusal of her face, finally lowering to her mouth and lingering there for an infinitesimal moment. The air felt charged, quickened by the current of sensual energy that arced between them.

Mutual attraction. Unmistakable. Powerful. Tempting.

Kat had been aware of it the first time they'd met. She was acutely aware of it now. She felt it in her body—the way her skin tightened and then lifted away from the scaffold of her skeleton; the way her breasts tingled as if preparing for his touch. Her insides quavered with a flicker of longing, shocking her because she had always been slow to arousal. She loved the intimacy of sex, of touching and being needed, but it always took her *so long* to get there.

But in Flynn's presence her body went on full alert, every erogenous zone flashing as if to say, 'Touch me!' Even the weight of his gaze on her mouth was enough to set her lips buzzing with sensation. She sent the tip of her tongue out to try and damp down the tingling but his hooded gaze followed every millimetre of movement, ramping up the tension in the air until she felt a deep, pulsing throb between her legs that echoed in her womb.

'Would you like to stay here tonight?' he said.

Kat laughed to cover how seriously tempted she was. 'I think I'll take my chances with the wildlife next door.'

'I wasn't asking you to sleep with me.'

Kat wished she could control the blush that filled her cheeks. A blush not so much of embarrassment, but of wanting what she wasn't supposed to want. And knowing he knew it. 'I'm not interested either way.'

'Liar,' he said. 'You were interested the moment I walked into that café that day with that cheque. That's why you haven't dated anyone since October.'

Kat wondered how on earth he had found out that information. Did he have someone tailing her? Keeping tabs on her? The last thing she wanted was anyone to find out she had mistakenly dated a married man. Her fledging career would be sabotaged if her affair with Charles Longmore were leaked in the press. Thankfully her partner in crime and grime was too frightened of his wife finding out to do his own press leak and cash in on her newfound fame as Richard Ravensdale's love child. 'I haven't dated because I made a celibacy pact with my best friend. We're off men until February.'

His eyes smouldered. 'I'll wait.'

Kat arched her brows. 'You don't strike me as a particularly patient man.'

'I know how to delay gratification,' he said. 'It makes the final feast all the more satisfying.'

No wonder he was a force to be reckoned with in court. He had a way with words that would leave most people's heads spinning.

But Kat was not most people. She too could delay gratification. Not only delay it but postpone it indefinitely. 'Don't set the table too early,' she said. 'Your guest might not show up.'

'Oh, she'll show up,' Flynn said with another glint in those bedroom eyes. 'She won't be able to stop herself.'

CHAPTER FOUR

IT WAS SNOWING in earnest when Flynn walked Kat back to the house next door. Even though it was only a few metres, she was conscious of his tall, warm body walking beside her along the footpath. In her flat shoes she barely came up to his shoulder. She didn't like admitting it but their playful banter was something she found intensely stimulating. Sparring with him was like being involved in a fast-paced fencing match. She had to be on her guard every second.

She wondered if he would come into the café tomorrow. A little spurt of excitement flashed through her at the thought of seeing him again. She didn't want to be attracted to him, or to even like him, but the way he had handled the 'rodent-ectomy' as he called it had lifted him in her estimation. She still couldn't get over the fact he hadn't mocked her for her phobia. It had been a perfect opportunity to tease her. But instead he had simply dealt with the problem with surprising expertise and tact, as if it were perfectly normal for her to be squeamish about removing an unwanted creature from beneath the sofa.

Kat unlocked the door and turned to look up at him through the falling snow. 'Thanks for tonight.'

'You're welcome,' he said. 'I closed the cat flap, by

the way. I put some duct tape over the catches. I think Monty must've worked them loose. He's a smart cat.'

Kat couldn't stop looking into his dark brown eyes with their thick fringe of lashes. Every now and again his gaze would flick to her mouth, the contact of his gaze making her lips feel tingly. 'Thanks for not making fun of me.'

His brow furrowed like a series of tide lines on a seashore. 'About what?'

'My silly phobia.'

He blinked away some snow and smiled, the flash of his white teeth making her stomach do a jerky little somersault. 'I used to be scared of the dark when I was kid. I slept with a night-light on for years. I got an awful ribbing about it at boarding school but eventually I got over it.'

'I can't imagine you being scared of anything.'

There was a long beat of silence.

Kat looked at his mouth—the way it was curved, the way his dark stubble surrounded it, the way his lean jaw with the sexy cleft in his chin made her ache to trail her fingertips over its rough surface. She sent the tip of her tongue out over her lips, watching with bated breath as his eyes tracked its journey. Her awareness of him sharpened. His stillness. As if he were waiting for her to make the first move. It had been months since she had felt a man's lips on hers. Months since she had felt a man's arms gather her close and remind her of how good it felt to be wanted. Needed.

Flynn's hands came down on the tops of her shoulders as softly as the snow cascading around them. His head came down, his foggy breath mingling with hers in that infinitesimal moment before contact. And yet, he didn't make that final contact. He hovered there as if he knew she would be the first to break.

If you kiss him, you lose.

But I want to kiss him.

Yes, but he knows that, and that's why he's waiting.

I haven't been kissed in months.

He probably knows that too.

But it's been so long, I've almost forgotten what it feels like to be a woman.

If you kiss him, you might not be able to stop.

Back and forth the battle with Kat's conscience and her flagging willpower went. And the whole time Flynn waited. She put a hand on his chest, then both hands. His coat was soft and warm to touch, but then, who could go past cashmere? Beneath the luxurious fabric she could feel the outline of his toned muscles. If she took a step, even half a step, she would be flush against his pelvis.

Even without closing that tiny distance she knew he was aroused. She *sensed* it. His body was calling out to hers, signalling to her, stirring hers to send the same message back. She became aware of her breasts, the way they seemed to swell, to prickle, to tingle. She became aware of her breathing; the way it stopped and started in little hitches and flows, swirling in a misty fog in front of her face, mixing intimately with his. She became aware of the pulsing throb between her legs, that most secret of places that ached for fulfilment. *Baboom. Baboom. Baboom.* The blood in her veins echoed the frantic need coursing through her.

'If you don't make up your mind soon, we're both going to freeze to death on this doorstep,' Flynn said.

Kat dropped her hands from his chest and stepped back. 'You thought you'd won that, didn't you?'

His glinting eyes and crooked smile made her insides twist and coil with lust. 'It's only a matter of time before I do.'

She gave him a scornful look. 'Dream on, Carlyon.'

His eyes darkened as if the challenge she'd laid before him privately excited him. 'Something you should know about me—I *always* win.'

Now it was Kat getting excited. She *loved* proving people wrong. It ramped up her determination. It fuelled the fire in her belly. If anyone said she *couldn't* do something, she made it her business to *do* it. If anyone said she *would* do something, she made sure she *didn't*.

Although there was a part of her that recognised the challenge of resisting Flynn Carlyon was right up there, as far as difficult challenges went. But as long as she kept her distance she would be home free. 'I'm sure that arrogance works well for you in court but it makes absolutely no impression on me,' she said.

He reached out his gloved hand and traced a fingertip along the surface of her bottom lip. 'I've thought about kissing you since the first day I met you.'

Me too! Me too! Kat kept her features neutral in spite of the excited leap of her pulse. 'I wouldn't have thought I was your type.'

His gaze went to her mouth as if savouring the moment when he would finally claim it. 'You're not.'

Why the heck not? 'Not used to slumming it, then?'

His brows came together, forming a two-fold pleat between his eyes. 'Is that how you see yourself?'

It was how others saw her. She had been the victim of classism since she'd been old enough to know what it was. Having a charwoman and barmaid for a mother didn't exactly get her high enough on the social ladder to suffer vertigo. 'I know what side of the tracks I come from,' Kat said. 'It's certainly not the same side as you.'

His frown was still pulling at his brow, as if invisible stitches were being tugged beneath his skin. 'I wouldn't know about that.' Then after a slight pause he added, 'I don't actually know who my parents are.'

Kat frowned in confusion. 'But you said your father is a builder and your mum is—'

'They're not my real parents.'

She looked at him blankly. 'Not your real parents… Oh, are you adopted?'

Something in his eyes became shuttered. His mouth was flat. Chalk-white flat. I-wish-I-hadn't-said-that flat. But, after a moment of looking at her silently, he finally released a breath that sounded as if he had been holding it a long time. A lifetime. 'Yes. When I was eight weeks old.'

'Oh… I didn't realise. Have you met your birth mother?'

He gave a twist of a smile that didn't reach his eyes. 'No.'

'Have you gone looking?'

'There's no point.'

'Why?' Kat said. 'Don't you want to know who she is? Who both your parents are?'

He huddled further into his coat as the snow came down with a vengeance. Kat got the feeling he was withdrawing into himself, not because of the cold but because he'd obviously revealed far more than he'd wanted to reveal. 'I've kept you long enough,' he said. 'Go inside before you catch your death. Good night.'

She watched him stride through the white flurry of snow back to his house. He didn't look back at her even once.

He unlocked his front door and disappeared inside, the click-click sound of the lock driving home as clear as if he had said, 'Keep Out.'

Flynn closed the door with a muttered curse. *What the hell were you thinking?* He wasn't thinking; that was the trouble when he was around Kat Winwood. He didn't think when he was around her. He *felt*. What was wrong with him, spilling all like that? He never talked about his adoptive family.

Never.

Cricket came slinking up on his belly as if he sensed Flynn's brooding mood. He bent down to ruffle the dog's ears. 'Sorry, mate. It's not you. It's me.'

Even his friends Julius and Jake Ravensdale knew very little of his background. They knew he was adopted but they didn't know he was a foundling. A baby left on a doorstep. No note pinned to him to say who he was and whom he belonged to. No date of birth. No mother or father to claim him. No grandparents.

Nothing.

That sense of aloneness had stayed with him. It was deeply embedded in his personality—the sense that in life he could only ever rely on himself.

Even his adoptive parents had lost interest in him once they had conceived their own biological children. Flynn remembered the slow but steady withdrawal of his parents' attention, as Felix and Fergus had taken up more and more of their time. He remembered how on the outside he felt at family gatherings, where both sets of grandparents would dote on his younger brothers but pay little or no attention to him. The blood bond was strong; he understood it because he longed to have it.

He ached to have knowledge of who he was and where he had come from.

But it was a blank.

He was a blank.

He was a man without a past. No history. No gene-alogy. No way of tracing the family he had been born into. In spite of extensive inquiries at the time of his abandonment, no one had come forward. He had spent years of his life wondering what had led his mother to leave him like a parcel on that doorstep. Why hadn't she wanted to keep him? Why had she felt she had no choice but to leave him on a cold, hard doorstep of a stranger's house? He had been less than a week old. His birth hadn't been registered. It was as if he had come out of nowhere.

What had happened to his mother since? Had she had more children? Who was his father? Had his mother and father loved each other? Or had something hap-pened between them that had made it impossible for his mother to envisage keeping the baby they had con-ceived? Did his father even know of his existence? The thoughts of his origins plagued him. He couldn't look at a baby without thinking of what had led his mother to abandon him.

It was one of the reasons he hadn't pursued a long-term relationship since Claire. Back in his early twen-ties he had wanted to fill the hole in his life by building a future with someone, by having a family of his own. When Claire had had a pregnancy scare a couple of months into their relationship, he had proposed on the spot. The thought of having his own family, of having that solid unit, had been a dream come true. But when Claire had found out she wasn't pregnant a couple of days later she'd ended their engagement. Her rejection had felt like another doorstep drop-off.

He hadn't been able to commit to another long-term relationship since. To have his hopes raised so high only to have them dashed had made him wary about setting himself up for another disappointment. Not knowing who he was made him worried about who he might become. What if he didn't have it in him to be a good father? What if there was some flaw in his DNA that would make him ill-suited as a husband and father?

But now, as he was in his thirties and he saw friends and colleagues partnering and starting their parenting, he felt that emptiness all the more acutely. With Julius and Holly married now, Jake and Jaz engaged and Miranda and Leandro preparing for their wedding in March, he was the last man standing.

Alone.

Why had he told Kat Winwood, of all people? Or was it because he saw something in her that reminded him of himself? Her tough-girl exterior. Her take-no-prisoners attitude. Her steely self-reliance. Her feisty determination to win at all costs.

Everything about her stirred his senses into overload. Her sexy little body. Even her starchy stiffness when she was stirred up excited him. Her beautiful eyes, the colour of sea glass, fringed with long, black lashes that reminded him of miniature fans. Her pearly white skin, luminescent and without a single blemish, not even a freckle. Her rich dark-brown hair, with its highlights of burnished copper, that fell to just past her shoulders in a cascade of loose waves. Her flowery perfume— a hint of winter violets, lilacs and something else that was unique to her.

From the first moment he'd met her he had wondered

what her lips would feel like against his own. He lay awake at night thinking about her. Imagining what it would be like to make love to her. He wasn't being over-the-top confident to think she was attracted to him. He could sense it in the way she kept looking at his mouth, as if a force was drawing her gaze there against her will. Even when she looked at him with those intelligent, defiant eyes he could see the flare of her pupils and the way her tongue sneaked out to moisten her luscious mouth. He enjoyed making her blush. It showed she wasn't quite as immune to him as she made out. He enjoyed sparring with her. The sexy banter was like foreplay. He got hard just thinking about it.

Every cell in his body delighted in the challenge she was laying before him. He thrived on the chase. The conquest was his lifeblood. It energised him. It excited him to think she was playing so hard to get. He was tired of the easy conquests. He could pull a date with just a look. It had lost its appeal. He wanted more. More depth, more intellectual stimulation, more time to explore the chemistry that sizzled and crackled between them.

Her strong will constantly clashed with his but that was what he found so attractive about her. She wasn't going to let anyone walk over her, or at least not without a fight.

Her indomitable stance on not meeting her father was a way of taking control—of being in charge. Richard had hurt her mother, Kat wanted justice and this was her way to get it. She was intent on punishing her father but what she didn't realise was, in the end, she was punishing herself and her half-siblings.

But Flynn wasn't going to stop until he had achieved

what he'd set out to achieve. He wanted Kat Winwood at that party.

He wanted Kat Winwood, period.

Kat watched from an upstairs window the next morning as Flynn took his little dog Cricket for an early morning walk. He must have been up first thing to shovel the snow from his footpath. But then she looked down at hers and saw it was clear as well. A warm, oozy sort of feeling spread through her insides. Had he done that for her?

He was rugged up in coat, hat and gloves and he had dressed Cricket in a little padded coat that only left his ridiculous tail, odd ears and stumpy little legs on show. She watched as the dog bounced around him with glee, his little feet stirring up the powdery snow like a miniature snow machine. Flynn bent down and ruffled the dog's ears affectionately before they continued along the footpath.

What was the story with that crazy little dog? He had mentioned his mother had got tired of Cricket once he'd ceased to be cute. Had that happened with Flynn? Had his mother—both his parents—lost interest in him once their other sons had come along? Was that why he had been sent to boarding school? Were Flynn's brothers adopted too? Or had his parents conceived their own children after adopting him? It sometimes happened when a couple adopted a child after years of infertility.

So many questions were crowding her thoughts. She wanted to know more about him. She wanted to know everything about him.

Oh no, here you go again.

What? I'm just interested in his background.

Sure you are.

I am!

You're interested in getting into bed with him. So much for your celibacy pact.

I'm not going to sleep with him. I just want to find out more about him.

You are so going to lose this.

I am not. I can resist him. I'm strong. I'm invincible. I'm disciplined.

You're toast.

Kat was late getting back from working at the café as she had worked an extra shift because one of the waitresses had called in sick. The traffic was horrendous because of another heavy snowfall. The roads were slippery and tempers were becoming frazzled, including hers. And there were no parking spaces outside the Carstairs house. She had to do three tedious circuits before one became available in front of Flynn's BMW, as he had arrived just before her. *Typical. He gets the celebrity car spot while I'm driving around in circles for hours.* He was standing on the footpath retrieving some papers off the passenger seat as Kat drew alongside the car in front in order to reverse park. She tried not to be put off with him standing there watching her but every time she went to reverse back she was either too close to the car in front or too far from the curb.

Flynn tucked his papers under one arm and came over to her driver's window, leaning down to speak to her. 'Do you want me to park it for you?'

Kat's pride came to her rescue. That was the second time he'd offered to park her car. What did he think she was? Useless? Sure, it was nice he'd scraped the snow away from her doorstep that morning, but she was perfectly capable of parking her car. If she let him do it for her, what else would she let him do? Allowing him to do stuff for her was a fast track into his bed and she was keeping off it. 'No thanks. I've got it.'

'I'll stand behind to guide you in. Take it slowly.'

Kat watched in the rear-view mirror as he positioned himself behind her car to stand in front of the BMW. She gave herself a pep talk. *You've parked a thousand times in spaces much tighter than this. Don't let him put you off. Just park the damn thing.* She put her indicator back on, positioned the wheels and then gingerly pressed her foot on the accelerator. She was doing brilliantly. *Yay!* The car was easing into the space like a dream but then another car flashed past, the driver called out something rude and Kat momentarily lost her focus. She forgot her foot was still on the accelerator until she felt the car go over a bump. The skin on her scalp shrank. She glanced behind her to see Flynn hopping about the footpath clutching one of his feet, a string of curse words coming out of his grimly set mouth.

Kat jumped out of the car, almost getting swiped by another car as it went past, spraying her with dirty, slushy snow. 'Oh, my God! Are you okay?'

He leaned one hand on the rear of her car as he put his foot to the ground, wincing as he tried to get it to take his weight. He frowned at her from beneath a single bar of eyebrows. 'Who taught you to park a car?'

Kat knew it wasn't the time to take umbrage with his tone but if he hadn't been there taunting her she would have parked the car just fine. Well, maybe. 'What were you doing standing *behind* my car? You should've stood on the footpath and directed me from there. That's what any sensible person would've done.'

'I wasn't going to stand by and watch you plough your car into mine,' he said. 'I've only had it a month.'

He pushed himself away from her car and took a couple of steps but his mouth had white tips around the edges and he was barely able to put any weight on his foot. She chewed at her lips, wondering what she should do. She might be doing her level best to avoid him but she could hardly leave him to fend for himself, especially since she had been the one to run over his foot. 'Do you want me to call an ambulance or… or something?'

'That won't be necessary.'

Kat tried not to be put off by his clipped tone. He was in pain. Of course he would be brusque. 'I'm sorry… I didn't mean to hurt you. My tyres are a little bald and I—'

'Your tyres are *bald* and you're driving on them in this weather?' He glowered at her. 'Do you realise how dangerous that is? Not just to yourself but to other innocent people on the road?'

Kat put up her chin. It was all right for him to bang on about new tyres. He could afford to buy any brand of tyre he liked. He could afford to buy any *car* he liked. She had to make do with whatever she could afford. She couldn't do without a car when she had to go to auditions all over the country. 'I bet your foot isn't even hurt. I bet you're one of those men that get man flu. One sniffle and I bet you go to bed all day.'

He shook his head at her like a frustrated parent does a wilful child. 'You're freaking unbelievable.'

Kat spun on her heel and stalked off without another word. She was glad she'd run over his foot. It served him right. She would do it again if she had half a chance.

Both feet.

CHAPTER FIVE

'BROKEN?' FLYNN ASKED, peering at the X-ray of his right foot that his friend Dr Joaquim Barrantes in A&E was showing him on the computer screen.

'In three places,' Joaquim said. 'How'd you do it again?'

Flynn gave him a speaking look. 'Don't ask.'

Joaquim grinned. 'So, how are things going with that hot little Scot? Got her to go out with you yet?'

'I'm working on it.'

'How many months has it been now?' Joaquim gave him a teasing look. 'Not like you to take so long to get down to business. You must be losing your touch.'

'I've changed my tactics,' Flynn said. '"Slowly but surely" is my new M.O.'

Joaquim nudged some crutches that were propped against the gurney. 'Yeah, well, these will slow you down a bit. But you'll be fine with a bit of rest. You don't need it plastered, just a firm bandage and crutches for four weeks. The bones are small, but you don't want to compromise healing with too much weight on them in the early stages of recovery.'

Crutches. Flynn smothered a curse. What was that going to do to his credibility in court? Limping around on a pair of crutches didn't suit his image of being in control. But taking time off while his foot healed would be pointless. What could he do? He wasn't the sit-around-the-house type. It was not as though he could go skiing. He wouldn't even be able to head to somewhere warm. Walking on a beach or lounging around a resort pool on crutches wasn't his idea of fun. And spending time with his family in Manchester wasn't something he was keen to repeat after the Christmas debacle. And who was going to walk Cricket twice a day?

The cogs of Flynn's mind began to tick over. He wasn't averse to twisting the odd emotional blackmail screw when it suited him. Besides, Kat owed him something, surely? She might not have deliberately injured him but he was a firm believer in do the crime, do the time. And it would be rather entertaining to have her play nursemaid. He would be able to see her several times a day. Every morning. Every night.

Who knew what he could talk her into with that amount of close contact?

'What about driving?' Flynn asked his friend.

Joaquim shook his head. 'It would be fine if it wasn't your right foot but your insurance company wouldn't cover you if you drove with it until you've been given the all clear. Just as well you filthy rich lawyers can afford to catch cabs everywhere.'

'Funny,' Flynn said. 'But us rich lawyers are the people you overworked medicos turn to when your patients want to sue you.'

Joaquim tapped his fingers on the wooden desk he was standing next to. 'So far, so lucky.'

Kat was glancing out of the front window to see if the snow had stopped when she noticed a cab pulling up outside Flynn's house. Her stomach dropped when she saw Flynn get out on crutches, his foot heavily bandaged. *Crutches?* Oh, dear Lord! What had she done? Would he sue her? He was a lawyer. A high-profile one. She would be taken to the cleaners… Not that she owned anything, but still… The thought of wounding someone—anyone—was anathema to her. Now she'd had time to cool down, she realised how rude she had been. Acting as if it was his fault his foot had got run over.

It was *her* fault.

She was lousy at parking. She always had been. She needed to eat a big slice of humble pie even if she choked on it. She let the curtain drop back and raced out, only stopping long enough to put on a coat. The icy air burned her cheeks but she figured it would counter the hot blush currently residing there.

Flynn had not quite made it to his front door when she came up alongside him. 'Oh, my God!' she said. 'Is it broken?'

'In three places.'

'I'll pay your health costs.' She swallowed convulsively, mentally checking her bank account and wondering how she was going to follow through on her promise.

'Forget about it.'

'But surely I can do something?'

He seemed to consider her question for a moment, his eyes studying her face as if committing it to memory. 'Can you cook?'

'Yes, but—'

'Good,' he said. 'I'll need a meal each evening and lunch and dinner on weekends, unless I go out, which I very much doubt I'll be doing much of now I'm on these damn crutches.'

Kat frowned. 'Don't you have a housekeeper?'

'Only to clean the house once a week,' he said. 'I'll need help with shopping and walking Cricket and running errands. You up for it?'

She tried not to look resentful, given her role in his predicament, but she couldn't help feeling he was orchestrating things to suit his ends. But spending time with him in any capacity was surely asking for the sort of trouble she could do without.

He was too confident. Too sure of himself. Too darned sexy. *Yes, even on crutches.*

He did something to her female hormones. They started humming with excitement. They did cartwheels in her belly when his dark eyes locked on hers. When he looked at her mouth her insides quivered at the thought of those firm but sensual lips coming into contact with hers. Not that she would let that happen. If he thought he could win her over with seduction then he was in for a big let-down.

You broke his foot on purpose.

I did not! It was an accident.

Now you'll have to spend hours with him, doing stuff for him. Acting like a wife.

I will not be like a wife. I'll walk the dog, put the rubbish out, pick up his dry cleaning and cook his meals... Eek! You're right—I'll be like a wife.

'Isn't there someone else you can get to help you?' Kat said. 'It's not like you couldn't afford to pay someone.'

'You're the one who broke my foot. Why should I be out of pocket for an inconvenience you caused?'

Kat would have liked to call his bluff but he was a high-powered lawyer and she was one job away from the dole queue. He was well within his rights to sue her for causing injury. She wouldn't stand a chance in defending herself, nor could she afford a defence lawyer to act on her behalf. Her space between a rock and a hard place had just got a little more cramped. Hippopotamus-in-a-hot-tub cramped. 'I don't suppose I have much choice.'

'That's settled, then. Why don't you come in now and I'll show you round the kitchen?' A glint appeared in his gaze and he added, 'I might even have an apron I can loan you—that is, unless you have one of your own?'

Kat gave him a beady look. 'No, funnily enough, that's one item that's missing from my wardrobe.'

As soon as Flynn opened the door Cricket came bowling out, spinning around Kat's legs, yapping volubly, bouncing up and down on his stubby little legs like his paws were on springs. She crouched down so she could pat him and got her faced licked for her trouble. 'Oh, you crazy little mutt.' She laughed and pulled back before he took off her make-up. 'Only a mother could love that little face.'

Kat looked up to see Flynn looking at her with a far-away look in his gaze. 'Sorry.' She got to her feet. 'That was a bit insensitive of me...'

He gave a brief smile. 'It's fine. He was a very cute puppy. Anyone would've fallen for him.'

Kat followed him and the dog inside. She took one of Flynn's crutches so he could take off his coat. She could feel the warmth of the hand rest where his fingers had just been, making her own hand tingle. She helped him take off his coat as if taking an explosive device from a would-be suicide bomber. She didn't touch his body, only the fabric of his coat, but she could feel the electric pulse of his proximity shoot through her body like a lightning zap. 'Are your brothers adopted too?'

He propped himself back on both crutches. For a moment she thought he was going to tell her to mind her own business. His dark eyes had a curtained look. A don't-bother-knocking-no-one's-going-to-answer look. But then his expression subtly changed. There came a slight relaxation of the muscles as if something tight and restricted inside his mind had loosened. 'No. My parents managed to conceive naturally three years after adopting me.'

Was that why he wasn't close to his family? Was that why he had been sent away to school? His parents hadn't needed him once they had created their own flesh and blood? He was like the cute little puppy that had failed to be cute once it grew up a bit and got a little more challenging to handle. 'Is that why you're not close to them?' Kat said. 'Did they treat you differently once they had their own kids?'

He gave a resigned lip-shrug. 'Sharing DNA with your kids is a powerful factor in bonding with them. Adoption works well when it works, but when it doesn't it can be a disaster.'

Kat's heart squeezed for the little boy he had been. How painful for him to have been shunted aside like a toy that no longer held its initial appeal. Small children picked up on the slightest change in dynamic with primary caregivers. The thought of Flynn recognising at such a young age he was no longer important to his parents must have had a devastating effect on him. 'Your adoptive parents shouldn't have treated you any differently,' she said. 'They made a commitment to you as a baby that was meant to be for life.'

He gave her a twisted smile that had a hint of sadness to it. 'It doesn't always work like that. Matching kids to parents isn't an exact science. I was a difficult baby, apparently. When my parents had Fergus and then Felix they realised it wasn't their parenting that was the problem—it was me. I simply didn't belong in that family.'

Kat frowned. 'I don't believe that for a second. They adopted you as a tiny baby. They should've bonded with you no matter what. You don't give up on a child just because it doesn't fulfil your expectations. A child is an individual. They have their own path to tread. It's the parents'—biological or adoptive—responsibility to make sure their child gets every opportunity to become the person they're meant to become.'

Cricket gave a loud yap, as if in agreement. Flynn smiled wryly as he scratched the dog's belly with the rubber end of his crutch. 'Not every kid gets that level of commitment, do they, Cricket?'

Kat chewed at her lip for a moment. 'You said the other day there was no point looking for your birth parents. What did you mean by that?'

He stopped scratching the dog and started hopping towards the kitchen. 'Cricket needs feeding. I usually take him out for half an hour morning and evening, after his breakfast and dinner.'

She followed him into the kitchen. 'Flynn, why won't you talk about your birth parents? You shut up like a clam with lockjaw every time I mention them.'

He pointed to the pantry with one of his crutches as if she hadn't spoken. 'His dry food's in there and his meat's in the fridge. There's more in the freezer.'

The drawbridge was up. She could see the tight muscles on his face. The set mouth. She had come too close and he was telling her not to come any closer. But the more he pushed her away the more she wanted to draw close. He was so much more than the arrogant my-way-or-the-highway man she had thought him on first appearances. He was deep. Deep and mysterious. Intriguing to the part of her that couldn't help feeling compassion for a fellow sufferer of the club of Not Belonging. 'Is your foot hurting you?' she said.

He rubbed his hand over his face loud enough for her to hear the rasp of his stubble. 'I had a couple of painkillers at the hospital. I might go and have a lie down. I'm feeling like a bit of a space cadet.'

'I'll sort out Cricket and then bring you up something to eat,' Kat said. 'Do you have a spare key so I can let myself back in?'

'There's one in the bowl on the hallstand. It's on a blue key ring.'

Kat let herself back in forty minutes later with Cricket panting at her feet. He had been a little darling, trotting by her side as if he had got first-class honours from obedience school. However, it had been a completely different story at the dog exercise area in the park. Cricket hadn't cared for the other dogs, especially the big ones. He'd strained at the leash and barked and snarled as if he'd been ready to rip them apart. It hadn't won him any friends. The other owners had quickly called their dogs back and given Kat looks, as if to say, 'Why don't you get control of your dog?'

It had been humiliating.

But for all that she couldn't help thinking it was a bit of a windfall having this one-on-one time with Cricket. The play she was auditioning for was A. R. Gurney's *Sylvia*, which was a play about a middle-aged married man who brought home a dog he found at the park, much to his wife's displeasure, because she wanted to enjoy their empty nest. Kat was auditioning for the role of Sylvia the dog, a wonderful part that was energetic and challenging on every level. A Canadian actor was playing the lead of Greg, the husband's role, but no one knew who was playing Kate, the wife, as it was apparently the director's secret. It would be announced once the auditions were over. An understudy would take the role until formal rehearsals started.

Kat wanted that role. It was a chance-in-a-lifetime role. A star-making role. Audiences loved Sylvia. It was the actor who played the dog that made or broke the performance. If she got that part it would be her chance to prove her mettle as an actor.

Kat tossed a salad and set it beside the fluffy cheese omelette she had made. Cricket followed at her heels as she carried it upstairs. She had no idea where Flynn's bedroom was but the layout was much the same as next door so she took a gamble. She found him fast asleep on the bed with one hand folded across his flat stomach and the other in a right angle flung back on the pillow at his head. His bandaged foot was propped on another pillow; the other one was still wearing a shoe—a black Italian leather zippered ankle boot. His handsome features were relaxed in sleep, giving him a vulnerable look that was at odds with his reputation as an intimidating courtroom king.

She approached the bed with caution, not wanting to wake him, but unable to stop herself from going closer. She leaned down to put the tray on the bedside table and then straightened to see if he had registered her presence. His eyelids flickered as if he was in the middle of a dream and his lips were slightly parted, enough for her to hear the soft, even rhythm of his breathing.

On an impulse she could neither explain nor control,

Kat reached out and gently brushed her fingers down the stubble-shadowed landscape of his jaw. The slight catch of her softer skin on his raspy one made something slip sideways in her stomach, like a stockinged foot on a shiny floor.

He opened his eyes and reached for her hand at the same time, his fingers wrapping around the slim bones of her wrist like a steel bracelet. He gave her a slow smile. 'Changed your mind about that kiss?'

Kat tried to pull out of his hold but his fingers tightened just a fraction—a delicious fraction that set her nerves tingling. 'I—I was checking to see if you had a temperature. You can never be too careful with fractures. There can be internal bleeding and infection and you might—'

'Am I hot?'

Way, way too hot. Way too hot for her to handle. 'I brought you some dinner. Just leave the tray—I'll clear it away in the morning.'

He released her hand and patted the bed near his thigh. 'Sit. Stay and talk to me.'

Don't do it.

Why not? He only wants to talk.

Yeah, right.

He needs some company. He's injured.

Not his mouth, or his hands, or his you-know-what. They're in perfect working order.

Kat felt the usual tug of war inside her mind, not to mention inside her body. She knew she should leave but another part of her wanted to stay. He drew her interest in a way no other man had done before. There was something about him that made her flesh sing just by being in the same room as him—from breathing the same air as him. He had a potent effect on her senses.

He made her aware of her femininity, of her needs—the needs that were proving rather difficult to ignore, especially when she was this close to him. Close enough to touch his face again, to trace the sensual contour of his tempting mouth. To lean down and press her lips to his and see what fireworks would happen—for they *would* surely happen. She knew it in her bones. 'Just for a minute, then…' She sat on the edge of the bed.

He surveyed her features for a moment. 'It was kind of you to stay and make me dinner. I wasn't sure you would.'

Kat gave a shrug. 'There's nothing to making an omelette.'

His thumb found her pulse and stroked over its frantic beat as his eyes held hers in a mesmerising lock. 'It's a pity we met the way we did. Perhaps if we'd met under different circumstances you wouldn't be sitting there but lying in here beside me.'

Kat felt a ripple of lust between her legs but disguised it by casting him a resentful glare. 'You cost me my job in that café.'

He gave a little grimace of remorse. 'I know. But I was lucky I didn't get burnt when you poured that coffee in my lap.'

She chewed at her lip when she recalled that day. Having Flynn show up at the café the day after her mother's funeral with that cheque from Richard Ravensdale had been like coarse salt rubbed into a festering wound. The thought of being paid to keep silent about something that should never have been a secret in the first place was an insult. So too was the fact that her father had sent his lawyer instead of coming to see her in person.

That hurt.

It shouldn't but it did. If her father wanted to have a relationship with her—a proper relationship—then why send someone else to set it up for him?

But, no, Richard had paid someone to pay her to keep her mouth shut about his dirty little affair with a hotel housemaid. Now Richard wanted to be a father to her. Why? To boost his popularity? To keep his fans happy? It certainly wasn't because he cared about her.

But Flynn had a point. If she and Flynn had met some other way she might well have considered getting involved with him. He was the most interesting man she had ever met. His looks made her go weak at the knees, but he was so much more than a good-looking man. She found his razor-sharp intelligence the biggest turn on. He was funny and charming, and yet there were layers to him, depths he kept hidden. Enigmatic depths that made her want to get as close as she possibly dared.

'I'm sorry about the coffee but it was all too much,' Kat said. 'I'd only just got back from Glasgow from the funeral. I didn't even know how anyone had found out about his affair with my mother. It was a shock to find it splashed all over the papers.'

'Apparently one of your mother's former workmates let something slip to a journalist,' Flynn said. 'The rest, as they say, is history.'

'Sometimes I wish I hadn't agreed to that paternity test. But I wanted to know for sure.'

'At least you know who your father is. Lots of people never find out.'

Kat looked at him again. There was a slight frown pulling at his brow, as if he was thinking about something that pained him. Twice now she had tried to draw him out about his birth parents but he had shut off the conversation. Why was he being so stubborn about it?

Lots of relinquished children managed to conduct loving relationships with their biological parents once contact was made. 'If your biological parents ever came looking for you would you want to meet them?'

His eyes didn't meet hers. 'I can't see it happening now. Not after thirty-four years.'

'It's never too late to give up hope.'

He gave her a movement of his lips that was almost a smile. 'That's exactly what your father keeps saying.'

Kat didn't want to think about the father she didn't want, and Flynn's father, whom he might never meet. In her mind the two situations were completely different. 'Is your foot troubling you?'

'Not much.'

She rose from the bed. 'I should let you have your food and go back to sleep.'

He captured her hand again, giving it a light squeeze that was perfectly timed with his on-off smile. 'Thanks.'

Kat bit her lip again as she looked at their joined hands. His skin was deeply tanned, as if he had been somewhere warm recently. She could see the paler band where his watch usually rested. His fingers were almost twice the thickness of hers, making her feel more feminine than she had in years. If she could just grow her nails instead of biting them back to the elbow she would feel even more feminine. 'I'm really sorry about your foot.'

But, when she looked back at him to see why he hadn't said anything, she saw he was soundly asleep.

Flynn swore as he came out of the shower the next morning. Not only had he overslept, which was going to make him late for his first client, the plastic bag he had wrapped around his foot hadn't done the job of keeping his bandage dry. And his foot was hurting. Badly. He limped out of the *en suite* to his bedroom with a towel around his hips to find Kat at his bedside collecting his tray from the night before.

She swung around and then quickly averted her gaze. 'Sorry. I thought you were still in the shower. I knocked but—'

'It's fine.' He reached for a pair of boxers and a shirt. 'I'm going to be late for work. Has Cricket been out yet?'

She kept her back turned to him as she straightened his bed, smoothing down the covers with meticulous precision, as if she did it for a living. 'Yes, I took him out first thing.'

'Why didn't you wake me?'

'I wasn't aware being an alarm clock was on my list of duties,' she said in a crisp tone.

'I got my bandage wet.'

She turned to look at him, her eyes giving a little flash. 'Poor baby.'

He clipped on his watch, snapping the catch in place. 'I haven't got time for breakfast. I have to brief a client before court. Can you hand me those trousers?'

'These?'

'No, the grey ones.'

'Here you go.'

Flynn winked at her. 'You'd make a great wife.'

She gave him an artic look. 'I have other ambitions.'

He slipped his belt through the lugs on his trousers whilst balancing on one crutch. 'You don't want to get married and have kids some day?'

'I want to establish my career first,' she said. 'Husbands have a way of getting in the way of career aspirations; kids even more so.'

Flynn wondered if she was being completely truthful. He had only met a handful of women who didn't want the whole package. He had wanted it himself until having it snatched away had made him reassess. But after he had come back to London on Christmas night after the usual palaver with his family—having rescued Cricket from being ignominiously dumped at the nearest dog shelter for almost certain euthanasia—the Carstairs family had invited him in for supper.

The difference in households had been nothing short of stunning. There was none of the stiffness and formality of his family, pretending to be comfortable with him when clearly they weren't. The Carstairses' kids, Josh and Bella, had run up to him and hugged him around his legs, grinning from ear to ear, excited beyond bounds he had come to join them. To see such unabated joy on their little faces had sent a rush of unexpected emotion to his throat, making him feel like he was choking on a pineapple. He had watched in silent envy as Neil and Anna had exchanged loving glances over the tops of the heads of their children who were miniature replicas of them.

It was fine now, being single and free to do what he liked, but what about in a few years' time? Would he still feel the same? Or would he feel a deep cavern of emptiness inside him where the love of a wife and family should have been? He was already tired of the dating scene. The thought of coming home to someone who wanted to be with him because they loved him, not because he was rich or well-connected, was something he couldn't stop thinking about lately.

It was like a door inside his mind he had thought he had closed and bolted had been prised open. A crack of light was shining through, illuminating the possibilities.

Possibilities like kids to go with the dog he already had. He loved coming home to Cricket. Seeing that funny little face beaming with excitement at seeing him had shifted something inside him. It made him see what an alternative life could be like. A life where not just a scruffy little dog would bolt up the hallway to greet him but a couple of grubby-faced kids like Josh and Bella. Kids who looked like him. Who carried the same DNA. Family was something he had seen as something other people had, not him. He was alone. Unattached. Without a blood bond.

But what if he made one?

He dismissed the thought, pushing it back behind the door in his mind, leaning his resolve against it to make sure it was closed.

'Can you choose me a tie?' Flynn said.

Kat went back to his wardrobe and selected a tie. 'Will this one do?'

'Perfect. Can you put it on for me?'

Her lips pursed. 'Why do I get the feeling you're making the most of this situation?'

He smiled as her hands looped the tie around his neck. This close he could smell her winter flowers fragrance as it danced and flirted with his senses. The temptation to press his mouth to hers was like a tug of war inside his body; every organ strained at the effort of keeping his willpower under control. 'Why do I get the feeling you'd like to strangle me?'

Her gaze went to his mouth. Her fingers worked on his tie but he could feel them tremble as they inadvertently touched the skin of his neck. His blood leapt at the contact, pulsing through his veins like rocket fuel. She took her bottom lip between her teeth in concentration—or was it because she was fighting an urge, the same urge he could feel barrelling through his body? She completed his tie and gave his chest a quick pat. 'There.' She gave him the briefest flash of a smile. 'All done.'

His gaze locked on hers, watching as the dark ink of her pupils in that sea of bewitching green widened. Watching too as the tip of her tongue came out and darted over the surface of her lips, the top first and then the bottom, leaving them moist, shining and tempting. His blood headed south, his groin swelling and tingling with the promise of contact. Any contact. He couldn't think of a time when he had wanted a woman more than her. But he wanted her to make the first move. She was oscillating; he could tell. The same battle he was fighting in his body was being played out over her features. Her gaze slipped again to his mouth. Her tongue did another circuit of her lips. Her breathing hitched just loud enough for him to hear it. He saw the rise and fall of her slender throat. He ached to press his lips to the thrumming pulse he could see hammering there. 'What have you got riding on this celibacy pact?' he asked.

She swallowed again. Audibly. 'Wh-why do you want to know?'

'Just wondering what's keeping your self-control in check.'

Her chin came up, her mouth pulled tight again. 'You think you're so damn irresistible, don't you?'

Flynn smiled at her. 'You want me *so* bad.'

Her eyes fired a round of ire at him. 'I. Do. Not. Want. You.'

'How many times do you reckon you'll have to say that to believe it?'

Her breath came out like a small explosion. 'You're unbelievable. You think just because every other woman you've ever smiled at fell at your feet that I will too. Well, guess what? I won't.'

'That's what the silly little celibacy pact is all about, isn't it?' Flynn said. 'You knew from the moment we met that we would end up in bed together so you thought of a plan to prevent it from happening. Cute plan, but it's doomed to fail.'

She laughed but it didn't sound authentic, more like someone acting as though they were amused when deep down they were anything but. 'No wonder those bones broke in your foot. They were probably weakened from carrying around your ego.'

'Speaking of my broken foot,' Flynn said. 'Can you carry my briefcase downstairs?'

She gave him a mutinous look, but then her gaze went to his crutches and she gave a tiny swallow. 'How will you get to work? You can't drive, can you?'

'Unfortunately, no.'

She bit her lower lip and glanced at his bandaged foot again. 'I could drive you if you—?'

'No.'

She gave him a steely glare. 'There's no need to be so emphatic about it.'

'I'll take my chances with a cab,' Flynn said. 'But don't worry—I'll keep the receipts for you.'

CHAPTER SIX

FLYNN WASN'T HOME when Kat arrived later that day to take Cricket out for his evening walk. She refused to acknowledge the little slump in her spirits. What did she care if he wasn't home? It was better if she *didn't* see him, especially after seeing him all but naked this morning. Every time she thought of coming across him in his bedroom in nothing but a towel hitched around those lean hips her stomach somersaulted. His body was as attractive as his mind. Toned and tanned with muscles in all the right places. And his sexy frame was sprinkled with just enough masculine hair for her hormones to start fanning themselves.

But, when she walked back from the park with a panting Cricket at her side, she noticed more lights on in Flynn's house than she had left on when she had let herself in earlier. The front door opened before she could use the key Flynn had given her but it wasn't him standing there—it was Miranda Ravensdale. *Gulp*. Her half-sister. Kat knew it was Miranda as she had seen numerous photos of her and her brothers when the news of her existence had broken.

Miranda smiled shyly. 'Hi. I'm Miranda. I hope you don't mind us dropping in like this but when we heard Flynn broke his foot Jaz and I thought we'd better drop off a casserole or something. We won't stay long. We're just going, aren't we, Jaz?'

Before Kat could think of anything to say, another young woman appeared. 'Hiya.' Jasmine Connolly gave a beaming smile. 'So, we finally meet. Hey, Cricket.' She bent down and cuddled the dog, who was in a paroxysm of delight. 'What do you think of your new neighbour, huh? Isn't she a sweetheart to take you out for walkies?'

Why had Jaz made it sound as if Kat had taken the dog out as a Good Samaritan favour? Kat couldn't stop looking at Miranda, searching the young woman's elfin features for any likeness to her own. Her half-sister. A relative. Someone to belong to. Family. 'Erm...nice to meet you.'

Miranda bit her lower lip. 'Is it too awkward for you? I mean, we can leave now, can't we, Jaz?'

'But I thought we were going to stay and have dinner with Flynn?' Jaz said.

Kat saw the two exchange glances. 'I'm just dropping off Cricket,' she said into the little silence.

'Oh, won't you stay and have dinner with us?' Miranda's gaze was a wide, enthusiastic, welcome-to-the-family one. 'We made enough to feed an army. Two armies, the navy and the air force, actually. Julius and Jake aren't here, if that's what's worrying you. Julius and Holly are in Argentina just now and Jake's out with Leandro, my fiancé, at a work thing.'

Kat knew it would look churlish of her to refuse. But meeting her half-sister without warning had thrown her completely. No doubt Flynn was behind this impromptu meeting. Her fury at him boiled in her blood like caustic soda until her veins felt like they were going to bust. How dared he engineer a meeting she didn't want? Wasn't emotionally ready for? What if he'd invited her father? The whole freaking family? 'Where is Flynn?' she said.

'In the sitting room with his foot up,' Miranda said. 'I insisted he rest it. It's awfully bruised and swollen. I think he's been putting weight on it against doctor's orders. Some men make terrible patients.'

Kat peeled off her gloves, studying both girls with a watchful gaze. 'Did he tell you how he broke it?'

'He said he tripped down the stairs,' Jaz said. 'Not like him to be so clumsy, is it, Miranda?'

'No.' Miranda laughed self-deprecatingly. 'That's the sort of thing I would do, not Flynn.'

Kat opened and closed her mouth, stuck for something to say. Why hadn't he told the girls the truth? Why hadn't he exploited the situation? Why tell them he'd tripped when he could have told them *she* was responsible?

Jaz's grey-blue eyes began to dance. 'So, how long have you two been seeing each other?'

Kat straightened her shoulders. 'I'm not. We're not. I'm just—'

'House-sitting next door—yeah, yeah, yeah,' Jaz said, still grinning. 'Kind of convenient, huh?'

Kat elevated her chin, her mouth set in a prim Sunday school teacher line. 'Mr Carlyon recommended me to the Carstairs family next door. That is and will remain the only connection I have with him.'

Jaz was undaunted and gave Miranda a little elbow-nudge. 'Mr Carlyon? That's cute. And does he call you "Miss Winwood"?'

Kat glanced at Miranda, who was looking at her with big, soulful Bambi eyes. It occurred to her then that this meeting must be as tricky for Miranda as it was for her.

She was the interloper. The new half-breed sister. The shameful secret that had come to light after twenty-three years of silence. How awful must it be for Miranda to have to face the living and breathing evidence of her father's betrayal of his marriage vows? Miranda was no longer the baby sister, the youngest child. Kat had taken that position from her. The press had even gone as far to say Kat was the more beautiful of the sisters. Before that Miranda had always been compared to her glamorous mother and found lacking, and now she had a half-sister to be compared to. How did Miranda feel about that? Was she angry? Upset? Did she project that negative emotion on Kat?

Not so far as Kat could see. If anything, Miranda looked like she wanted to make a good impression. She looked like she was keen to establish a bond with her but was uncertain about how she would be received.

'What does a guy have to do to get a drink around here?' Flynn's deep voice called out from the sitting room.

Jaz turned on her heel and marched off to the sitting room. 'You're not supposed to drink when you're taking prescription painkillers,' she said.

Miranda looked at Kat with a shy grimace. 'I know this must be just awful for you...meeting me like this... I know you've not wanted any contact. I understand that. I really do. The whole situation is just ghastly for you but I do want us to be friends if at all possible. None of this is your fault. None of us blame you for it—well, apart from Mum, but let's not even go there.'

'Thanks.' Kat forced a smile. 'It's kind of weird but not awful. I've just needed some time to get my head around it all.'

Miranda's features relaxed ever so slightly. 'Please

don't be offended by Jaz's teasing just now. She just wants everyone to be as happy as she is, now she and Jake have got engaged. You're the last Ravensdale to be single… I mean, not that you probably think of yourself as a Ravensdale or anything, but…' She bit down on her lip again and blushed. 'I'm sorry. I'm making such a dreadful hash of this. I always talk too much when I'm nervous.'

'I go quiet when I'm nervous,' Kat said.

Miranda's eyes bulged. 'Really? That's exactly like Julius. I can't wait until you meet the boys. They're awesome big brothers. They're really looking forward to meeting you. But only if you want to, of course. You mustn't feel pressured to meet Dad. He can be a bit overpowering.' She gave a little eye-roll. 'Not to mention Mum—but don't get me started.'

Kat felt her smile relax. 'She's actually one of my favourite theatre actors.'

'Really?'

'She's amazing onstage,' Kat said. 'She's spellbinding to watch live. I could watch her all day.'

Miranda did that lip-chewing thing again and a small frown pulled at her smooth forehead. 'I've always found my mother's fame a bit of a burden. I know she's super-talented and all that but sometimes I just wanted her to be a mum. A normal one, you know?'

Kat gave her a wry look. 'What's normal? My mum certainly wasn't a soccer mum.'

Miranda touched Kat's arm, those big brown eyes warm and compassionate as they held hers. 'I'm really sorry about your loss. You must miss her dreadfully.'

Kat was a little ashamed to realise she didn't miss her mother. Not in the way one should miss a parent. It was almost a relief not to have to deal with her mum's issues.

The drinking. The depression. The never knowing what she would find at the end of the phone when she called. Morose moods. Mania. Mayhem. 'Thanks,' she said.

Cricket came bolting back out, did a couple of crazy spins and yapped three times at Kat. Miranda gave a light laugh. 'Looks like he's taken a bit of a shine to you.'

Kat smiled back. 'It's mutual.'

Miranda went off to join Jaz in getting dinner organised, so Kat took the opportunity to speak to Flynn in private. As soon as she entered the sitting room, his gaze met hers from where he was sitting on one of the plush sofas. 'So, you've met half of the family.'

She sliced him a glare. 'Feeling pretty proud of yourself, are you?'

He gave her a lazy smile. 'It had to happen sooner or later. Miranda and Jaz are like sisters to me. I've known them since they were in pigtails.'

Kat folded her arms. 'I suppose you'll have Richard just drop in next. If he does, I'm out of here. I don't care how rudely I come across.'

He studied her for a beat. 'I didn't know the girls were going to show up. I was speaking to Jake about a legal matter and I mentioned I'd broken my foot. He must've told Jaz and she told Miranda. They arrived just as I was getting out of the cab.'

Kat kept her gaze trained on his. 'Why did you tell them you tripped down the stairs?'

He gave a light shrug. 'I didn't want to make things awkward for you.'

'I thought the whole point of this exercise was to make things as awkward for me as possible.'

'The girls are keen to have an amicable relationship

with you. Why would I go and tell them you maimed me? They might never speak to you again.'

'*Maimed* you?' It's three tiny little bones, for God's sake. Talk about a drama queen.'

'It hurts like the very devil.'

She went over and whipped the glass of Scotch out of his hand. 'That is not allowed. You heard what Jaz said. You shouldn't mix alcohol with prescription drugs.'

His lazy smile made the base of her spine shiver. 'I'm having a hot fantasy of you dressed in a nurse's uniform. Ever played one?'

'Will you *stop* it? The girls will hear.'

His dark eyes glinted. 'We can't have the girls thinking anything untoward is going on between us, now can we, Miss Winwood?'

She gave him a look that would have withered marble. 'As if I would stoop so low.'

Jaz came breezing in with a tray loaded with nibbles. She looked at Kat's glowering expression and then at Flynn, who was smiling like a cat with an empty bowl and whiskers dripping with cream.

Jaz gave him a cheeky grin. 'That Carlyon charm not quite hitting the mark, eh, Flynn?'

'You know me,' he said. 'The harder I have to work for something the more I enjoy the victory.'

'Looks like you might've met your match,' Jaz said. 'I haven't seen you so hooked on anyone since Claire.'

The atmosphere changed as if an unpinned grenade had been dropped.

Flynn's expression turned to stone, his eyes to flint and the atmosphere to freezing. Kat glanced at Jaz but if Jaz was put off by Flynn's demeanour she showed no sign of it.

Miranda came in at that point and gauged the stiff

little tableau with a worried flicker of her gaze. 'What's going on?'

'I mentioned the C word.' Jaz took one of the nibbles and crunched into it loudly. Defiantly loudly. He-should-get-over-himself loudly.

Flynn reached for his crutches. 'Excuse me, but I'm going to give dinner a miss.'

Kat stood back as he limped past without once glancing her way. But she didn't have to see his face to know it was as tense as the muscles in his back and shoulders. *Interesting.* She waited until he was well out of earshot. 'Who is Claire?'

Jaz handed her a platter of nibbles. 'His ex-fiancée. Eleven years ago, to be precise. He's been gun-shy about commitment ever since.'

'Jaz, you really shouldn't have said anything,' Miranda said. 'You know how he hates anyone reminding him.'

Jaz shrugged off her friend's reproach. 'So, what's he got to be so uptight about? I've got three ex-fiancés and you don't see me getting upset if anyone mentions them by name.' She gave a twinkling grin and reached for her drink. 'Anyway, I've just about forgotten their names now I've got Jake.'

'How long was Flynn engaged?' Kat asked.

'Only a few weeks,' Miranda said. 'But he must have really loved her. He was devastated when she broke it off. He wouldn't talk about it, not for ages. I don't think he even told Julius or Jake all the ins and outs of what went wrong. He can be pretty tight-lipped at times.'

'I think it comes from him being adopted,' Jaz said, and at Miranda's cautionary look added, 'What?'

'You know he doesn't like everyone knowing about that,' Miranda said.

'It's all right,' Kat said. 'He told me he was adopted.'

Miranda's eyes went wide. Not saucer wide. Satellite-dish wide. 'Did he?'

Jaz gave Miranda another little conspiratorial nudge. 'See? What did I tell you? He's got it bad.'

'Have you met his family?' Kat asked, trying to ignore the traitorous little flutter of excitement Jaz's comments evoked. 'I mean, his adoptive one?'

Jaz bent down to give Cricket a snippet of smoked salmon. 'I met his mother last year when I was in Manchester for a bridal show. She was nice in a standoffish way. I got the feeling she didn't really get Flynn. I think he intimidates her with his intelligence. Not that it's his fault he's so smart and has done so well for himself. He's always been driven and superfocused.'

'He said he has no interest in meeting his biological parents,' Kat said. 'Do you know why?'

'I think a lot of men who've been adopted are like that,' Miranda said. 'I guess they find it hard to understand what it's like for a woman to have to make that impossibly difficult decision to relinquish a baby.'

'Maybe he'll tell you since you're getting on so well,' Jaz said to Kat with a spark in her gaze.

Kat gave her a speaking look. 'Don't hold your breath.'

The girls left after an hour of eating and chatting on lighter topics. Kat found it a surreal experience to be on such familiar terms with the two young women she'd spent the last three and a half months actively avoiding. She even felt a little sad once they'd left. Their tight unit reminded her of all she had missed out on as a child. She hadn't had close friends growing up, or at least not as close as Jaz and Miranda were. She had moved around too much when her mother had changed jobs or relationships. It had been hard to create a bond with friends when in the back of her mind she knew it wouldn't be long before she would be taken away to some other place where she would have to start all over again. Her friend Maddie was the only exception, but even then they had met as adults, when Kat had visited Maddie's beauty salon when she'd first moved to London, and their friendship had grown from there.

She wondered if she would see Miranda or Jaz again or if by seeing them it would bring her into contact with her father. She wasn't ready to meet Richard Ravensdale. She didn't think she would ever be ready. How could she stand in front of a man who had wished her existence away?

But the thought of meeting her half-brothers was tempting. Miranda had spoken so highly of them. What would it be like to have twin older brothers to watch out for her? To have a family who included her in their lives?

Who actually *wanted* her in their lives?

Kat put some food on a tray and carried it upstairs with Cricket at her heels. Flynn's door was closed so she had to put the tray on a hall table outside before she could knock. 'Flynn? Are you awake? I brought you some dinner.'

There was no answer so she opened the door. Flynn was lying on his back with his foot elevated, his eyes closed, but she could tell he wasn't asleep. There was too much tension in his body. She could see it in the terrain of his face: the twin lines running down either side of his mouth, the groove between his brows, the in and out flare of his nostrils, as if he was carefully measuring each breath. Was it his foot giving him grief or had Jaz's mention of his ex-fiancée done that to him? Eleven years was a long time to be bitter over a relationship break-up. She tried to imagine him as a man in love. He didn't seem the type to let his emotions rule his head. He was charming and laid-back, but always in control. Or was his bitterness anchored in the fact that Claire had been the one to walk out? Some men found rejection hard to take. Perhaps his being adopted had made him even more sensitive to it.

Kat came and sat on the edge of the bed feeling a bit like a kitten approaching a lion. 'So, I take it Jaz struck a raw nerve?'

'Not raw. Dead and buried.' His tone was flat, emotionless, but she could hear a speed hump of hurt. 'I hate having it exhumed. It stinks.'

Kat hadn't realised how close her hand was to his where it was resting on the bed. If she moved her pinkie a few millimetres it would come into contact with his. Something shifted in her belly at the thought of his darkly tanned skin touching hers. 'She's quite a personality, isn't she?'

He grunted something unintelligible.

'I liked Miranda too,' Kat said. 'A lot. I didn't expect to but she's nothing like I expected. I thought she'd hate me, but she made me feel like she really wants us to have a connection.'

'She's a sweetheart. Leandro's a lucky man.'

Kat looked at their hands again. Watched as the distance between their fingers got smaller. Was she moving her finger or was he moving his? 'Were you in love with her?'

'Who?'

'Claire.'

His lips folded inward like he was filtering his response. Blocking it. Banning it. The silence boomed with the beats of the muscle flicking in his jaw. In. Out. In. Out.

'If you'd rather not talk about it…' Kat left the words hanging. Dangling like a dare.

His gaze hit hers. Hard. Two-can-play-at-that-game hard. 'Do you want to talk about your affair with a married man?'

Shame turned Kat's stomach sour and made her face burn. 'You *know* about that?'

'Men like Charles Longmore can't help boasting about bedding a celebrity.'

Panic took an ice-pick to her spine and a sledgehammer to her heart. If Flynn knew then who else knew? Would her shame be splashed on every tabloid? Everyone would blame her. They always did. The Other Woman always got the blame. No one ever blamed the philandering husband. Kat would be cast in the role of home wrecker and there would be no way to defend herself. 'Oh no…'

'It's all right.' Flynn's voice had a reassuring steadiness to it. 'He and I have come to an understanding.'

Kat swallowed back bile, her hammering heart going back to where it belonged in her chest. 'How do you know him?'

'Mutual acquaintance.'

She looked down at her clenched hands. 'I didn't know he was married. He lied to me. Lie after lie after lie. I broke it off as soon as I found out. The worst thing was I'd always been so annoyed with my mother for getting involved with married men. I feel like *such* a hypocrite.'

Flynn put his hand over her white-knuckled ones

and gave them a light squeeze. 'Don't be so hard on yourself. He was a jerk. A cheat. No one will believe him anyway.'

'Why do you say that?'

'You're way out of his league.'

Kat cocked her head at him. 'Is that a compliment, Mr Carlyon?'

His smile tugged on her resolve like a child pulling at its mother's skirt. 'Yes, Miss Winwood. It is.'

Another small silence ticked past.

Kat relaxed her hands and smoothed them against her bent thighs. 'I guess I should let you rest…'

'I wasn't in love with Claire.'

Kat wondered why that should make her feel such an odd sense of relief. It wasn't as if she was worried about whether his emotions had taken a battering. Why should she care if he'd had his heart banged up?

You do care. You like him.

No, I don't. Well…maybe a little…but only because he was so good about that creep Charles.

'Claire thought she was pregnant,' Flynn said. 'I wanted to do the right thing by her and our child.'

'At least you didn't pay her to have an abortion.'

He gave her a fleeting half-smile before his expression went back to neutral. 'It was way earlier than I'd planned to settle down, but I thought it would work out if we both were committed to doing the best thing for the baby. But she found out a couple of days later it was a false alarm. She ended our relationship then and there.'

Kat searched his inscrutable face. What emotions was he screening from view? How had he felt at having the future he had planned with Claire cut so abruptly? Or had he been privately relieved he was off the hook, so to speak? Many young men would be terrified at the thought of fatherhood being thrust upon them before they were ready. 'You weren't relieved?'

He gave a soft laugh. 'No. Maybe later, when I'd got over myself a bit. But not then.'

'Why was doing the right thing by her and the baby so important to you? Because you were adopted?'

He met her gaze in a lock that made something in her chest ping. 'I wasn't a straightforward adoption.'

'What do you mean?'

Kat saw his deepening frown, the slow blink, the tight swallow, the shadow of something pass through his gaze. Several somethings. It looked like he was shuffling through his thoughts, deciding whether he should reveal what he had stored inside the filing system of his mind.

'I was a foundling,' he finally said. 'An abandoned infant with no name, no registration of birth or any other details pinning me to another soul on this planet. All I had was the ratty old bunny rug I was wrapped in and a soiled cloth nappy. And the worst case of nappy rash the authorities had ever seen.'

Kat stared at him in shock, her heart jolting at the thought of him as a tiny baby, suffering, abandoned, alone. 'Oh dear, that's so sad. Didn't anyone ever come forward?'

'Nope.' The way he said the word made it sound as if he had long ago given up hope. Maybe he hadn't had it in the first place.

Kat covered his hand with hers. Not that she did a great job of covering much of it, given her hand was so much smaller. He turned her hand over and entwined his fingers with hers. The heat from his hand warmed her body from her fingertips to her toes. 'I can't imagine what that must be like for you,' she said. 'Not know-ing. Never knowing.'

His thumb moved back and forth against the fleshy base of hers. 'Maybe it's better not to know, or so I keep telling myself. I can't see myself turning up any famous actors as my parents.'

Kat pulled her hand out of his. 'I suppose you think I'm being petty about my father.'

'He's the only one you'll ever have.'

'He's not the one I want.'

'We don't get to choose.'

She got off the bed and stalked to the window, fold-ing her arms across her body. 'I'm not ready.'

'That's another thing you might not have much choice over,' he said. 'What if you run in to him some-time?'

Kat swung back to face him with a look that would have curdled milk. 'You mean with another impromptu dinner party at your house?'

'I didn't engineer the girls turning up.'

'You engineered me house-sitting next door.'

'So?'

'So how can I trust you?'

He let out a long breath. 'The question is, can I trust you?'

Kat frowned. 'Why would you ask that?'

His gaze was direct. Don't-mess-with-me direct. 'I've told you stuff I've told no one. Not even the Ra-vensdales know I was abandoned as a baby. They only know I was adopted.'

Kat shifted her mouth from side to side, wondering if he regretted telling her. She seemed a strange ally for his secrets. She had made it clear she didn't like him and yet he had told her things he had told no one else.

Or did he suspect she *did* like him? That she liked him more than she wanted to admit to herself? 'Why did you tell me?'

One side of his mouth lifted in a wry smile and he reached for his crutches to get off the bed. 'I have absolutely no idea. Maybe it's the painkillers and alcohol combination.'

Kat wondered if it was because he saw something in her that he saw in himself: the bone-deep sense of aloneness, of not belonging anywhere or to anyone. Of always having to rely on yourself with no one as backup. 'I won't tell anyone. You have my word.'

'And when you make a promise you keep it, right?'

She glanced at his slanted mouth. Right now she wished she had never made that crazy promise to her friend Maddie. Right now all she wanted to do was press her lips against his and taste the sensual heat of him, to feel the potency of him awakening every female pore of her body into an inferno of lust.

He came to stand in front of her but because he was on crutches his mouth was closer than normal. She could see every line and contour, the way the edges turned up at the corners, as if he was used to smiling far more than not. It impressed her that he was so positive in outlook, considering his tragic beginnings and the way his adoptive family held him at arm's length. Most people would be bitter and angry at the world. *A little like me.* So many people from difficult backgrounds became difficult people. The cycles of neglect and abuse often went on for generations.

But Flynn had made something of himself, refusing to let his tragic background stop him from achieving all he set out to achieve. He had qualities she couldn't help admiring. Most of the men she had been involved with had exploited her in some way. But Flynn hadn't sabotaged her fledging relationship with Miranda and Jaz, even though he'd had a perfect opportunity.

Why had he done that?

What did it mean?

Why was he treating her as if he had plans for building a future with her?

Kat looked into the dark-brown depths of his eyes, her stomach free-falling when they went to her mouth. He leaned one hand on his crutch and lifted the other to her face in a *fainéant* movement from the top of her cheekbone to just beside her mouth, his fingertip leaving a trail of fire against her skin. She sent her tongue out over her lips, swallowing deeply as she sensed him leaning closer. Her pelvis registered his proximity, her inner core contracting with a pulse of vicious need.

His mouth hovered above hers, his warm, faint-hint-of-whisky breath wafting over her tingling lips. His nose bumped against hers, a soft nudge that was powerfully, shamelessly, erotic. His stubble-shadowed skin grazed her cheek, sending her senses into a swishing, swirling tailspin. The tip of his tongue stroked the vermillion border of her bottom lip, a caress so intoxicating, so arousing, it nearly knocked her off her feet.

But somehow Kat managed to gather her scattered senses long enough to realise she had won a vital point against him. 'You kissed me.'

His eyes contained a dark glitter that put that point she'd scored in jeopardy. 'That's not a kiss.'

'You touched my lips with your tongue.'

'Nah-ah. I touched the edge of your lip.'

'You're taking hair splitting to a whole new level,' Kat said. 'You did so kiss me.'

His mouth lifted in that devilish smile that did so

much lethal damage to her self-control. And her resolve…*wherever the hell it was.* 'That's not a kiss.' He
leaned closer. 'But this is.'

CHAPTER SEVEN

IN THE END, Kat wasn't entirely sure if he or she had closed that final distance. All she knew was as soon as Flynn's mouth came into contact with hers every thought of resisting him flew out of her head like bats out of a cave. His lips moved against hers with gentle pressure, not crushing, but cajoling hers into a passionate exchange that made every knob of her spine loosen. Her mouth flowered open beneath the first stroke of his tongue, the intimate invasion a toe-curling reminder of the act both their bodies craved—had craved from the moment they'd first met.

Was that not why it was so hard to step away and tell him to back off? Was that not why she had made that celibacy pact, because from the first moment she had laid eyes on him she had *wanted* him? She had recognised the danger he represented to her—the danger of being involved with someone where she wasn't the one in control.

Her body was dizzy with longing for more of his drugging kiss. Her tongue tangled with his in a heated duel; it was a combat of wills, a collision of personalities, a celebration of all that was physically arousing between a man and a woman. Her mouth was on fire with the potency of his, the assault on her senses unlike any other kiss she had received in the past.

For one thing, he wasn't holding her, on account of his crutches. It was only his mouth that was connected to her. His lips were fused to hers, drawing from her a response that was wild, hungry and desperately needy. Was it because she hadn't been kissed in weeks and weeks—months, even? Or was it because Flynn's kiss spoke to her on a level no one had ever been able to reach? She wanted to melt against his body but his crutches were an impediment. He was tilted towards her but if she pushed against him she was concerned he would fall. She wound her arms around his waist, her breasts coming into contact with the hard wall of his chest, but even that was enough to put him off-balance.

He lifted his mouth off hers and clutched at his crutches to rebalance himself. 'This isn't working quite the way it should.'

Kat lowered herself back on her heels, her hands falling away from his body, her cheeks hot as a bonfire. Two bonfires. Possibly three. What was she doing? Where was her self-control? Her resolve? *Where the heck was her flipping resolve?* 'I suppose you think I'll fall into bed with you now you've kissed me.'

His eyes were dark and glinting. Victory glinting. I-want-you-and-I-know-you-want-me glinting. 'You could fall or you could walk the couple of steps. I'd offer to carry you but I'm not sure I could pull it off with these sticks.'

'I'm not going to sleep with you.'

'But you want to.'

Kat laughed but even to her own ears it sounded fake. *So much for the actor's handbook.* She was going to have to brush up on the not-interested-in-you look.

She *was* interested in him.

He excited her. He challenged her. He thrilled her.

She had never met a more mesmerising man. Her senses were still reeling from having experienced the heart-stopping heat and passion of their first kiss—a kiss that had been months in the making. The chemistry between them had built each time they had been in contact. Every look, every bantering word exchanged, every locked gaze, had led to a kiss beyond anything she had experienced before.

What would happen if she allowed things to go further?

Making love with Flynn Carlyon would be dangerous. How could she keep her heart disengaged when he was already ambushing her with his wit, his humour, his intelligence, not to mention his Olympic-standard determination? He wanted her and wasn't afraid to let her know it. The knowledge of his desire for her spoke to her own desire for him like a secret code embedded in her body. She could feel the electrifying shockwave of longing every time he looked at her with that smouldering gaze. The silent message he conveyed moved through her body, making her pulse race and her heartbeat escalate. 'I'm not getting involved with you.'

'Because I'm too close to your father?'

Kat knew it wasn't just because of her father. It wasn't even because of her celibacy pact with Maddie. It was because she knew getting involved with Flynn would not be a simple affair. The way he made her feel was so different from anyone else. She hadn't fallen in love with anyone before. But then she had never got to know anyone so well before. She'd had infatuations and mild crushes, but she hadn't learned anything about them as people.

But with Flynn it was completely different.

She had got to know him over the last few months, finding out more and more things about who he was, what he wanted, what he represented. The values he held. The information about his background was deeply personal stuff and yet he had chosen to reveal it to her. It made her feel as if their relationship was on a completely different footing from any she'd had before. No one had ever come close enough to make her want the fairytale. She had always been career focused, not marriage-and-family focused.

But Flynn made her *feel* stuff. Stuff she didn't want to feel. Not just a potent attraction but a sense of relating to someone who understood what it was like always to be on the outside.

But what did *he* want?

He was a commitment-phobe, or so Miranda and Jaz had intimated. Was he interested in her only so he could get her to Richard's party by fair means or foul? She was a task he had to accomplish, a box that had to be ticked.

Or did he want her because he too felt this powerful connection that pulled and tugged at every organ in her body?

Kat gave him a pointed look. '*Are* you close to my father? Are you close to anyone?'

The glint dulled in his eyes. 'Don't try and analyse me, Kat.' He turned away on his crutches to settle back in a sitting position on the bed.

'Why haven't you had a serious relationship since Claire?'

'Been there, done that, packed away the tuxedo.'

'So you're not interested in ever settling down?'

'Nope.' The word sounded like it was underlined. In bold.

'Once bitten, twice shy?' Kat said. 'Seems a bit defeatist, if you ask me. What if you fall in love?'

'I won't.'

'Is that something you can control?'

'I've never met anyone I want to spend the rest of my life with.'

'But that could change,' Kat said. 'You could meet someone tomorrow who completely rocks your world.'

His eyes held hers for a beat. 'So could you.'

She looked away first, watching out of the corner of her eye as he made his way back to the bed. He lay back on the pillows, propping his arms behind his head. 'Can you unzip my boot for me?'

Kat approached the bed with a scowl that would have sent a drill sergeant running for cover. 'Would you like me to bring your pipe and slippers while I'm at it?'

He smiled a breath-snatching smile. 'If I told you what I'd like you to do you'd blush to the roots of your hair.'

She pressed her lips together, undid the zip on his leather boot and slipped it off his foot. His bandaged foot was swollen and there were purple and black streaks running between his toes. She touched her fingers to his foot to check for excessive heat. 'Do you need more painkillers?'

'No, I'm fine, but you can take the food away.' He closed his eyes as if signing out for the night. 'I'm not hungry.'

Kat hovered at the end of his bed. 'Are you sure you're okay?'

He opened one twinkling eye. 'A goodnight kiss wouldn't go astray.'

Her lips hadn't stopped tingling from the last one. She wasn't game to do a repeat. Her self-control was on a precarious knife-edge as it was. 'You don't give up easily, do you?'

His smile was one of those lazy, spine-melting ones. The ones that made her want to dive headfirst into his bed and crawl into his skin. 'We want the same thing,' he said. 'Sex without complications.'

'Sex is always complicated.'

'Maybe you haven't had the right partner.'

Kat put her hands on her hips. 'So you think you are?'

His eyes kindled. 'I'm damn sure of it.'

She tried to ignore the pulse of lust that throbbed in her core. Throbbed and ached. 'How can you be so confident?'

His eyes moved over her flushed features, lingering the longest on her mouth. 'One kiss told me all I needed to know. That's why you won't do it again, because you're frightened you won't be able to control yourself.'

'*Really?* Is that what you think?'

'Come here and prove me wrong.'

Kat knew she should resist his challenge but she wanted to prove it to herself as well as him. She would show him she could press her lips to his and feel nothing. No fireworks. No shooting stars. No fireballs of lust ripping through her body.

She stood next to him and lowered her mouth to his smiling one. It was the only point of contact, lips on lips. But he didn't respond. He didn't do anything to prolong the kiss. In fact, he didn't do anything but lie there like a mummified body.

Wasn't he *feeling* anything?

Anything at all?

She pressed her lips back down again, moving them

against the firm warmth of his in a slow-moving caress. She couldn't remember a time when she had kissed a man with such concentrated intensity. It was as though all the nerve endings in her body had gathered in her lips, heightening their sensitivity. She sent out the tip of her tongue to trace the seam of his mouth, the touch slow, sensual and soft. She did it again, once, twice, and then the third time he gave a swift intake of breath and took control of the kiss. His arms came around her, bringing her down on the bed beside him, his mouth clamped to hers in a searing kiss, their tongues teasing and tangling, their lips sliding and sucking, their teeth nipping and tugging. She felt the full force of his arousal against her thigh, the potent power of it triggering her own intimate moisture.

He rolled her so she was half under him, his mouth still pressed hotly to hers. She swallowed a gasp as he slid one of his hands across her breast in a light skating touch that left her aching for more. She stroked his hair, his face, his back and shoulders as he plundered her mouth, inciting her desire to a level she had not thought possible. Never had desire rushed through her at such a breakneck pace. It was as if a drug had invaded her system, powering her up to do things she normally would never dream of doing. She reached for his belt and unhooked it, then went for his zipper. She wanted to feel the throb of him in her hand, to feel the desire he felt for her skin-on-skin.

He made a guttural sound when she got his zipper down, responded by slipping a warm, dry hand up under her sweater to cup her breast. Even though she was still wearing a bra her senses went wild. Off-the-scale wild. Scarily out-of-control wild. The promise of more was there in his hand as he cradled her. It was there in the roll of his thumb over her lace-covered nipple, making it go pebble-hard.

He left her mouth to bring his down to her breast, sucking on her through the lace, then when she thought she could stand it no longer he deftly unhooked her bra and drew on her with his warm, moist, tantalising mouth.

Kat reached for him with desperate fingers, peeling back the fabric of his underwear to access the satin-covered steel of his flesh. He made another deep sound of approval as she explored his length, concentrating on the blunt tip where his pre-ejaculate fluid had gathered.

His mouth left her breast to concentrate on the other one, subjecting it to the same delicious torture until she was writhing with longing beneath him. Such swift arousal was unusual for her. She wasn't used to her body aching with such urgent pressing need, as if she would die if he didn't follow through and complete their union. She could feel her clitoris stirring, swelling and aching for contact, for friction. The frustration of being so close and yet not close enough was making her resolve melt like a sugar cube dropped in a pot of hot tea.

Who cared about the stupid celibacy pact?

She wanted him. She wanted him with every cell in her body. She wanted the release his kiss hinted at, the release his hard body promised.

Flynn's mouth came back to hers in another passionate onslaught that made her senses sing like a choral symphony. A thousand-member choral symphony. But just when she thought he would take it to the next level he drew back, breathing heavily but still in control. 'As much as I'd like to finish this, I'm going to call a halt.'

Kat called on every bit of acting expertise she possessed to look cool and composed when inside she was screaming, *Don't stop now!* 'Because you think I wasn't going to?'

He brushed a strand of hair off her face, his eyes holding hers in a lock that made her insides wobble like a jelly near a jackhammer. 'It's something else, isn't it? This thing we have going on.'

Kat edged out from under him and put some order to her clothes. 'There's no *thing* going on. We kissed and fooled around a bit, that's all.'

'I want you, Kat, but I'm prepared to wait until you're willing to admit you want me too. We do this as equals or not at all. Your choice.'

'What is it you want?' Kat said. 'A fling? A future? A one-off? Or is this just a ploy to butter me up so I agree to meet my father?'

'This is about us.' The deep, coming-from-beneath-the-floorboards pitch of his voice made her insides shiver. 'It's been about us from the first moment we met. That's why you were about to rip my clothes off just then and have your wicked way with me.'

Kat kept her gaze away from his unzipped trousers but it took a mammoth effort. Two mammoths and a couple of weightlifters thrown in. 'I have to go. I'll see you in the morning when I take Cricket out.'

'Do you want to meet for lunch tomorrow? I have a space between clients between one and two.'

'I'm working.'

'Then I'll have lunch at the café with you. You get a lunch break, don't you?'

'I'm not working at the café tomorrow,' Kat said. 'I have…an audition.'

Interest sharpened his gaze. 'What for?'

'Just a pantomime thing.'

'If you reached out to your father you'd be able to—'

'I do not need his help to get a job,' Kat said. 'If I can't get it on my own merit then I'll quit altogether.'

'Acting is in your blood,' Flynn said. 'You won't be happy unless you achieve what you've set out to achieve.'

Kat raised one of her brows. 'That sounds more like a description of you rather than me.'

'It's a description of both of us,' he said. 'Good luck tomorrow.' He gave her a wink. 'Break a leg. Or should I say, foot?'

Kat was on her way to the audition when she got a call from her friend Maddie. She was going to ignore it but she had already been a bit slack at responding to a couple of texts, which she knew would make her friend suspicious. 'Hi, Maddie.' She injected brightness into her tone. 'I've been meaning to call. Just been crazily busy, you know how it—'

'What's this I hear about you living next door to Flynn Carlyon?' Maddie said.

'Where did you hear that?'

'There's a photo of you on Twitter. You two are trending.'

'It's not what you think—'

'Have you broken the pact?' Maddie 's voice had a note of suspicion. A whole stave of suspicion.

'No-o-o-o.' Kat strung her answer out like she was stretching a piece of string. Or the truth.

'Have you kissed him?'

'I…erm…he kissed me.'

'Did you respond?'

What a question. What choice had she had? It had been the best kiss she'd ever experienced. Everything in her had responded—every cell, every pore, every atom. Every kiss henceforth would be measured against Flynn's searing sensuality and found lacking. 'I didn't let it go too far,' Kat said.

He didn't let it go too far—not you.

I would have stopped eventually.

Like when? After he'd given you the big O?

'How far?' Maddie said.

Far enough to want more. Far enough for Kat's body to be aching with the need to feel his arms around her, his mouth pressed to hers, his hard body doing all the things to hers she craved. Like the big O. 'Where was the photo taken?' she asked.

'Aha! Diversionary tactics. You are *so* going to lose this bet.'

'Kissing is allowed,' Kat said. 'We agreed on that.'

'There's kissing and there's kissing,' Maddie said. 'Which side does Flynn fall on?'

'You don't want to know.'

Maddie laughed. 'I knew you'd be the first to break. You just can't help yourself, can you? A handsome man takes a shine to you and you fall madly in love.'

'I'm not in love with Flynn Carlyon,' Kat said. 'I just have a body-crush on him.'

'He is rather gorgeous,' Maddie said. 'Even on crutches.'

'You've seen him on crutches?'

'That's the photo on Twitter I was telling you about,' Maddie said. 'You were standing outside his house with him with the snow falling down around you with a weird little dog at your feet. It looked like a shot for a Hollywood romantic comedy.'

There was nothing comedic about their relationship. It was turning into high drama. How could she possibly avoid the temptation of him when she was forced to spend time with him? Time she *looked forward to* in spite of her misgivings about him and his connection with her father. 'I ran over his foot.'

'On purpose?'

'By accident. You know what I'm like at reverse parking,' Kat said. 'He was standing behind the car and—never mind. It's a long story. I'm helping him walk his dog and run errands for him while he's out of action.'

'Ah, but is he out of action in the bedroom?' There was a teasing lilt in Maddie 's voice. 'I can't see a pair of crutches getting in the way of what Flynn Carlyon wants.'

'What about you?' Kat was desperate to steer the conversation away from her nemesis. 'Have you fallen off the wagon?'

'No,' Maddie said. 'Not even tempted by anyone.'

'Sure?'

There was a tiny silence.

'Well, I do have to visit my great-grandfather this weekend for his birthday and you know who will be there.'

'Why will Byron be there?' Kat asked. 'You guys broke up months ago.'

'I know, but Gramps's dementia has worsened since his stroke,' Maddie said. 'He thinks we're still together and Mum thinks it will stress him out if we tell him any different. It's just a weekend. I can handle that. Anyway, good luck with the audition. Call me as soon as you hear, okay? And remember—I knew you before you were famous.'

CHAPTER EIGHT

KAT WAS THE last person to audition, which meant by the time her name was called her stomach had grown teeth and they were gnawing all the way to her backbone. The director asked her to take position, but instead of feeling the buzz of being onstage she felt sick. What if she blew it? What if she made an idiot of herself? Who was she kidding? She was an amateur. She hadn't been to a performing arts school. She had rehearsed in front of a mirror, not an acting coach. All she was good for was toilet-paper ads. She was rubbish at acting.

She was rubbish, period.

'Ready when you are, Miss McTaggart.'

It took Kat a moment to realise the director was speaking to her. She had used her grandparents' surname instead of her own. 'Erm…right.' She stepped into position. The contents of her stomach curdled and began to crawl towards her windpipe. Sweat broke out on her brow. Her throat felt like someone had put a choke collar around it. A studded one, around the wrong way. The stage lights were making her eyes water. Or maybe it was because she felt ridiculously out of her depth. The spotlight was focused on her but she felt like it was shining on all of her faults. The irregularities of her features, the figure she wished was fuller in some places and more toned in others. The hair she hadn't had time or money to have professionally styled. The supermarket brand of make-up she'd used instead of a designer brand.

The stalls were in darkness but Kat noticed a woman sitting at the back of the theatre. The woman was dressed in nondescript clothes but she had an aura about her that suggested she wasn't one of the theatre or ancillary staff. She looked vaguely familiar but because the lights were off in the stalls it was hard to make out any distinguishing features.

'Is there a problem, Miss McTaggart?' The director's voice contained a thread of impatience. A steel-cable thread.

'Sorry.' Kat wriggled her shoulders to shake off the tension. 'I'm just getting into character.'

'Would you like a bone to chew on?' the woman at the back of the theatre asked in a tone dripping with sarcasm. Not dripping—flooding.

Kat bristled like a cat, which wasn't all that helpful, given she was supposed to be a dog. She took a deep breath and channelled her angst at the woman into her performance, using it to galvanise her into the performance of her life. She *became* Sylvia. She used every bit of Cricket's quirkiness she had born witness to: his pleading looks, his energy, his over-the-top excitement and his frantic rear-end wagging and wriggling. She felt so authentic in the scene she wished she had a tail when it was over so she could wag it.

'Thanks, Kathy,' the director said. 'I'll let you know what we decide in a day or two.'

The woman at the back of the theatre rose from the chair she was sitting on. 'I've already decided,' she said in an accent that this time Kat recognised as none other than Elisabetta Albertini's. 'I want her. She was by far the best.'

Kat's eyes widened as Elisabetta came out of the low light of the stalls towards the stage. Her dream felt like it was balanced on a high wire without a safety net. As soon as Elisabetta recognised her it would plummet to the cold, hard floor of reality. There was no way Elisabetta would want to star alongside her husband's love child. No way in the world. It wouldn't matter how brilliant a job she had done of the audition. It would be better to get in first to save everyone from embarrassment. 'Erm…my name isn't really Kathy McTaggart,' she said. 'My name is—'

'Katherine Winwood,' Elisabetta said. 'Yes, I know.'

Kat fought hard not to be intimated by that cold, dark-brown, assessing stare. Was Elisabetta searching for her husband in Kat's features? As much as Kat knew it must be galling for Elisabetta to face the living, breathing evidence of her husband's betrayal, she still wished she could be accepted at face value, for herself, not for the trouble she had inadvertently caused. 'I really want the part but if you'd rather not work with me then—'

'Didn't you just hear me say I wanted you?' Elisabetta gave an imperious arch of her brow.

'Yes, but I thought since—'

'I want you in that part,' Elisabetta said. 'Fix it, will you, Leon?' she said to the director. She turned back to Kat. 'Rehearsals start on Monday. Be on time.'

Kat had trouble keeping her jaw off the floor as Elisabetta walked out with regal poise. Had that just happened? Had Elisabetta Albertini just insisted *she* get the part?

But why?

Was it because of her talent or was this some sort of publicity stunt? She hadn't shown a skerrick of talent until Elisabetta had insulted her. How could she know for sure what Elisabetta's motivations were? What if Elisabetta wanted to sabotage her career? What better way to get back at her husband Richard than by publicly humiliating his love child onstage?

'Looks like you got the part,' Leon said. 'Congratulations.'

'Thanks.' Kat mentally chewed at her lip. What if this was not about her acting merit? What if this was all about revenge? Wasn't it the director's or casting agent's decision as to who got the part? Or had Elisabetta insisted on choosing whom she would front up with onstage? She had a reputation as a diva. And she certainly had the star power to call the shots. No one would ever employ Kat again if this turned out to be a stitch-up.

Why had Elisabetta chosen her other than to use it as an opportunity to get back at her?

The self-doubts sat like anvils on her shoulders. Her dream of being onstage was turning into a nightmare. The whole world would watch Elisabetta cut her down. It was risky but the determined streak in Kat's personality thrived on the chance to prove to Elisabetta and to everybody she was made of stronger mettle. She would not be rattled or thrown off her game by a vindictive attempt to ruin her one chance at stardom.

'Ruby the costume designer will measure you in Dressing Room B,' Leon said. 'I'll email the contract to your agent.'

Flynn was sitting on his sofa with his foot up after work, reading through a client's brief, when he got a call from Jake Ravensdale. 'Jaz tells me you're done like a dinner over Kat Winwood,' Jake said. 'Want to double up at my stag night? Half the cost, twice the fun.'

Flynn pushed the papers off his knee and Cricket promptly rested his furry chin on them, looking up at him with hopeful eyes. He reached out, absently stroked the little dog's ears and was rewarded with a blissful puppy sigh. 'My plan is to get her to your father's party, not into church.'

'Come on, man, you know Dad only wants her there to placate his fans,' Jake said. 'He doesn't care a jot about her. Miranda and Jaz were quite taken with her. Do you reckon she'll agree to meet Julius and me sometime, like at your wedding?'

'Very funny,' Flynn said. 'But I want Kat to meet your father. I think it would be good for her. It will give her some closure. Even if she tells him to his face what she thinks of him.'

'That's going to be fun to watch,' Jake said. 'So, how's the foot? Must be tricky sweeping her off her feet when you're on crutches.'

Flynn eyed his bandaged foot with a scowl. 'You can say that again.'

'So is she The One?' Jake said.

Flynn let out a swift curse. 'What is it with you Ravensdales? You all get hitched within a month or two of each other and then try and recruit everyone else in your circle to do the bloody same.'

'Just want you to be happy, mate.' Jake adopted a serious tone for once. 'You're so jaded about settling down because of all those dirty divorces you handle. But life is short. Before you know it, you'll be staring down the barrel of retirement. Is that all you want to show for your life? Work, work and more work?'

'Listen,' Flynn said. 'I'm glad you and Jaz got your

stuff sorted. You're a great couple. Perfect for each other in every way. But leave me to my miserable life with work, work and more work, okay? I'm fine with it.'

Was he fine with it? Flynn thought once he had signed off on the call a moment or two later. Ever since Kat had come into his life he felt…different. Like the colours in his day were brighter, which was weird, since it was one of the bleakest, greyest winters on record. He felt sharper within himself, more switched on. More focused. He enjoyed life more, felt more potent, even though he hadn't had sex in… When *had* he last had sex? He screwed up his face as he tried to recall his last relationship, not that it had been a relationship in any sense of the word. He had only slept with the woman a couple of times way back in September at a law conference in Newcastle before he'd lost interest.

September? Had it really been that long? He had been so focused on Kat Winwood since early October that no one else had taken his eye. He couldn't even bear the thought of trying it on with anyone else. Who would match her for intelligence and feistiness? The chemistry between them was phenomenal. He had only to look at her and he wanted her. But it was more than a physical lust. Over the last few months he had got to know her. Getting to know a partner other than in the biblical sense was not usually high on his priorities.

But with Kat he felt he understood her. He could read her mood, even when she did her best to hide her emotions. Underneath all that feistiness and shtick was a sensitive girl who hadn't had it easy.

And Cricket loved her, which was the best litmus test of all.

There was that word 'love' he usually steered clear of. Love was an emotion that had let him down from as young as he could remember. Sometimes he wondered if his abandonment as a baby had done something to his brain, changed its architecture or something, making him distrustful of any bonds no matter how genuine they appeared.

But he didn't want to be tied down with the responsibility of a relationship... *Did he?* The thought kept returning like a tongue to an irritable tooth. Before he'd met Kat he had been perfectly at peace with his decision to keep his relationships casual. He knew marriage was something that worked well for some people. Even his adopted parents, for all their other faults, were committed to each other and there was every indication they would remain that way for the rest of their lives.

But he saw plenty of other marriages. Horrible marriages. Bitter marriages. Marriages where the warring parties tore each other to shreds and where children were used as pawns and payback.

He wanted no part of it.

Cricket whined and wriggled up closer to put his head on Flynn's knee with a look of complete and utter devotion, as if to say, 'I love you and will never let you down.' Flynn ruffled the dog's ears again. 'I love you too, buddy,' he said, a little shocked to find his voice catching slightly over the words.

Kat let herself into Flynn's house to save him the trouble of having to answer the door on crutches. She was later than usual, as the audition had run over time, plus she'd had to feed Monty and convince him to sit on her knee long enough for the Carstairs family to be assured their beloved pet was being looked after properly. Thankfully Monty hadn't scratched her this time, but he'd coughed up a fur ball in her bedroom, which seemed a little too deliberate for her liking.

Cricket came like a NASA rocket out of the sitting room, his toenails scrabbling on the marbled hallway, his little body skidding like a drunken skater on loose ice skates. She bent down and he leapt into her arms and gave her face a virtual baptism. 'Yes, you crazy little excuse for a dog,' she said, laughing. 'I love you to bits, too.'

She looked up to see Flynn had limped to the doorway after all. 'Sorry I'm so late,' she said. 'I had to feed Monty and quickly Skype the Carstairses before I came over.'

He glanced at her hands. 'No scratches? Things must be looking up between you two.'

Kat gave him a rueful smile. 'We're getting there, slowly but surely.'

There was an enigmatic twinkle in his eyes. 'Not a bad way to do things.'

She reached for Cricket's lead. 'I'll just take Cricket out now.'

'Don't worry about taking him out tonight,' Flynn said. 'It's foul outside. How did your audition go?'

She put Cricket's lead back on the hallstand. 'I got it...'

'You don't sound too excited.'

Kat let her shoulders down on a sigh and faced him. 'I'm not sure I got it for the right reasons.'

'Did the director recognise you?'

She didn't bother hiding her worry. She had a feeling he knew it anyway by the way he was looking at her. Softly. Understandingly. 'No, but Elisabetta Albertini did. She's playing the role of Kate in *Sylvia*. I didn't know that otherwise I would've thought twice about auditioning. She was sitting at the back of the theatre and, after insulting me when I took a bit of time getting over my nerves, she insisted the part was given to me.'

'You must've done a good job. She's picky about who she works with.'

'I can't help feeling I'm being set up,' Kat said. 'I looked like such an amateur up there. I was quaking in my shoes. I've never felt so nervous in my life. What if she only wants me in that part so she can make a fool of me?'

His gaze lost none of its softness; if anything it got softer. Tender, almost. 'You need to work on your confidence, sweetheart. She'll eat you alive if you show you're intimidated by her.'

Kat's heart was still skipping over the word 'sweetheart.' Lots of men used terms of endearment and they usually meant nothing. Sweet nothing. But somehow the way Flynn said it gave it weight. Substance. A foundation she could stand on while the rest of the world trembled with uncertainty. 'Do you think she'd do it? Ruin opening night to get back at me?'

'Do you want me to have a chat with her?'

She gave him a horrified look. 'No!'

'You're not really frightened of her, are you?'

Kat tossed her hair back off her shoulders—a gesture of bravado straight out of the actor's handbook. She just wished she felt the indifference she was portraying. 'Of course not.'

'How about we go out to dinner tonight?'

Kat frowned. 'Dinner?'

'To celebrate you getting the part.'

She chewed at her lip. 'I don't know…'

'Ouch.'

Kat looked up at him in concern. 'Is your foot okay?'

He grinned at her. 'That was my ego, not my foot. How many times does a guy have to beg a girl to go out to dinner with him?'

She looked at him narrowly. 'Just dinner?'

'I'd offer to take you dancing, but can you see me burning up the dance floor on these sticks?'

Kat's conscience and willpower went into battle again.

Dinner will be fine.

You think?

Of course it will. We'll have a drink, eat a meal. Go home. Simple.

You'll sip champagne while gazing into his dream-boat eyes and start planning how many of his babies you'll have.

I will not. Anyway, he's not the settling down type.

But you are.

Am not. I want a career. Stardom. My name up in lights.

And then what?

And then I'll be happy.

Yeah?

Kat forced a smile. 'I'm not much of a dancer myself. I've never been able to get through a waltz without pulping my partner's toes.'

He smiled with his eyes, making her stomach free-fall. 'Sounds like you just haven't found the right partner.'

The restaurant Flynn took her to in a cab was owned by one of his clients. They were given the best table in the house in a romantic corner that gave them privacy from the other diners. Flynn ordered champagne and, once it was poured, raised his glass to hers in a toast. 'To your brilliant career.'

Kat took a sip of the delicious bubbles whilst looking into his eyes that were dark as pitch, yet soft and melting. How on earth was she going to stop herself from falling in love with him when he looked at her like that?

You're well on your way.

No, I'm not. I'm just aware it could be a danger, that's all.

Stop looking at his mouth. Dead giveaway.

Kat put her glass down and shifted in her seat, keeping her gaze trained on the cleft in his chin. 'So…how was your day?'

'Look at me, Kat.'

She looked. Felt her heart kick at the way his knowing smile curved up the corners of his mouth. The mouth that had kissed hers—kissed it and made it hungry for more. So hungry it was all she could do to keep herself on her side of the table. Her knees bumped against his, sending a shockwave of awareness through her body, concentrating in the heated core of her womanhood. Warmth flooded her, need oozing, the ache of lust building with every beat of the silence as his gaze tethered hers. 'Wh-what?'

'You're nervous.'

'I'm not.'

'When was the last time you went out to dinner with a guy?'

Kat let out a long sigh and looked at the salt-and-pepper shakers on the crisp snow-white tablecloth. 'September last year. Charles the creep. I was so ashamed I was physically sick when I found out he had a wife and three little kids, one of them only a few weeks old.'

She brought her gaze back up to his. 'How can men do that to their wives?'

Flynn made a twisting movement with his mouth. 'There are some prize jerks out there, that's for sure. I come across them all the time in my line of work. You'd be shocked at how many men try and wriggle out of paying for their kids once their relationship with their mother is over.'

Kat fiddled with the stem of her glass. 'I just hate how I didn't see it. That I didn't see *through* him. How could I have got it so wrong?'

He placed his hand over her restive one, the warmth and steadiness of it moving through her entire body like a soothing wave of a calming, cleansing drug. 'You did the right thing by getting out of it as soon as you found out. But I can see how it would make you cautious.'

She looked at their entwined hands, hers so light against the tan of his. 'I've always prided myself that I'm nothing like my mother. She was hopeless at reading men. She was in and out of dysfunctional relationships all through my childhood. I never knew who would be there when I got home from school. Sometimes it was so scary. I couldn't understand why she couldn't see the innate badness in some of the men she brought home. *I* could see it and I was just a kid.'

Flynn's expression was gravely serious. 'Were you ever in danger? Did any of your mother's men friends hurt or interfere with you?'

Kat pulled her hand out of his light hold on the pretence of brushing back a wayward strand of hair. She didn't trust herself to touch him for too long. His touch made her body hunger for him. Hunger and ache. 'A couple of times I had to fight off some unwanted attention, mostly when I was a teenager. It was worse when

Mum was drinking. She just didn't pick up on stuff. I couldn't talk to her about it, as she would get angry and blame me for being too mouthy or whatever.'

His frown formed a bridge between his eyes. 'But in spite of it all you still loved her?'

She gave him a crooked smile. 'Yeah, well, that's what kids do, isn't it? Their survival depends on it—loving their caregivers. Not that she was great at caregiving or anything. But, yes, I loved her.'

'Is that why you don't want kids?' he said after a moment. 'Are you worried you won't do a good job of mothering your own kids?'

Kat picked up her glass for something to do with her hands. 'I guess on some level… But I really want to achieve what I set out to achieve first. If I get tied down with kids and marriage, I'll never reach my goal.'

'What if fame isn't everything you think it will be?'

'It's not just the fame,' Kat said. 'I've wanted to act for as long as I can remember. I know I won't be satisfied until I exhaust every opportunity to make it onstage. It's not like I want to prove it to anyone else. I need to prove it to myself.'

'It's a tough life, working for weeks and then nothing for months,' Flynn said. 'There are good years and bad years. Plays fold without notice or run for season after season until you're bored out of your brain for the want of something fresh and more challenging. Then there are the great reviews and the awful ones. You have to have a tough skin.'

She met his dark gaze across the table. 'And you don't think I have one?'

'Underneath that tough exterior is a girl with a soft heart. I see it. Cricket sees it. Miranda and Jaz saw it.

Probably Elisabetta saw it, which is why you're feeling so threatened by her.'

Kat had always prided herself on the impenetrable armour she wore around her heart. But in his presence she could feel it falling away, piece by piece, like a glacier fracturing. He seemed to understand her in a way no one had ever done before. It was hard to keep her defences up when he was so strong and supportive, so intuitive and accepting of her. 'Do you think I should meet Julius and Jake?'

'They wouldn't want you to do anything you're not comfortable with. But they're on your team, Kat. We all are.'

'Apart from Elisabetta,' she said with a downturn of her mouth.

He reached across the table and covered her hand with his. 'Let your talent do the talking. You have no reason to doubt yourself.'

Kat stroked her fingers over the flesh of his thumb, feeling a rush of lava-hot heat go from his body to hers. His eyes held hers in a lock that said all that needed to be said. The message was erotic, exciting, thrilling. Urgent. The need that pulsed between them made her inner core vibrate with a longing no amount of celibacy pacts could withstand.

Resisting him any longer was pointless. They had been moving towards this moment from the first time they'd locked gazes. She wanted him and couldn't bear prolonging the agony. She could no longer find any reason not to explore the chemistry between them. So what if he wasn't the settling down type? She wasn't ready for the white picket fence and cottage flowers either. All she wanted was to feel his arms around her, to feel alive in the way a man can make a woman feel when they both like and respect each other. She couldn't think of a man she liked and respected more than Flynn.

Maybe that was what she had been doing all wrong with dating up to this point. She had dated men who weren't her equal intellectually, not strong enough to stand up to her and *for* her. They had only been interested in her body, not her mind, her emotions, her ambitions, her drives and aspirations.

'If we were to get involved…hypothetically speaking…' Kat chanced a quick glance at him. 'What would you want out of it?'

His thumb found the nerve-rich centre of her palm and began stroking a mesmerising caress across the sensitive flesh. 'You mean apart from sex?'

Kat's belly quivered at his touch, at his words, at his smouldering-coals look. 'I mean…would we be having a fling or be in a…a relationship?'

'You said "relationship" like it was a prison sentence.'

'Yes, well, some of mine have been a bit like that.'

His stroking continued, stoking a fire within her body she could feel deep and throbbing in her core. 'What about your celibacy pact?'

'I've proven my point to my friend. Besides, I think she's going to break it herself this weekend. She's going to be within arm's reach of her ex. Always a dangerous prospect for her.'

'Whose idea was the pact?'

'Mine mostly,' Kat said. 'I just got tired of getting involved with men who were shallow and not interested in me as a person. Or ones who told blatant lies.'

'Well, if it's any comfort, I'm not married, haven't been and was only engaged for forty-eight hours eleven years ago,' Flynn said. 'Every other relationship—and I use that term loosely—has been temporary.'

Kat stroked her fingertip over the blunt end of his thumb, watching as his dark ink-like pupils flared with molten heat. Even the candle on the table flickered, as if it was tired of competing with the flame of attraction glowing between them. 'So…if we get involved what will we call it?'

His mouth slanted in that spine-tingling manner. 'How about a flingsationship?'

She gave him an answering smile. 'I've never heard of one of those. What does it involve?'

He winked at her. 'Let's go back to my place and I'll show you.'

CHAPTER NINE

IN THE CAB on the way back to Flynn's house Kat could feel desire flooding every inch of her body like the wash of a warm tide. Flynn was holding her hand against the strong muscles of his thigh, an intimate anchoring of her to him that made her fingers itch to creep closer to the hot, hard, tempting heat of him. He glanced down at her with a teasing glint in his eyes. 'Don't even think about it,' he said in a sexy undertone. 'There are security cameras.'

Touching him was all she could think about. Touching him, stroking him with her fingers, licking him with her tongue. Tasting him. She communicated it with her gaze, a kind of visual foreplay that made his pupils flare and his hand tighten over hers. 'Just wait till I get you alone,' she said.

'You'll have to be gentle with me. I've got fractures.'

Kat bit her lip as she glanced at his bandaged foot. 'Will it make it…?'

'Awkward but not impossible,' he said, holding her gaze.

She saw the hunger there, the need, the longing. *For her.* Had any of her partners looked at her like that? As if she was the only woman in the world he wanted to make love to? 'When was the last time you...?' She left the question hanging open.

'September.'

Kat raised her brows. 'Why so long between drinks?'

He kept his eyes trained on hers, the heat in his fuelling the fire already raging in her flesh. 'Because when I set my mind to something I don't allow distractions to take my focus off my goal.'

Kat licked her lips with a quick dart of her tongue. 'How long were you prepared to wait?'

'However long it took.'

'What if I didn't play ball, so to speak?'

'I knew from the moment we met you would.'

It wasn't just hubris on his part. Kat had known it too. Deep in her body she had known he was the one man she would not be able to resist. She reached up with her hand and stroked his lean and tanned cheek, his light stubble catching on her fingers. 'I hope I'll be worth the wait.'

Something softened in his expression. 'Is that a lack of confidence I hear again?'

Kat puffed out a little sigh. 'It's easier for guys. Simpler. For women it's a little more complicated...or at least, it is for me.'

He cupped her cheek with his warm hand, his eyes holding hers in an intimate lock. 'I'll make it good for you. I promise.'

'Even with crutches?'

The look in his eyes made every knob of her spine shudder in anticipation. 'Count on it, baby.'

Keeping Cricket out of the bedroom proved to be more of a challenge for Flynn than getting her into it, Kat thought wryly as she listened to the little dog whining and scratching on the other side of the door. 'Do you think he'll settle down?'

Flynn reached up to loosen his tie. 'I'm not making love to you with a dog breathing down my neck.'

'But he sounds so miserable.'

'He'll get over it.' He tossed the tie to one side. 'Now, come here so I can undress you.'

She looked at him balanced awkwardly on his crutches. 'Maybe we should switch it around. I'll undress you.'

His dark eyes gleamed. 'Be my guest.'

Kat made him sit on the bed and knelt down between his spread thighs to unbutton his shirt. She peeled it off his broad shoulders, leaning into him to press kisses to his warm, tanned, muscular flesh, from the base of his neck to the tightly whorled cave of his bellybutton.

She heard him snatch in a breath as her tongue circled his navel, but he put his hands on her shoulders to stall her from going any lower. 'That's not the way I plan to do this,' he said. 'You're pleasure is my priority. My goal.'

Kat shivered at the steely intent in his gaze. 'What do you want me to do?'

'Take your clothes off. Slowly.'

Kat got to her feet, balancing on one foot and then the other as she removed her heels. She slid her tights down from beneath her simple black dress, letting them fall in a twisted heap on the floor next to her shoes, all the while holding that dark-as-night, hungry gaze. She reached behind her back to pull down the zipper on her dress, letting the fabric shimmy down her body before it too landed in a puddle at her feet. She lowered one bra strap and then the other, her breasts still cupped in their black lace. She unhooked the back of her bra and watched as his eyes devoured their shape. She had body issues, just like any other young woman her age, but somehow standing in front of him in nothing but her knickers made her feel as if she was the most beautifully proportioned woman he had ever seen.

Cricket gave a piteous whine from the other side of the door, scratching at the woodwork as if he was determined to dig his way through to his beloved master.

Flynn muttered a curse. 'I can't freaking believe this.'

Kat laughed at the agitated look on his face. 'Let him in. I don't mind. Really.'

He mock-glowered at her. 'I'm not having a threesome with a dog.'

She moved closer to the bed, hooking one finger under the edge of her knickers. 'Have you ever had one?'

He frowned. 'A threesome? No. Not my thing at all. You?'

Kat shook her head. 'A guy I was dating asked me to a while back but I refused. Needless to say, that relationship didn't last long.'

'Nice to know I'm not the only conservative lover around.'

She arched a brow and eased her knickers a little further down. 'How conservative are you?'

His smile made her insides shift and shudder in delight. 'Come over here and I'll show you.'

Kat stepped out of her knickers and moved within touching distance, her breath leaving her chest in a little gasp as his hands settled on her hips. She stood between his legs, her hands resting on his shoulders, her heartbeat tripping like a foot missing a step when his mouth came to her breast. He glided his lips along the sensitive flesh, his tongue passing over her budded nipple in a teasing, barely touching stroke that made every nerve ending beg and plead for more. He suckled on her gently before switching to her other breast, torturing her spinning senses with the promise of fulfilment.

There was a building storm in her body—a storm of need that refused to be ignored. She could feel the tension in her lower body, the delicious pulse and contraction of her womanhood, the deep ache that begged to be assuaged.

He guided her to lie down with him on the bed, somehow removing his trousers and underwear before he came down beside her, his damaged foot off to one side out of harm's way. He stroked the seam of her body with a slow-moving fingertip, his touch like fire against bone-dry tinder. He explored her more intimately, sliding one and then two fingers into the secret cavern of her body, coming back to the swollen bud of her clitoris, massaging it with such deft skill she came apart within seconds. The sensations rippled through her body, fanning out from her core to all of her limbs, even to her very fingertips, in wave after wave of spine-tingling pleasure.

He planted a warm hand on her belly. 'But wait. There's more.'

Kat sucked in a breath as he brought his mouth to her. The feel of his lips and tongue on her most intimate flesh made her whole body shake and shudder. The earth-shattering orgasm thundered through her body, hurtling her into a vortex unlike anything she had experienced before. She was breathless when it was over, stunned that her body could respond with such violent fervour.

Flynn gently lifted a strand of hair away from her

mouth and tucked it behind her ear. 'Was that as good as it looked?'

Kat touched his mouth with a fingertip. 'You know it was.'

He captured her finger and pressed a soft kiss to her fingertip. 'You could've been pretending.'

'I'm not *that* good an actor.'

He kissed her fingertip again. 'Repeat after me: I. Am. A. Brilliant. Actor.'

Kat tried to pull her hand away but he held firm. 'This is silly…'

'Say it, sweetheart.' His eyes wouldn't let hers go. 'Say it for me.'

She took a breath and released it in a whoosh. 'I. Am. A. Brilliant. Actor.'

He smiled and inched up her chin. 'I want you.'

Kat drew in another sharp breath as his eyes seared hers. She could feel the swollen heat of him against her thigh and reached down to take him in her hand. She moved her hand up and down his shaft, watching as he fought for control with every movement of her hand.

'Hold that thought,' he said and rolled away to retrieve a condom from the bedside drawer.

See? He's done this a thousand times.

So?

You're just another notch on his bedpost.

Firstly, he doesn't have a bedpost—he has a bedhead. Secondly, he's waited months for me. That makes it different.

What makes you think you're so special?

He likes me. And I like him.

You're falling in love with him.

I'm doing no such thing.

Flynn paused once the condom was in place. 'Are you okay?'

Kat quickly rearranged her features. 'Sure.'

A tiny frown appeared between his eyes. 'We don't have to continue this if you'd rather not.'

She smoothed out the crease of his frown. 'I guess being a lawyer and all you'd be pretty pedantic about consent.'

'It's not about me being a lawyer. It's about me being a man who respects a woman's right to say no at any stage of the encounter.'

You are so going to fall in love with this guy.

Kat ignored the debate with her conscience to gaze into his dark eyes. 'I want you. I really, truly want you.'

His mouth came down to hers in a slow burn of a kiss, stoking the fire of her need until her entire body was shaking with it. She whimpered, she begged, she clawed at his back and urged him to put her out of her misery, but still he took his time pleasuring her with his mouth, with his tongue, playing, flirting and teasing hers.

'Don't be so impatient,' he said against her lips.

'Aren't you…you know…?'

His erection moved against her folds, potent, thick and heavy with desire. 'I am, but I want you to be ready for me.'

I was ready for you the first time I set eyes on you, Kat wanted to say out loud. But instead she used her body to do the talking, pushing herself against his swollen heat, her breath catching as he entered her slickly in one deep thrust that made every hair on her scalp tingle and twirl. He groaned as he surged again, the rocking movement of his body triggering powerful sensations in her core. She was close but not quite close enough.

But, as if he could read her every need, he reached down between their entwined bodies and found the throbbing heart of her desire. His fingers worked their magic and suddenly she was flying, spinning, rolling over and over, losing track of anything but the explosive release pulsing through her entire body.

Flynn followed with a series of thrusts that signalled his own release. Kat felt the tension of him just before he pitched into the abyss, heard the guttural groan, felt the hot breeze of his expelled breath against her neck. She felt him relax against her when it was over, his arms still holding her as if he never wanted to let her go.

She tiptoed her fingers up and down the musculature of his back, exploring every knob of his spine, from between his shoulder blades to the base just above his taut buttocks. She felt his skin quiver like a horse shaking off an insect. 'Am I tickling you?' she said.

He leaned on his elbows to look at her. 'You have beautiful hands. But then everything about you is beautiful.'

Kat traced the outline of his mouth with her fingertip. 'This is kind of weird…'

'What is?'

'Me being in bed with you.'

'Doesn't feel weird to me. It feels amazing.'

She looked into his coal-black gaze. Had he felt anything like the cataclysmic release she had felt? 'Better than usual?'

His expression was closed for a nanosecond, as if he had retreated to some place in his mind where no one else was allowed access. But then he smiled a lopsided smile. 'Fishing for compliments, Miss Winwood?'

Kat pulled at her lower lip with her teeth. 'Will you tell Jaz and Miranda and the twins about us?'

His eyes moved between each of hers, as if he too were searching for something she was trying to conceal. 'Would it bother you if they found out?'

She thought about it for a moment. 'Not really…as long as they know this isn't heading anywhere serious.'

Something about his expression looked tight. Pulled back. 'Wedding fever might've hit the Ravensdales but it's not going to hit me.'

Kat studied the taut line of his mouth for a moment. 'I would've thought you'd be the first person to want to settle down and have a family.'

'Why's that?'

'Because you didn't have one growing—'

'I did have one.' He rolled away from her to dispose of the condom. 'I still have one.'

'But you're not close to any of them.'

'So?' He threw her a glance. 'Lots of people aren't close to their families. It doesn't mean they don't love them.'

Kat pulled her knees up to her chest and wrapped her arms around her legs. 'You love them?'

He let out an impatient breath. 'Of course I do. They raised me, educated me, provided for me.'

'Do you ever tell them you love them?'

He reached for his trousers, sitting on the bed with his back to her and pulled them on. 'We're not that sort of family.'

Kat watched as he got awkwardly to his feet to shrug on his shirt. 'Are you angry with me?'

He turned to look at her. 'Why do you think that?'

'Because you're getting dressed. It's like you're putting up a barrier.'

He drew in a long breath and then released it in a

measured stream. 'It's late. I thought you'd want to go back next door to your own bed.'

He's dismissing you. He's done the deed, now he wants you gone.

No, he's not. He's protecting himself. I've touched a nerve.

Kat unfolded her legs and got off the bed. She didn't reach for her clothes but went over to where he was balanced on his crutches with his shirt hanging open. She slid a hand over the taut muscles of his chest, right up to the back of his neck to bring his head down towards hers. 'Do you really want me to go back next door?' she whispered against his mouth.

'Not yet,' he said and covered her mouth with his.

CHAPTER TEN

FLYNN WOKE SOMETIME during the night to realise Kat was still in bed beside him. It wasn't that he didn't have the occasional sleepover but he was choosy about who stayed and who didn't. He had wanted Kat to stay. Had wanted it so much it spooked him. He kept telling himself it was okay; she wanted what he wanted—a flingsationship—something between a fling and a relationship. It could last days, weeks or months and he was fine with that.

He looked at her sleeping beside him, her hair in a tangled mess across the pillow, her soft mouth settled in a half-smile as if she was dreaming about something pleasant. She gave a tiny murmur and nestled a little closer. It was as if she had sensed there was someone in the bed beside her and couldn't bear not to be touching them. He shivered as her arms and legs wrapped around his, her head burying against his chest as she gave a kittenish purr of satisfaction.

He found himself stroking the back of her head while he listened to the sound of her breathing, feeling each soft breath waft over his skin like a caress. One of her hands slipped down between their bodies, her fingers finding him as hard as stone.

She opened her eyes and looked up at him with a sultry smile. 'You're up already?'

Flynn shuddered as her hand tightened around him. 'Been up a while, actually.'

She sat up and pushed her hair back off her face, her beautiful breasts drawing his gaze like an industrial-strength magnet. He touched each one with his hand, cupping them, stroking them, watching as she expressed her pleasure with little sighs and moans. He leaned forward to take her nipple in his mouth, rolling his tongue over and around it, drawing on it with gentle pressure. Her hands came down to grasp his head, her fingers digging into his scalp as if to anchor herself against the powerful sensations his touch evoked.

He moved his mouth to her other nipple, then to the underside of her breast, licking the sensitive flesh with his tongue until she pulled him away to look at him with eyes bright with desire.

She pushed him back down on the bed and straddled him, taking care not to bump his bandaged foot. Her hair half-covered her breast like she was a mermaid, which somehow was even more sexy than straight-out nakedness. He slid his hands up from her hips to her waist, his erection pressed up against her naturally separated folds. He could feel her wet heat, the temptation of her making his body hum with overwhelming longing to thrust in without protection.

But that was a line he wouldn't cross.

'Want to put a condom on for me?' he asked, nodding to the bedside drawer where he kept them.

She reached over, the lithe stretch of her body making his all the more frantic with excitement. She was slim and yet femininely rounded in all the right places. She undid the packet with her teeth as she held his gaze with the sensuous heat of hers. Then with torturous slowness she applied it to him, stroking it down his length, securing it in place with a couple of massaging strokes that nearly blew the top of his head off.

Then, when he thought he could take no more, she gave him a look from beneath her half-mast lashes and shimmied down his body so her mouth was within reach of his erection. 'I thought you were a conservative lover,' he said in a strangled voice.

She gave him a naughty girl look and got down to business. He took as much as he could before he pulled her away with a gentle but firm hand fisted in her hair. 'Enough,' he said. 'I won't be able to pleasure you.'

'We can take turns, can't we?'

Flynn stroked his hands up and down the silk of her arms. Her cheeks were rosy, her mouth wet from where she had sucked on him, her eyes sparkling with sexual excitement. 'I want to watch you come,' he said.

She looked momentarily uncertain. 'You mean while I'm on top like this?'

'If you're comfortable doing it that way.'

She came back over him and positioned herself so he could enter her, guiding him in with her hand. He felt the tight grip of her body, the slick heat drawing him in until he was mad with the need to let fly. He let her control the depth by holding her by the hips, thrusting up to meet her downward movements. The pleasure built to a crescendo, and for the first time since he'd been a teenager he wasn't sure he could hold on to his control.

He watched as her orgasm played out over her face, felt it in her body where it rippled and contracted around his. She was gasping, crying, whimpering, shaking and shuddering all at once, her head, with her wild hair, thrown back as she gave a primal sound that made him feel more of a man than he had ever felt before.

His own release was just as earth-shattering. It rocketed through him, leaving him breathless and boneless once it was over.

Kat slumped over him with her head nestled against his neck, her hair splayed across his chest in a silky wave. He stroked her slim back in long, gentle strokes, loving the feel of her satin-smooth skin against his palm.

His mind began to drift… What would it be like to lie with her like this for morning after morning? To wake and see her lying beside him? To see her gorgeous face smile at him as if he was the only person in the world she wanted to wake to? To see her face at the beginning and at the end of each day? And not just her face but the faces of the children they could make together—a girl and a boy, or two girls or two boys. They could even foster or adopt. Make some kid's life a blessing instead of a curse.

Flynn snapped the lid down on his thoughts like someone shutting a Jack-in-the-box. Why did he have these thoughts around Kat of all people? She wasn't interested in settling down any more than he was. She was happy with a temporary relationship because she wanted to focus on her career.

She was young, eleven years younger than him. He had never had a lover that much younger. But she was far more mature than some of his previous partners who had been similar in age to him. He liked her sense of humour, her intelligence and her determination to succeed. He even liked the fact she was standing up to Richard Ravensdale. So many women in her shoes would have milked the situation for all it was worth. Milked it and made butter, yoghurt and custard out of it. But she had stood her ground. Refused to be bought. Refusing to be manipulated into doing anything she didn't believe was right for her.

Flynn wanted her at that party but not just to please Richard. He wanted her to feel connected to her siblings. To feel a part of the family, because he knew it would be good for her. She had no one in the world now her mother was dead. It would give her a safe haven to have older half-brothers and a half-sister to turn to. Even Jaz with her runaway tongue would be good for her. It would give Kat a community of love that appeared to have been sadly lacking in her childhood.

'I'd better get back to check on Monty,' she said into the silence.

Flynn stroked his hand up to the nape of her neck, her hair tickling the back of his hand where it was resting against it. 'He'll be fine. Cats are pretty self-sufficient.'

She lifted her head to look at him. 'Are you sure you want me to stay the rest of the night?'

He brought his hand round to cup her face. 'Isn't that what people who are having a flingsationship do?'

'I wouldn't know, as this is my first.'

'Mine too,' he said and brought her head back down to his chest.

Kat woke to the feel of someone licking her face but when she opened her eyes it wasn't Flynn but Cricket. 'Eeeww!' She laughed and pushed him away.

Flynn came in on his crutches, showered and dressed for work. 'I would've brought you breakfast in bed but I haven't figured out how to do that whilst on crutches.'

'It's the thought that counts,' Kat said, getting out of the bed, picking up Flynn's shirt from the night before and slipping it on. She could smell him on the fabric, but then she could smell him on herself. Something shifted in her belly at the memory of all they had shared the night before. It wasn't just the physicality of sex, the mind-blowing release or the sensual touches and caresses. It was the sense of having drawn closer to him than to any other person. She wondered if he felt the same.

'I have an early meeting with a client,' he said. 'Will you be okay to take Cricket out?'

'Sure,' Kat said. 'I'm using him as research. I think that's why I nailed the audition.'

Flynn smiled crookedly. 'Good to know he's come in useful. Last night I was ready to drive him to the dog's home.'

'You would never do that. You love him and he loves you.'

His eyes moved away from hers and he picked up something from the top of a chest of drawers. 'Dinner tonight?'

'I'll cook something for us here,' Kat said.

He turned to look at her. 'Sure you want to go to that much trouble?'

'It was part of the deal, wasn't it?'

A small frown pleated his brow. 'I wouldn't have held you to it. I could've found someone else to walk Cricket, and I can afford to eat out or have it delivered to me.'

'So why did you insist I do it?'

His expression had a hint of ruefulness to it. As if she had uncovered something about him he hadn't expected. 'I wanted to spend time with you. To get to know you.'

A warm glow spread through her. 'Do you spend time getting to know all of your lovers?'

'Occasionally.'

Somehow his answer disappointed her. She wanted to be the only one he took the time to get to know. She wanted to feel as special to him as he felt to her.

See? What did I tell you? You're falling for him.

I'm not in love with him.

Not yet, but it won't be long.

Flynn came over to her and eased up her chin so her eyes couldn't escape his. 'Where did you go just then?'

'Go?'

'In your mind,' he said. 'Every now and again you get this faraway look in your eyes, as if you're thinking about something.'

Kat pulled out a relaxed smile from her actor's handbook. 'I was thinking about tonight's menu.'

His eyes did that back-and-forth thing between each of hers. Left eye. Right eye. Left eye. Right eye. Then he looked at her mouth, making her belly turn over. 'Am I on it?' he said.

She stepped up on tiptoe and pressed a kiss to his mouth. 'You're the main course.'

Flynn came back home after a long day at work to find his house filled with delicious home-cooking smells. Cricket bounded up to him, spinning in circles in unmitigated excitement. The sense of home, of security, of belonging, was like a warm blanket on a cold winter's night. It settled around his shoulders, wrapping him in a cloak of contentment unlike anything he had felt before, if ever.

Kat came out of the kitchen. 'How was your day?'

'Long and tiring.'

'Dinner won't be long. I just have to carve the roast.'

'You cooked a roast?'

Her face fell. 'You don't like roasts?'

He brushed his fingers down her cheek. 'Love them.'

Her smile lit up her face. It was like sunshine after a month of cloudy weather. 'Go and put your feet up and I'll fix you a drink.'

'I feel like I've stepped into a nineteen-fifties time warp,' Flynn said. 'By the way, the apron looks great on you.'

She looked at him with a pursed mouth. 'I'm not going to ask you who wore it before me.'

'No one,' he said. 'It was a present from Jake a couple of birthdays back. He likes to joke around.'

'When is your birthday?'

'May. I don't know the exact date but apparently it's anywhere between the tenth and fifteenth.'

'Taurus,' she said, nodding. 'That makes sense.'

'Stubborn as a bull?' Flynn said. 'Yeah, that's me.'

She chewed at her lip for a moment. 'Is it weird not knowing the exact day you were born?'

'Birthdays aren't that important to me.' He had made them unimportant. He no longer ruminated over which day, hour, minute he was born and to whom. Well, not often.

'I guess you already know when my birthday is,' she said with a little frown. 'It seems like the whole world knows I was born two months after Miranda.'

He touched her face again. 'Any more thoughts about meeting Richard?'

She pulled away as if his fingers had burned her. 'No.'

'What about Julius and Jake? Would you be prepared to meet them?'

'Maybe.'

That was a win if nothing else. But the clock was ticking on that party date and he wanted her there. Everyone was expecting him to pull this off. She didn't have to stay long, just meet her father and get out of there, if that was what she wanted. 'I'll organise something when Julius and Holly come over from Argentina. They'll arrive a few days before Richard's party. Jake might catch up with you sooner but it'd be nice if you met them together.'

'Whatever.'

He brushed his thumb over her pouting mouth. 'They're good people, Kat. Don't put them in the same class as your father. He's in a class all of his own.'

She stretched her lips into a smile that didn't show her teeth. 'I'll get that drink for you.'

When Kat brought in a glass of wine to Flynn he was sitting with his feet up, Cricket curled up by his side. He was checking something on his phone but put it down when he saw her. He smiled as she handed him the glass. 'It's going to be tough going back to microwave meals.'

'Can't you cook?'

'I can but I don't always bother. Too much fuss for one person.'

'I know,' Kat said. 'I'm a bit the same.'

He patted the seat beside him on the other side of where Cricket was lying. 'Got a minute?'

'Sure.'

She sat down and he put his arm around her shoulders to draw her closer. 'I've been thinking about your job at the café,' he said. 'It's going to be tough getting to and from rehearsals.'

'I can manage.'

A little silence passed.

'What if I were to pay you?'

Kat swung her gaze to his. 'For what?'

He gave a little roll of his eyes. 'Not *that*. For helping me around the house. Walking Cricket and so on.'

She didn't have to think about it. Her pride wouldn't allow her to accept money off him or any man. Not unless she was officially employed, as in a proper job. 'No. Absolutely not.'

'But what if your shift runs overtime or you have a clash?'

'I'll cut back my hours,' Kat said. 'I'll swap shifts. I'll *make* it work.'

He let out a breath that had a hint of frustration to it. 'It's just money, Kat. I have plenty of it.'

'That's not the point.' She sprang up off the sofa and folded her arms as tight as a steel band across her body.

'What about if I gave you an interest-free loan?'

She gave him a wintry look. 'I'm not a charity case.'

He studied her for a beat. 'Oh, I get it. You don't want to be beholden to me in case I turn the screws on you attending Richard's party.'

Kat pressed her lips together. 'It's not about that stupid party.'

'It's about your pride, isn't it?'

She didn't answer.

'Are you nervous about rehearsals on Monday?'

'A little.'

'Need any help with your lines?'

'I can manage.'

'Kat.' The way he said her name in that achingly gentle way brought her gaze back to his. 'You've been doing everything on your own for so long you've forgotten how to recognise a genuine desire to help,' he said. 'I want you to do well in that play.'

'Why?'

'Because I think you deserve this chance to show the world what you're made of.'

Kat released a breath she hadn't realised she'd been holding. 'Okay...if you don't mind. It would be good to run through my lines a few times.'

'I don't mind at all,' he said. 'I haven't seen the play live but I've seen a couple of YouTube clips. We can work on it over the weekend.'

This will be the clincher. Helping you with your lines. Sheesh... What's next? A wedding rehearsal?

What's wrong with helping me with my lines? Any friend would do that.

Friend? Is that what he is?

Well, he's not my enemy. Not now.

Flynn tapped her on the end of her nose. 'You'd better not zone out like that onstage. Elisabetta will eat you for breakfast and spit out the leftovers.'

Kat blinked and pasted on a smile. 'I'll go and dish up. Don't move. I'll bring it in on a tray.'

The weekend passed so quickly it was Monday morning before Kat was ready. Not because she hadn't rehearsed her part in the play, but more because the time she'd spent with Flynn had been one of the happiest times of her life. He was such easy company, funny and relaxing to be around. He settled her nerves by getting her to go through her part numerous times. He had even gone to the trouble of downloading and printing the script so he could take Kate or Greg's part when needed.

Kat couldn't stop herself thinking what an amazing partner he would make. The way he supported her, encouraged her, challenged her to give more than she thought herself capable of giving. The evenings, they'd spent lingering over dinner and chatting over current affairs or life in general. His sharp mind kept her on her toes; he saw the flaw in any argument and had the mental flexibility to adopt any other position and argue from that corner with just as much skill as from the opinions he held himself.

But it was the nights in his arms she enjoyed the most. Not just the wonderful sex, which seemed to get better and better, but the closeness she felt to him. The sense of him understanding her on a level no one had taken the time or effort to do before.

Even the way he had rescheduled his first client so he could have breakfast with her on Monday morning made her realise how well he knew her. How had it happened? How had the man she had seen as her mortal enemy now become her biggest ally?

Kat could still taste his kiss when she walked through the back door of the theatre. Elisabetta was already there, talking with the director Leon and the other cast member playing Greg. There were stagehands about, as well as the costume designer called Ruby, whom Kat had met on the day of the audition.

It was clear from the moment they began the rehearsals that nothing Kat could do would please Elisabetta. She kept insisting on Kat redoing the scene, even though Leon had been reasonably happy with it. But apparently Elisabetta's demands overruled his opinion and he meekly allowed his biggest star to call the shots.

It was beyond exhausting but Kat hadn't fought this hard and for this long to be bullied by a woman who should have been professional enough to put personal issues aside for the sake of the theatre company and the sponsors. Kat called on every bit of determination she possessed to get through the session without biting back. She withstood the stinging criticism, she turned a deaf ear to the insults and she channelled her frustration into her acting.

'That's it for the day,' Leon finally announced. 'We're back on set at ten tomorrow. Well done, everyone.'

Elisabetta gave Kat a haughty look. 'You'll have to work harder. I'm not impressed by what I've seen so far.'

'You liked what I did in the audition,' Kat said. 'What's changed?'

Elisabetta's gaze could have stripped three decades of wallpaper off a wall. 'You think because you're his bastard child you can talk to me like that?'

Kat aligned her shoulders. Raised her chin. 'We're not on set now. I'll talk to you any way I like.'

Elisabetta's black eyes flashed with venom. 'He doesn't want you in his life, you know. He's only doing it for the publicity. To make his fans think he's a good man.'

'I know,' Kat said. 'That's why I don't want anything to do with him.'

Elisabetta's brows snapped together. 'You're not coming to his party?'

'Nope.'

Something hard in the older woman seemed to give way. It was visible in the small almost imperceptible sag of her shoulders, in the way her tautly held features ever so slightly relaxed. 'Why not?'

'Would you want to meet someone who paid to get rid of you?' Kat asked.

Elisabetta shifted her mouth back and forth as if she was shuffling words like cards inside her mouth. 'What's going on between you and Flynn Carlyon?'

'Nothing.'

Elisabetta smiled—the smile of a cat standing beside an empty birdcage. 'So he's managed to do it, then.'

'Do what?'

'Get you into his bed.'

Kat ground her back teeth together to try and control her temper. 'My private life is none of your business.'

'Don't get too cosy in his bed,' Elisabetta said. 'He won't offer you anything but a quick tumble when it suits him.'

'You know something, Ms Albertini?' Kat said. 'You're a wonderful actor, one of my all-time favourites. I've admired you from afar for as long as I can remember. But as a person? You're a bitter disappointment.'

At first Kat thought Elisabetta was going to slap her. The colour rose in the older woman's face in twin spots on her regal cheekbones, but then she tossed her glorious mane of salt-and-pepper hair back and laughed. Kat stood there waiting for it to end, sure another insult would follow and mentally preparing for it. Had she gone too far? Who in their right mind would insult one of London's most adored theatre actors? Was this the end of her career? Was it over before it had even begun?

An apology was forming on Kat's lips when Elisabetta stopped laughing and smiled at her instead. 'I like you, Kat Winwood,' she said. 'You've got G and D.'

Kat frowned in puzzlement. 'G and D?'

'Guts and determination,' Elisabetta said. 'Believe me, in this business you'll need it. I'll see you tomorrow. *Ciao.*' And with a wave of her hand and a swish of her plush velvet coat she disappeared through the stage curtains.

CHAPTER ELEVEN

KAT HAD JUST returned from walking Cricket and was hanging up his lead when Flynn came in from work.

'How did today go?' he asked.

It occurred to her then how comforting it was to have someone to debrief with at the end of the day. Under normal circumstances she would have gone home to an empty bedsit. Sure, she could have called a friend or have a friend call her, but to have someone on site who was genuinely interested in her made her feel supported. Grounded. Safe. Protected. 'It was…interesting,' she said.

'Did Elisabetta behave herself?'

Kat took Flynn's coat from him and held it against her. She could easily have hung it up next to hers but she wanted to savour the warmth and smell of his body still trapped in the cashmere. 'She was hell on wheels during rehearsals, but after everyone left we sort of came to an understanding.'

One of his dark brows lifted in an arc. 'That sounds intriguing. Tell me what happened.'

Kat gave him a quick run-down on the conversation she'd had with Elisabetta. 'Mind you,' she said. 'I wouldn't trust her, for all her charming friendliness. She's like a chameleon. She changes when it suits her.'

'That's why she has the reputation she has as an

actor,' Flynn said. 'She can morph into any character she wants. But you did well to stand up to her. Not
many people do. They're too frightened of her celebrity
to connect with the person under the façade.'

Kat frowned. 'You think it's a façade? That she's not
like that normally? Bitchy and unfriendly to anyone she
perceives as a threat?'

He leaned on one crutch as he brushed his bent
knuckles down her cheek. 'She's a bit like you. You
can be prickly and unfriendly until you establish trust.
Maybe she recognised that same quality in you.'

Kat turned and hung up his coat as she thought about
it. She straightened out the sleeves, dusted off an imagi-
nary bit of lint from the back and turned to look at him
again. 'What would you like for dinner?'

He was looking at her strangely. There was a slight
frown between his eyes and his mouth had lost its easy
smile. Then he did a slow blink and refocused. 'Sorry,
did you say something?'

'I asked what you wanted for dinner,' Kat said. 'I
didn't have time to pick anything up after the rehearsal,
but I can go out now to the convenience store and—'

'No,' he said. 'This has gone on long enough. You
don't need to wait on me hand and foot. I can order
something in but only if you'll stay and share it with
me.'

Would that be all that she was sharing? The thought
of spending another night in his bed was tempting. More
than tempting. But what if what Elisabetta had said was
true? That he would only have her in his bed when it
suited him? How long would it suit him? A week? A
month? Until Richard's party was over?

Why are you stressing about how long he wants

to sleep with you? It's a fling. They're not meant to last long.

I'm not stressing. I'm just wondering...

You're in too deep. You know you are. You've got feelings for him, deep, scary feelings that involve weddings and babies and a white picket fence.

I want a career first. It's all I've ever wanted.

So you keep saying.

When the food arrived, Kat set it up in the dining room. Once they were both seated, Flynn raised his wine glass to hers. 'To the most beautiful new talent to hit London's West End.'

Kat gave a self-deprecating snort. 'I don't know about that. I've got so much to learn. It's a big step up from toilet-paper ads to playing Sylvia.'

'You got that part on your merit.'

She fingered the bottom of her glass. 'Did I? Or did Elisabetta choose me because she wants to get back at Richard by publicly humiliating me?'

He put his hand over hers, stilling its restless fidgeting. 'Look at me, Kat.' His eyes were dark and serious. 'Whatever her reasons were, you have to take control now. It's up to you. Actors have to deal with difficult casting arrangements all the time. Good actors don't bring their personal life to the stage. You have to be Sylvia on that stage, not Richard Ravensdale's love child. Understood?'

Kat let out a wobbly breath. 'You're right. You're so right.' She smiled. 'Thanks for the pep talk. If ever you get sick of practising law, you could be a life coach.'

His smile was rueful as he pulled his hand back from hers. 'Yeah, well, I'm good at sorting out other people's problems. It's different when it's closer to home.'

Kat searched his features for a beat. 'Is there something you're struggling with? Personally, I mean?'

His expression closed like curtains on a stage. 'No.'

His answer was too abrupt, too definite. Was he having second thoughts about their relationship? Did he want it to end sooner rather than later?

They ate in a companionable silence but Kat got the feeling he was mulling over something. Every time she glanced at him he was frowning. It would relax whenever he caught her looking at him, and his smile would quickly replace it, but it only lifted half of his mouth.

Was his foot annoying him? Slowing him down at work? Her guilt over injuring him came back with a vengeance. Everything had changed between them once she had run over his foot. The dynamic of their relationship had changed. They had gone from enemies—at least on her part, that was—to lovers. Intimate partners in a fling-relationship that had a scarily loose time frame. It never used to bother her when she'd had temporary relationships in the past. It was just how things were. She had never felt a pressing ache in her chest at the thought of it ending. She had never envisaged a future together where she could have it all: the career, the loving and supportive husband, the kids, the house and the pets.

But now, after just one night sleeping in Flynn's bed, she realised how much she wanted to repeat it. To spend not just one night but many nights, all the nights that were allotted to her on this earth.

But what did he want? He had made it clear he wasn't going to settle down. Even Elisabetta, who knew him well, had said the same.

'I bought you something today,' Flynn said into the silence.

Kat looked up in surprise. 'What? Why?'

He leaned back in his chair to reach for a small package on the sideboard she hadn't even noticed was there when she'd come in to set the table. He handed the package to her with an unreadable look. 'Actually, it's from Cricket,' he said. 'For taking him for all those walks.'

Kat unpeeled the satin ribbon and the paper to find a jewellery box from a well-known jeweller inside. Her heart flip-flopped. Jewellery? What sort of jewellery? She tentatively opened the box and found a beautiful tortured pearl on a delicately crafted white-gold chain. The pearl was irregular in shape but she knew from reading about them somewhere that each one was completely unique. Was he telling her something by this lovely gift? That he saw *her* as unique and special? She looked across at him. 'I don't know what to say…it's beautiful. But you shouldn't have bothered.'

'Cricket insisted,' Flynn said. 'Anyway, it's just a trinket.'

A trinket? Kat looked back at the gorgeous pearl. This was no throwaway trinket. This would have cost a packet. She had never been given jewellery as a gift before. In fact, as far as gifts went, she had received very few over the course of her twenty-three years. Her mother had never had enough spare cash for presents, and certainly none of Kat's past boyfriends had ever gifted her with anything—not so much as a bunch of flowers.

Kat leaned down to where Cricket was sitting at her feet waiting in hopeful enthusiasm for a titbit to be offered his way. 'Thank you, Cricket,' she said, ruffling his funny ears. 'You've made me feel very special. I'll treasure this for always.'

Cricket yapped as if he understood every word she said and then did one of his crazy little twirls.

'Mad dog,' Flynn said with a relaxed smile.

Kat met his gaze across the table again. 'I think he's the nicest dog I've ever met.'

Are you talking about the dog or him?

The dog... Okay, both.

Sucker.

Kat lifted the pearl and its chain out of the box and trailed it across her palm. 'Does Cricket buy all your lovers gifts?'

'You're the first because I've only had him since Christmas.'

She put the pearl back in its box and gently closed the lid. She was the first but wouldn't be the last. Why should that make her feel empty inside? As if a giant hole had been gouged in her stomach? 'What happened with your family that you ended up with Cricket?'

He picked up his wine glass and looked at the contents for a moment. 'There was a scene. There usually is at Christmas and birthdays—any occasion, really.'

'What happened?'

He took a slow breath in and released it in a whoosh. 'I didn't like the way my parents were treating Cricket. He's not the sort of dog you can lock outside, especially as they'd had him in the house since he was a puppy. We got into an argument and things escalated. My father's solution was to have Cricket euthanised.'

'Oh, no!'

'Oh, yes.' His look was grim. 'I left with Cricket and drove back here and had a perfectly lovely evening with the Carstairses and their kids. It was the best and worst Christmas, if you know what I mean.'

'I do,' Kat said. 'But how lovely that you've got him now. He adores you. It's like he's always been yours.'

That smile that made her insides melt was back. 'I haven't quite figured out the logistics of what to do with him when I go away on holidays or business,' he said. 'He doesn't strike me as the boarding kennel type.'

Kat reached down to scratch Cricket underneath his chin. 'Is your daddy calling you fussy, my sweet? You're not a fusspot, are you? You just love the comfort of home and I don't blame you one little bit.'

When she looked up again she caught Flynn looking at her with that odd look on his darkly handsome features. 'What's wrong?' she said. 'Why do you keep looking at me like that?'

His expression became blank. Unreadable. The stage curtains not only pulled across but the lights turned out as well. 'How am I looking at you?'

'I don't know…as if you're uncertain about something…about me.'

He reached for the wine bottle to refresh their glasses. 'It's just work stuff playing on my mind. Big cases, big egos, big bucks involved.'

'I guess it's another good reason to avoid marriage,' Kat said. 'You see the other side of it—the dirty and bitter side. No wonder it puts you off.'

He put the wine bottle back in the silver cooler. 'Not all marriages end up in the divorce court. Some couples manage to last the distance, but you can never know if you and your partner are going to be the success story or the soul-destroying showdown.'

'True,' Kat said. 'But do you think it's more about good luck than good management?'

'A bit of both, probably,' he said. 'When I look at your brothers and sister and their partners, I can't imagine any of them ever wanting a divorce. But life can throw up some curve balls. Relationships can get knocked off course by all sorts of things. Bad health, financial stress, kids or the lack thereof, interfering relatives… The list is endless.'

'I guess communication is the key,' Kat said. 'Being able to talk about stuff—really talk, I mean. Not locking stuff away only for it to blow out in an argument when it's too late to fix it.'

He gave a wry smile. 'Listen to us. The experts on the institution both of us are actively avoiding.'

Kat smiled back but for some reason it felt false. 'Yeah, well, I didn't rule it out entirely. Just not right now.'

A long silence passed.

All Kat could hear was the ticking of the mantle clock in the sitting room next door.

'It's tough finding a partner once you're famous,' Flynn finally said. 'You can never know if people want you for you or for the social esteem it gives them to be associated with you. Both your brothers have struggled with that.'

'Has Miranda experienced it too?'

'She lost her boyfriend Mark when they were teenagers,' he said. 'Cancer. She hadn't dated since. She martyred herself until Leandro whisked her away to Nice to help him sort out his late father's estate. He's had a thing for her for ages. Everyone could see it except Miranda.'

Another silence ticked past.

'Does it happen to you?' Kat asked. 'The celebrity thing? I mean, you're so close to the Ravensdales. Do people use you to get to them?'

'Lovers, you mean?' he said. 'Occasionally, I guess. It doesn't really bother me, to be perfectly honest.'

'Because you only want them for sex?'

He looked at her for a beat or two. 'Putting it baldly, yes.'

Was that all he wanted from her? Their relationship was based on the physical chemistry they had, not on anything else. No lasting bond was being formed. No future path was being laid out. No plans were being made for continuing their relationship indefinitely. 'I guess I should count myself privileged you want me for other things as well,' she said, and held up her hand to tick off a list. 'Dog walking, cooking, running errands, scintillating conversation.'

His smile was a little twisted. 'I want you for lots of reasons.'

Her insides slipped sideways at his deep and husky tone. But common sense raised a red flag. 'You want me to go to Richard's party,' Kat said. 'Be honest. That's your primary goal. It has been from day one.'

'I'm not denying I want you there,' he said. 'But it's no longer my primary goal.'

She moistened her suddenly dry mouth. 'What is?'

His eyes smouldered as they held hers. 'Why don't we clear away here and I'll show you?'

Flynn woke from a disturbing dream later that night. It took him a moment to realise it had only been a dream. His heart was pounding, his skin was clammy and his pulse was racing like he'd had four energy drinks back to back. He had dreamt he was left alone on an island in the middle of the ocean. There was no power. No lights. No food. No shelter. No way of contacting anyone. A cruise ship was in the distance but it was too far for him to swim. There were sharks in the water. Menacing dorsal fins everywhere, circling the island. Every escape route was seething and swirling and swishing with danger.

He turned his head expecting to see Kat beside him in the bed but the space where she had been earlier was empty…well, apart from Cricket, of course. 'What are you doing in here?' he said. 'You're supposed to be sleeping in your basket downstairs.'

Cricket sank his undershot chin even lower onto his paws, his eyes taking on a beseeching look that would make anyone with half a heart think twice about removing him.

But that was the trouble. Flynn had more heart than he wanted right now. It was taking up more and more room in his chest, making him feel things he didn't want to feel. He couldn't explain why suddenly everything had changed when for so long he had been perfectly happy with his life. Seeing Kat arrive home earlier that evening had shown him what his life could be like if they were a couple. Not just dating or having a fling, but a committed couple.

He had been excited all day at the thought of coming home. The thought of sharing a meal with her, talking to her, watching her with Cricket, making love to her, had distracted him all day. He had bought her that pearl in his lunch hour. A completely spontaneous thing he still couldn't explain. He had walked past that jeweller's hundreds if not thousands of times and never once had he looked at the display in the window. But that day he had felt compelled not only to look but to go inside. He had seen the pearl and instantly known it was perfect for Kat. It was unique and beautiful, just as she was.

He tossed the bedcovers aside and reached for his

crutches beside the bed. He was completely over his foot. It wasn't so much the pain now but the inconvenience. He was tired of how it slowed him down.

Where was Kat? Had she gone back next door? He made his awkward way downstairs and saw that her coat was no longer hung up next to his. Her hat and gloves were not on the hall table. A cavern of emptiness spread in his chest like a flesh-eating stain.

He was alone.

Kat knew Flynn was in a foul mood as soon as she arrived the next morning. She had left his bed the night before because he'd seemed restless while he slept. She'd assumed his foot was giving him trouble so she'd left so he could have the bed to himself without having to worry about her bumping him during the night.

There were other reasons she had left. One big reason, actually. Not that she wanted to examine it too closely.

He was in the kitchen stirring a cup of coffee, which seemed a little pointless, as he didn't take milk or sugar. His back was turned towards her and even though he was wearing a business shirt and trousers she could see the tension in his body. She could even sense it in the air, crackling like static. Even Cricket was acting a little subdued. He wasn't bouncing around and twirling in excitement but had a baleful look on his funny little face.

'Good morning,' she said with Pollyanna brightness.

'Morning.'

'How did you sleep?'

'Fine.'

She waited a beat but he still didn't turn around to greet her. 'Is something wrong?'

'No.'

Kat rolled her eyes. 'So why are you giving me the cold shoulder?'

He turned but in doing so he lost hold of one of his crutches. It clattered noisily to the floor, terrifying Cricket in the process. The poor little mutt went careening out of the room as if someone had taken a baseball bat to him. Flynn swore and tried to pick up his crutch but Kat got there first. 'Here you go,' she said.

'Thanks.' It was little more than a brooding mutter.

'Clearly someone got out of the wrong side of the bed. Am I supposed to play twenty questions or will you tell me?'

'Why didn't you stay last night?'

'I'm being paid to house-sit next door,' Kat said. 'That means I'm meant to actually house-sit. Pardon me for being a little pedantic about these things but accepting money from someone without doing the work is not something I'm all that comfortable doing.'

His tight frown relaxed slightly but didn't completely disappear. 'I'm sorry. I'm being unreasonable. Of course you have responsibilities next door.'

Kat put her hand on his forearm where he was leaning on his crutch. 'I was worried I was disturbing you last night. You were tossing and turning so much I thought your foot would get hurt if I stayed.'

There was a flicker of wryness in his smile. 'You don't take up that much space.'

'I'd better check on Cricket,' Kat said. 'Is he usually so jumpy around fallen objects?'

'My father threw a shoe at him at Christmas. I got the feeling it wasn't the first time.'

'I don't think I like either of your parents very much,' she said. 'I hope I don't have to meet them. I'm not one for keeping my opinions to myself.'

His smile set off a twinkle in his dark eyes. 'So I've found out.'

Kat reached up and planted a kiss to his mouth before she could stop herself. 'Good morning,' she said softly.

'Good morning,' he said with equal softness. 'Do you want some breakfast? I've made coffee.'

She gave him a look of mock reproach. 'Coffee is not breakfast. You need proper nutrition when your body is repairing itself.'

He tugged on a tendril of her hair. 'Yes, dear.'

Kat laughed off his hen-pecked husband imitation. 'As if you'd ever allow a woman to tell you what you could and couldn't do. Or a man, for that matter.'

He didn't answer when she turned to go and search for Cricket, but when she glanced at him as she got to the door he was no longer smiling and that brooding frown had settled back between his brows.

The next two weeks flew past with Kat juggling rehearsals and shifts at the café. She spent most evenings with Flynn but insisted on returning to her own bed next door. The Carstairs family was coming back the following week and she wanted to make sure everything was in tip-top shape for their arrival.

On set, Elisabetta was her usual demanding self, but Kat came to look forward to their scenes together onstage. She felt inspired by the older woman's talent and knew when Elisabetta pulled her up for something it was because she knew Kat could give more, could dig deeper, could perform from her heart and soul instead of simply acting out a role. Elisabetta loved acting the way Kat loved it. It was a driving passion, an ambition she'd had since she was young.

Kat found it a little weird to have struck up a tentative friendship with her biological father's wife, but over the course of the rehearsals she felt a bond growing between Elisabetta and herself that she never would have predicted. She wouldn't have described them as friends, by any measure of the word, but she liked to think Elisabetta respected her for her willingness to learn. In a rare moment in the dressing room, Elisabetta even told Kat some of her anguish over finding out about Richard's affair with Kat's mother.

'I hated her and I hated him,' Elisabetta said, leaning forward to apply a fresh coat of lipstick. She pressed her lips together. 'The worst thing was, he was still seeing her when he'd reconciled with me.'

'I know,' Kat said. 'I don't know how you could stay married to him after that. I would've divorced him in a flash.'

Elisabetta turned on her chair in front of the lighted mirror, her expression a little wistful. 'Have you ever been passionately in love?'

Kat opened and closed her suddenly dry mouth. 'I… erm…'

'I loved Richard from the moment I met him,' Elisabetta said. 'I looked into his eyes and wham. That was it. But I hate him too. Some days the hate wins, other days the love does. Right now, I'm undecided.'

'Do you think he's learned his lesson?' Kat asked.

Elisabetta sighed as she picked up her hairbrush. She examined it for a moment before absently drawing a couple of hairs free from the bristles. 'Who knows? Some men never do.'

Kat let a little silence pass before she asked, 'Do you think I should go to his party on Saturday? I mean, would it upset you if I did?'

Elisabetta's hand tightened on the hairbrush, the tendons on her hand standing out like white cords. But then she relaxed her hand and began brushing her hair as casually as you pleased. Swish… Swish… Swish… 'It's no skin off my nose what you do. I don't care either way.'

If Kat hadn't been an actor herself she would have believed Elisabetta. She would have taken her answer at face value. But something about the older woman's indifferent tone rang an alarm bell. What if by going to the party Kat upset Elisabetta? What could be worse at your husband's Sixty Years in Showbiz party than his dirty little secret showing up? Her friendship with Elisabetta—if you could call it that—was too fragile, too new, to compromise it. Her career was balanced on the high wire of Elisabetta's approval. She couldn't risk it. Not for the man who hadn't wanted her to be born in the first place.

But what about Flynn?

He'll understand.

You think?

Kat didn't want to think about it. The topic of Richard's party was the elephant in the room whenever she was with Flynn. An elephant with halitosis. Neither of them had mentioned Richard's party in the last couple of weeks. But as she walked Cricket later that day she knew she would have to give Flynn an answer one way or the other.

Flynn listened as his male client ranted about his soon-to-be-ex-wife in between raving about his replacement of her with a woman half his age. This was his fourth client today, all of them desperate to extricate themselves out of their marriages, and yet, strangely, Flynn could think of nothing but the good side of marriage.

When he heard his client try and justify his actions in taking a mistress, because his wife had been sick during her pregnancy for a couple of months and not interested in sex, Flynn's back came up. What about the promise of 'in sickness and in health'? Wasn't that supposed to mean something?

He thought of Kat coming day in and day out to help him. Sure, he'd playfully blackmailed her, but she could have easily told him where to go. But instead, she had adjusted her timetable to see to his and Cricket's needs.

His needs...

His needs were not just physical. He could have those met in the way he used to—with a casual date for a week or two. His needs now were more cerebral. He looked forward to seeing Kat, talking to her, listening to her. Watching her. Loving her.

Loving her.

For once, Flynn didn't push the thought aside. He didn't shove it back behind the locked door in his brain. He didn't fight it. He let it flow through his mind, sweeping away the doubts that had lingered for too long. Of course he loved her. Hadn't he fallen in love with her that first day? Her feisty little stand-off had made him fall like a pebble kicked off a cliff. Kissing her had sealed the deal. Making love with her had cemented it. Now there was one last step he had to take to set it in stone.

To set it in stone for ever.

'Till death do us part' was a promise Flynn wanted to make. Ached to make. He had shied away from it all those years because he hadn't met the right person. The person he felt he could live with for the rest of his life. Before now, the promises had seemed claustrophobic, strangling, suffocating.

Now they made sense.

With Kat *everything* made sense.

Flynn was home by the time Kat got back from her walk with the dog. He was in the sitting room but instead of sitting on the sofa with his foot up he was standing on his crutches looking out of the window. He turned when she came in but his expression was difficult to read. 'Hi.'

'Hi.'

Was he going to come over and kiss her like he usually did? Why was he standing all the way over there? He didn't even seem aware of Cricket, who was dancing around his ankles in a frenzy of delight. But then, as if the little dog sensed the gravity of Flynn's mood, he lowered himself to the floor in a submissive 'stay' position, his scruffy little head resting on his paws.

'Is…is something wrong?' Kat asked. 'You seem a little tense. Not just today but for the last couple of weeks. Is it work? Your foot? Your family?' *Me?*

He gave her a smile that only involved half his mouth. 'I've been waiting for you.'

Kat hung up her coat, pulled off her gloves and put them on the hallstand. 'I told you I was going to be late. We had to do a dress rehearsal and then Elisabetta had an issue with the way her hair was done. Honestly, she can be such a pain in the butt.'

There was a weird little silence.

She looked at him again, her heart jerking as if it had been kicked. 'Why are you looking at me like that?'

His expression lost its surface tension, as if something deep inside him had softened. Melted. 'I never thought I'd do this again.'

'Do what?'

'Ask someone to marry me.'

Kat stared at him in a stunned silence. She blinked and opened her mouth to speak but no words came out. Shock ran through her like a stupefying drug. She couldn't get her thoughts to process properly. It was as though someone had scrambled her brain, shaken it up until none of her synapses were connecting. Why would he ask her to marry him? He wasn't in love with her… was he? He had never said. Never hinted. Not one word.

Flynn came closer and, leaning on one crutch, cupped her cheek in his hand. 'I'm sorry I can't get down on bended knee but I love you, Kat. I want you to marry me. Please will you do me the honour of becoming my wife?'

He's only asking you because of the party.

No, he's not. He said he loves me.

Yeah, right. The party is on Saturday. This is his insurance policy.

Kat felt like she was balanced over a canyon on a toothpick. How could she know for sure what his motives were? He had set his mind on getting her to that party. She would not be able to say no if she was officially engaged to him. It would look odd if she didn't show. He was Richard's legal advisor, a part of the family— a close friend to all the Ravensdales. 'This seems rather…sudden…'

His mouth did that rueful half-twist again. 'I know, but once I make my mind up about something I have to act. Let's not waste any more time pretending we don't care for each other. We belong together, darling. We both felt it the first time we met.'

Don't do it.

But I want to say yes!

You need more time. What about your career? 'Fools rush in' and all that.

The tender look on Flynn's face overrode her doubts. 'You love me?'

His smile made her heart squeeze as tightly as a child's hug. 'How can you doubt it?'

Kat stepped up to him and wrapped her arms around his waist, looking up at his adoring expression. How could this be happening? It was so much more than she'd expected. She hadn't dared expect anything. She had tried to keep her heart out of reach but it had been impossible. Resisting Flynn Carlyon had been impossible. Stopping herself from falling in love with him had been impossible. 'But I thought you were against marriage?'

He cradled her face in one of his large hands. 'Not when it involves you. I can't think of anyone else I would want to spend the rest of my life bantering with. Can you?'

Kat smiled. 'No.'

His black-coffee eyes twinkled. 'So, is that a yes?'

She brought her mouth up to meet his descending one. 'Yes. A thousand, million, squillion times yes.'

The kiss was getting a little more serious when Kat became aware of Flynn's phone ringing. He had different tones for different people but she had never heard this ring tone before. She eased back to look up at him. 'Are you going to answer it?'

'It's not important. It's just Richard.'

A cold handprint touched the back of her neck. 'Why's he calling you now?'

'He calls me most days.'

Kat searched his expression…for what, she wasn't sure. Something didn't feel right. She couldn't explain it. It had been fine until that phone had started ringing. She couldn't help feeling it was like the sounding of an alarm bell. She could see the rectangular outline of his phone inside his shirt pocket.

She heard it ping with a left message.

She reached for it at the same time Flynn did, his hand stilling hers. Warning hers.

'I want to see that message,' she said.

'No.'

Kat raised her brow at his intractable tone. 'Why not?'

'It's private.'

'But I'm your fiancée. You get to share everything with me.'

Something hardened in his jaw. A muscle. A ligament. It travelled all the way to his mouth. 'Not about my clients.'

'He's my father, so surely that's different?'

'It's not.'

Kat knew he was right to insist on client confidentiality but she couldn't get rid of the cloud of doubt blurring her vision of the future. Their future. 'So does that mean you won't allow me access to your phone once we're married?'

The tension around his mouth tightened. 'Trust is a huge part of being married.'

'Does that mean I get to keep my phone and emails private too?'

She could see the battle played out on his face. It was like a tug of war between logic and emotion. Push. Pull. Push. Pull. 'If you insist.'

'I do.'

The phone rang again. Same tone. Same insistent clarion call. Flynn took it out of his pocket and, giving Kat an unreadable look, answered it. 'Richard, I'm busy right now. I'll call you ba—'

'Did you get her to agree to come to the party?' Richard's voice carried like a foghorn.

Kat's spine went rigid. Ice-block rigid. Don't-mess-with-me-rigid. She held out her hand for the phone. 'I want to speak to him.'

Flynn held the phone against his chest. 'I don't think that's such a great idea.'

She kept her hand out, her eyes locked on his, her determination on fire. 'Give me the damn phone.'

'Is that Kat I can hear in the background?' The fabric of Flynn's shirt only faintly muffled Richard's theatre-trained voice. 'Let me talk to her.'

Flynn handed her the phone with a look that suggested he felt like he was handing over a live bomb.

'This is Kat Winwood.'

'Kat, my dear.' Richard's voice was all treacle, honey and sickly-sweet jam. 'How lovely to hear your voice at last. Are you coming to the party? Did Flynn make it impossible for you to refuse, as I instructed him?'

Kat's hand tightened on the phone. She wanted to throw it at the wall. To smash it on the floor. To stomp on it until the screen shattered, like her dream had been shattered. 'No,' she said, casting Flynn a look that said, *This includes you.* 'I've decided not to come to the party and my decision is final.'

'But my sweet child,' Richard said, 'it won't be the same without you there.'

'You'll get over it,' Kat said and handed the phone back to Flynn.

Flynn clicked off the call and put the phone back in his pocket without saying anything to Richard. 'Come on, Kat. You surely don't think I staged my proposal to get you to—?'

'Why ask me today? Why not ask me after the weekend when the party is over?'

A muscle worked like a hammer in his jaw. Tap. Tap. Tap. 'How can you possibly *think* that? Haven't the last few weeks shown you how much I care about you? What does it matter when I ask you? The important thing is that I ask you. I love you. Why would I wait?'

Kat reached for her coat, shoving her arms through the sleeves so roughly the lining tore. How could she trust he was being genuine? She was torn; she wanted to believe he loved her but what if it was all a ruse to get her to meet her father in person? Flynn didn't like losing. He had set himself a goal and he let nothing and no one get in his way of achieving it. There was a streak of ruthlessness in him. She had seen that from the first time she'd met him.

But would he really go so far as to *propose* to her to achieve his mission?

'I'm not going to ask you again,' Flynn said in a hard, tight voice. 'Take it or leave it.'

Kat turned to look at him with an implacable set to her features. 'You should know me well enough by now to know I don't tolerate ultimatums.'

His frown turned his eyebrows into a single intimidating line. 'I'll make arrangements for someone else to walk Cricket. You're relieved from your responsibilities here as of now.'

Kat kept her spine straight, her shoulders aligned, her resolve rimmed with steel. 'You're acting like a child who's thrown its favourite toy out of the sandpit.'

He gave a rough laugh. '*I'm* acting like a child? What about you? You won't admit to your feelings about me because you're frightened of allowing someone close in case they let you down.'

'I'm not in love with you.' Kat used every ounce of acting ability she possessed. 'I'm in love with my career. That's all I want for now. It's all I've ever wanted.'

His top lip curled, his dark eyes flashed. 'I hope it keeps you warm at night because, after all the lights are down and the adoring fans have all gone home, you'll be on your own.'

CHAPTER TWELVE

FLYNN COULDN'T WAIT for the party to be over. It was a slow, miserable torture watching the Ravensdale siblings with their partners. It was a painful reminder of what he had lost. No one was looking at him with love shining in their eyes. He had no one he could slip his arm around and draw close. No one to exchange a look with that spoke of love, hope, the future.

He was alone.

Miranda approached with a plate of nibbles. 'Shame about Kat not coming.'

'Yeah, well, can't say I didn't try.'

'Maybe she just needs more time.'

'How much time?' Flynn couldn't keep the frustration out of his tone. 'When you know, you just know, right?'

Miranda's eyes rounded. 'You asked her to *marry* you?'

He swiped a hand down his face as if to swipe away the memory of his failure. How could he have got it so wrong? 'Maybe I need proposal lessons or something.'

'It's probably not your proposal that's the issue,' Miranda said. 'It's your timing.'

Flynn looked down at her heart-shaped face with those big Bambi eyes brimming with concern. Had he mistimed it? Would he get a different answer if he asked again? 'Maybe. Maybe not.' *Maybe I'm destined to be alone.*

'Dad's party was always going to be an issue for her,' Miranda said. 'She saw it as your mission. She probably couldn't separate it from her feelings for you.'

Hope flicked a match inside his chest, the warmth spreading as it took hold. 'You reckon she has feelings for me?'

Miranda gave him a 'get real' look. 'You men can be so blind at times. Of course she loves you. All the signs are there.'

'She hasn't said anything… I mean, she never actually said the words.'

'In the best relationships you don't need to.'

As if to confirm it, Leandro looked at Miranda from across the room where he was standing next to Richard. His look said it all: 'I love you and I can't wait for this evening to be over so we can be alone'.

Miranda's cheeks blushed a dusky rose. 'I'd better rescue him. That's the third soliloquy he's suffered tonight about Dad's brilliance.'

Flynn's chest cramped when he saw Leandro's arm slip around Miranda's waist and draw her close. Flynn shifted his gaze and saw Julius and Holly, and his heart squeezed again. Harder. Like a vice squashing an overripe peach. One of the waiters passed with a tray of drinks and Holly shook her head, one of her hands going protectively over her abdomen. The look Julius gave her was so proud, so full of love, it made Flynn feel all the more achingly alone.

Jaz appeared by his side with her usual impishness. 'Why the long face?'

He sent her a look that told her to back off. 'Where's Jake? Chatting up one of the waitresses?'

She laughed a tinkling-bell laugh. 'No, he's still re-covering from meeting me in the cloakroom. Here he comes now.'

Jake strutted into the room, straightening his tie, his eyes meeting Jaz's with a satisfied gleam. He pulled Jaz to his side. 'Find your own girl. This one's mine.'

Flynn gave him a rictus smile. A been-dead-for-a-month rictus smile. 'I'm working on it.'

Jake swept his gaze around the room. 'No Kat?'

'Nope.'

'Pity.'

'Yeah.'

The silence stretched.

'You're really serious about her.' Jake didn't say it as a question, more of a statement. An observation of truth.

'Yes. I am.'

'You going to ask the big question?'

'I already have.'

Jake's dark brows shot up. 'You did?'

'Yep. She said no.'

Jake's chin went back against his neck in disgust. 'You asked her *before* the party? Are you out of your freaking mind?'

He was out of his mind. Out of his mind with love. Out of his mind with impatience for this wretched party to be over so he could go to Kat and sort this out. 'I know, I know, I know. Bad timing.'

'You could skip the speeches and head back to Lon-don,' Jack said.

'I made a promise to your father.'

'Yeah, well, does it look like he's disappointed his

love child didn't show?' Jake's tone was cynicism on steroids. 'At least Mum's here.'

Flynn looked across to where Elisabetta was working the floor like the superstar she was. She was never happier than when she was centre-stage. Even though she'd threatened not to turn up, she couldn't help herself. Any chance to take the spotlight off Richard and shine it on her instead was too tempting.

A thought took hold. What if Kat couldn't stop herself from attending? What if she had changed her mind? What if her desire to meet her half-brothers had overridden her desire to distance herself from her father?

Flynn swept his gaze over the crowded room. There was no sign of her. But for the last few minutes the back of his neck had prickled, like radar picking up a faint signal.

But then he heard something... Cricket was barking outside on the terrace with the smokers, where he had ordered him to stay. Barking madly. Joyfully.

Flynn smiled. He knew what that bark was.

It was a bark of recognition.

Kat had decided to gatecrash the party but not as herself. She wanted to see her family without them seeing her. She wanted to see Flynn too. To see if he had moved on in the two days since she had rejected his proposal. Would he be flirting with one of the beautiful people at the party? Or would he be feeling like she did? Miserable and empty, as if someone had scraped out her heart and her belly?

But she hadn't factored in Cricket.

Her disguise had fooled the paparazzi hanging around the entrance to Ravensdene. It had fooled the catering staff manager when she'd signed on for duty in the kitchen. She hadn't tested it on Flynn because she had been assigned the back half of the house for the first half of her shift. But she was no match for Cricket. As soon as she came outside with a tray of drinks for the smokers on the terrace, he recognised her. He danced around her ankles, spinning and leaping and panting in excitement. She put the tray she was carrying on a table and bent down to him. 'Hush. Don't blow my cover. I'm not meant to be here.'

Then why are you?

Because I might have been a bit hasty in my judgment.

You've blown it. He said he was only going to ask you once.

I know, but I need to see him. Just the once. Just in case I've got it wrong.

Kat straightened once Cricket had settled down. Well, marginally, that was. He kept following her like a devoted slave, his tongue hanging out, his little beady eyes dancing as if he knew he was in on her secret.

Kat was about to go back inside when Flynn came out on the terrace. 'Cricket, leave the waitress alone.'

The waitress?

Of course he won't recognise me. I'm blonde tonight, with glasses. And heaps of make-up.

If he were truly in love with you, he'd recognise you anywhere in any disguise.

Flynn leaned against the balustrade on the terrace, resting his crutches beside him. 'Could you bring me a drink?'

Kat approached him warily. 'Orange juice is all I have left.' She was quite proud of her English accent. Maybe she wouldn't need a voice coach after all.

He took the glass and, without looking at her, knocked half of it back. 'Thanks.'

Kat knew she should have moved on but it annoyed her that he hadn't recognised her. Really annoyed her, which was ridiculously inconsistent of her. But still. 'Will that be all?'

'Yep.' He knocked back the rest of his drink and handed her the glass, again without looking at her.

She waited a beat. 'Would you like me to bring you some food? A plate of nibbles?'

'No thanks.'

'Another drink?'

'Not in the mood for celebrating.'

'Oh?'

He let out a long-drawn-out breath. 'It's a long story. I won't bore you with it when you've got work to do.'

'I'm not busy.' Kat mentally kicked herself. 'I mean… I've got a minute or two…'

He gave her a brief glance, the sort of glance you gave catering staff that you expect never to see again. 'Ever been in love?'

Kat looked down at Cricket who was looking up at her with that black-button gaze. 'I have, actually.'

'It sucks.'

She glanced back at Flynn. He was studying his bandaged foot with a frown so deep it had joined his eyebrows. 'Why do you think it sucks?' she said.

'If the person you love doesn't love you back, then it sucks. Big-time.'

'How do you know she doesn't love you back?'

'She never said the words.'

'But that doesn't mean she doesn't love you,' Kat said. 'It just means she was a little uncertain of the circumstances under which you proposed.'

He looked at her then in puzzlement. 'How do you know I proposed?'

Kat gave a short, uncertain laugh. 'Flynn…it's me. It's Kat. Don't you recognise me?'

A smile began in his eyes well before it appeared on his mouth. 'Of course I recognise you, you little goose. You love me? Really?'

Happiness burst inside Kat's chest like a flower exploding. 'I do.'

'That's twice you've said "I do" to me. Do you reckon you could say it one more time in front of a minister of religion so I can get a ring on your finger?'

Kat was torn between wanting to punch his arm for messing with her head and throwing her arms around him and kissing him. Kissing him won. She threw her arms around him, almost knocking him backwards off the terrace. 'You want to get married in church?'

'Anywhere that makes it official.'

She couldn't wipe the smile off her face. 'I'm sorry for rejecting you the first time. I just had to make sure you really loved me.'

He brushed a strand of blonde wig back behind her ear. 'I didn't think it was possible to love someone as much as I love you. Life loses all its colour without you in it.'

Kat stroked his face. 'These last couple of days have been torture. I've been so lonely and miserable. I couldn't bear another minute without seeing you.'

'How did you land the waitress job without alerting Richard's security team?'

She gave him a sheepish look. 'Well, I had to tell someone, otherwise I would never have got in. He said he would keep it a secret but I didn't factor in Cricket.'

'Yeah, well, I still haven't figured out boarding arrangements for him,' Flynn said. 'I knew as soon as I heard him barking that you were here.'

'Do you think you would've recognised me anyway?'

He touched her nose with his fingertip. 'Sure of it. My body picks you up like radar.'

Kat grinned. 'Mine too.'

Flynn took her hand and held it against his chest. 'Time to meet the family...or would you like to stay incognito?'

Kat pulled at her lip with her teeth. 'Do you think it would annoy Elisabetta? I don't want to upset her. I have to get through a season with her, remember.'

'You could stay disguised, but I'm going to have a heck of time explaining to your brothers why I've been kissing the blonde waitress.' Flynn gave a rueful grimace. 'Too late. Here they come now.'

Kat turned to see her twin half-brothers come out of the French doors. It was a surreal moment to meet them in the flesh. They were exactly alike, especially when they both smiled once they realised what was going on.

'Welcome to the family,' Julius said. 'I hope you know what you're letting yourself in for.'

'I think I'll cope,' Kat said.

Jake gave her a brotherly hug. 'Welcome to Mayhem Manor.'

Miranda and Jaz came out with Holly close behind. There were lots of hugs and words of welcome. The warmth of her family made Kat's heart swell so much, she had difficulty drawing breath.

Her family.

But then another person walked out to the terrace.

Her father.

Kat took a deep breath as he came towards her. She wasn't sure what she was supposed to feel. She didn't love him. She didn't even like him. But for the sake of appearances and the rest of the family she held out her hand to him. 'Hello.'

Richard ignored her hand and hugged her, just long enough for the cameras to document it. 'Welcome to the family, my dear.'

Elisabetta sauntered out with a glass of champagne in one hand, her expression one of acute boredom, although Kat was sure she could detect a hint of secretive delight in that dark-brown gaze. 'So, you've sorted it all out, Flynn?'

'Not quite.'

Kat glanced at Flynn who had hopped on his crutches to where she was standing surrounded by her family. 'What else needs to be sorted?' she said.

'You haven't said you love me. I'm not going back inside the house until you do.'

Kat gave him a teasing smile. 'Is that an ultimatum?'

His answering smile made the backs of her knees tingle. 'Something I should warn you about before we marry—I *always* win.'

Kat took him by the tie and pulled his head down. 'Guess what? So do I.'

* * * * *

LEGACY OF HIS REVENGE

CATHY WILLIAMS

CHAPTER ONE

'THERE'S A DAUGHTER.'

In receipt of this revelation, Matias Rivero looked at his friend and trusted associate, Art Delgado. Like Matias, Art was thirty-two. They had gone to school together and had formed an unlikely friendship with Matias the protector, the one who always had his friend's back. Small, asthmatic and bespectacled, Art had always been an easy target for bullies until Matias had joined his class and, like a dangerous, cruising shark, had ensured that no one came near the boy who had spent the past two years dreading the daily onslaught of beatings.

Now, all these years later, Matias was Art's boss and in return Art was his most loyal employee. There was no one Matias trusted more. He motioned for Art to sit and leaned forward to take the mobile phone handed to him.

He scrolled down the three pictures capturing a small, homely, plump little creature leaving Carney's mansion in an old car that looked as though its only wish was to breathe its last breath and depart for the great automobile parking lot in the sky.

Matias vaguely wondered why she wasn't in a car befitting a man who had always made social climbing his priority.

But more than that he wondered who the hell the woman was and why he hadn't heard of her before.

'How is it that I am only now finding out that the man has a child?' Matias murmured, returning the mobile phone to his friend and relaxing back in the chair. 'In fact, how do you know for sure that the woman is his daughter?'

At a little after seven, his office was empty. It was still summertime hot, it was Friday and everyone else had better things to do than work. There was nothing pressing to hold his attention. His last lover had been dispatched a few weeks ago. Right now, Matias had all the time in the world to think about this development in his campaign.

'She said so,' Art told him, pushing his wire-rimmed spectacles up his nose and looking at his friend with some concern. 'But I don't suppose,' he added uneasily, 'it makes any difference, Matias. Does it?'

Matias pushed his chair back and stood up. Seated, he was formidable. Standing, he towered. He was six feet three of solid, packed muscle. Black-haired and black-eyed, the product of an Argentinian father and a dainty Irish mother, Matias had resoundingly come up trumps in the genetic lottery. He was sinfully beautiful, the hard lines of his lean face wonderfully chiselled into absolute perfection. Right at this moment, he was frowning thoughtfully as he strolled towards the floor-to-ceiling bank of glass that overlooked the busy London streets in the heart of the city.

From this high up, the figures down below were matchstick small and the cars and taxis resembled kids' toys.

He ignored the latter part of his friend's remark and

instead asked, 'What do you mean "she said so"? Surely I would have known if the man had offspring. He was married and it was a childless union.' But in truth, Matias had been uninterested in the personal details of James Carney's life.

Why would he care one way or another if the man had kids or not?

For years, indeed for as long as he could remember, he had been focused on bringing the man to his knees through his company. The company that should never have been Carney's in the first place. The company that had been founded on lies, deceit and Carney's outright theft of Matias's father's invention.

Making money and having the power associated with it within his grasp was so entwined with his driving need to place himself in a position to reach out and wrench Carney's company from under his feet, that it would have been impossible to separate the two. Matias's march towards wealth had also been his march towards satisfying his thirst for revenge. He had gained his first-class degree, had bided his time in an investment bank for two years, making the money he needed to propel himself forward, and then he had quit with money under his belt and a black book stuffed with valuable connections. And he had begun his remorseless rise to the top via mergers and acquisitions of ailing companies, getting richer and richer and more and more powerful in the process.

Throughout it all, he had watched patiently for Carney's company to ail and so it had.

For the past few years, Matias had been circling the company, a predator waiting for exactly the right time. Should he begin the process of buying shares, then flooding the market with them so that he could plunge the company into a premature meltdown? Should he wait until the company's health deteriorated beyond repair so that he could instigate his hostile takeover? Choices, choices.

He had thought about revenge for so long that there was almost no hurry but the time had finally come. The letters he had recovered from his mother's possessions, before she had been admitted to hospital three weeks previously, had propelled him towards the inevitable.

'Well?' he prompted, returning to his chair although he was suddenly restless, itching now to start the process of retribution. 'You had a convivial conversation with the woman? Tell me how you came to your conclusion. I'm curious.'

Matias looked at Art, waiting for clarification.

'Pure coincidence,' Art admitted. 'I was about to turn into Carney's drive when she came speeding out, swerved round the corner, and banged into the car.'

'The woman crashed into my car? Which one?'

'The Maserati,' Art admitted. 'Nasty dent but her car, sadly, was more or less a write-off. No worries. It'll be sorted.'

'So she banged into my Maserati,' Matias hurried the story along, planning on returning to this little episode later down the line, 'told you who she was and then…what?'

'You sound suspicious, Matias, but that's exactly what happened. I asked her if that was the Carney residence and she said yes, that her dad lived there and she had just seen him. She was in a bit of a state because of the accident. She mentioned that he was in a foul mood and that it might be a good idea to rearrange whatever plans I had with him.'

'So there's a daughter,' Matias said thoughtfully. 'Interesting.'

'A nice girl, Matias, or so it would seem.'

'Impossible.' That single word was a flat denial. 'Carney is a nasty piece of work. It would be downright impossible for him to have sired anything remotely *nice*.' The harsh lines of his face softened. For all his friend's days of being bullied, Art had an instinctive trust in the goodness of human nature that he, Matias, lacked.

Matias had no idea why that was because they were both mixed race, in Art's case of Spanish descent on his mother's side. They had both started at the bottom of the pecking order and had had to toughen up to defend themselves against casual racism and snobbery.

But then, Matias mused not for the first time, he and he alone had witnessed first-hand the way criminal behaviour could affect the direction of someone's life. His father had met James Carney at university. Tomas Rivero had been an extraordinarily clever man with a gift for all things mathematical. He had also been so lacking in business acumen that when, at the age of twenty-four, he invented a computer program that facilitated the analysis of experimental drugs, he was a sitting duck for a man who had very quickly seen where the program could be taken and the money that could be made out of it.

James Carney had been a rich, young thing with a tribe of followers and an eye to the main chance. He had befriended Tomas, persuaded him into a position of absolute trust and, when the time was right, had accumulated all the right signatures in all the right places that ensured that the royalties and dividends from the software went to him.

In return, Tomas had been sidelined with a third-rate job in a managerial position in the already ailing family business Carney had inherited from his father. He had never recovered mentally.

This was a story that had unfolded over the years, although, in fairness to both his parents, nothing had ever been said with spite and certainly there had never been any talk of revenge on the part of either of them.

Matias's father had died over a decade previously and Rose Rivero, from the very start, had not countenanced thoughts of those wheels turning full circle.

What was done, was done, as far as she was concerned. The past was something to be relinquished.

Not so for Matias, who had seen his father in those quieter moments, seen the sadness that had become a humiliating burden. You didn't have to be a genius to work out that being shoved in some dingy back office while you saw money and glory heaped on undeserving shoulders had damaged his father irreparably.

As far as Matias was concerned, his father had never fully recovered from Carney's theft. He had worked at the company in the pitiful job condescendingly given to him for a couple of years and then moved on to another company, but by then his health was failing and Rose Rivero had had to go out to work to help make ends meet.

If his mother had cautioned against revenge, then he had had enough of a taste for it for the both of them.

But he knew that over the years the fires had burned a little less brightly because he had become so intensely consumed in his own meteoric rise to the top. It had been propelled by his desire for revenge but along the way had gathered a momentum of its own, taken on its own vibrant life force…distracted him from the goal he had long ago set himself.

Until he had come upon those letters.

'She must have produced her insurance certificate,' Matias mused, eyes narrowing. 'What's the woman's name?'

'I'll email you the details.' Art sighed, knowing without having to be told the direction of his friend's thoughts. 'I haven't had a chance to look at it but I took a picture of the document.'

'Good,' Matias said with some satisfaction. 'Do that immediately, Art. And there will be no need for you to deal with this matter. I will handle it myself.'

'Why?' Art was the only person who would ever have dared ask such a forthright question. Especially when the question was framed in a tone of voice that carried a warning.

'Let's just say that I might want to get to know her better. Knowledge is power, Art, and I now regret that I didn't dig a little deeper into Carney's private life. But don't look so worried! I'm not the big bad wolf. I don't make a habit of eating innocent young girls. So if she's as *nice* as you imply, then she should be as safe as houses.'

'Your mother wouldn't like this,' Art warned bluntly.

'My mother is far too kind for her own good.' For a few seconds, Matias thought of Rose Rivero, who was recuperating from a near fatal stroke at one of the top hospitals in London. If his father had never recovered from Carney's treachery, then his mother had never recovered from his father's premature death. When you looked at it, Carney had not only been responsible for his family's unjust state of penury, but beyond that for the stress that had killed his father and for the ill health and unhappiness that had dogged his mother's life. Revenge had been a long time coming but, if only James Carney knew it, it was now a juggernaut rolling with unstoppable speed towards him...

Sophie Watts stared up at the soaring glass tower in front of her and visibly quailed.

The lovely man whose car she had accidentally *bruised* three days previously had been very accommodating when she had phoned the number he had given her when they had exchanged details. She had explained the situation with her insurance policy and he had been sympathetic. He had told her in a friendly enough voice that she would have to come and discuss the matter personally but he was sure that something could be sorted out.

Unfortunately, the building in front of her did not look like the sort of user-friendly place in which cheerful and accommodating people worked, sorting out thorny situations in a cordial and sympathetic manner.

She clutched her capacious bag tightly and continued staring. Her head told her that she had no option but to move forward with the crowd while her feet begged to be allowed to turn tail and flee back to her low-key corner of East London and her little house in which she did her small-scale catering and baking for anyone who needed her services.

She didn't belong here and the clothes she had carefully chosen to meet Art Delgado now felt ridiculous and out of place.

The young women sweeping past her with their leather computer bags and clicking high heels were all dressed in sharp black suits. They weren't dithering. They were striding with purpose into the aggressive glass tower.

A small, plump girl with flyaway hair wearing a summery flowered dress and sandals didn't belong here.

Sophie propelled herself forward, eyes firmly ahead. It had been a mistake to come here *first thing* so that she could *get it over with*. That idea had been great in theory but she hadn't banked on the early rush-hour stampede of city workers. However, it was too late now to start chastising herself.

Inside, the foyer was a wondrous and cruel blend of marble, glass and metal.

Arrangements of sofas were scattered here and there in circular formations. The sofas were all very attractive and looked enormously uncomfortable. Clearly management didn't want to encourage too much lounging around. Ahead of her, a bank of receptionists was busily directing people while streams of smartly dressed worker bees headed for the gleaming lifts opening and closing just beyond an array of stunted palm trees in huge ceramic pots.

Sophie felt a pang of physical longing for her kitchen, where she and Julie, her co-worker, chatted and baked and cooked and made big plans for the upmarket bakery they would jointly open one day. She craved the feel of her apron, the smell of freshly baked cake and the pleasant playing around of ideas for meals they had booked in for catering jobs. Even though she was now talking to one of the receptionists, explaining who she wanted to see, confirming that an appointment had been made and stuttering over her own name, she was unhappily longing to be somewhere else.

Frayed nerves made her miss what the snappily dressed girl in front of her had just said but then she blinked and registered that a mistake had been made.

'I don't know a Mr… River,' she said politely.

'*Rivero.*' Eyebrows arched up, lips tightened, eyes cooled.

'I'm here to see a Mr Delgado.'

'Your meeting is with Mr Rivero.' The receptionist swivelled the computer towards her. 'You are to sign in. Anywhere on the screen will do and just use your finger. Mr Rivero's secretary will be waiting for you on the tenth floor. Here's a clip-on pass. Make sure you don't remove it because if you do you'll be immediately escorted out of the building.'

In a fluster, Sophie did as she was told but her heart was hammering inside her as she obeyed instructions, allowing herself to be swept along in a group towards the nearest lift and then staring fixedly at nothing in particular as she was whooshed up to the tenth floor, as directed.

Who was Mr Rivero? She had banked on the comfort of explaining her awkward situation to the very nice Mr Delgado. What sort of hearing was she going to get from a complete stranger? She was as tense as a bow string when, disgorged into the plushest surroundings she had ever seen, she was taken in hand by a very tall, middle-aged woman whose expression of sympathy did nothing to quell her escalating nerves.

And then she was being shown into an office, faced

with a closed door, ushered through it and deposited like an unwanted parcel in a room that was simply breathtaking.

For a few seconds, eyes as round as saucers, Sophie looked around her. She hadn't budged from where she had been placed just inside the door of a gigantic office. She cravenly recoiled from actually being bold enough to walk forward. Bag clutched tightly in front of her, she gradually became aware of the man sitting behind the desk. It was as if, suddenly, she focused, and on focusing felt the thudding impact of shock because the guy she was staring at was the most stunningly drop-dead gorgeous specimen she had ever seen in her entire life.

Her breathing slowed and even though she knew she was staring, she couldn't help herself. His hair was raven black, his eyes the colour of the darkest, richest chocolate, his features lovingly and perfectly chiselled. He oozed the sort of stupendous sex appeal that made heads swing round for a second and third look.

The silence stretched and stretched between them and then it dawned on her that she was making an absolute fool of herself.

'Miss Watts.' Matias was the first to speak. 'Do you intend to hover by the door for the duration of this meeting?' He didn't get up to shake her hand. He didn't smile. He did nothing to put her at ease. Instead he nodded at the chair in front of his desk. 'Sit down.'

Sophie shuffled forward, not knowing whether she was expected to shake his hand as a formality, but his expression was so forbidding that she decided against it and instead sank into the leather chair. She almost immediately leaned forward and rushed headlong into the little speech she had earlier rehearsed.

'I'm really sorry about the car, Mr…er… Rivero. I honestly had no idea that your friend was turning into the drive. It's so difficult to see round that bend, especially in summer. I admit I may have been driving a little faster than usual but I want to impress upon you that it was *unintentional*.' What she could have added but didn't was that her vision had been blurred because she had been doing her utmost not to cry after a stormy and upsetting meeting with James Carney.

Matias was watching her intently, his dark eyes narrowed on her flushed and surprisingly pretty face. He was a man who went for catwalk models, with long, angular bodies and striking, photogenic faces, yet there was something alluring about the woman sitting in front of him. Something about the softness of her face, the pale, vanilla shade of her unruly hair, the perfect clarity of her aquamarine eyes, held his attention and he could only assume that it was because of her connection to James Carney.

He hadn't known the woman existed but the minute he had found out he had recognised the gift that had landed in his lap for what it was.

He thought back to those letters he had unearthed, and his jaw tightened. That soft, wide-eyed, innocent look wasn't going to fool him. He didn't know the full story of the woman's relationship to Carney but he certainly intended to find out, just as he intended to exploit the situation he had been handed to discover if there were any other secrets the man might have been hiding. The broader the net was cast, the wider the catch.

'Employee,' Matias replied. This just in case she got

it into her head that special favours were going to be granted because of Art's personal connection with him.

'I beg your pardon?'

'Art Delgado is my employee. He was driving my Maserati. Miss Watts, do you have any idea how much one costs?'

'No, I don't,' Sophie said faintly. He was having the most peculiar effect on her. It was as though the power of his presence had sucked the oxygen out of the air, making it difficult to breathe.

'In that case, allow me to enlighten you.' He named a sum that was sufficiently staggering to make her gasp. 'And I have been told that your insurance policy is invalid.'

'I didn't know,' Sophie whispered. 'I'm usually so good at dealing with all that stuff but things have been a bit hectic recently. I know I cancelled my old policy and I had planned on renewing with somewhere cheaper but...'

Matias held up one imperious hand to stop her in mid flow. 'I'm not interested in the back story,' he informed her coolly. 'To cut to the chase, the damage you have done to my car will run to many, many thousands.'

Sophie's mouth dropped open. 'Thousands?' she parroted.

'Literally. I'm afraid it won't be a simple case of sorting out the dent. The entire left wing of the car will have to be replaced. High-performance cars charge high-performance prices.'

'I... I had no idea. I haven't got that sort of money. I...when I spoke to your friend...sorry, your employee Mr Delgado on the phone, he said that we would be able to work something out.'

'Sadly working something out really isn't in his remit.' Matias thought that his old friend would raise a sardonic eyebrow at that sweeping statement.

'I could pay you back over time.' Sophie wondered what sort of time line would be acceptable to the unforgiving man staring coldly at her as though she were an undesirable alien that had suddenly invaded his personal space. She somehow didn't imagine that his time line was going to coincide with hers. 'I run a little catering business with a friend,' she hurtled on, desperate to bring this uncomfortable meeting to an end and even more desperate to find some sort of solution that wouldn't involve bankruptcy for her and Julie's fledgling start-up company. 'We only opened up a year and a half ago. Before that we were both primary school teachers. It's taken an awful lot of borrowing to get everything in order and to get my kitchen up to the required standard for producing food commercially, and right at this moment, well…there isn't a great deal of spare change flying about.'

'In other words you're broke.'

'We're really making a go of things, Mr Rivero!' Heat flared in her cheeks. 'And I'm sure we can work something out when it comes to a repayment schedule for your car…'

'I gather you're James Carney's daughter.' Matias lowered his eyes, then he pushed back his chair and stood up to stroll across to the impressive bank of windows, in front of which was a tidy sitting area complete with a low table fashioned in chrome and glass.

Sophie was riveted at the sight of him. The way he moved, the unconscious flex of muscle under the expensive suit, the lean length of his body, the casual strength he exuded that was frankly spellbinding. He turned to look at her and it took a big effort not to look away.

His throwaway remark had frozen her to the spot.

'Well?' Matias prodded. 'Art was on his way to pay a little visit to James Carney on business,' he expanded, 'when you came speeding out of his drive like a bat out of hell and crashed into my car. I had no idea that the man even had a family.' He was watching her very carefully as he spoke and was mildly surprised that she didn't see to ask him a very fundamental question, which was why the heck should Carney's private life have anything to do with him?

Whatever she was, she clearly didn't have a suspicious nature.

Sophie was lost for words. She had been shaken by the accident, upset after the visit to her father, and Art Delgado, so different from this flint-eyed guy assessing her, had encouraged her into a confidence she rarely shared with anyone.

'Of course…' Matias shrugged, curiosity spiking at her continued silence '… I am not primarily concerned with the man's private life but my understanding was that he was a widower.'

'He is,' Sophie whispered, ashamed all over again at a birthright she hadn't asked for, the consequences of which she had been forced, however, to live with.

'So tell me where you fit in,' Matias encouraged. 'Unless, of course, that was a little white lie you told my employee on the spur of the moment.' He appeared to give this a little thought. 'Maybe you were embarrassed to tell the truth…?'

'Sorry?' That garnered her attention and she looked at him with a puzzled frown.

'Young girl having an affair with an old man? I can see that you might have been embarrassed enough to have said the first thing that came to your head, anything that sounded a little less unsavoury than what you really are to Carney.'

'How dare you?' Sophie gasped, half standing. 'That's disgusting!'

'I'm just trying to do the maths.' Matias frowned and tilted his head to one side. 'If you're not his lover, the man must have had a mistress while he was married. Am I right? Are you Carney's love child?'

Sophie laughed bitterly because nothing could have been further from the truth. Love had never come into the equation. Before her untimely death, her mother, Angela Watts, had been an aspiring actress whose great misfortune had been her Marilyn Monroe blonde-bombshell looks. Prey to men's flattery and pursued for her body, she had made the fatal error of throwing her net too wide. James Carney, young, rich and arrogant, had met her at a club and, like all the others, had pursued her, but he had had no intention of ever settling down with someone he considered a two-bit tart with a pretty face. Those details had been drummed into Sophie from as soon as she was old enough to understand. He had had fun with Angela and she had foolishly thought that the fun would actually go somewhere, but even when she had contrived to trap him with a pregnancy he had stood firm, only later marrying a woman he considered of the right class and social position.

'He met my mother before he was married,' Sophie confessed, belatedly adding, 'not that it has anything to do with...well, *anything*. Mr Rivero, I would be more than happy for you to draw up a schedule for repayment.

I will sign it right here and right now and you have my word that you will have every penny I owe you back. With interest if that's what you want.'

Matias burst out laughing. 'That's very obliging of you,' he drawled lazily. 'Believe it or not, I haven't become a successful businessman by putting my faith in the impossible. I have no idea what you owe the bank but I suspect you're probably barely making ends meet. Am I right?'

He tilted his head to one side and Sophie looked at him with loathing. He might be sinfully handsome but she had never met anyone she hated more on the spot. She wasn't stupid. He had all the money in the world, from the looks of it, but he wasn't going to be lenient when it came to getting back every penny she owed him and she knew that he wouldn't give a hoot if he drove her little company into the ground to do it.

Right now, he was toying with her like a cat playing with a mouse.

'We could work out a schedule,' he mused, 'but I would be on my walking frame before you made the final payment.' She really had the most wonderfully transparent face, he thought. Impossible though it was, she looked as pure as the driven snow.

But perhaps she wasn't fashioned in the same mould as the father. Certainly, she wouldn't have had the example set by him on a daily basis if she was the product of a youthful affair. He was surprised, in fact, that she had any contact with the man at all and he wondered how that had worked when Carney's socially acceptable wife had been alive.

Matias wasn't going to waste time pondering stuff like that, however. Right now, he was working out how best to use her to his advantage. When he pulled the plug on Carney, he intended to hit him on all fronts and he wondered whether she could be of use to him in that.

What other secrets was the man hiding? Matias knew that the company was beset with financial problems but, in the ether, there had been rumours of foul play… Sometimes skeletons were hard to find, however hard you dug, and Carney was a man who was sly and smart enough to cover his tracks. Wouldn't it be satisfying if all his dark secrets were to be exposed to the cruel glare of light…?

Could this fresh-faced girl be the key to unlock more doors? And what if there were personal skeletons? An attack on all fronts was certainly worth considering. He was honest enough to acknowledge that this level of revenge was probably beneath him, but those letters he'd found…they had made this personal…

'You could always ask Daddy for the money,' he ventured smoothly, knowing what the answer would be.

'No!' This time she did stand up. Her full mouth was drawn into a thin, obstinate line. 'I won't have… my father involved in this. Bankrupt me if you want.' She reached into her bag, pulled out one of the business cards, remembering how filled with optimism she and Julie had been when they had had them printed. 'Here's my business card. You can come and see the premises. It's just in my kitchen but the equipment must be worth something. I have a number of big jobs lined up, so if you're patient I can do those and you can have the money. As for the rest… I will sell my house and I should be able to sort out the rest of the debt with money left over after the mortgage has been covered.'

Matias looked at her, every line of his powerful body

indicating a man totally relaxed, totally unfazed by her emotional outburst.

Dark eyes roamed over her. She had tried to do something businesslike with her hair but somewhere along the line it had rebelled and tangled, white-blonde strands already curling around her cheeks. Her eyes were wide and a curious shade of turquoise and fringed, he noted, with thick dark lashes, which was at odds with the colour of her hair. And her body…

He shifted in his chair, astonished that he was even bothering to notice that she had curves in all the right places and luscious breasts that were prominent against the truly appalling flowered dress she was wearing.

She lacked sophistication and clearly had no style gene whatsoever, so what, he wondered, with a certain amount of irritation, was it about her that captured his attention so completely?

'You're overreacting,' he told her as she remained standing, her blue eyes dark with worry, anger and distress.

'You've just told me that you're not willing to come to any kind of arrangement with me about the money I owe you for your stupid car!' Easy-tempered by nature, Sophie was shocked at the stridency of her voice and the fact that she *was yelling at him*! 'I can't go to my bank and draw out the kind of money I would need to make good the damage. So, *of course I'm going to be upset.*'

'Sit down.'

'No. I'm going. You can get in touch with me on the number on the card! I'm going to have to talk this through with Julie. I don't know what she's going to say. She's put in most of her savings to try and get this business of ours going, as have I, so I'm going to have to find the money to pay her back too and make sure she doesn't have to pay for my mistake.' Her voice was wobbling and she stared off into the distance in an attempt to stop herself from crying.

Matias squashed all feelings of guilt. Why should he feel guilty? He was staring at a woman whose father had destroyed his family. In that scenario, guilt didn't exist. After all, all was fair in love and war, wasn't it?

'You could do that,' he murmured, 'or you could sit back down and listen to the proposition I have for you.'

CHAPTER TWO

'GO EASY ON THE GIRL,' Art had urged his friend the previous day. 'Because Carney's her father, doesn't mean that she has been cut from the same cloth.'

Matias hadn't argued the point with his friend, but he had privately held the view that the apple never fell far from the tree and an innocent smile and fluttering eyelashes, which he was guessing had been the stunt the woman had pulled on Art, didn't mean she had a pure soul.

Now, however, he was questioning the judgement call he had made before he had even met her. He was seldom, if ever, wrong when it came to summing people up, but in this instance his friend might have had a point. Matias wasn't going to concede that the woman spent all her spare time helping the poor and unfortunate or that she was the sort who wouldn't have recognised an uncharitable thought if it did a salsa in front of her. What he *did* recognise was that he would be better served in his quest for revenge by getting to know her.

She was an unexpected piece of a puzzle he had thought was already complete and he would have to check her out.

He had waited years for retribution. Waiting a couple

of weeks longer wasn't going to kill him and it might put him in an even stronger position than he already was.

He looked at her anxious face and smiled slowly. 'There's no need to look so worried,' he soothed. 'I'm not a man who beats about the bush, Miss…it *is* Miss, isn't it?'

Sophie nodded and automatically touched her ring-free finger. Once upon a time, she had had a boyfriend. Once upon a time, she had had dreams of marriage and kids and a happy-ever-after life, but reality had had something different to say about that.

'Boyfriend?' Matias hadn't missed that unconscious gesture. No ring on her finger. Had there been one? Once? Was she divorced? She looked far too young, but who knew? It wasn't his business but it paid to know your quarry.

Sophie sat on her hands. 'I don't see what that has to do with…your car, Mr… Rivers…'

'*Rivero.*' Matias frowned because it wasn't often that anyone forgot his name. In fact, never. 'And in point of fact, it has. You owe me money but if you're telling the truth, then it would seem that you have little to no hope of repaying me.'

'Why wouldn't I be telling the truth?'

Matias debated whether he should point out that her father would surely not be keen to see his child slaving in front of a hot oven cooking food for other people, so how likely was it that catering was her full-time occupation? Or maybe she was the sort who rebelled against their parents by pretending to reject money and everything it stood for? When you came from money and had comfort and security as a blanket to fall back on, it was easy to play at enjoying poverty. From what he knew of the man, keeping up appearances ran to a full-time occupation and surely his offspring would have been dragged into that little game too?

However, he had no intention of laying any of his cards on any tables any time soon. At any rate, it would be a matter of seconds to check her story and he was pretty sure she was telling the truth. Her car, for one thing, did not suggest someone with an enviable bank balance and the oversight with the insurance added to the impression.

He shrugged. 'Maybe you imagine that pleading poverty will touch some kind of chord in me.'

'That never crossed my mind,' Sophie said honestly. 'I can't think that anyone would be mad enough to try and appeal to your better nature.'

'Come again?' Momentarily distracted, Matias stared at her with outright incredulity.

The woman was here on the back foot, staring bankruptcy in the face if he decided to go after her, and yet she had the cheek to *criticise him*? He almost couldn't believe his ears.

Sophie didn't back down. She loathed arguments and avoided confrontation like the plague, but she was honest and forthright and could be as stubborn as a mule. She had had to be because she had had to take up where her mother had left off when it came to breathing in deep and pursuing what she felt James Carney owed her.

Right now, she had no idea where Matias was going with some of his remarks. He had mentioned a solution to the problem staring her in the face, but she couldn't help noticing that he hadn't actually said what that solution might be.

If he was stringing her along only to pull the rug

from under her feet, then she wasn't going to sit back and allow him to bully her in the process.

'If you had a better nature,' she pointed out, 'then you would try and understand what it's like for me. You probably don't have a clue about what it's like to struggle, because if you did then you would be able to put yourself in my shoes, and if you did that you might try and find a solution to the problem instead. If you give me a chance, then I will pay you back, but first you have to give me a chance.'

'Is this your idea of buttering me up?' Matias said coldly. 'Because if it is, then you're heading in the wrong direction. Let's not forget that you're here with a begging bowl.' He would come back to her father and exactly how hard he'd made Matias's family *struggle* in due course.

Sophie's soft mouth tightened. She had a lot of experience when it came to begging bowls and she had learned the hard way that buckling under threat never got anyone anywhere.

'You said that you had a proposition for me,' she reminded him, clinging to that lifebelt and already willing to snatch at it whatever the cost. Perhaps if she had had only herself to think about, she might have backed off, but there were more people at stake here than just her.

Matias was already pleased that he had decided to go with the flow and exploit the opportunity presented to him. Soft and yielding she might look, but it had quickly become apparent that she was anything but.

He felt the kick of an unexpected challenge. So much of his life was predictable. He had reached the pinnacle of his success and he was still in his early thirties. People kowtowed to him, sought his advice, hung onto his every word, did their utmost to please him. Bearing in mind that financial security and the power that came with it had been his ambition for as long as he could remember, he was now disappointed to acknowledge that there was something missing from his life, something that not even the glowing fires of revenge had been able to fulfil.

He had become jaded over time. When he thought back to the hungry young man he had once been, his whole body alive for the task he had set himself, he felt as if he were staring backwards at a stranger. Certainly, on a personal level, the fact that he could have any woman he wanted was something that had long lost its novelty value. Now, for the first time in ages, he was facing a challenge he could sink his teeth into and he liked the feeling.

'In two weeks' time…' Matias had returned to his desk and now he pushed back his leather chair and relaxed with his hands folded behind his head '… I am due to host a long weekend party at one of my houses. Around eighty people will be descending and they will be expecting the highest standard of catering. I will provide the food. You will handle everything else. Naturally, you won't be paid. Succeed and we can carry on from there. I have no intention of exercising my right to frankly bankrupt you because, for a start, driving without being insured is illegal. If I went the whole way, you'd be in prison by dusk. Instead, I will play it by ear.'

'In other words,' Sophie said stiffly, 'you'll own me until you consider the debt to be paid off.'

Matias tilted his head to one side and smiled coolly. 'That's one way of putting it…' Okay, so it was the only way of putting it. He would be able to take his

time finding out about her and thereby finding other
ways back to her father. Were those rumours of foul
play in the company vaults true? Was that something
the man had confessed to his offspring? If so, if that
level of information could somehow be accessed, then
he would have the most powerful weapon for revenge
within his grasp. He couldn't care less about the damage to his car. He could take it to the nearest scrapyard
and buy a replacement without even noticing any dent
in his limitless income.

'And when you think about the alternatives,' he
mused, 'you'll conclude, pretty fast, that it's a sweet
deal for you.' He gave a gesture that was as exotically
foreign as he was. 'You might even be able to...' he
flicked out the business card she had earlier given him
'...distribute these discreetly during the weekend.'

'And will I be able to bring my business partner?'

'I don't think so. Too many cooks and all that. I will
ensure that you have sufficient staff to help but essen-
tially this will be your baby.' He glanced at his watch
but didn't stand, leaving it to Sophie to deduce that
he was done with her. She stood up awkwardly and
looked at him.

How could someone so effortlessly beautiful be so
utterly cold-hearted?

Although, she had to acknowledge, at least he hadn't
done what he had every right to do and contacted the
police. She could have kicked herself for that little window during which she had forgotten to renew her insurance with a different company. So unlike her but then
she had had so much on her mind.

'Will there be something...er...in writing?'

'Something in writing?'

'Just so that I know how much of the debt will be covered when I handle the catering for you that weekend...'

'You don't trust me?'

Sophie gazed off and thought of her father. She'd had to learn fast how to manage him. Trust had never been in plentiful supply in their relationship and she thought that it would be prudent not to rely on it in this situation either.

'I don't trust many people,' she said quietly and Matias's ears pricked up.

He looked at her carefully. 'No?' he murmured. 'I don't trust many people either but then, as you've pointed out, I don't have a better nature whereas I expect you probably do. Am I right?'

'I've found that people inevitably let you down,' Sophie told him painfully, then she blinked and wondered what on earth had induced her to say that. 'So it would work if I could have something in writing as I go along...'

'I'll get my secretary to draw something up.' All business now, Matias stood up, signalling that her time was up. 'Rest assured, you won't be required to become my personal slave in return for a debt.'

His dark eyes flicked to her as she shuffled to her feet. She gave the impression of someone whose eyes were always downcast and he could see how Art had been knocked sideways by her meek persona, but he wasn't so easily fooled. He had seen the fire burning just below the surface. She blushed like a virgin but those aquamarine eyes flashed like a siren call and he couldn't wait to get to the bottom of her...and discover in the process what she could contribute to the picture he had already compiled of her father.

* * *

'But I just think that there must have been *some other way* of sorting this situation out! I'm going to be left here for *several days* on my own and I just don't know whether I can manage the Rosses' cocktail party on my own!'

Sophie's heart went out to Julie and she looked at her friend sympathetically. Sympathy was about all she could offer. She had signed up to a deal with the devil and it was a better deal than she might have hoped for. Even though she hated it.

She had been over all the pros and cons of the situation, and had apologised profusely to her friend, who was not as confident in the kitchen as she was.

'But on the bright side,' she said in an upbeat voice, 'think of all the possible connections we could make! And,' she felt compelled to repeat because fair was fair, 'he could have just taken everything from us to sort out the damage to his car. I honestly had no idea *that a car* could cost that much to repair! It's mad.'

He was sending a car for her and Sophie looked at her watch with a sense of impending doom. A fortnight ago, his secretary had emailed her with an extensive list of things she 'should bring, should know and should be prepared to undertake'.

There was to be no veering off from the menu and she would have to ensure that every single dish for every single day was prepared to the highest possible specification.

She was told how many helpers she would have and how they should behave. Reading between the lines, that meant *no fraternising with the guests*.

She was informed of the dress code for all members of staff, including herself. The dress code did not include jeans or anything that might be interpreted as casual.

She gathered that she was being thrown in at the deep end and this detailed information was his way of being kind to her. She assumed that he had diverted his original catering firm to some other do specifically so that he could put her through her paces and she had spent the past two nights worrying about what would happen if she failed. Matias Rivero wasn't, she thought, callous enough to take the shirt off her back, but he intended to get his money's worth by hook or by crook. He might be unwilling to throw her to the sharks, but he wasn't going to let her get off lightly by agreeing to monthly payments that would take her decades to deliver what was owed.

This was the biggest and most high-profile job she had ever got close to doing and the fact that he would be looking at her efforts with a view to criticism filled her with terror. She wondered whether he hadn't set her an impossible task just so he could do his worst with a clear conscience when she failed. He struck her as the sort of man who saw ruthlessness as a virtue.

His car arrived just as she was giving some final tips to Julie about the catering job she would be handling on her own, and Sophie took a deep breath and reached for her pull-along case.

There would be a uniform waiting for her at his country house, which was in the Lake District. However, his instructions had been so detailed that she had decided against wearing her usual garb of jeans and a tee shirt to travel there and, instead, was in an uncomfortable grey skirt and a white blouse with a short linen jacket. At a little after ten in the morning, with the sun climbing in the sky, the outfit was already making her perspire.

She hung onto the hopeful thought that she would probably find herself stuck in the kitchen for the entire time. With any luck, she wouldn't glimpse Matias or any of his guests and she knew that, if that were the case, then she would be all right because she was an excellent chef and more than capable of producing the menu that had been emailed to her.

She wouldn't even have to bother about sourcing the ingredients, because all of that would already have been taken care of.

Her high hopes lasted for as long as the very smooth car journey took. Then nerves kicked in with a vengeance as the car turned between imposing wrought-iron gates to glide soundlessly up a tree-lined avenue on either side of which perfectly manicured lawns stretched towards distant horizons of open fields, shaded with copses. It was a lush landscape and very secluded.

The house that eventually climbed into view was perched atop a hill. She had expected something traditional, perhaps a Victorian manor house with faded red brick and chimneys.

She gasped at the modern marvel that greeted her. The architect had designed the house to be an organic extension of the hill and it appeared to be embedded into the side so that glass and lead projected as naturally from rock and foliage as a tree might grow upwards from the ground.

The drive curved around the back, skirting a small lake, and then they were approaching the house from the side where a sprawling courtyard was large enough to house all those important guests she had been expecting to find. Except the courtyard was empty aside from three high-performance cars parked haphazardly.

All at once, a quiver of nervous tension rippled through her. She could have become lost in a crowd of people. In an empty mansion, and it certainly looked empty, getting lost wasn't going to be that easy.

And for reasons she couldn't quite understand, reasons that extended well beyond the uncomfortable circumstances that surrounded her presence here, Matias made her feel…awkward. Too *aware of herself*, uncomfortable in her own skin and on edge in a way she had never felt before.

Her bag was whipped away from her before she had time to offer to take it herself and then she was being led through a most marvellous building towards the kitchen by a soft-spoken middle-aged woman who introduced herself as Debbie.

It was a cavernous space of pale marble and pale walls on which were hung vast abstract canvasses. She could have been walking through the centre of a fabulous ice castle and she actually shivered because never had she felt so removed from her comfort zone.

It had been hot outside but in here it was cool and quite silent. When she finally turned her attention away from her impressive surroundings, it was to find that Debbie had disappeared and instead Matias was lounging in the doorway of the kitchen.

'You're here,' he commented, taking in the prissy outfit and the flat black pumps and the neat handbag, which had apparently replaced the Santa's sack she had been carrying the last time he had seen her. He straightened and headed straight back in the direction of the kitchen, expecting her to follow him, which she did.

Sophie was tempted to retort where else would she be when she'd had no choice, but instead, she said politely to his back, 'I expected it to have been a bit busier.'

'The first of the guests don't arrive until tomorrow.' Matias didn't bother to turn around. 'I thought you might find it helpful to acquaint yourself with the kitchen, get to know where everything is.'

They had ended up in a kitchen that was the size of a football field and equipped to the highest possible standard. Sophie felt her fingers itch as she stared around her, dumbstruck.

'Wow.' She turned a full circle, eyes as wide as saucers, then when she was once again looking at him, she asked, 'So are you going to show me where everything is?'

Matias looked blankly around him and Sophie's eyebrows shot up.

'You don't know your way around this kitchen at all, do you?'

'I'm not a cook so it's true to say that I've never had much time for kitchens. I'm seldom in one place for very long and I tend to eat out a great deal. I'm a great believer in the theory that if someone else can do something better than you, then it would be cruel to deny them the opportunity.'

Sophie laughed and was surprised that he had managed to make her laugh at all. Her cheeks warmed and she looked away from those piercing dark eyes. Her heart was beating fast and she was confused because once again she could feel the pull of an attraction that went totally against the grain.

For starters, he had proven himself to have all the characteristics she despised in a man. He was arrogant, he was ruthless and he had the sort of self-assurance that came from knowing that he could do what he wanted and no one would object. He had power, he had money and he had looks and those added up to a killer combination that might have been a turn-on for other women but was a complete turn-off for her.

She knew that because he was just an extreme version of the type of men her mother had always been attracted to. Like a moth to an open flame, Angela Watts had been drawn to rich, good-looking men who had always been very, very bad for her. She had had the misfortune to have collided with the pinnacle of unsuitable men in James Carney, but even when that relationship had died a death she had still continued to be pointlessly drawn to self-serving, vain and inappropriate guys who had been happy to take her for a ride and then ditch her when she started to bore them.

Sophie had loved her mother but she had recognised her failings long before she had hit her formative teens. She had sworn to herself that, when it came to men, she would make informed choices and not be guided into falling for the wrong type. She would not be like her mother.

It helped that, as far as Sophie was concerned, she lacked her mother's dramatic bleached-blonde sex appeal.

And if she had made a mistake with Alan, then it hadn't been because she had chosen someone out of her league. It had just been…one of those things, a learning curve.

So why was she finding it so hard to tear her eyes away from Matias? Why was she so aware of him here in the kitchen with her, lean, indolent and darkly, dangerously sexy?

'Why don't you look around?' he encouraged, sitting at the kitchen table, content to watch her while he worked out how he was going to engineer the conversation into waters he wanted to explore.

She was very watchable. Even in clothes that were better suited to a shop assistant in a cheap retail outlet.

He was struck again by how little sense that made considering who her father was, but he would find out in due course and in the meanwhile…

He looked at her with lazy male appreciation. She had curves in all the right places. The hazy picture he had seen on Art's phone had not done justice to her at all. His eyes drifted a little south of her face to her breasts pushing against the buttons of the prissy, short-sleeved shirt. At least the jacket had come off. She was reaching up to one of the cupboards, checking the supply of dishes, he presumed, and the shirt ruched up to reveal a sliver of pale, smooth skin at her waist, and a dormant libido that should have had better things to do than start wanting to play with a woman who was firmly off the cards kicked into gear.

'Everything looks brand new.' Sophie turned to him, still on tiptoes, and he could see that indeed the crockery and the glasses in the cupboards could have come straight out of their expensive packaging. 'How often has this kitchen been used?'

'Not often,' Matias admitted, adjusting position to control his insurgent body. He glanced away for a few moments and was more in charge of his responses when he looked at her once more. Her hair was extraordinarily fair and he could tell it was naturally so. Fine and flyaway—with her heart-shaped face it gave her the look of an angel. A sexy little angel.

'In summer, I try and get up here for a weekend or so, but it's not often possible. Taking time out isn't always a viable option for me.'

'Because you're a workaholic?' Not looking at him, Sophie stooped down to expertly assess what the situation was with pots and pans and, as expected, there was no lack of every possible cooking utensil she might need. Next, she would examine the contents of the fridge.

With her catering hat firmly in place, it was easy to forget Matias's presence on the kitchen chair and the dark eyes lazily following her as she moved about the kitchen.

'I've discovered that work is the one thing in life on which you can depend,' Matias said, somewhat to his astonishment. 'Which, incidentally, is how I know your father.'

Sophie stilled and turned slowly round to look at him. 'You know my father? You actually *know* him?'

'I know *of* him,' Matias admitted, his dark eyes veiled. 'I can't say I've ever met the man personally. In fact, I was contemplating a business venture with him, which accounts for Art heading towards the house when you came racing out of the drive and crashed into my Maserati.' The delicate bones of her face were taut with tension and his curiosity spiked a little more.

'You had an appointment with my father?'

'Not as such,' Matias told her smoothly. 'Art was going to…let's just say…lay the groundwork for future trade…' In other words, he had sent Art to do the preliminary work of letting Carney know that his time was drawing to a close. He, Matias, would step in only when the net was ready to be tightened.

'Poor Art,' Sophie sighed, and Matias looked at her with a frown.

'Why do you say that?'

'I don't think he would have got very far with James even if he'd managed to gain entry to the house.'

'*James?* You call your father *James*?'

'He prefers that to being called Dad.' Sophie blushed. 'I think he thinks that the word *dad* is a little ageing. Also…'

'Also,' Matias intuited, 'you were an illegitimate child, weren't you? I expect he was not in the sort of zone where he would have been comfortable playing happy families with you and your mother. Not with a legitimate wife on the scene.'

Sophie went redder. What to say and how much? He was being perfectly polite. He wasn't to know the sort of man her father was and, more importantly, the reasons that had driven her mother to maintain contact with him, a legacy she had passed on to her daughter. Nor was she going to fill him in on her private business.

But the lengthening silence stretched her nerves to breaking point, and eventually she offered, reluctantly, 'No. My mother was a youthful indiscretion and he didn't like to be reminded of it.'

'He got your mother pregnant and he refused to marry her…' Matias encouraged.

Sophie stiffened because she could see the man in front of her was busy building a picture in his head, a picture that was spot on, but should she allow him to complete that picture?

The conversation she had had with her father just before she had blindly ended up crashing into Matias's car had been a disturbing one. He was broke, he had told her.

'And don't stand there with your hand stretched out staring gormlessly at me!' he had roared, pacing the magnificent but dated living room that was dark and claustrophobic and never failed to make Sophie shudder. 'You can take some of the blame for that! Showing up here month in month out with bills to settle! Now, there's *nothing left*. Do you understand me? *Nothing!*'

Cringing back against the stone mantelpiece, truly fearful that he would physically lash out at her, Sophie had said nothing. Instead, she had listened to him rant and rave and threaten and had finally left the house with far less than she had needed.

What if he was telling the truth? What if he *was* going broke? Where would that leave her…? *And more importantly, where would that leave Eric?*

As always, thinking of her brother made her heart constrict. For all her faults and her foolish misjudgements, her mother had been fiercely protective of her damaged son and had determined from early on that she wasn't going to be fobbed off by a man who had been happy enough to sleep with her for four years before abandoning her as soon as the right woman had finally appeared on the scene. She had used the only tool in her armoury to get the money she had needed for Eric to be looked after in the very expensive home where his needs were catered for.

Blackmail.

How would those fancy people James mixed with like him if they knew that he refused to support his disabled son and the family he had carelessly conceived, thinking that they would all do him a favour and vanish when it suited him?

James had paid up and he had continued paying up

because he valued the opinion of other people more than anything else in the world, not because he felt any affection for either the son he had never seen or the daughter he loathed because she was just an extension of the woman who, as far as he was concerned, had helped send him to the poorhouse.

If there was no money left, Eric would be the one to pay the ultimate price and Sophie refused to let that happen.

If Matias was interested in doing a deal with her father, a deal that might actually get him solvent once again, then how could it be in her interests to scupper that by letting him know just how awful James was? If her father had money then Eric would be safe.

'That's life.' She shrugged, masking her expression. 'There aren't many men who would have found it easy to introduce an outside family to their current one.' She took a deep breath and said, playing with the truth like modelling clay, 'But he's always been there for my mother... And now...er...for me...financially...'

Matias wondered whether they were talking about the same person. 'So you would recommend him as someone I should have dealings with?'

Fingers crossed behind her back, Sophie thought of her brother, lost in his world in the home where she visited him at least once a week, her brother who would certainly find life very, very different without all that care provided, care that only money could buy. 'Yes. Of course. Of course, I would.' She forced a smile. 'I'm sure he would love to have you contact him...'

CHAPTER THREE

MATIAS LOWERED HIS stunning dark eyes. So she either had no idea what kind of man her father was or she knew perfectly well enough and was tainted with the very same streak of greed, hence her enthusiasm for him to plough money into the man.

He wondered whether, over time and with her father's finances going down the drain faster than water running down a plughole, she had found herself an accidental victim of his limited resources. She had just declared that her father had supported her and her mother and Matias had struggled to contain a roar of derisive laughter at that. But she could have been telling the truth. Perhaps the dilapidated car and the debt owed to the bank were the result of diminishing handouts. She might have been an illegitimate child but it was possible that Carney had privately doted on her, bearing in mind that his own marriage had failed to yield any issue. Advertising a child outside marriage might have been no big deal for many men, but a man like Carney would have been too conscious of his social standing to have been comfortable acknowledging her publicly.

For a moment and just a moment, he wondered whether he could notch up some extra retribution and

publicly shame the man by exposing a hidden illegitimate child, but he almost immediately dismissed it
because it was...somehow unsavoury. Especially, he
thought, shielding the expression in his dark eyes, when
the woman sitting in front of him emanated innocence
in waves. There was such a thing as a plan backfiring
and, were a picture of her to be printed in any halfway
decent rag, a sympathetic public would surely take one
look at that disingenuous, sensationally sincere face
and cast *him* in the role of the bad guy. Besides, Carney's close friends doubtless knew of the woman's existence already.

'I will certainly think about contacting your father,'
Matias intoned smoothly, watching her like a hawk. He
became more and more convinced that she was playing him for a sap because she was suddenly finding it
seemingly impossible to meet his eyes. 'Now, you've
looked at the menu. Tell me whether you think you're
up to handling it.'

Sophie breathed a sigh of relief at the change of subject. She hated the little white lie she had told, even
though she was surely justified in telling it. Matias
might be disgustingly rich and arrogant but he still
didn't deserve to be deceived into believing her father
was an honourable guy. On the other hand, if the choice
was between her brother's future safety and well-be-
ing and Matias investing some money he wouldn't ever
miss, then her brother was going to win hands down
every time.

But that didn't mean that she'd liked telling Matias
that fib.

She jumped onto the change of topic with alacrity.
'Absolutely.' She looked around her at the expensive

gadgets, the speckled white counters, the vast cooking range. 'And it helps that your kitchen is so well equipped. Did you plan on doing lots of entertaining here when you bought the house?'

'Actually, I didn't buy the house. I had it built for me.' He went to the fridge, extracted a bottle of chilled white wine and poured her a glass. It seemed wildly extravagant to be consuming alcohol at this hour of the afternoon but she needed to steady her nerves, which were all over the place. 'And I had no particular plans to use the space for entertaining. I simply happen to enjoy having a lot of open space around me.'

'Lucky you,' Sophie sighed. After two sips of wine, she was already feeling a little less strung out. 'Julie and I would have a field day if we had this sort of kitchen. I've done the best with what I've got, but getting all the right equipment to fit into my kitchen has been a squeeze and if the business really takes off, then we're definitely going to have to move to bigger premises.'

Matias wondered whether that was why she had encouraged him to contact her father and put some work his way. Was it because she would be the happy beneficiary of such an arrangement?

Suspicious by nature and always alert to the threat of someone trying it on, he found it very easy to assume the worst of her, in defiance of the disingenuous manner she had. Judge a book by its cover and you almost always ended up being taken for a ride.

Not only did he have the example of his father to go on, who had paid the ultimate price for judging a book by its cover, but he, Matias, had made one and only one catastrophic misjudgement in his heady youth. On the road to the vast riches that would later be his and caught up in the novel situation of being sought after by men far older than himself who wanted to tap his financial acumen, he had fallen for a girl who had seemed to be grounded in the sort of normality he had fast been leaving behind. Next to the savvy beauties who had begun forming a queue for him, she had seemed the epitome of innocence. She had turned down presents, encouraged him to sideline the sort of fancy venues that were opening up on his horizon and professed a burning desire to go to the movies and share a bag of popcorn. No boring Michelin restaurants for her!

She had played the long game and he had been thoroughly taken in until she had sprung a pregnancy scare on him. Talk had turned to marriage pretty quickly after that and God knew he might just have ended up making the biggest mistake of his life and tying the knot had he not discovered the half-used packet of contraceptive pills in her handbag. Quite by accident. Only then, when he had confronted her, had her true colours emerged.

That narrow escape had been a turning point for him. A momentary lapse, he had discovered, was all it took for your life to derail. Momentary lapses would never again occur and they hadn't. Matias ruled his own life with a rod of steel and emotions were never allowed free rein. He took what he needed out of life and discarded what ceased to be of use to him.

Art was the only person on earth who knew about that brief but shameful episode and so it would remain. Matias had had little time for the perils of emotional roller-coaster rides, having grown up as witness to the way his father's emotional and trusting nature had led him down a blind alley, and his disastrous love affair had been the final nail in the coffin, after which he had entombed his heart in ice and that was exactly the way he liked it.

'You said you've only been in the catering business for a year and a half. What prompted the change of career?'

'We both enjoyed cooking.' Sophie realised that her glass of wine was empty and he appeared to have topped it up. She moved to sit at the wonderful kitchen table fashioned from black granite and metal. 'We became accustomed to friends asking us to cater for them and bit by bit we came to the conclusion that, in the long run, we might very well be better off doing something we both loved and were good at. Julie was fed up with her teaching job and I guess I just wanted a change of career.'

'It must have been a leap of faith for you. Changing career that dramatically takes guts.' Had she embarked on that career change with the mistaken impression that her father was still wealthy enough to fund her? Had she had to resort to borrowing from the bank when she found herself out of a job and unable to turn to her parent for a handout? Was that why she was struggling financially?

Lucas knew that James Carney's financial position had been poor for a few years.

'Maybe. Haven't *you* ever had to change career or were you born with a silver spoon in your mouth?' she asked.

'You say that as though you're not familiar with that situation yourself.'

'I'm not,' Sophie said flatly and Matias looked at her through narrowed eyes.

'I confess I find that hard to believe, given your father's elevated lifestyle.'

'I'd really rather not talk about him,' Sophie hedged warily.

'You don't like talking about your father? Why is that? I grant you, it must have been a nuisance living in the shadows, if indeed that was the case, but surely if, as you say, he helped you and your mother through the years...well, he must be quite a character because many men in a similar situation would have walked away from their responsibility.'

Sophie muttered something inaudible that might have been agreement or dissent.

'Of course, life must be altogether easier for you now,' Matias continued conversationally. 'I gather his wife died some years ago, so presumably he has taken you under his wing...'

'We don't have that sort of relationship,' Sophie admitted stiffly and Matias's ears pricked up.

'No?' he encouraged. 'Tell me about him. The reason I ask is simple. If I'm to have any financial dealings with him, it would be useful to try and understand the sort of person he is.'

'Do you take this close an interest in *all* your...er... clients?' This more to divert the conversation than anything else. Sophie had no real idea how people in the business world operated.

'I have slightly more elaborate plans for your father's company,' which wasn't exactly a lie, then he shrugged.

'Is that what you do?'

Matias frowned. 'Explain.'

'Well, do you...er...invest in companies? The truth is I honestly don't know the ins and outs of how companies operate. I've never had much interest in that sort of thing.'

'I see…so you don't care about money…'

'Not enough to have gone into a career where I might have made a fortune. Life would have been a lot easier if I had.' For starters, she thought, she wouldn't have had to endure the monthly humiliation of picking up where her mother had left off, and going to her father with cap in hand because Eric's home was costly and there was no other choice. 'I don't suppose I'm ruthless enough.'

'Is that a criticism of me?' Matias asked wryly, amused because it was rare for anyone to venture any opinion in his presence that might have been interpreted as critical. But then, as she had pointed out, whatever better nature he had was seldom in evidence and things weren't going to change on that front any time soon.

Sophie was caught between being truthful and toeing the diplomatic line. Talking about her father was out of bounds because sooner or later she would trip up and reveal exactly the sort of man he was. Telling Matias Rivero what she thought of him was also pretty questionable because he had thrown her a lifeline and he could whip it back whenever it suited him. If she succeeded in this task, a good proportion of her debt to him would be wiped out. As agreed, she had received a detailed financial breakdown of what she could expect from her weekend's work.

Getting on the wrong side of him wasn't a good idea. But he *had* asked…

And something about the man seemed to get her firing on cylinders she didn't know she possessed.

'Well, I *am* here,' she pointed out and Matias frowned.

'Where are you going with that?'

'You intend to get your pound of flesh from me by

whatever means necessary and if that's not ruthless, then I don't know what is.'

'It's not ruthless,' Matias informed her, without a hint of an apology. 'It's good, old-fashioned business sense.' On more levels than she could ever begin to suspect, he thought, dispelling a fleeting twinge of guilt because all that mattered was getting her despicable father to pay for what he had done all those years ago.

Matias thought back to the slim stash of letters he had found shoved at the back of his mother's chest of drawers. He would never have come across those letters if she hadn't been rushed to hospital, because he had had to pack a bag without warning for her. Her housekeeper had had the day off and Matias had had no idea what sort of things his mother might need. He had opened drawers and scooped out what seemed to be appropriate clothing and in doing so had scooped out those unopened letters bound with an elastic band.

His mother's writing. He had recognised that instantly just as he had noted the date on the stamps. They had all been sent over a period of a few weeks at a time when his father had been taking what were to be his last breaths before the cancer that had attacked him two years previously had resurfaced to finish what it had begun.

Curiosity had got the better of him because all those letters had been addressed to the same man. James Carney.

In actual fact, he need only have opened one of the letters because they had all contained the same message.

A plea for help. A request for money for an experimental treatment being carried out in America for precisely the sort of rare cancer his father had contracted.

None of the letters had been opened—they had just been returned to sender. It was plain to see that the man who had defrauded Matias's family and reaped the financial rewards that should have, at the very least, been shared with his father, had not had the slightest interest in what his mother had wanted to say to him.

Carney had been too busy living it up on his ill-gotten gains to give a damn about the fate of the family who had paid the price at his hands.

There and then, Matias had realised that retribution was no longer going to be on the back burner. It was going to happen hard and fast. The time for dragging his feet was over.

If Carney's illegitimate daughter now found herself caught in the crossfire then so be it. He wasn't going to lose his focus and the woman sitting opposite him was all part of his bigger plan. He could bring the man down the routine way, by bankrupting him, but he was getting a feeling...that there was more to the saga of his hidden daughter than met the eye. What could she tell him? Any whiff of a financial scandal, any hint that the health of his ailing company was tied up with fraud, would be the icing on the cake. Not only would such public revelations hit Carney where it hurt most, but a long prison sentence would loom on the horizon for him. All in all, a thoroughly satisfying outcome.

'Julie, my partner, wouldn't agree with you.' Sophie stuck her chin out at a mutinous angle. 'I've left her barely coping with one of the biggest contracts we've managed to secure since we started our catering company. We could really harm our business if she doesn't succeed because one poor job has a knock-on effect in the catering world.'

'You don't have my sympathy on that score,' Matias told her bluntly. He was unwillingly fascinated by the way she coloured up when she spoke and the way her aquamarine eyes, fringed by the lushest lashes possible, glittered and sparkled like precious gems.

Her skin was as smooth as satin and she didn't appear to be wearing a speck of make-up. She oozed *natural* and if he wasn't the cynical guy that he was, he would be sorely tempted to take her at face value because that face appeared so very, very open and honest.

Step up the memory of the ex who had almost got his ring on her finger on the back of appearing open and honest! Good job he wasn't the sort of idiot who ignored valuable learning curves.

'Here's a free piece of advice…never go into business with anyone. However, considering you've passed that point, you should have made sure that you weren't going into business with dead wood. Have you got anything signed allowing you to disentangle yourself from a ruinous partnership without feeling the backlash?'

Two bright patches of colour stained her cheeks and she glared at Matias without bothering to conceal a temper that was rarely in evidence. She looked at him, furiously frowning, all the more irate because he returned her glare with a lazy, amused smile. Her skin tingled as he held her gaze and kept on holding it, sucking the breath out of her and making her agonisingly aware of her body in ways that were confusing and incomprehensible.

Her breasts felt heavy and *full*, her nipples were suddenly sensitised, their tips pebble hard and scratchy against her bra, and there was a tingling between her legs that made her want to touch herself.

Sophie was so shocked that she looked away, heart hammering hard, barely able to breathe normally.

What on earth was going on with her? It was true that she hadn't had any interest in men since she had broken up with Alan, but surely that wouldn't make her susceptible to a man like Matias Rivero? He epitomised everything she disliked and if he was, physically, an attractive guy then surely she was sensible enough to be able to get past outward appearances?

'Julie is *not* dead wood,' she denied in a voice she barely recognised.

'If she's panicking because you're not there to hold her hand, then she's incompetent.'

'Thank you for your advice,' she said with sugary sarcasm, 'although I won't be paying much attention to it because I actually haven't asked for it in the first place.'

Matias burst out laughing. Against all odds, he was enjoying himself with the one person on the planet he should have wanted to have as little to do with as possible. Yes, he was on a fact-finding mission but he hadn't anticipated having fun as he tried to plumb her depths for some useful information on her father.

'Would it shock you to know that I can't think of anyone who would dare say something like that to me?'

'No,' Sophie told him with complete honesty and Matias laughed again.

'No?'

'Men with money always surround themselves with people who suck up to them and, even if they don't, people are so awed by money that they change when they're around rich people. They behave differently.'

'But you're different from them?' Matias inserted

silkily. 'Or are you just someone who can afford to make penury their career choice because there has always been a comfort blanket on which to rely should push actually come to shove?'

'I don't expect you to believe me,' Sophie muttered. 'James supported us because he had to. I was grateful for that, but there was never any question about there being any comfort blanket for the…for us…'

Matias looked at her narrowly, picking up *something* although he couldn't quite be sure what.

'Because he had to…' he murmured. 'You're not exactly singing his praises with that statement.'

'But like you said,' Sophie pointed out quickly, 'he could have just walked away from his responsibility.'

'Unless…' Matias let that single word hang tantalisingly in the air between them.

'Unless?' Sophie gazed at him helplessly and thought that this was what it must feel like to be a rabbit caught in the headlights. There was something powerful and *inexorable* about him. His head was tilted to one side and his midnight-dark eyes were resting lazily on her, sending little arrows of apprehension racing through her body like tiny electrical charges.

'Unless he felt he had no choice…'

Sophie stilled. She was caught between the devil and the deep blue sea. Tell him everything and he would have nothing to do with her father, who would probably have to declare bankruptcy if everything he said was true, and where would that leave Eric? Yet say nothing and who knew where this conversation would end up?

She remained resolutely silent and thought frantically about a suitable change of subject. Something innocuous. Perhaps the weather, although that alert expression in Matias's dark, brooding eyes didn't augur well for some inconsequential chit-chat at this juncture.

He looked very much like a dog in possession of a large, juicy bone, keen to take the first bite.

'Is that it?' he pressed softly. 'Did your mother apply a little undue pressure to make sure she was taken care of? Is that the relationship you have with your father now? I expect a man like him, in a reasonably prominent position, might have found it awkward to have had the mother of his illegitimate child making a nuisance of herself.'

Lost for words, Sophie could only stare at him in absolute silence.

How on earth had he managed to arrive at this extremely accurate conclusion? And more to the point, how had the conversation meandered to this point in the first place?

'I thought you might have been the secret child he spoiled, bearing in mind his marriage failed to produce a suitable heir.' Matias was shamelessly fishing and not at all bothered at Sophie's obvious discomfort.

'I really don't want to talk about James,' Sophie eventually said, when the silence had become too much to bear. 'I know you're interested in finding out what you can before you sink money into…er…his company, but you're really asking the wrong person when it comes to business details and I don't feel comfortable discussing him behind his back.' Something her father had said, in the rush of anger, rose to the surface of her addled brain…something about *where* all the money he had given them over the years had come from, a paper trail that should have been brushed under the carpet but was threatening to re-emerge under the eagle eyes of independent auditors. She shivered.

Matias debated whether to press the issue or fall back on this occasion and he decided that, with time on his hands, there was no point trying to force her into revealing secrets that might be lurking just below the surface.

For sure, something wasn't quite right but he'd discover what that was sooner or later.

In the meanwhile…

'Is there anything you need to know about the job?' he asked briskly, finally changing the subject to her obvious relief. The details could very well be left to his head housekeeper, who was busy with preparations in the vast house somewhere, but Matias was drawn to continuing the conversation with her.

His life had become very predictable when it came to women. He had made one youthful mistake, had learnt from it and ever since his relationships had all had two things in common. One was that they followed exactly the same pattern and the second was that they were all short-lived.

The pattern involved mutual attraction with the expected lavishing of expensive presents, in something of a brief courtship ritual, followed by a few weeks of satisfying sex before he began getting bored and restless.

It didn't matter who he dated or what sort of woman happened to catch his eye. From barrister to catwalk model, his interest never seemed to stay the course.

Was Sophie right? People behaved differently in the presence of the powerful, influential and wealthy. Were the women he dated so awed by what he brought to the table that they were unable to relate to him with any kind of honesty?

Unaccustomed to introspection, Matias, for once, found himself querying how it was that he was still so resolutely single at his age and so jaded with the revolving door of relationships he enjoyed. When had no-strings-attached fun turned into liaisons that seemed to get shorter and shorter and become less and less satisfying?

He frowned, disconcerted by this *breach of protocol* and refocused on the woman in front of him.

'Would you be able to help me if I had any questions?' Sophie quipped and he dealt her a smile that was so sudden and so devastating that she had a moment of sheer giddiness.

She blinked, owl-like, mouth parted, her cheeks tinged with delightful colour.

She wasn't angry...she wasn't defensive...she wasn't on the attack...

She was *aware*.

Matias felt that kick of his libido again, forbidden, dangerous but, oh, so pleasurable.

It had been a little while since he had had a woman. His most recent girlfriend had lasted a mere two months, at the end of which he had been mightily relieved to see the back of her because she had gone from compliant to demanding in record time.

Was his brief sexual drought generating a reaction that was as thrilling as it was unexpected?

There was certainly something undeniably sexy about Sophie and he couldn't put his finger on it. Maybe it was because he knew that he shouldn't go anywhere near her.

A thought entered his head like quicksilver. Why not? She was attractive. Indeed, it was a while since he had had his interest sparked by a woman who appeared to be uninterested in the usual game playing. There had been no coy looks, fluttering lashes or suggestive remarks. Admittedly, she was here under duress because he had placed her in an impossible situation, but even so she was doing a good job of keeping him at arm's length.

Matias watched her with brooding interest. If he wanted information on the Carney man, then surely pillow talk would yield everything he wanted to know?

Just like that, his imagination took flight and he pictured her in his super-king-sized bed, her tangle of long white-blonde hair spread across his pillow, her voluptuous pale nakedness there for his enjoyment. He wondered what her abundant breasts might look like and he imagined suckling at them.

An erection as solid as steel made him twinge in discomfort and he did his utmost to drag his mind away from imagining salacious, tawdry details about her.

'You're right,' he drawled, settling further into the chair, his big body relaxed, his hands loosely linked on his lap, his long legs extended to one side. 'If you want help, you're going to have to talk to my housekeeper. I have next to no interest in the workings of a kitchen, as I've already mentioned.'

'How lovely for you to be in a position like that,' Sophie said politely, still reeling from the way he *got to her* and made her whole body vibrate and rev up and behave almost as though it didn't belong to her at all.

'In case you're thinking that I was born with a silver spoon in my mouth, you're wrong.' He frowned because it wasn't in his nature to tell anyone anything about him that wasn't strictly essential. He didn't do confiding, especially not in women who could take one small slip-up and celebrate it as a signpost to the nearest bridal shop.

'I never said that,' but Sophie had the grace to blush because she'd certainly been thinking it. Rich, arrogant and privileged from birth had been her assumption.

'You have a very transparent face,' Matias told her wryly. 'You don't have to spell it out. It's there in your expression of disapproval. You think I'm an arrogant, ruthless tycoon who has it all and has never suffered a day's hardship in his entire life.'

Sophie didn't say anything. She was busy trying to get her body to behave and to look past Matias's devastating and unwelcome sex appeal. However, no matter how hard she tried to tell herself that she was only responding the way any normal, healthy young female would respond to a guy who would have been able to turn the head of a ninety-year-old woman with failing eyesight, she still could scarcely believe that he was capable of having that huge an impact on her.

To combat the drag of her disobedient senses, she even did the unthinkable and disinterred the mental image of her ex, Alan Pace. On paper, he had been the perfect life partner. Sandy-haired, blue-eyed and with just the sort of even, friendly disposition that had made her feel safe and comfortable. Sophie had really begun to nurture high hopes that they were destined for the long run.

She was always careful to vet the people she introduced to her brother; when, after three months, she'd filled Alan in on Eric, he had been surprised that she hadn't said anything sooner and had been happy to meet him.

Unfortunately, meeting Eric had marked the begin-

ning of the end for them. Alan had not been prepared
for the extent of her brother's disabilities and he had
been quietly horrified at the thought that taking Eric
out was a very regular activity and one which Sophie
enjoyed and did without complaint. He had envisaged
the possibility of him having to become a joint carer at
some indeterminate point in the future, and although
Sophie had squashed that suggestion because Eric was
very, very happy where he was, she had not been able,
in all good conscience, to rule it out altogether. After
that, it had just been a matter of time before Alan had
begun heading for the nearest exit.

Yet harking back to Alan, she had to admit to herself that not even *he* had affected her the way Matias
seemed capable of doing. And before it all went belly
up, Alan had been the perfect boyfriend! So what the
heck was going on with her?

Not only was the man gazing at her with dark-eyed
intensity very much *not* the perfect *anything*, but the
last thing she felt in his presence was *safe and comfortable*.

Privately Sophie was appalled that she might bear
any resemblance to her wayward mother, who had spent
a lifetime making all the wrong choices and going for
men just like the one sitting opposite Sophie, men who
had *Danger, health hazard* stamped all over their foreheads in bright neon lettering.

'It doesn't matter what I think of you,' she said
quickly, because this was the only way she could think
of to bring their interaction to an end and she desperately wanted to do just that. 'I'm here to do my duty
and now, if you'll excuse me, might I go and freshen
up? And then perhaps I could talk to the person I will

be working alongside? Also someone who can show me how everything works here?'

He was being dismissed! Matias didn't know whether to be amused or outraged.

He stood up, as sleek and graceful as a panther, and shoved his hands in the pockets of his trousers.

Sophie looked away. She knew that her face was bright red and that she was perched on the edge of her chair, rigid with tension and so aware of him that she could hardly breathe. He was just so staggeringly good-looking that she had to consciously *not* look at him and even *not* looking at him was making her go all hot and cold.

'Excellent idea,' Matias drawled, his keen eyes taking in every sign of her discomfort and also the way she was pointedly avoiding his eyes. He felt the thrill of a challenge and was already circling it, playing with thoughts of what happened next in this little scenario. 'Wait here. I will ensure that you are shown the workings of the kitchen and then to your quarters, which I trust you will find satisfactory.'

And then he smiled, slowly and lazily, and Sophie gave a jerky nod of her head, but he was already turning and striding out of the kitchen.

CHAPTER FOUR

SOPHIE HAD ONLY dimly speculated on what a long week-end party might be like. She had mostly thought along the lines of one of those upper-class country affairs where a dozen people wafted around in flowing robes, smoking cigarettes in long cigarette holders and talking in low, restrained, cut-glass accents. She had seen stuff like that in period dramas on television. Generally speaking, there was always an unfortunate death at some point.

Matias's party, she could tell as soon as guest number one had arrived, was not going to be quite like that.

Through the kitchen windows, which overlooked the spread of lawns at the back of the house and the long avenue and courtyard where the cars would be parked, the first guests arrived in a roaring vintage car, which disgorged a couple who could have stepped straight out of a celebrity magazine.

Debbie, the lovely housekeeper in her fifties who had, the day before, showed Sophie the ropes, had been standing next to her and she had said, without batting an eyelid, that everyone in the village had been waiting for this party with bated breath because the guest list was stuffed full of celebrities.

And so Sophie had discovered as the day had continued and the guests had begun piling up. All told, there would have been getting on for eighty people. Many would be staying in three sumptuous hotels in the vicinity, where chauffeurs were on standby to take them there at the end of the evening and return them to the house in time for breakfast and whatever activities had been laid on.

Through a process of clever guesswork, Sophie deduced that this wasn't so much a weekend of fun and frolic with Matias's nearest and dearest, but something of a business arrangement. The scattering of A-list celebrities from the world of media and sport was interspersed with a healthy assortment of very rich, middle-aged men who oozed wealth and power.

Sophie guessed that this was how the fabulously wealthy did their networking.

The supply of food was constant, as was the champagne. Having had a brief respite the day before, when Matias had done as asked and introduced Sophie to the people she would be working with, Sophie had been hard at it since six that morning.

Brunch was the first thing on the menu. An elaborate buffet spread, then tea before supper made an appearance at seven-thirty in the evening.

Sophie had no idea what these people did when they weren't eating and she didn't have time to think about it because she was rushed off her feet cooking and giving orders and hoping and praying that nothing went wrong.

She didn't glimpse Matias, even in passing. Why would he venture into the bowels of the kitchen where the lowly staff were taking care of his needs when he had the movers and shakers there to occupy him?

Strangely Art, Matias's employee, *had* put in an appearance in the kitchen and he had been as lovely as she recalled. Kind, gentle, almost making her think that there might be a purpose to his surprise visit, even though he had just briefly passed the time of day with her. And she wasn't quite sure why Matias had made sure to make the distinction that Art was only his *employee*, because it was clear, reading between the lines, that the two had a close bond, which, in turn, made her feel, stupidly and disturbingly, that Matias couldn't possibly be the cruel ogre she thought him to be. Didn't people's choice of friends often tell a story about *themselves*? Crazy.

Nose to the grindstone, she nevertheless still found herself keeping an eye out for Matias just in case he put in an appearance and when, at a little after eleven that evening, she made her way up to her quarters, she was foolishly disappointed not to have seen him at all.

Because she needed to make sure that everything was on target for her repaying some of the stupid debt she owed him, she reasoned sensibly. She had worked her butt off and she wanted to know that it hadn't been in vain, that day one had definitely wiped out the amount that had been agreed on paper.

The last thing she needed was to be told, when it was all over and done with and she'd shed a couple of stone through sheer stress, that he wasn't satisfied or that he'd had complaints about her or that the food had given his guests food poisoning and so she would have to cough up the money she owed him even if it meant her going bust.

She, herself, had no idea what the reaction to all her hard work was because she didn't emerge from the bowels of the wonderfully well-equipped kitchen for the entire day and night.

Waiters and waitresses came and went and an assortment of hired help made sure that dirty crockery was washed and returned for immediate use.

In addition to that plethora of staff on tap, Sophie also had a dedicated sous chef who was invaluable and did all the running around at her command.

But it was still exhausting and she had two more days of this before the first of the guests would start departing!

Surely, she thought, she would see Matias *at some point*! Surely he wouldn't just leave her to get on with it without poking his nose into the kitchen to see whether he was getting his pound of flesh!

It was simply her anxiety given the circumstances that resulted in Matias being on her mind so much.

She was cross with herself for letting him get under her skin. She recalled the way her body had reacted to his with a shudder of impatience. He'd given her the full brunt of his personality in all its overpowering glory when there had been no one else around, but now that he was surrounded by his cronies he couldn't even be bothered to check up on her and make sure he was getting value for money.

It infuriated her that, instead of being relieved that he wasn't hovering over her shoulder or popping up unexpectedly like a bad penny, she was disappointed.

By the time the festivities were coming to an end and the end of the long menu was in sight, she had reconciled herself to the fact that she would leave without seeing Matias at all and would probably find out the outcome of this exercise in repaying the money she owed him via his secretary.

He'd made his appearance and he wasn't going to be making another one.

She hadn't even had a chance, with everything happening, to have a look around the house! Not that she'd wanted to mingle with the guests. She knew her place, after all, but she'd hoped that she might have had a chance, last thing at night, to peep into some of the splendid rooms. No such luck because there had always been someone around or else the sound of voices from one of the rooms had alerted her to the presence of people who seemed to think nothing of staying up until the early hours of the morning.

The guests finally departed during the course of Monday in a convoy of expensive cars. The sound of laughter and chatter filtered down to the kitchen where most of the hired help had tidied, cleaned and left to go back to the village, where they would no doubt regale their family and friends with excited tales about what and who they'd seen.

Had Matias gone? By five-thirty, with just Sophie and Debbie left on the premises doing the final bits of tidying, she knew that he had. Without telling her how she had performed.

For some reason, she was booked to remain in the sprawling mansion until the following morning, and she had naturally assumed that there would be guests to cook breakfast for on that morning, but now she realised that she had been kept on to do cleaning duties after the guests had left.

He'd bought her lock, stock and barrel. She hadn't been asked to simply prepare meals, which was her speciality, but he had also kept her on to do basic skivvy work and he knew that she had no choice but to comply.

'You take the left wing of the house,' Debbie told her kindly. 'I've checked and all the guests have gone. There shouldn't be anything much to do at all because the rooms have all been cleaned on a daily basis. This is just a last-minute check to make sure nothing's been forgotten…and you've been saying that you wanted to have a peep at some of the rooms. It's worth a look. Mr Rivero doesn't come here very often but it's always a treat for us when he does because it's such a grand house.'

Finally back in her comfortable jeans and tee shirt, Sophie decided to do just that. Having not stuck her head over the parapet for the past three days, she took her time exploring the various rooms she had been allocated.

Debbie had been right: there was hardly any tidying to be done at all. Rooms had already been cleared of debris and vacuumed. She wound her way up the marble and glass staircase, admiring the canvasses on the walls as she began checking the bedrooms on the first floor.

The house looked untouched, having been completely tidied by a small army of staff.

Her mind was a complete blank as she pushed open the final door at the end of a long corridor that offered spectacular views of the lake from behind vast floor-to-ceiling panes of reinforced glass.

The first thing she noticed was the feel of pale, thick carpet under her feet as most of the house was a mixture of marble, wood and pale, endless silk rugs. Automatically, she kicked off her sandals and then stepped forwards.

Her eyes travelled to the huge bed…the white walls…
the chrome and glass built-in wardrobes…the window
that was just one massive pane of glass, uninterrupted
by curtains or even shutters, through which Nature in
all its lush green glory stretched towards the still black
waters of the lake.

Then, to the left, a door she hadn't even noticed because it so cleverly blended into the pale paint opened
and she was staring at Matias.

In pure shock, she took a few seconds to appreciate
that he was semi naked. Obviously, he had just had a
shower. His dark hair was still damp and a white towel
was loosely draped around his lean hips. Apart from
that scant covering…nothing. Bare chest, bare legs, bare
everything else.

Sophie wanted to look away but she couldn't. Her
mouth fell open and her eyes widened as she took in
the broad muscularity of his shoulders, the width of his
hard chest, the arrowing of dark hair down towards that
low-slung towel. He was so absurdly, intensely *masculine* that all the breath left her in a whoosh.

She knew that she was staring and she couldn't do a
thing about it. When she finally looked him in the face,
it was to find him staring back at her, eyebrows raised.
'Inspection over?'

Matias had made a point of steering clear of her for
the past few days. He'd regrouped and realised that what
he had viewed as an interesting challenge that could
lead to a number of pleasurable destinations with Sophie was in fact a poorly thought-out plan generated by
a temporary lapse in his self-control.

She might be intensely attractive and he might very
well be able to rationalise his visceral response to her,

but taking her to his bed could only be a bad idea. Yes, pillow talk might result in him hitting the jackpot when it came to finding out more about Carney but there had been no point kidding himself that that had been the overriding reason for his sudden desire to act like a caveman and get her between the sheets. She'd done something to him, cast some spell over him that had made him lose his formidable self-control and that wasn't going to justify whatever jackpot it might or might not lead to.

So he'd kept away. He'd even considered sleeping with one of the single women who had been at the party, a model he had known briefly several months previously, but in the end had ditched the idea.

Because having entered his head, Sophie had stubbornly lodged there like an irritating burr and he'd found he didn't want anyone else.

And now here she was. His dark eyes roved over her flushed face and then did a quick tour of her body. These were obviously the clothes she was most comfortable in and she looked sexy as hell in them. The faded jeans clung to her curves like a second skin and the tee shirt revealed breasts that were gloriously abundant.

The kick of his libido demolished every single shred of common sense. Matias had no idea what it felt like to operate without self-imposed boundaries. He was finding out now as he looked at her and surrendered to a surge of lust that could not be forced into abeyance.

The thrill of a challenge waiting to be met was one that wasn't going to go away until it was dealt with.

He padded across to the bedroom door and quietly shut it and Sophie's head swung round in alarm.

'What are you d-doing?' she stammered, frozen to the spot.

'I'm closing the door,' Matias told her gently. 'In case you hadn't noticed, I'm not exactly dressed for visitors.'

'I was going to leave…' Sophie shuffled a couple of paces back but it was laborious, like swimming against a strong current. 'I had no idea that you were still here.'

'Where else would I have been?'

'I thought you'd left with all the other guests.'

'And not had a talk to you about your performance?'

'Have I done something wrong?' Sophie asked in a rush, red as a beetroot, torn between wanting to flee and needing to stay to hear whatever criticisms of her work that he had.

Matias didn't answer. He turned around and headed towards his wardrobe and Sophie broke out in a film of nervous perspiration.

'I'd rather talk to you…s-somewhere else,' she stuttered. 'If I'd known you were in here, I would never have entered.'

'I make you uncomfortable,' Matias said flatly, spinning round to look at her and at the same time throwing on a snowy white shirt without yet removing the towel. He didn't button it up but left it hanging open over his fabulous chest and Sophie's mouth went dry.

'You're barely clothed,' she pointed out breathlessly. 'Of course I feel *uncomfortable* and I certainly don't imagine I'll be able to have a conversation about my duties in your bedroom!' She went a shade redder. 'What I *mean*…is that this is…*isn't* the place for a serious conversation. If I've failed in the task you set me, then… then…' She looked in horror as he hooked one finger over his towel.

She turned away and Matias laughed softly. Okay, so the woman had somehow reduced him to a level of dithering unheard of. Normally, he approached women and relationships with just exactly the same assured directness with which he approached work. Both were a known quantity and neither induced anything in him other than complete certainty of the outcome.

But with *her*...his taste for revenge had been diluted by desire. What should have been clear-cut had become cloudy. He had vacillated like a hapless teenager between pursuit and withdrawal and had tried to reclaim the loss of his prized self-control only to find it now slipping out of his grasp.

He'd acted out of character and that disturbed him because it never happened.

'You haven't failed,' he said quietly. 'If you give me five minutes, I'll meet you downstairs in the kitchen and we can debrief.'

He headed towards the en-suite bathroom and Sophie fled back down the stairs to the kitchen where she had to take a few seconds to regain her self-control. She was sipping a glass of water when the kitchen door slid open and there he was, drop-dead gorgeous in a white shirt cuffed to the elbows and a pair of black jeans that showed his powerful body off to perfection.

'Have something a bit more exciting than water.' He headed straight for the oversized wine cooler and extracted a bottle of wine and then two glasses. 'You must feel as though you need it. I've thrown you in at the deep end and you've risen to the occasion.' He poured them both a glass of wine, sipped his and then, eyes on her face, tilted his head in a salute.

Sophie cleared her throat. 'Were you expecting me to fail?'

'I thought you would pull through. I didn't think that you would handle the situation with such efficiency. Everyone raved about the food and I was impressed with the way the timetable was adhered to.'

'Thank you.' She blushed and drank some of the wine.

'Naturally, the past few days only cover a proportion of the debt but you've made a start.'

'Will you be in touch about…er…another arrangement so that I can try and schedule my jobs accordingly? Julie did very well handling the cocktail party on her own but she was very nervous and I would rather not put her through that. If I know when you need me, then I can make sure I'm only missing food preparation on the premises rather than in situ at a client's house.'

'No. I can't tailor my timetable to suit your partner, I'm afraid.' He paused, gazed at her, again felt the fierce kick of desire and wondered how he could have been sufficiently short-sighted to have imagined that he could make it disappear on command. It would disappear but only after he'd had her, only when he'd sated a craving that made no sense and had sprung from nowhere. 'Did you enjoy the long weekend?'

'I was under a great deal of pressure,' Sophie confessed stiffly. 'But it was challenging catering for that amount of people. It was the largest party I've ever done.'

'I didn't see you put in an appearance.'

'I was busy overseeing the food. Besides…'

'Besides?'

'What would I have done out there? Asked everyone if they were enjoying the food?'

'You could have circulated, handed out your business cards.'

'I would have felt awkward,' Sophie admitted truthfully. 'Those sort of big bashes aren't my thing. I wouldn't have fitted in.'

'You underestimate your...charms,' Matias said softly. 'I imagine you would have fitted in a great deal better than you think.'

Sophie looked at him and wondered whether she was imagining *something* in his voice, something low and speculative that was sending a shiver down her spine and ratcheting up her painful awareness of him and her heightened reaction to his proximity. Was he actually *flirting* with her? Surely not.

Confused, she stared at him in silence and he stared right back at her, holding her gaze and making no effort to look away. He sipped his wine, gazed at her over the rim of the glass and the effect was devastating.

She was utterly defenceless. She didn't know what he was playing at. This made no sense at all. She was lower than the hired help! She was the hired help plus some!

'I sh-should head upstairs,' she stuttered, half standing on wobbly legs. 'If it's all the same to you, there's nothing left here for me to do. Er...and...if you're satisfied with...with my efforts...then maybe your secretary...can contact me...'

She ran her fingers through her tangled hair and licked her lips because *he was still looking at her with that brooding, veiled expression and it was doing crazy things to her nervous system.*

'And if...if it's okay with you, then I shall get a cab to

the station tonight. I was under the impression that there would be some guests here until tomorrow morning, which is why I was…ah…booked to stay for one final night…' She took a deep breath and exhaled slowly. 'I wish you wouldn't stare at me like that,' she said, licking dry lips.

'Why?'

'Because it makes me feel uncomfortable.'

'Funny, I've never had any complaints from a woman because I haven't been able to keep my eyes off her. On the contrary, they're usually at great pains to make sure that they position themselves directly in my line of vision in the hope that I'll notice them. This is the first time I can genuinely say that I've found myself in the presence of a woman I can't seem to stop looking at.'

Shocked, Sophie literally could find nothing to say. Her vocal cords had dried up. All she could do was stare. He was so ridiculously beautiful that it seemed utterly mad for him to be saying this sort of stuff to her. Even more crazy was the fact that her whole body was surging into overdrive and melting like wax before an open flame.

She wasn't this person! She was level-headed and practical and she knew when and where to draw lines. Not that she had had to draw any since her break-up with Alan. Since then, and that had been over three years ago, men had been put firmly on the back burner and she hadn't once been tempted to dip her toes back into the dating pool. Not once. So why was her body on fire now? Because a guy with too much money, too much charm and too much in the looks department was coming on to her?

'Don't you feel the chemistry between us as well?'

'I don't know what you're talking about,' Sophie whispered and Matias raised his eyebrows in an expression of frank incredulity.

'Of course you do,' he corrected her casually. 'Although,' he continued, 'I understand that you might want to deny it. After all, it's not exactly something either of us bargained on, is it?' No truer words spoken, Matias thought wryly. All things considered, he would have placed greater odds on him catching a rocket to the red planet.

He shrugged eloquently. 'But there you are. These things happen.'

So he fancied her and wanted to have sex with her. Sophie's brain finally cranked into gear and anger began building inside her with the force of suppressed molten lava. He was a rich, powerful man who had her on the run and, because of that, he figured he could come onto her because he happened to find her attractive.

And the worst thing was that he had picked up vibes from her, vibes that had informed him that the pull was mutual. But if he thought that she was now going to fall into bed with him then he had another think coming!

'I'm sorry,' she said coldly, 'but I'm not interested.'

Matias laughed as though she'd cracked a hilarious joke. 'Telling me that you don't feel that electric charge between us?' He noted the blush that crept into her cheeks. 'Ah, yes. Of course you do. You're feeling it now. Why deny it?'

'I won't be…doing anything with you.' She wanted to walk through that door, head held high with contempt and hauteur, because he could buy her services but he *couldn't buy her*, but her feet were nailed to the ground and she found herself standing up but going nowhere.

'You're mistaking me for one of those women who *plant themselves in your line of vision*,' she continued, voice shaking with anger and mortification, 'but I'm not. Yes, I'm here because there's no other way I can pay off the money I owe you, and I can't let my colleague down because she would stand to lose out financially, just as I would if you called the debt in, but that doesn't give you the right to sit there and make a pass at me!'

Her feet finally remembered what they were there for and she stalked towards the door.

The sound of his voice saying her name brought her to an immediate stop. As noiseless as a predator stalking prey, he was right behind her when she spun round and she stumbled backwards a couple of steps, heart beating wildly behind her ribcage, her every sense alert to his commanding presence.

Her nostrils flared, an automatic reaction to the clean, woody scent of whatever aftershave he was wearing.

'Do you honestly think,' Matias asked in a voice that managed to be measured and yet icily condemnatory at the same time, 'that I might actually believe your body comes as part of the repayment schedule for the damage you did to my car?'

Sophie went bright red. Put like that, she could see what an idiot she'd been because when it came to women he certainly didn't need to use any unnecessary leverage. The guy could have whomever he wanted, whenever he wanted.

And he'd wanted her.

That treacherous thought slithered into her head, firing her up against her will.

'I suppose not,' she grudgingly conceded, 'but I

feel vulnerable being here, singing for my supper.' She looked away and then raised her bright blue eyes to his. 'I'm not anything like those women who were here this weekend…'

Matias's eyebrows shot up. 'I didn't think you'd noticed who was here and who wasn't.'

'I saw them coming and going through the kitchen window and some of the guests came on kitchen inspection a few times over the weekend.'

'And?'

'And what? They were all clones of one another. Tall and skinny and glamorous. I assumed that one of them might have been your…er…girlfriend.'

'If I had a girlfriend, we wouldn't be having this conversation.'

'We don't even like one another,' Sophie breathed, 'and *that's* why we shouldn't be having this conversation!'

'Do you have a boyfriend?'

'What if I had? Would it make a difference?'

'Possibly.' He tilted his head to one side. 'Possibly not. Why do you compare yourself to other women?'

'I'm just saying that I'd imagine those women you asked to your house here were exactly the sort of women you normally dated…and so what would you see in someone like me except *easy availability*?' She was playing with fire but the sizzling danger of this treading-on-thin-ice conversation was weirdly and intensely seductive. It was the sort of conversation she had never in her life had before with any man.

'Want me to spell it out for you?' Matias husked. 'Because I will, although I'd rather do that when you're lying naked in my bed.' He vaguely recalled when he had originally played with the notion of getting her be-tween the sheets because pillow talk might reveal se-crets he could use to his advantage. Standing here now, with a fierce erection that was demanding release, the only talking he wanted to do in bed was of the dirty variety. In fact, just thinking about it was driving him completely nuts.

He didn't know what it was about this woman but she made him lose his cool.

'And that won't be happening,' Sophie informed him prissily, edging back, away from the suffocating radius of his powerful personality. 'Ever!'

'Sure about that?' Matias laughed softly, fired up on every possible cylinder. 'Because that's not a con-cept I recognise.'

'Too bad,' Sophie muttered, and then she turned tail and fled before she could get even more sucked into a conversation that was dangerously explosive and *dangerously, dangerously exciting*.

Not even the luxury of her accommodation, which still made her gasp after four nights, or the calming, long bath she had could clear her head.

Matias's dark, brooding, insanely sexy face swam in her head, stirring her up and making it impossible for her to fall asleep and when, finally, she did, it was a restless, broken sleep until eventually, lying in the darkened room at nearly two in the morning, she de-cided that counting sheep wasn't getting her anywhere.

She made her way as quietly as she could towards the kitchen. Aside from the security lights outside, the house was shrouded in darkness, which should have been spooky but was strangely reassuring.

She already knew her way round the kitchen like the

back of her hand and there was no need for her to switch on any lights as she padded unhesitatingly towards the fridge to get some milk so that she could make herself a mug of hot chocolate. Time to find out whether it was true that hot chocolate encouraged sleep.

Stooping and reaching to the back of the shelf for the milk, Sophie was unaware of footsteps behind her and certainly, with only the light from the fridge, there were no helpful warning shadows cast so the sound of Matias's voice behind her came as a shock.

She straightened, slammed her head against the fridge shelf, sent various jars and bottles flying and stood up as red as a beetroot to confront a highly amused Matias staring down at her with his arms folded.

CHAPTER FIVE

BROKEN GLASS LAY around her. One of the jars had contained home-made raspberry jam. Sophie had remarked on how delicious it was when she had first had it on a slice of toast a few mornings ago and had been told that Mrs Porter, who lived in the village, made it and sold it in one of the local shops.

Sophie didn't think that Mrs Porter would have been impressed to see her hard work spilled all over the tiled kitchen floor like blobs of gelatinous blood. It joined several gherkins and streaks of expensive balsamic vinegar.

'Don't move,' Matias commanded.

'What are you doing here?' Sophie said accusingly, remaining stock-still because she was barefoot, but horribly aware of her state of undress. She hadn't dressed for company. It was a mild night and she had forsaken her towelling dressing gown and tiptoed downstairs in the little skimpy vest she wore on warm nights and the tiny pair of soft cotton pyjama shorts that left an indecent amount of thigh and leg on display.

Indecent, that was, if you happened to be in a kitchen with the man who had been haunting your dreams kneeling at your feet carefully picking up bits of glass.

He didn't look up at her. He seemed to be one hundred per cent focused on the spray of broken glass around her. Looks, however, could be deceiving for Matias was acutely aware of her standing there in a lack of clothing that was sending his blood pressure through the roof.

'I own the house,' he pointed out with infuriating, irrefutable logic as he continued with his glass retrieval while trying to divert his avid gaze from her fabulously sexy legs, pale and shapely in the shadowy darkness of the kitchen. 'I find that seems to give me the right to come and go as I please.'

'Very funny,' Sophie said tightly.

'I'm here for the same reason you are.' He sat back on his haunches to cast a satisfied look at his cleaning efforts, then he raised his eyes to hers and took his time looking at her. 'I couldn't sleep.'

'Actually, I was sleeping just fine.'

'Which is why you're here at a little after two in the morning?'

'I was thirsty.'

'Stay put. There are probably fine shards of glass on the ground still and I suppose I should clear up all this mess.' He seemed to give that a little thought. 'No. Scratch that. I'll leave the mess but I meant what I said about staying put and the shards of glass. Get a sliver of glass in your foot and you'll probably end up having to be taken to hospital.'

'Don't be ridiculous!' But she daren't move. Bleeding in his kitchen wasn't going to do. Coping with her embarrassing state of semi-nudity was definitely the better option. She would just have to stand here while he took his time removing every piece of glass from the floor.

She could have kicked herself for being so stupid but bumping into him was the last thing she had expected.

Meanwhile, she could barely look down at herself because all she could see was her pale skin, her braless breasts, which were unfashionably big, and her nipples poking against the fine ribbing of her vest.

And all she could do was to make unhelpful comparisons in her head. Comparisons between herself and the women who had been at his party. Next to most of the women there, she was the equivalent of a walking, talking dumpling, and while none of them had been his girlfriend Sophie had no doubt that those were exactly the sort of women he went for. Long and thin with poker-straight hair and faces that seemed to resent the business of occasionally having to smile.

'This could take for ever,' Matias gritted, standing up and peering down at the floor. 'I don't have for ever.' He stepped forward and before she had time to even open her mouth in protest he was scooping her up as though she weighed nothing.

'Good job I was sensible enough to come down here wearing shoes,' he murmured, grinning as he looked down at her.

'Put me down!'

'Not until you're safe and sound and not until I make sure that those very pretty feet of yours are free from any slivers of glass…'

'I'd know if I'd stepped on glass,' Sophie all but sobbed, acutely aware of the way her scraps of clothing were rucking up everywhere. One of her breasts was practically popping out of her vest. She couldn't bear to look. She wasn't wearing underwear and she could feel the petal softness of her womanhood scraping against the side of the pyjama shorts.

And worst of all was what her disobedient body was doing. Turned on by the strength of his arms and the iron-hard broadness of his muscular chest, her nipples were tight and pinched, the rosebud tips straining against the vest, and she was so wet between her legs.

She could only hope that he didn't notice any of that on the way to her room.

She squeezed her eyes shut and didn't open them when she felt him push open a bedroom door.

'Ostrich.' Matias was fully aware of her body, every succulent inch of it, soft and warm in his arms. He could just about see the rosy blush of a nipple peeping out. 'Why have you got your eyes shut?'

Sophie duly opened her eyes, glared at him and then, slowly but surely, it dawned on her that they weren't in her bedroom. He had taken her to a bedroom that was unapologetically male, from the chrome and glass of the fitted wardrobes to the walnut and steel of the bed, over which hung an abstract painting that was instantly recognisable, the bedroom she had frantically backed out of a few hours ago.

'Your bedroom.' She gulped, when her vocal cords finally decided to play ball.

'Let me check your feet.'

'Please, Matias…'

'Please, Matias…*what*?' He deposited her very gently on his bed, as though she were as fragile as a piece of porcelain, but he wasn't looking at her. Instead, he was once again kneeling in front of her and he then proceeded to take one foot in his big hand, to inspect it closely for wayward glass.

It was ludicrous!

But the feel of his hands on her...wreaked havoc with her senses and also felt just so...*sexy*.

Something that sounded very much like a whimper emerged from her throat and their eyes met.

Understanding passed between them, as loud and clear as the clanging of church bells on a still Sunday morning.

Desire. Loud and thick and electric and definitely mutual.

'We can't,' was what Sophie heard herself whimper, breaking the silence between them. She didn't even bother to pretend that she didn't know what was going on any more than he pretended not to recognise the capitulation behind that ragged, half-hearted protest.

'Why not?' Matias had thought about sleeping with her for his own purposes but now he couldn't remember what those purposes were because cold self-control had been replaced with a raging urgency to take her to bed whatever the cost.

'Because this isn't a normal situation.'

'Define normal.'

'Two people who want to have a relationship.'

'I won't deny that I don't do relationships, but sex doesn't always have to lead to a once-in-a-lifetime relationship.'

'Not for you,' Sophie whispered as her resolve seeped away the longer he looked at her with those dark, sinfully sexy eyes. 'But for me...' She turned away and swallowed painfully.

Matias joined her on the bed and gently tilted her head back to his. 'For you?'

'My mother wasn't careful when it came to men,' she

told him bluntly. 'She was very attractive…she had that *something* that men seem to find irresistible…'

'You talk as though that *something* is something you don't possess.'

'I don't,' she said simply, raising her eyes to his and holding his gaze with unwavering sincerity. 'Men have never walked into lampposts when I sauntered past, they've never begged or pleaded or shown up with armfuls of roses in the hope that I might climb into bed with them.'

'And they did all those things for your mother?'

'She had that effect on them.'

'If that were the case, why didn't she and your father marry…considering he fathered a child with her?'

Sophie opened her mouth to tell him that James Carney had fathered more than one child but something held her back. What? Was it her fierce protectiveness over Eric? A need, born of habit, to save him from the curiosity of other people, even though he wouldn't have cared less?

Or was it a hangover from the way Alan had ended up reacting to her disabled brother?

Sophie told herself that she didn't care one way or another what a perfect stranger thought of her situation, least of all someone like Matias. She told herself that if he planned on doing business with her father, then the presence of her disabled brother wouldn't matter a jot, and yet she pulled back from the brink and swallowed down the brief temptation to spill her guts. She was a little startled that she had even been tempted to tell him at all.

'James always thought that he was too good for my mother.' Sophie hid the hurt behind that crisply delivered statement of fact. 'He was rich and he was posh and he didn't think that my mother was the right sort of woman for him.'

Matias's jaw clenched because this came as no surprise at all to him, and Sophie saw his instinctive reaction with a trace of alarm as she remembered how important it was for him to inject money into her father's nearly bankrupt company.

'It happens.' She shrugged and moved on quickly. 'You might fancy me, but you can't pretend that you don't feel the same way about me as he did about my mother. You're rich and powerful and it doesn't matter who my father is or isn't—the fact is that I have never grown up in the sort of circles you would have moved in.'

'You don't know what sort of circles I moved in as a child,' Matias heard himself say. He was uneasily aware that this was a deviation from his normal handling of any sort of *situation* with a woman. Since when had he turned into the sort of touchy-feely person who wanted to waste time talking when a perfectly good bed beckoned?

'I can guess. I'm not stupid.'

'You're anything but stupid. Although it *was* fairly stupid of you to be driving without insurance.'

'Please don't remind me.'

'My parents had no money,' Matias said abruptly. 'They should have but they didn't. I grew up as the kid on the wrong side of the tracks. I went to a tough comprehensive where I learned that the only way to get out in one piece was to be tougher than everyone else, so I was.'

Sophie's mouth fell open, partly because this was so

unexpected but mostly because he was confiding in her and everything was telling her that this was a proud, arrogant man who never confided in anyone.

She felt a little thrill and her heart turned over because the unexpected confidence marked something more between them than *lust*. You didn't confide like that in someone you just wanted to take to bed and throw away afterwards.

Sophie didn't work that out in any way that was coherent or analytical. It was more of a *feeling* that swept through her and in the wake of that *feeling* she softened. *This was how barriers got broken down; this was how defences were surmounted.*

Except she wasn't thinking any of that right now, she was just ensnared by a desire to know more about him.

'Enough talking,' Matias said gruffly, meaning it. 'Because I'm rich and powerful now doesn't mean that I don't fancy you for all the right reasons.'

'Which are what?' Sophie whispered, and Matias dealt her a slow, slashing smile that sent every nerve in her body quivering in high excitement.

'You have a body I would walk over broken glass to touch,' he expanded, not touching her but wanting to with every pore in his body.

'Don't be silly.' She laughed shakily, driven to bring this whole crazy situation down to a prosaic, pedestrian place because she just couldn't quite believe that she was impressionable enough to be swept off her feet by a man like him. 'I'm short and I'm…well covered. The world is full of short, plump women like me. We're a dime a dozen.'

'You're doing it again, running yourself down. You shouldn't, because what you have is more than just a body I could find anywhere.' He laughed. 'You might think that your dear mama failed to pass on that special *something* but you'd be wrong because you definitely have it in bucketloads.'

Don't say that, something in Sophie wanted to yell, but over and above that was a hot yearning at the soft, lazy timbre of his voice and a melting feeling at the way he was looking at her. This was the sort of textbook situation she had always cautioned herself against and yet here she was, blossoming like a flower in the sunshine and wanting this inappropriate man more than she could have ever believed possible.

Belatedly, she realised that her clothes were still askew, her vest tugged down, her shorts scrunched up at the crotch. She shifted and just like that words melted away, replaced by the delicious frisson of burning desire.

Matias straightened. A full moon streamed through the floor-to-ceiling panes of glass, casting a silvery glow through the room. She was so beautiful that he could barely contain himself. And *still* he wasn't sure what she would do if he touched her.

Or what *he* would do if he touched her and she turned away. A cold bath wouldn't begin to sort it out.

He didn't have long to ponder the problem because she took the decision right out of his hands. She reached up and stroked the side of his face, her huge eyes wide, her full mouth softly parted.

Matias caught her hand and drew her finger into his mouth. His gaze didn't leave hers as he sucked it, sucked it so that she knew that that was just how he was going to suck her nipple and, without even realising it, she responded by pushing her breasts out. Her nipples were tingling. Eyes half closed, she gasped when he slid his hand under the vest and cupped her breast.

He still had her finger in his mouth and was still sucking it, and still holding her gaze, his dark eyes lazy and hypnotic as he rolled his finger over the stiffened bud of her nipple. That was all he did and it was enough for her body to shriek into a response that was a hair's breadth away from orgasmic.

It was electrifying.

Sophie moaned. 'I want you.'

Matias held her hand, playing with the wet tip of her finger. 'Your wish is my command. You want me? Rest assured that you will have me, as hard and as often as you want.'

She'd expected him to drive into her without further ado. She could see the hunger in his dark eyes and it matched hers. He didn't. Instead, he arranged her on the bed, straddled her for a few seconds and then slowly pulled down her shorts.

She was so soft, so silky smooth, her skin so pale in the moonlight. He had to stare and even as he stared he did his damnedest to control his breathing, but he was so turned on that he had to make an effort to remember that breathing involved sucking air in and releasing it out.

In one swift movement, he stood up, holding her riveted attention, and stripped off.

Sophie had never seen anything so magnificent in her entire life. No artist would have been able to do justice to the sheer perfection of his body. A broad chest tapered down to a washboard-flat stomach and then lower, to an erection that was impressively huge, a thick, long shaft of steel that made her want to pass out because she was so turned on.

She'd had one serious boyfriend. Her level of experience was very definitely on the lower end of the spectrum and nothing had prepared her for the impact of being in the grip of true, shameless, wanton desire. Desire shorn of everything but a need to live for the moment and take what was on offer. Desire that was looking for nothing beyond the next sixty seconds and the sixty seconds after that.

Sophie would never have believed herself capable of actually *being here and being this person* because it contravened all her principles. But now that she *was* here, she felt wildly, wickedly decadent.

Naked, Matias spread apart her legs and then lowered himself to do something that felt so intimate that she froze for a few seconds.

'Problem?' he purred and she blushed madly.

'I've never had anyone do…that…'

'Then relax and enjoy. Trust me, you'll be begging for more.' With which, he flattened her thighs wide open, hands placed squarely on them, and he lowered his dark head between her legs. His tongue was delicate between her wet folds and then, delving deeper, he found and teased her clitoris until he could feel it throbbing. Her whimpers became cries mixed with moans. Her fingers dived into his dark hair. One minute, she was pushing him down to suck her harder, the next she was tugging him up and squirming in a futile attempt to control her reaction.

Sophie had never, ever felt anything like this before. She hadn't known that this level of pleasure even existed. She half opened her eyes and his dark head moving between her legs made her shudder and gasp. She bucked against his mouth as the rush of building pleasure began to consume her, began to take over her body, then she was coming and she could no more stop the crescendo of her orgasm than she could have stopped a runaway train with the palm of her outstretched hand.

She cried out and then panted and arched and cried out again as she spasmed against his mouth.

It seemed to last for ever.

'Matias…' this when she was finally back down on planet earth '…you shouldn't have…'

'Shouldn't have what?' He had moved up to lie alongside her and he tugged her so that their bodies were pressed so closely against one another that they could have been joined. 'Pleasured you? I wanted to. I wanted to taste you in my mouth when you came.'

'It's not just about me.'

'Kiss me and hold me. You're so beautiful. I want to feel your mouth on me…but first I need to taste your breasts. I've been fantasising about them for so long. I want to see if they taste the way I imagined they do.'

'You've been fantasising about my breasts?'

'It's hardly my fault that they're so damned gloriously big.'

'Too big.'

Matias propped himself up on one elbow to examine them. He circled one nipple with his finger, watched it pinch and stiffen. She had generous full breasts and her nipples were boldly defined circular discs. He leant down and delicately darted his tongue over one and then he suckled on it. It tasted better than his wildest imaginings. Sweet as nectar, yet with the tang of salt.

It throbbed in his mouth as he drew it in and the touch of her hand at the nape of his neck and then curled into his hair was the most powerful aphrodisiac imaginable.

She was so headily responsive and yet she wasn't doing the usual gymnastics that so many of the women he bedded performed, gymnastics they always hoped would impress him enough to cement their staying power in his life.

Sophie was honest in all her responses and her little whimpers of pleasure carried a note that was almost of surprise, as if every touch was new and pretty sensational.

Good God, he thought, hanging on to restraint by a thread, a man could get addicted to this sort of thing. It was just as well that he was cool-headed enough to recognise this for what it was and to recognise himself for what *he* was. He was immune to being snared even by a woman who was driving him crazy.

He guided her mouth to his erection and knew, in the way she hesitated at first, that this was probably new to her as well, and that gave him a kick as powerful as a rocket launcher.

Sophie licked his shaft and enjoyed the way he shuddered. It made her feel more comfortable about coming into his mouth the way she had, with such wild abandon. Then she took him in her mouth and built up a rhythm of sucking that had him groaning out loud as his fingers tangled in her silver-blonde hair.

Her experience ran to the very basic when it came to sex. Her innocent fumblings with Alan, the guy she had thought she might end up marrying, were a thousand light years away from…*this*.

Her body was aching and yearning and tingling all

over again. She released him and lay down again, her back arched, her hair fanning out on the pillow, her eyes closed. He was watching her. She could feel it and it thrilled her.

When she sneaked a peek, she blushed shyly and was tempted to cover her breasts with her hands but she didn't.

'I want you,' Matias groaned heavily and she sighed and smiled at the same time, not quite believing what they were doing but wanting more of it and wanting it *now*.

'Then take me,' she whispered.

The seconds it took for him to fetch a condom and put it on felt like hours because she was so hot for him.

She parted her legs and then the joy and pleasure of him entering her made her heart swell and turned her on in every corner of her body. He thrust long and deep and hard and built a rhythm that started slow, getting firmer and stronger until their bodies were moving as one.

She was so tuned into him…it felt as though they had been lovers for ever. She knew when he was going to come as surely as she knew when *she* was, and when he groaned and arched back, his big, powerful body shuddering, she, too, felt her own body ascending to a climax, coming along with him, moving to the same primitive beat.

Spent, Sophie lay in his arms. His breathing was still a shallow rasp and she could feel the perspiration binding their bodies, making them hot and slippery. It felt so good and she wriggled and nestled into him, enjoying the way his arms clasped around her.

Did she fall asleep? She must have done although when she drowsily opened her eyes she was still wrapped in his arms, his thigh between her legs, her breasts squashed against his chest.

Half asleep, she reached down to touch him and felt the immediate stir of his body as he came to life in her hands. He was no more awake than she was. He was warm and half asleep and so was she, and the merging of their bodies was as natural and instinctive as the rising and setting of the sun or the changing of the tides.

When she woke the following morning, the sun was creeping into the room, weak and grey. There was a fine drizzle of rain. Where was Matias? Not lying next to her. Sophie yawned and shifted, turning onto her side to find him working at the desk by the window.

Matias heard the sound of her stirring and immediately stiffened because this whole situation had unnerved him. The sex had been amazing but afterwards…

Hell, they had fallen asleep together, wrapped around one another like clambering vines. Sleeping was something he did on his own. Women lay in his bed for sex but retreated to another bed for sleep or, better still, cleared off. Yet he had thought nothing of falling asleep with her in his arms, and then, in the middle of the night, they had made love again, and without protection. He'd barely been awake and it had been the most mind-blowing experience of his life, almost dreamlike and yet at the same time so exquisitely *real*. Their bodies had joined together and fused and he'd come explosively.

And now…

'We didn't use contraception.' He swivelled to face her, his body already responding to her warm, flushed face and the peep of her soft, generous breasts. He wanted to have her again immediately and that unnerved him as well.

'Huh?'

'Last night. You woke me up and we made love without protection.'

Sophie shot up into a sitting position, pulling her knees towards her. 'I—I didn't think…' she stammered. She wouldn't be pregnant. She *couldn't* be pregnant. Alarm and dismay flooded her face. 'There's no way there could be an accident,' she shot back, eyes huge. 'It's the wrong time of the month for me…'

Was it? She was too fraught to do the maths.

'And I couldn't be *that* unlucky.'

Disconcerted, Matias frowned. 'Unlucky?'

Sophie leapt out of the bed, belatedly remembered that she was buck naked and dragged the duvet out to cover her. Having sex with no protection had catapulted him right back to the conniving girlfriend who had almost booked herself a trip down the aisle on the back of a fake pregnancy scare, but the horror writ large on Sophie's expressive face was telling a different story and as she scuttled away from him his instinct wasn't to pursue his accusations. His instinct was to chase her right back into his bed.

'Do you honestly think I would *want* to find myself pregnant by *you*?' Her voice was high and unsteady.

Matias stood up, as sleek and graceful as a panther, and as dangerous to her state of mind. 'Why are you bothering to try and cover yourself? I've seen you in your birthday suit and, besides, your left breast is out.'

Sophie looked down and was confronted by the sight of her pink nipple perkily defying her attempts at concealment. When she raised her eyes again it was to find Matias standing right in front of her. He had slipped on his boxers to work but aside from that he was gloriously naked and she almost fainted at the surge of desire that swept through her like a tidal wave.

'You don't mean it when you say that you'd be unlucky if you discovered you were pregnant by me,' he grated and Sophie glared at him.

'You're *so* arrogant.'

'You like it.'

'You're *so* not my type.'

'You like that too. It's boring when you're with someone who's just like you. Where's the excitement in that?'

'I don't want exciting. I've *never* wanted exciting. My mother wasted most of her life *wanting exciting.*'

'You're not your mother,' Matias returned without skipping a beat, settling his hands on her soft shoulders and gently massaging them. 'And you may not want *exciting* but that doesn't mean that your goal in life should be to settle for *deadly dull*. I'm taking it,' he continued, the low, lazy drawl of his voice sending shivers up and down her spine, 'that you're putting me in the *exciting* category.'

'This isn't funny, Matias!'

'It's anything but,' he agreed. 'Especially,' he surprised himself by adding, 'considering I had a narrow escape with a woman who claimed to be pregnant so that she could get me to put a wedding band on her finger.'

'What?' Sophie tried to recapture some of the anger she had felt but his fingers were doing things to her body and she was relaxing and unbending and turning into a rag doll at his touch.

She was also, she discovered, heading back to the bed, a fact she only realised when she toppled back onto the mattress, with the duvet flying off her, leaving him in no doubt that, for all her protests, she was most definitely turned on by him. The tips of her nipples were stiff peaks and the rub of wetness between her legs was practically audible.

Matias didn't give her time to think. He'd never considered himself the sort of guy who could fall prey to the mindless demands of his body, but he was discovering that that was just the sort of guy she turned him into. It wasn't going to last longer than a heartbeat so why, he thought, shouldn't he just yield and enjoy the once-in-a-lifetime experience?

He shoved her over so that he could take up position lying next to her and before she could start protesting he slipped his hands between her legs and edged his finger into her, feeling her wetness with a soft moan of satisfaction.

'Stop doing that,' Sophie protested, squirming half-heartedly to distance herself from his exploring fingers. 'I can't think when you do that. You're arrogant and you have a nerve implying that I would be the sort of girl who would engineer a pregnancy to try and get you up the aisle!'

'Did I imply that?'

'Yes, you did! What girlfriend?'

Matias lay back and stared up at the ceiling. 'I was young and cocky and on my way up. I thought I knew it all and could take on anything. Turned out I was no match for a woman who wanted to start at ground zero with me. She'd spotted my potential. I was already a massive earner by then and driving around like a strutting bull in a red Ferrari.'

'Obnoxious, in other words,' Sophie muttered darkly, but she was secretly won over by the way he could mock himself.

'Very,' Matias confirmed drily. 'She told me she was pregnant. Turned out she wasn't but that was something I only discovered by accident.'

'You told me I'm not my mother,' Sophie ventured, still on the defence and still smarting but wanting him so badly it hurt, 'and I'm not your ex-girlfriend.' She wasn't going to curl into him, which was what she wanted to do, but she wasn't turning away either. She couldn't.

'And now that we've established that…' he moved his hand away from the dampness between her legs to her breast and the teasing pink nipple begging to be licked '…why don't we skip breakfast and carry on with our magical mystery tour of one another?'

'I have to get back to London,' Sophie said raggedly, her body already quivering in acquiescence.

'No, you don't. Have you forgotten that you have a debt to settle?'

'Not like this!'

'No,' Matias agreed seriously, 'not like this, but I *would* like to commission you to cook me breakfast and I'm not hungry yet, at least not for food.'

'Matias…'

'I want you in my bed, Sophie, and then, when we've made love and I've pleasured you in every way I know how, I would like to employ you to prepare breakfast for me because there's still the matter of that pesky debt to be paid off. Will you do that?'

'I'll do that.' Sophie frowned. 'But when we leave here…'

Matias raised his eyebrows and teased the fluff between her legs until he could see her thoughts getting all tangled up in her head. 'Hmm…?'

'When we leave here,' she panted, giving in as he

knew she would, 'none of this happened. Okay? I go back to being the caterer you employ so that I can pay off the money I owe you. It's back to business.'

'Sure,' he agreed smoothly, wanting her even more now that she was setting just the sort of rules and regulations that should, in theory, appeal to him, because they were exactly the ones he would set himself. 'But enough talking…'

CHAPTER SIX

FOR THE FIRST time since she had arrived, Sophie was able to appreciate Matias's sprawling mansion at leisure because she stayed to cook him breakfast the following morning and the morning after that.

'But I thought all the guests had gone,' Julie had proffered in a puzzled voice, when Sophie had phoned and told her the situation.

Sophie had muttered something and nothing about not all the guests having gone just yet, and what choice did she have considering she was indebted to the man and so had to do as he commanded or else face having their business dismantled like a house of Lego bricks in the hands of a hyperactive toddler.

She could just about extrapolate sufficient truth from what she had said to paper over her guilt at playing truant, because that was what it felt like.

She was preparing breakfast for Matias but that was just a nonsense excuse for what she was really doing. She was his lover and she was enjoying every second of it. Having curled up into herself after her experience with Alan, she was feeling liberated in a way she had never hoped to be. She was, she felt, on a journey of self-discovery and she had stopped asking herself how that was possible when Matias was so unsuitable. She just knew that he gave something to her, added some crazy dimension to her life that made her forget all the principles she had spent her life nurturing.

She was being reckless for the first time in her life and she was liking it.

You're not your mother, Matias had told her and she had actually listened and allowed herself to unbend and live a little without beating herself up about it. Okay, so Matias wasn't going to be around for ever but that didn't mean that she was going to suddenly develop a taste for inappropriate men. No, Matias was her walk on the wild side and why shouldn't she enjoy him while she had the chance?

He was rich, he was powerful, he was arrogant and he was self-assured to the point of ridiculous, but he was also, she had discovered, an extremely thoughtful lover, a good laugh, was weirdly tuned into her thoughts and just so, so unbelievably clever.

Hovering on the fringes of her enjoyment, however, was the looming certainty that he wouldn't be around for much longer, although when she thought about that a guilty little voice whispered in her head, *But won't he be...? After all, you'll still have to pay off the rest of your debt...maybe there'll be more breakfasts to be prepared...*

Breakfast this morning had been an elaborate concoction of eggs, spinach, ham and a hollandaise sauce on freshly baked bread.

The smell of the bread still lingered in the kitchen as Sophie tidied away the dishes while Matias reclined at the kitchen table like a lord and master, replete after having his appetite sated.

She turned around and he beckoned her across and patted his lap.

'Sit,' he commanded with a grin, watching as she sashayed towards him, fresh as a flower without make-up and sexy as hell in some cut-off faded jeans and a baggy tee shirt.

She wasn't wearing a bra. He liked her without one. He liked being able to reach out and touch her without having to go through the bother of unclasping boring fastenings.

They'd been larking around for two days like teen-agers and Matias still couldn't get enough of her. He hadn't steered the conversation towards her father again. Hadn't even thought about it. The only thing on his mind had been her fabulous body and what it did to him.

'Nice breakfast,' he murmured as she settled obedi-ently on his lap. He slipped his hand under the tee shirt, found the generous swell of her breast and the tight bud of her nipple, then he lifted the shirt and angled her so that she was straddling him and began suckling at her breast.

He had no idea what she possessed that could make him act like a horny teenager but she had it. In his saner moments, he remembered who she was and what his original plan had been in getting her to repay her debt by working for him. Unfortunately, those saner mo-ments had been rarer than hen's teeth.

Watching her bustle about his kitchen, in a parody of domesticity that should have sent him running for the hills, had kick-started a nice little erection and suck-ing her nipple now was intensifying it to the point of painful.

He shifted under her and felt her smile as she reached

down and found his hard shaft, holding it firmly but getting little traction because of his jeans.

Too little traction. He adjusted his big body and, reading him and responding instinctively, Sophie slid off his lap, discarding her tee shirt along the way, and then she eased off his trousers with a little help from him.

He was so beautiful he took her breath away. She couldn't believe that in a space of just a few days she had moved from novice to wanton, had blossomed under his touch like a plant given life-saving nutrients. He'd encouraged her to touch, to experiment, to wallow in his open adoration of her body. He'd been a masterful teacher. He'd lavished attention on every inch of her body and taught her just how to touch him and where to make him feel good.

Now, with his trousers and boxers in a heap on the ground, she took his thick shaft between her hands and played with him, absolutely enjoying the way he slid a little further down the chair and loving the guttural moan that escaped his lips. His hand cupped the crown of her head as she took him into her mouth and his fingers curled into her hair as she began to suck.

They were in their private paradise, a delicious bubble where they had been able to indulge their appetite for one another without interruption, a bubble in which thoughts and conjectures and *reality*, at least *for her*, had not been allowed to intrude.

She stood up, noting that his eyes were closed, those thick, lush lashes casting shadows on his razor-sharp cheekbones. His nostrils were flared. He knew what she was going to do and was lazily waiting to be pleasured.

Sophie couldn't get her jeans and underwear off fast

enough. He did that to her, made her whole body agitate with an urgency to be satisfied. She was wet between her legs, dripping, aching to have him inside her.

She knew where he kept his condoms and quickly fetched one from the wallet in his trousers on the ground. They had made love without protection that one single time and never again. Now, she slipped a condom out of its foil and took him between her hands so that she could put it on him.

His eyes were slumberous on her, hotly working her up to a peak of excitement, and she groaned out loud as she lowered herself onto him, her every nerve ending tingling as he circled her waist with his big hands, then she was moving on him, pressing down to feel him deep inside her, letting him take her to places only he could.

He levered her head towards him and kissed her as she moved on him, a deep, hungry, urgent kiss that made her moan and then she was coming, hurtling towards that peak of satisfaction, her body moving in perfect rhythm with his until the world exploded and all she could feel was the intense pleasure of her climax that went on and on, subsiding eventually in little, erotic waves that left her shaking and trembling.

She sagged against him, head against his chest, listening to his slow, ragged breathing that very gradually returned to normal. They were both practically slipping off the chair and she reluctantly climbed off him and began sticking back on her clothes.

He looked so peaceful there, his big body relaxed, his eyes half closed as he watched her scramble to put on her tee shirt and then hop into her underwear.

He wasn't at all self-conscious about his body. Where, even now that they had made love what felt like a thousand times, she still needed to put on her clothes rather than parade her nudity, he couldn't care less.

He stood up, flexed his muscles and looked at her sideways with a satisfied smile.

'Work is beginning to call,' he drawled, eyeing the puddle of clothes on the ground and deigning to put on his jeans but nothing else. 'She's an extremely demanding mistress.'

'Yes, I have to get back as well.' Sophie's heart sank but she smiled brightly at him. 'Julie's beginning to tear her hair out because we've just landed a pretty big order and it's hard planning a menu together over text or on the phone.'

'You still owe me for my car...' He swerved round her and, standing behind, wrapped his arms around her waist and leant down so that he was talking into her hair, his voice a little muffled.

Sophie literally thrilled. She couldn't help grinning from ear to ear. She knew that this situation wasn't going to last and was probably the least sensible thing she could be doing but the pull of having fun was irresistible. She couldn't think beyond it.

'But,' Matias continued gravely, 'you're paying off the debt quickly. That said... I might still need you to do some catering for me and I rather enjoy the private catering you've been providing, by which I mean those excellent breakfast options you've presented to me.'

Sophie swivelled round so that they were facing one another and she looked up at him. 'I like cooking you breakfast,' she told him. 'Do we...er...put a date in the diary? How does this work?' She sighed and reached up to link her fingers behind his neck. 'I mean, Matias, how does this *really* work? Is there a time frame? And if I choose to stop…*this*…then what happens? I feel vulnerable thinking that we've entered new territory.'

'Do you think I'm going to penalise you if you decide you want to stop being my lover? I won't. I'm not that kind of guy. You're free to make your choice. I still want you, Sophie, but there's no way I want you to feel that you're somehow committed to pleasing me for fear of what I might do if you change your mind.'

The bubble was beginning to burst. They weren't going to be in one another's company twenty-four-seven, making love, talking, making love again. True, Matias had taken himself off for brief periods to work, during which time she had video called Julie so that she, too, could remember that real life was going on outside his glasshouse mansion, but most of their time had been spent in one another's company.

Living in the moment had been easy. She had been able to turn a blind eye to real life because real life was located somewhere outside the glass and concrete of his house. Real life was back in London. Well, they were returning to London soon and although she had told him that, once they left, what they had would come to an end, she didn't want it to end and that frightened her.

They hadn't mentioned actual numbers at all in terms of the money she still owed him for the damage to his car. She didn't care about that because she had discovered that, despite the fact that he could be stunningly arrogant, he was also incredibly fair and incredibly honourable.

What did concern her was the deal he was considering making with her father. That, too, was a subject that hadn't been raised, but it would be just as soon as they drove away from their little bubble and the real world started to intrude. She had promoted James Carney as someone he *should* deal with, had sidestepped most of the truth about her father because what was at stake was the fate of her beloved brother.

Suddenly it was vitally important that she tell him about Eric. She didn't have to compromise any deal Matias wanted to do with her father, but at least when the deal was done and should her father show his true colours, *which wasn't inevitable because he would be on the back foot*, Matias would put two and two together and understand why she had done what she had, why she hadn't warned him off.

Not that, Sophie feverishly told herself, there would be any problems. Her father was broke. He needed Matias. He would be on best behaviour.

'Good,' she said vaguely, wondering how to send the conversation in the direction in which she wanted it to go and finally deciding to just say what she had to say. 'And about my father...'

'Yes?' Matias's ears pricked up. He marvelled that this was the first time Carney had been mentioned in their couple of days alone together when the original purpose of her being here was to provide information that he could use. It irked him that he had been so sidetracked by her that he had taken his eye off the ball.

'Will you still...er...be interested in investing money in his company?' Sophie had the whole back story about Eric prepared for Matias and was a little taken aback at the sudden deathly silence that greeted her question.

'Ah. We haven't discussed that, have we?'

'I guess there have been a few distractions.' She laughed nervously.

'So there have.' Matias looked at her coolly, his quick

brain putting two and two together and not liking what he was coming up with.

'What's wrong?'

'What makes you think that something's wrong, Sophie?'

'I don't know. What have I said? I just thought that… we're going to be leaving here and I wanted to talk about what happens next.'

'Why would that lead to a discussion of my plans for your father? But now that we're on the subject…you've, apparently, no idea about the ugly business of making money, but did you know your father is…shall we say… battling one or two financial problems…?' Matias was watching her intently and he was as still as a statue.

She knew. It was there, written plainly on her face. She'd played the clueless card, but she'd known all along that her old man was broke. She wasn't even trying to deny it.

'And,' Matias continued, testing the ground as the steady burn of rage began to build inside him, 'of course, if any deal is to go through, then there will have to be certain background checks…'

'Background checks?' she squeaked.

Matias shrugged but he was picking up everything he wanted to know and more from her reaction. 'The business community is a small world. There have been certain rumours of shady dealings…'

Sophie's face drained of colour. Her legs felt shaky. Her brain was in meltdown as she thought of what would be revealed in *background checks*. She knew nothing for sure, but she suspected…

'Surely that wouldn't be necessary,' she whispered.

'Oh, dear.' Used. He'd been used. She'd slept with

him to facilitate a deal with her father whom she knew to be penniless and crooked. She was clearly running scared from background checks that she must know could open up a can of worms. He'd got the information he'd wanted after all, but the fury of finding himself played once again was volcanic in its intensity. 'You seem apprehensive. Did you think that you could *distract* me into putting money into your bank account without doing my homework thoroughly?'

Sophie's face drained of colour as she tried to make sense of what he was saying but the dots weren't joining up. What was he implying?

Some part of her was desperate to give him the benefit of the doubt and to find a reasonable explanation for the cold, veiled expression on his handsome face but a chill was growing inside her and it make her feel sick and giddy.

'I d-don't know what you're talking about,' she stammered.

'Don't you?' Not even his duplicitous ex-girlfriend from long ago had managed to produce a rage like this. He'd learned *nothing* because he'd been conned again. If he'd smashed his fist against the wall, he would have driven it right through the brickwork, so powerful was the torrent of emotion coursing through his body. 'I don't know why I didn't stop to question your sudden departure from shy and blushing to hot and ready for sex.'

'That's an awful thing to say!'

'If memory serves me right, you had your claws out when we first met…'

'Because you were horrible to me! Because you threatened to shut down my business to pay off a debt!'

'But then we came to a satisfactory conclusion, didn't we? But when did you decide to hop in the sack with me? Was it when you found out that I might decide to have business dealings with your father? Did you think that you were clever in trying to withhold the true state of your father's coffers and the fact that he's a crook? Did you think that your sexy body would seal the deal for me regardless of that?'

Sophie stared at him round-eyed. She was looking at a stranger. Gone was the teasing, seductive guy who could turn her off and on like a light switch.

'No! I would never do something like that! The only reason I mentioned my father and…well…is because I wanted to tell you something that…'

Matias held up one imperious hand. 'Not interested. The fact is there's something you should know.' He killed the tight knot in the pit of his stomach. Sex was sex but business was business and this was the business of retribution and he'd been a fool to have ever been distracted by her gorgeous body and beautiful, duplicitous face.

Sophie was spellbound, filled with creeping dread and apprehension. He was pacing the kitchen, restless and somehow vaguely menacing in the soft prowl of his movements.

'Regrettably, you've got hold of the wrong end of the stick. The fact is, the only interest I have in your father won't be leading to any lucrative deals that might result in more money lining your pockets.' He looked at her flushed face narrowly and it got on his nerves that he half wanted her to deny that she had any interest in any of her father's money that might come her way, but she remained silent and he could tell from the expression on her face that money trickling down into her grasping little hands had been exactly what she had hoped for.

She'd turned into his compliant lover because sex was a most persuasive tool. His mouth tightened and cold hostility settled like glacial ice in his veins.

'You don't understand,' Sophie protested weakly, but everything seemed to be moving at bewildering speed and her brain couldn't keep up.

'I think I understand very well indeed. But here's what *you* don't understand. Not only will I *not* be putting money into your father's business, but my intention couldn't be more different. I won't be the making of your bankrupt, disreputable scumbag of a father. I will be the ruination of him.' He clenched his jaw as her mouth fell open and the colour drained away from her face. 'You may not remember but I mentioned in passing to you that my parents should have had money and all the little luxuries that go with the sort of well-oiled lifestyle your daddy dearest enjoyed, but sadly they didn't.'

'I remember… I meant to ask you about that…but…'

'Distractions…ah, yes, they got in the way.' Matias smiled coldly. 'Let me fill in the gaps. Your father stole my father's invention and used it to prop up the sad sack company he had inherited that was already on its last legs, and in the process made himself rich beyond most people's wildest dreams. My father was naïve and trusting, a simple emigrant who believed the rubbish your father told him about them going in as partners, jointly reaping the financial rewards of something my father invented. I know, because I've seen the proof of those conversations with my own eyes in letters that were kept in a folder. It never occurred to my parents that they could have taken the man through the courts and got what they deserved.'

'No.' But she already believed every word that was being said because that was very much the sort of thing her father would have done.

'My father never recovered from the betrayal of his trust. What your father did infected every area of my family's life. My father died prematurely from a rare cancer and do you want to hear the worst of it? I recently found more letters, hidden away amongst my mother's things, begging letters from my mother to your father, pleading for some money to send my father to America where groundbreaking work was being done in that area, clinical trials that were beyond my parents' meagre means.'

'I'm so sorry,' Sophie whispered brokenly.

'So,' Matias rammed home, every syllable filled with icy condemnation made all the more biting because he knew that he had allowed himself to drift into territory he should never have occupied, 'my intention was always to make your father pay for what he did.'

'What are you saying?'

'I think you know. I knew about Carney's penury. I wanted more information and I got it. A stint in jail seems appropriate considering what he did, wouldn't you agree? So thank you for corroborating what I suspected. Now I know exactly which rocks to turn over when I have your daddy's company in my hands.'

A wave of sickness swept through her. She had accepted that they were ships passing in the night and had justified her extraordinary response to him on all sorts of grounds about lust and desire, but now that the extent of his deception was unravelling in front of her she knew that she had felt a great deal more for him than lust or desire.

He had managed in drawing out a side of her that she hadn't known existed. He had made her laugh and forget all the worries that plagued her. When she had been with him, she had stopped being the girl who had been let down by an ex, the girl who had to grovel for handouts, the girl with the disabled brother whom she fiercely protected, the girl whose career could crash and burn at any moment, leaving her nowhere. When she'd been with Matias, unlikely as it was, she had been carefree and sexy and *young*.

But that had been an illusion because he had used her to get information about her father out of her, and the depth of her hurt was suffocating.

'I played right into your hands with that accident, didn't I?' Her voice was stilted but despair, as toxic as acid, was filling every corner of her. 'You don't care a jot that *I* never hurt your family.' She wasn't going to try and explain anything about Eric to him now, nothing at all, and she hated herself for allowing him to get so close, close enough for her to have been tempted to open up about her beloved brother. This ruthless, unfeeling man in front of her wouldn't even care. 'Did you even fancy me?' Tears stung the backs of her eyes. She was asking questions and she didn't want to know the answers but she couldn't help herself.

Matias flushed darkly. It pained him to see the wounded hurt in her eyes but he wasn't going to be sidetracked by that. This time he was going to stick to the brief. No way was he going to let her swing the tables round and cast him in the role of the criminal.

She'd been after money and that was the long and short of it, end of story.

'I should have stopped to ask myself why a man like you would have looked twice at me,' Sophie continued bitterly.

'Can you deny,' Matias intoned coldly, 'that you wanted me to pour money into your father's company because you knew that, if I did, some of it would inevitably come your way?'

Sophie closed her eyes.

She had needed that money but she would die before she explained it to him now. Instead she had to accept that she had been a tool to be exploited by him in his search for revenge. They hadn't been getting closer. That had all been in her stupid mind because he hated her for a crime she hadn't committed.

Matias noted that she couldn't even meet his eyes and he bunched his fists, resisting the urge to punch something very, very hard. He was uncomfortable in his own skin and that enraged him. He moved to the door, remained there for a few seconds, his body deathly still and yet seeming to exude a savage, restless energy.

'Our return to London will mark the end of any relationship between us.'

'But what about the money I still owe you?' Panicked, she licked her lips nervously.

'Do you honestly think that I would want to set eyes on you ever again, Sophie?'

Tears gathered at the backs of her eyes and she swallowed painfully, not wanting to cry in front of him but fearing that she would. Her heart was thundering inside her and her head was beginning to hurt.

'You're going to take my company away from me,'

she said flatly. 'You don't care who you hurt in your desire for revenge. It doesn't matter that I had nothing to do with whatever my father did to your father.'

Matias's jaw clenched. His eyes drifted down from her defiant heart-shaped face to the body he had so recently taken and he was furious that, in defiance of the hostile atmosphere simmering between them, his body was still insisting on responding to hers with un-bridled gusto.

He harshly reminded himself that whatever she trot-ted out, nothing could excuse the fact that she had tried to encourage him to open dealings with her father be-cause she'd wanted his money. Whatever guise it took, the apple never fell far from the tree. Greed was in her blood and nothing else mattered.

'Consider the debt to me paid in full,' he gritted. 'I won't be going after your company so you can breathe a sigh of relief. I walk through this door and all deal-ings between us, as I've said, come to an end. I will in-struct my secretary to email you confirming that you no longer owe me anything for the damage to my car and you should consider yourself fortunate, because there are no limits for me when it comes to getting jus-tice for what your father did to mine. In life, there is always collateral damage.'

Being referred to as *collateral damage* just about said it all, Sophie thought, devastated. Thank goodness, she hadn't confided in him about Eric. Thank goodness she hadn't allowed him even further into her heart.

'I shall go and pack my stuff up and then I think I'll get a taxi to the station and take the first train back to London.'

'My driver will deliver you to your house. In the

meantime, I have ignored work demands because of certain *distractions*.' His mouth curled into a sardonic smile. 'It's time for me to return to normality and not a moment too soon.'

Every word that passed his beautiful mouth was a dagger deep into the core of her but, no, she wasn't going to break down in front of him. She wasn't going to let him see how far he had already burrowed into her.

She nodded curtly and remained where she was as he turned his back on her and walked out of the kitchen.

Then and only then did her whole body sag, like a puppet whose strings had been abruptly cut.

But only for a few minutes, a few minutes during which she breathed deeply and did her best to find the silver lining in the cloud. It was what she had spent a lifetime doing. She'd done it every time she visited her brother and reminded herself that life with him in it, however damaged he was, was so much better than life without him in it. She'd done it every time she'd gone to her father, cap in hand, to beg for the money needed to keep Eric safe and happy, and left with the cash.

She would do it again now, and she would thank her lucky stars that she hadn't had the opportunity to emotionally invest even further in a guy who'd used her. And she'd thank her lucky stars that her debt to him was repaid in full.

But, as she got ready to leave, flinging her possessions in the case she had brought with her, her heart was still telling her that life was never going to be the same again.

CHAPTER SEVEN

Sᴏᴘʜɪᴇ ʟᴏᴏᴋᴇᴅ ᴀᴛ the innocuous white stick with the two bright blue lines and felt a wave of nausea surge through her all over again.

This was the third pregnancy test she had done and still her mind refused to compute the enormity of what was staring her in the face. She was sorely tempted to use the last one in the box but she knew that she had to accept the horrible, terrifying truth that she was pregnant. One reckless mistake had resulted in the baby growing inside her. She could do a hundred more tests and nothing was going to change that inalterable fact.

She was having Matias's baby.

A guy who had played her, used her and then discarded her without a backward glance. It had been a little over five weeks since she had last seen him, disappearing through the kitchen door of his over-the-top hillside mansion. Since then she had received a formal email from his secretary informing her that all monies owing to him had been cancelled. Since then, her father's company had gone into liquidation and was now in the process of being eaten up by Matias's sprawling empire. Sophie knew that because it had been on the news. Her father, needless to say, wanted no more to do with her because of the situation he was in. He had no more money to give her and the last time she had seen him, he had angrily accused her of helping to send him to the poorhouse. He'd conveniently overlooked the fact that the failure of his company had been down to his own incompetence and she had not reminded him, choosing instead to walk away and deal with the problems the bankruptcy presented to her brother's future.

Had Matias put the final nail in the coffin and sent the police after her father as well? She didn't know. If so, that was a further public humiliation to come.

Released from having to maintain appearances for the sake of his peers, she and Eric had been cut loose and Sophie had spent every night for the past fortnight trying to find a solution to the problem of how to keep her brother in the safe home he had grown accustomed to.

She was stressed beyond belief and now this had happened.

'You'll have to tell him,' was the first thing Julie said to her later that morning when she showed up at the house.

Sophie looked at her friend, utterly defeated and without a silver lining in sight. 'How can I?' she asked, remembering how they had parted company and feeling the stamp of pride settle in her like a stone. 'You know what happened, you know…' her voice cracked and she took a deep breath and continued in a rush '…what his motives were for getting involved with me.'

'But this is no longer about your father, Soph, or whatever revenge Matias Rivero was after. This is about a new life growing inside you that can't be made to take the blame for a situation he or she had nothing to do with.'

Sophie knew that in her heart of hearts. How could she withhold the baby's existence from his own flesh and blood? Matias would have to know but only because she could see no other way around it. She would have to make sure he knew that she *wanted nothing from him*. She didn't care how much money he had. As far as she was concerned, she would do the right thing and tell him about the baby, but after that she would walk away.

And he would be able to breathe a sigh of relief because she knew that the last person he would want to see show up at his office, again, would be her.

First time, she had shown up having crashed into his car. Now, she would be showing up with a baby-shaped wrecking ball solidly aimed at his life.

She could remember just how she had felt that first time she had shown up at his impressively scary office headquarters and spoken to the receptionist. Sick with nerves at an uncertain outcome, and yet with just enough hope that everything would be okay because although she wasn't going to be seeing the very empathetic Art Delgado, deep down she had clung to the belief that the guy she *would* be seeing might be cut from the same cloth.

One day later, as Sophie yet again stood outside the impressive building that housed Matias's legendary empire headquarters, hope was nowhere in existence.

She had had several hours to get her head round her situation and yet she was no nearer to locating any silver linings.

She strode into the glass building with a great deal more confidence than she was feeling and asked for Matias with the sort of assurance that implied an audience would be granted without argument.

'It's a personal matter,' she added to a frowning young blonde girl, just in case. 'I think Matias... *Mr Rivero*...would be quite upset if you don't inform him that I'm here. Sophie Watts. He'll know who I am and it's urgent.'

Would he see her? Why should he? His parting shot had been that he never wanted to set eyes on her again, even if that involved kissing sweet goodbye to the thousands of pounds she still owed him.

About to go to the boardroom to close a multimillion-pound deal, Matias was interrupted by his secretary and told that Sophie was in the foyer several stories below.

For approximately two seconds, he debated delivering a message back that he was unavailable.

He didn't. He'd walked away from her weeks ago but hadn't managed to escape whatever malign influence she had over him. She'd lodged under his skin like a burr, appearing like a guilty conscience just when he least needed it and haunting his dreams with infuriating regularity.

Everything was going nicely when it came to dismantling her father's company, ensuring that the man was left standing out in the cold with no shelter in sight. Behind the scenes, further revelations would come when he moved to phase two, which would involve the long arm of the law. An eye for an eye.

It should have given him an additional sense of satisfaction that his daughter, whose greed had matched her father's, would also be standing in the same cold spot, without any shelter on the horizon. Unfortunately, every time he tried to muster the appropriate levels of satisfaction at a job well done, the image of her soft heart-shaped face popped into his head, giving him pause for thought.

Revenge had been served cold, but it was not as sweet as it should have been.

It didn't help that his mother had read all about the takeover in the newspapers and had summoned him to the hospital where she was recovering nicely. She'd never agreed with his thirst for retribution and nothing had changed on that front.

All in all, he was pleased that he had done what he had done, because as far as he was concerned those wheels of justice had to turn full circle, but he was surprised at how dissatisfied he remained at what should have been a stunning victory of the present over the past. And he knew it was all down to Sophie.

'Show her up,' he told his secretary in a clipped voice, instantly deciding to put his meeting on hold, regardless of the value of the deal. 'And tell Jefferies and his team that Bill Hodgson will be handling the initial closing stages.' He ignored the startled look on her face because such an about-face was unheard of.

His mind was already zooming ahead to what Sophie might want from him.

Money was the first and only thing that came to mind. She had encouraged a deal with her father so that she could benefit from the financial injection. No deal meant no financial injection, which meant that she still wanted money, except it wasn't going to come from her dear papa.

He was outraged that she would try her luck with him. He knew that he certainly shouldn't be allowing her any chink through which she might try and slip. But he couldn't resist the opportunity to see her and he was, he acknowledged, curious to see what approach she would take to try and wheedle cash out of him.

Would she shoot him one of those sweet, innocent, butter-wouldn't-melt-in-her-mouth smiles? The kind of smile that instantly went to his groin and induced all manner of erotic, dirty, sexy scenarios in his head? He got a kick imagining her sashaying into his office, hot for sex. He'd send her on her way, but he still experienced a massive surge of desire playing with the thought.

The single knock on his door found him relaxing in his chair, his hands loosely linked on his washboard-flat stomach, his expression one of mild curiosity.

'Yes.' The door opened, his secretary stood to one side and there she was, tentatively walking into his office, blushing in the way that would send any normal, red-blooded man's pulse through the roof. She was wearing a pair of grey trousers and a white blouse and his eyes immediately dropped to the soft swell of her breasts and, right on cue, his brain lurched off at a predictable tangent, remembering exactly what those luscious breasts had felt like, had tasted like. 'What have you come for?' he asked abruptly, putting paid to the raunchy turn of his thoughts. He pushed himself away from the desk but did nothing to make her feel comfortable. Why should he?

'Can I sit down?'

Matias nodded to the chair. 'I wouldn't make myself too comfortable if I were you,' he drawled. 'Time is money, after all. On the subject of which, I'm taking a stab in the dark here at the reason for your sudden, unexpected visit. Because this isn't a social call, is it?'

'No.' Her voice was steady and Sophie was proud of

that, although that, in fairness, was the only part of her that felt remotely controlled. She hadn't laid eyes on him for weeks but she hadn't stopped thinking about him, and, seeing him in the flesh now, she was shocked that she could have so massively underestimated the impact of his physical presence.

His lean, dark face was even more stunningly beautiful than she recalled, his mouth more cruel, more sensuous, his body...

Sophie didn't want to think about his body. She just wanted to say what she had come to say and leave before her steady voice went the way of the rest of her. She reminded herself of the man he had turned out to be, vengeful and ruthless, and a lump of ice settled inside her, the cold knot of hatred, which she welcomed.

'Didn't think so.' Matias's lips thinned. He was recalling in vivid detail the mind-blowing sex they had shared... He was also recalling the reason she had slept with him. 'I expect you read all about your father's downfall in the financial pages.'

'You must be pretty pleased with yourself.'

Matias flushed darkly, nettled by the cool disdain in her voice. 'Your father got what he deserved.' He shrugged. 'And yes, I'm quietly pleased with myself, although I have to say that had he not let his company run aground, my job would have been considerably less easy. He was a thief, a conman and eventually an idiot who let go of the reins and never thought that the horse might bolt. A great deal of highly suspect financial dealings is being uncovered, but that won't come as any surprise to you. In due course, your father and Her Majesty will be more than nodding acquaintances, but not in the way he would doubtless like. But you haven't come here for a chat. I'm a busy man so why don't we just cut to the chase, Sophie? No deal with your father means no rescue of his terminally ill company, which means no cash in hand for you. So I'm guessing that you're here to see whether there isn't another way to elicit money out of me.'

'I wouldn't accept a penny from you if my life depended on it,' she snapped. Every word that had passed his beautiful lips stung, every word was a reminder of exactly what he thought of her.

If she could have turned tail and run for the hills, she would have, but Julie had been right. A father deserved to know about the existence of his child, even if he chose to do nothing with the knowledge. However much she hated him for how he had treated her, she was fair enough to recognise that simple fact.

'We're going round the houses here, *querida*. In one sentence, why don't you just tell me what the hell you're doing in my office?'

'We had unprotected sex, Matias. Do you remember?'

Two sentences that dropped into the still silence between them with the power of an unexploded bomb.

Usually quick on the uptake, Matias could literally feel his brain slowing down, skidding to a halt in the face of what she had said and what she hadn't.

'I remember...' he said slowly. It was strange but that languorous bout of lovemaking, in that quiet surreal lull between sleeping and waking, had stayed right there, between the sheets, trapped in a moment in time. Had he subconsciously shoved it to the back of his mind rather than face the possibility that taking her without protection might have had consequences? Or had it just seemed unreal in the light of day and therefore easily forgotten?

He was remembering now, remembering the way their bodies had fused, warm and lazy and barely awake.

'I'm pregnant, Matias,' Sophie told him flatly.

She'd not envisaged what sort of reaction she would get from her announcement. In her head, she said what she had to and then walked away. Now, as she watched the vibrant bronze of his face slowly pale, she found herself riveted to the chair into which she had sunk.

'You can't be,' he denied hoarsely.

'I've done three tests. I didn't even think about it until I started feeling nauseous every morning and realised that my period hadn't come.'

'It's impossible.' Matias raked his fingers through his hair and realised that his hand was shaking. Pregnant. She was having his baby. Just like that, his eyes darted to her still-flat stomach, then to her breasts, which now, suddenly, seemed bigger and lusher than he remembered. 'And if this is your attempt to try and get money out of me, then you're barking up the wrong tree. You seem to forget that I've had ample experience of a woman who will use a so-called pregnancy to worm her way into my bank balance.'

Sophie rose on shaking legs. 'I'm going now, Matias. I know you had a poor experience in the past and I'm very sorry that I've had to come here and spring this on you, but I'm not your ex-girlfriend, I'm not lying and I certainly don't want a penny from you. After what you did to me, do you honestly think that I could ever want anything from you? *Ever?* I'm here because I felt you should know about your baby.'

Matias watched as she began walking towards his office door. Everything seemed to be happening in slow motion or maybe it was just that his brain had now totally seized up, unable to deal with a situation for which he had not, in any way, shape or form, prepared himself. He didn't move as she opened the office door but then he did, suddenly galvanised into action.

He caught her as she was barrelling along the corridor towards the bank of lifts and he placed his hand on her arm, forcing her to a stop.

Who cared whether his bizarre behaviour was being observed?

'Where do you think you're going?' he gritted.

Sophie's eyes flashed. 'Back home! Where do you think? I can't believe you would have the nerve to accuse me of faking a pregnancy to try and extort money out of you. What sort of person do you think I am? No. Don't bother answering that! I know already!' She yanked her arm out of his grasp and hit the button on one of the lifts, which obligingly opened at her command. She stepped in, eyes firmly averted from Matias, but she was all too aware of him stepping into the lift with her and slamming his fist on one of the buttons, which instantly brought it to a shuddering stop between floors.

'What are you doing?' Alarmed, Sophie finally looked him squarely in the eyes and then blinked and made a huge effort to drag her eyes away because, even when she was seething with hatred, she still couldn't help finding him so impossibly attractive. It wasn't fair!

'We need to talk about this and if this is the only way to get you to talk to me, then I'll take it.'

'You can't just *do that*.' Sophie was shocked because

wasn't that breaking the law? Normal people didn't just *stop a lift to have a conversation*! But then since when was Matias Rivero a *normal human being*?

'Why not?'

'Because…because…'

'Are you going to have a conversation with me about this or are you going to put on your running shoes the second we're out of this lift? Because you can't drop a bombshell like that in my lap and then try and dodge the bullet.'

'I don't want anything from you,' Sophie repeated fiercely. 'I hate you!'

'Message received loud and clear.'

'And I didn't engineer getting pregnant to try and get money out of you! That's a vile thing to say even from you, but why should I be surprised?'

'Let's not waste time going down that road. It's not going to solve anything.'

'And I have no intention of getting rid of this baby, if that's what you're thinking!'

'Did I insinuate that that was what I wanted?' Matias raked frustrated fingers through his hair. Her colour was high, her eyes were glittering like aquamarines, and she was the very essence of bristling feminine fury. He set the lift back on its way down. 'We're going to go to a small wine bar five minutes' walk from this office. I know the guy who owns it. I'll make sure we get a good seat at the back somewhere and we can have a civilised conversation about this problem. Agreed?'

Sophie scowled. 'You used me just to get dirt on my father.' She looked at him narrowly and with hostility. 'We can talk about this if you like but I don't want you to forget how much I detest you for doing what you did.'

Matias hung onto his temper. He had no doubt that she was telling the truth and, with the dust settling, the grim reality of what had happened was beginning to take shape. He was going to be a father. When it came to his bucket list, having a kid had never been on it and yet here he was, with only a few months left of sweet independent singledom because of one crazy mistake.

Life as he knew it was about to undergo a seismic change and getting wrapped up in blame and counter-blame wasn't going to alter that.

The wine bar was half empty and they were, indeed, afforded utter privacy at the very back, where they were tucked away from the other tables. Matias ordered a coffee for them both and then looked at her directly.

'When did you find out?' he asked quietly, shunning anything that might lead to another emotive outburst.

'Yesterday.' Sophie glared bitterly at him and fiddled with the handle of her cup before taking a sip and grimacing because her taste buds were no longer quite the same. 'And don't think that it wasn't as big a shock for me as well! Don't think that I haven't thought about how Fate could have been so cruel!'

'Whatever has happened in the past, we have to put behind us or else we'll be stuck on a treadmill of never moving forward and the only way we can deal with this problem is to move forward towards a mutually agreeable solution.'

Sophie stared coldly at him because every word he said, while making perfect sense, left her feeling angry and defensive. Problem? Mutually agreeable solution? She rested her hand protectively on her stomach, a gesture that Matias keenly noted, just as he understood that treading on eggshells about summed up where he was right at this moment. She had come to his office under duress and was not inclined to give him the benefit of any doubts, but she was hardly the saint she made herself out to be, he thought. She talked a lot about him using her but hadn't she been after his money? No, she wouldn't be in line for a halo any time soon, but, like it or not, he had to listen to his own words of advice and approach the situation dispassionately.

'That's easier said than done,' Sophie said tonelessly and Matias heaved an impatient sigh.

'You wanted me to engineer a deal with your father because you thought he might be able to help you financially if he wasn't in financial trouble himself. Am I right?' His voice was level and cool. 'So when you rant and rave about what a bastard I am, take a long look at yourself and try and put things into perspective.'

He hadn't wanted to raise this thorny issue because he didn't see what the point of raising it might be, considering it wouldn't advance any sort of solution to their problem, but raise it he had and he was disconcerted by the absolute lack of suitable apology on her face. Clearly a sense of guilt didn't feature in her repertoire.

And yet that seemed strangely at odds with the person she came across as being. Surely his judgement couldn't be that skewed?

'You *are* a bastard.' But she flushed because he'd never given her the chance to explain about Eric and it was understandable that he had somehow ended up with the wrong end of the stick. She looked at him, her bright eyes filled with unspoken challenge. 'And how very lucky you are that I won't be hanging around and making a nuisance of myself by demanding anything from you. I'm not the nasty gold-digger you seemed to think I am and I wouldn't touch a penny from you if my life depended on it!'

'You're telling me that you weren't after money from me by trying to encourage me to do a deal with your father? Even though you knew that his company was on the brink of collapse? Even though you knew that he was probably criminally involved in skimming cash from the till?' Matias laughed shortly. 'Let's have your definition of a gold-digger, then, Sophie…'

'I don't care what you think of me,' Sophie said tightly. She'd had her tale to tell, had been ready to spill the beans about Eric because she had been seduced by Matias on an emotional level, had taken him for being someone he had not been. She'd had a narrow escape— so should she spill the beans *now*?

No way, she decided grimly. He was still after her father and there was no way she would allow Eric's privacy to be invaded by the press, which was exactly what could happen should Matias choose to publicise her brother's existence. Her darling, fragile brother was not going to be part of Matias's retribution or even unintentional *collateral damage*.

Matias instantly realised that that simple statement held the distinct possibility of opening up another quagmire and so he opted for silence.

'So what is your explanation for your behaviour?' he eventually demanded, grudgingly curious to find out what she would be able to come up with that didn't begin and end with her need to have money injected into her company.

'I don't have to provide you with an explanation,' Sophie retorted quickly, cringing back from a vision of reporters banging on the window of her brother's bedroom, terrifying him because he would be hopelessly confused and panicked.

'I just need to take everything you say at face value and believe you. Is that it?'

'You don't have to do anything you don't want to do. I haven't come here because I want anything from you and there's no *we* in this situation. I came here because I felt it was the right thing to do but this isn't a problem that I'm forcing you to face. I don't trust you, Matias, but you deserved to know about the pregnancy so here I am.'

'We're back to this again. Let's move away from that and focus on the present and the future. And just for your reference, there very much *is* a *we* in this situation because half of my chromosomes, whether you like it or not, happen to be inside you right now in the form of a baby neither of us expected but which both of us have to deal with.' His instinct was to qualify what he had to say by telling her that everything depended on whether she was telling the truth, but he decided that silence on that subject was definitely going to be the diplomatic course. 'You're having my baby...' For a few seconds he was stunned again by the impact that had on him. Matias Rivero, a father. He still couldn't quite get his head round that. 'If you thought that you could just pass on that information and then walk away, job done, then you were sorely mistaken. I won't be walking away from my responsibility, Sophie.'

'I don't want to be your responsibility.'

'You're not but my unborn child is, whether you like it or not. I didn't sign up to this but it's happened and we have to deal with it. You have an unhappy family background so maybe that's led you to imagine that stability is overrated, but I haven't and I am a firm believer in the importance of having parents in a child's life. Both parents.'

'I happen to believe very strongly in stability,' Sophie corrected him tightly, '*because* I've had an unhappy family background. I didn't know how you would react when I came to see you, bearing in mind the way we parted company, but you can rest assured that I won't stand in the way of your seeing your child.' She hated the way he made her feel. She didn't want to be here, and yet, in his presence, she felt so *different*, as though she were living on a plane of heightened sensation. She felt *alive*. She wanted to walk out but felt compelled to stay. She wanted to ignore his staggering, unwelcome impact on her senses but was drawn to him by invisible strings that she couldn't seem to sever. She loathed him for what he had done and loathed herself almost as much for knowing that somewhere inside her he still stirred something…something only he could somehow manage to reach.

'That's not good enough, *querida*.' Matias had never contemplated marriage and now here he was, facing marriage as the final frontier, and not simply marriage, but marriage to the woman who was the daughter of his sworn enemy. And yet what other solution was there? He had no intention of being a bit player in his child's life, forking out maintenance payments while having his visiting rights restricted and curtailed by a vengeful mother. Sophie wouldn't forget the circumstances that had brought him into her life and she would have the perfect opportunity, should she so choose, to wreak a little healthy revenge of her own by dictating how much or how little influence he had over his own flesh and blood.

He thought of his mother, recovering in a private hospital in London. She would be so upset if she ended up as only a part-time grandparent, snatching moments here and there with a grandchild caught in a tug of war between two warring parents. Matias might have been put off emotional commitment thanks to a conniving ex and the lessons learnt from his own emotional father and where it had got him in the long run. That said, he hadn't been lying when he'd told Sophie that his childhood had consisted of a strong and supportive family unit and now, in the face of this unexpected development, that strong family bond locked into place to override everything else.

'Twenty minutes ago, you were telling me that time was money, so I'd better go now.'

'Things change. Twenty minutes ago I didn't realise that you were carrying my baby.' His sharp eyes were glued to her face while he programmed his brain to accept the news she had broken to him, to start thinking outside the box. 'You're now set to be a permanent feature in my life. I want to be there for my child twenty-four-seven and the only way that can be achieved is if we marry.'

Deathly silence greeted this extraordinary statement and Sophie's mouth inelegantly fell open in shock.

'You've got to be kidding.'

'You might have come here out of a sense of duty but I have no intention of going away like an unpleasant smell because you refuse to accept that the past is over and done with.'

'I will never forget how you used me in your quest for revenge. You used me once and who's to say that you won't use me again?' She thought of Eric, the secret that Matias could not be allowed to uncover because what if his desire for revenge hadn't been sated? She looked at him from under lowered lashes and shivered. So beautiful, so powerful and so incredibly ruthless.

'Sophie, that story has ended. We are travelling down a different road now.' But Matias was genuinely puzzled by her statement. What else could he possibly use her for? For better or for worse, he had uncovered everything there was to uncover about her father.

He continued to look at her and noted the way her cheeks slowly coloured, arrowed in on the soft tremble of her full lips. The air between them was suddenly filled with a charge he recognised all too well, a sexual charge that made him immediately harden for her. He vividly recalled the silky wetness that always greeted his exploring fingers, his questing mouth, and he clenched his jaw.

He motioned, without looking around, for the bill and wondered whether she was conscious of the signals she was sending out under all the hostility and mistrust, signals that were as powerful as a deep sea-depth charge, signals that advertised a connection between them that was founded on the oldest thing in the world…sexual attraction.

'Think about it, Sophie, and I will call you tomorrow so that we can pick up this conversation.' He smiled slowly and watched intently as a little shiver went through her. 'I think we both need to do a little private reflection, don't you?'

CHAPTER EIGHT

SHE'D TURNED DOWN his extraordinary marriage proposal and she'd done the right thing.

Of course there were pros and there were cons. Every decision was always laced with pros and cons! But she had done the right thing. She'd been to see Eric, sat in his soothing presence, watched his contentment in his peaceful surroundings. Somehow she'd find the money to pay for him carrying on living there, but she would never expose him to the cruel glare of a curious and judgemental public.

Was she being selfish? Was she failing to consider the reality, which was that a child would always be better off with two parents as opposed to one and that was something that should override every other concern?

No. How could you hitch your wagon to a man you didn't trust? A man you felt might betray you again? And anyway, trust issues aside, two parents only worked if the glue that bound them together wasn't a child, but love. Matias didn't love her and he had never pretended that he did. He felt responsible for her, responsible for the child he had sired, and was admirably willing to step up to the plate and do his duty, but duty was a far cry from love.

Duty would wear very thin at the edges as time marched on. Duty would be the very thing he would come to resent when he found himself harnessed to a woman he would never have voluntarily chosen to spend his life with.

But three weeks had gone by and Matias just seemed to *be around so much*.

He hadn't said it in so many words, but there had been no need because every look he gave her and every word that passed his lips said *don't fight me*.

She'd turned him down but, like a predator waiting for the right moment to strike, he was simply biding his time.

He didn't realise, she thought, that he would never wear away her defences because there was more than just her and their baby at stake. At stake was a brother he knew nothing about and never would and that bolstered all her resolve when his presence just felt *too overwhelming*.

Nothing he could say, no logic he could use, could ever make her do anything that might jeopardise her brother's privacy and happiness.

She was congratulating herself on being strong as she sat, the first to arrive, at the posh restaurant where Matias had arranged to meet her for lunch. He had been away for the past three days and her stomach was already tightening in nervous knots as she braced herself for that first glimpse of him. On the one hand, she had been relieved that, although he had been scrupulous about maintaining contact with her by phone, he hadn't imposed his presence on her on a daily basis. On the other hand, she wondered whether she might have become more blasé about his physical presence if he were around more, if she had a chance to get accustomed to him. She didn't like the way he still made her feel and she hated the memories of him touching her that refused to go away. They weren't on that page any longer! Things had changed and they were never going to be on that page together again.

Lost in thought, she looked up to find that he had arrived and he wasn't alone.

Art was with him. She hadn't seen him since the weekend party in the Lake District and she rose to her feet, already smiling as he walked towards her. Behind him, Matias towered, unbearably sexy in his work clothes, one hand in his trouser pocket, the other hooked to his jacket, which was slung over his shoulder.

Seeing that warm, genuine smile on her face as she looked at Art, Matias sourly thought that it was something *he* hadn't seen for a while. She'd repeatedly thrown his marriage proposals back in his face and he'd been sharp enough to realise that the harder he pushed, the faster she would back away.

There was no way he was going to let her run out of his life because it suited her. Pride refused to let him forget that she had slept with him as a ruse to get him to invest in her father's company, but common sense dictated that he get her onside because he was never going to be persuaded into the role of part-time father.

He watched, his expression shuttered, as she and Art chatted away like the old friends they weren't and something hit him hard, something so unexpected that it was like a punch to the gut.

He didn't like seeing her relaxed interaction with his friend. He didn't like the way she was so at ease in his company. He didn't care for the tinkling of her laughter as they found God only knew what to talk about, considering they'd known each other all of five seconds.

Jealousy and possessiveness rammed into him with the weight of a sledgehammer and he interrupted their conversation to coolly inform her that Art wasn't going to be joining them for lunch.

'That's a shame.' Sophie sighed with genuine disappointment, which got on Mátias's nerves even more.

He scowled, met Art's curious eyes and scowled even more. 'Don't let us keep you,' he said abruptly, and Art grinned broadly but stood up, moving to drop a kiss on Sophie's cheek before heading out.

'That was *so* rude,' she said. 'It was lovely seeing Art again! I had no idea you two were so close. You never said! I can't believe you *grew up together*!' They were like brothers and it had brought her up short to acknowledge that Art adored Matias. Even in the space of half an hour, she had been able to glean that from their interaction and seeing them together had unwillingly reminded her of just why she had been seduced by him. There was a side to Matias that wasn't a bastard, a side that could elicit a depth of affection from a loyal friend who was clearly a wonderful human being. It was suddenly confusing to admit that he was also many other things, a complex guy with so many dimensions, it made her head swim.

Not that she was going to let that deflect her from the path she had decided to take.

'I had no idea I had a duty to tell you every detail of my life just because you're carrying my baby,' Matias drawled lazily, sitting back as menus were placed in front of them. Her cheeks were still flushed and she looked so damned sexy that the jealousy that had attacked him from nowhere five minutes ago staged another onslaught. He knew he was being irrational but he couldn't help it.

'You never said that you were going to visit your mother...'

'I could hardly let her find out about us via the grapevine.'

'She must have been disappointed,' Sophie said quietly. 'No mother likes to think that her child has... well...is going to have a family...you know...so unexpectedly...and without the usual build-up...'

Matias allowed her to run aground. Seeing his mother had reinforced his belief that the only solution was to marry the woman blushing opposite him. If she was going to dig her heels in, then he would have to work along the lines that there was more than one way to skin a cat. He'd seen the way she still looked at him. 'Naturally,' he murmured smoothly, 'she would have preferred the love and marriage scenario...'

'But you told her how it was? That this isn't that sort of situation?'

Matias didn't say anything because he had told his mother no such thing. 'Pregnancy becomes you, Sophie,' he said instead, relaxing into the chair and staring at her until the faint colour in her cheeks deepened and he saw the latent *awareness* of him that she was always so careful to try and conceal. 'Your body's changing. You're wearing looser clothes. Are your breasts getting bigger?'

'Matias!' Sophie was shocked because he hadn't been direct like this before.

Heat blossomed inside her. Her breasts ached and she felt the tingle of awareness stickily making its presence felt between her legs. *That* was what those casual words were doing to her!

'It doesn't get more intimate than having my baby...' he shrugged, his fabulous eyes not leaving her face '... so why are you so surprised that I am curious about the physical changes occurring to you? It's natural. I'm fifty per cent responsible for those physical changes.'

'This conversation is not appropriate! We no longer have that kind of relationship!'

'You think that we are more like...*what*?'

'Well, *friends*. At least, that's what we should be aspiring to become! We've talked about this and we both agree that it would be best for our child if we remain on good terms.' She cleared her throat and tried to ignore the suffocating effect his intense gaze was having on her nervous system. 'Remember we agreed that you would be able to see him or her any time you wanted?'

'So we did...'

'We may not have expected this...' she dug deep to repeat the mantra she had told herself '...but we're both adults and um...in this day and age, marriage isn't the inevitable solution to dealing with an unexpected pregnancy... We discussed this.'

'Indeed...'

'There's too much water under the bridge between us.'

'I won't deny that.' She had deferred, for once, and he had ordered for both of them, a sharing platter that was now placed between them. 'But I'm curious. What do you suggest we do with the mutual desire that's still putting in an unwelcome appearance?'

Sophie's mouth fell open. He had brought out into the open the one thing she had desperately tried to shove into a locked box. 'I don't know what you're talking about!'

'Liar,' Matias said softly. 'I could reach out and touch you right now and you'd go up in flames.'

'You couldn't be further from the truth,' Sophie denied weakly. 'I could never be attracted to someone who used me like you did. Never!'

'*Never* is a word that has no place in my vocabulary.'

'Matias…' She thought of Eric and the importance of hanging onto her resolve, but seeing Matias with Art had weakened that resolve, had reminded her of those sides to him that could be so wonderfully seductive, so thoughtful and unexpectedly kind.

'I'm listening.'

'I know you find it funny to make me uncomfortable.'

'I think about you all the time. I wonder what your changing body looks like under those clothes.'

'Don't say things like that! We don't have that kind of relationship! We talked about that.' She sought refuge in the platter in front of her but she could feel him staring lazily at her, sending her into heady meltdown. Her whole body was throbbing with the very awareness he was casually dragging out into the open and forcing her to acknowledge.

'I don't like to stick to the script. It makes for a boring life.' Matias sat back. He let his eyes drift at a leisurely pace down her curvaceous body and felt his mouth twitch because she was as rigid as a plank of wood, as if her posture were fooling him. 'In fact,' he drawled, 'I'm taking the afternoon off.'

'Why?'

'Do I have to provide a reason? And stop looking at

me like that. You should be thrilled at the prospect of spending time in my company. And do me a favour and refrain from telling me that we *don't have that kind of relationship.*'

'I can't leave Julie in the lurch.'

'She's going to have to get used to you no longer holding her hand when you finally decide to listen to me and quit working. She's a big girl. She'll cope.'

'I can't *quit working*, Matias.'

'Let's not go there. You don't need the money.'

Sophie thought of Eric and her mouth firmed. The irony was that Matias wanted to throw money at her. Once upon a time not all that long ago he had turned his back on her and tossed her to the kerb but now that she was pregnant, everything had changed. They had not discussed money in any great depth yet, but he had already made it clear that his child, and her by extension, would want for nothing.

And yet, how could she allow herself to ever become financially dependent on him? Her pride would never allow it and, more than that, what if she began to trust again only to find that she had once more made a mistake? What if, by then, she was totally reliant on the money he was so keen for her to have because she'd stopped working? No, there was no way she could give up her job. Maternity leave was one thing. Resignation was quite another.

Another roadblock, Matias thought with frustration. He impatiently wondered why she couldn't just recognise that his solution was the best and only way to move forward. What woman wouldn't want a life of luxury? What woman wouldn't want to be able to snap her fingers and get whatever she wanted? It wasn't as though they didn't have an electric connection still thrumming between them like a live charge. What more advantages did he have to bring to the table for her to accept his proposal? Why, he thought, did she have to be so *damned stubborn*?

'I've taken the afternoon off, *querida*, because I have a surprise for you.'

'I hate surprises,' Sophie confessed.

'I know. I'm not a big fan of them myself but I am hoping you'll like this one. It's a house.'

'A house?'

'For you,' he said bluntly and her eyes widened in surprise.

'You've gone and bought a house *for me*?' She bristled. 'Why would you do that?'

Matias sat back, taking his own sweet time, and looked at her evenly. 'Because,' he said calmly, 'you won't be bringing up our child in that tiny box of yours with its converted kitchen.'

'There's nothing wrong with *that box*,' Sophie cried hotly as pride kicked in and lodged inside her.

'Don't argue with me on this.' Matias's voice was forbidding. 'You've turned down my marriage proposal, in defiance of common sense. You've dug your heels in and dismissed all financial help I've offered as unnecessary handouts. You've insisted on working long hours even though you're unnecessarily putting our child at risk. You are *not* going to wage war with me on this.'

'How have I been putting the baby at risk?' Sophie asked furiously.

'You don't have to work until midnight baking cakes for anyone's anniversary party.'

'*Once.* I've done that *once*!'

'Or,' Matias ploughed on remorselessly, 'waste three hours in traffic delivering a four-course meal for a dinner party.'

'That's my job!'

'You're overexerting yourself. You need to take it easy.'

Sophie released a long sigh but… *Had anyone ever really looked out for her? Ever really cared whether she was taking on too much or not?* Of course, this wasn't about *her*, but about the precious cargo in her stomach, and it would be downright foolhardy to start thinking otherwise *but still…*

'I know you're not a gold-digger, Sophie. You don't have to keep trying to prove it to me over and over again.'

'That's not what I'm doing.'

'No? Then what is it?'

'I won't rely on you financially. I can't. I need to have my own financial independence.' Suddenly she felt small and helpless. She wished she were able to lean on him and just accept what was on offer. He made it sound so easy. Clean break from what had happened between them in the past and onward bound to the future he wanted her and his child to have, but there was so much more to the story than he knew.

'Well, you're going to have to compromise on this, whether you like it or not, *cara*.' His voice was cool and unyielding.

Their eyes tangled. He reached out and brushed a speck of something from the side of her mouth, then left his finger there for a few seconds to stroke it over her lips. 'A little bread,' he said roughly, his big body firing up immediately because it was the first time he'd touched her in weeks.

Sophie's eyes widened. For a minute there she had leaned towards him and her whole body had burned from the inside out, as though molten lava were running through her veins. *The way he was looking at her, with those deep, dark, sexy eyes...*

Yearning made her weak and it was a struggle to pull away from the magnetic drag on her senses.

'You have no idea what my taste is like. In houses.' Which was as good as accepting whatever over-the-top house he had flung money at, in defiance of the fact that he must have known that she would have kicked up a fuss about it. Her heart was still hammering and she lowered her eyes and took a few deep breaths before looking at him once again. She could still feel the burning of her skin where he had touched her. 'Don't get me wrong, Matias.' Her tone crisped up but her body, awakened by his touch, *wanted more*. 'You have a lovely place in the Lake District but I couldn't imagine living in a massive greenhouse like that. I don't know what your apartment's like but I'm guessing it's along the same lines...'

'Damned by faint praise,' Matias murmured, wanting her more than he had ever wanted anything or anyone in his life before and damn well determined to have her because he could *smell* the same want radiating from her in waves.

'What I'm saying is you and I obviously don't have the same taste in houses so it's unlikely I'm going to like whatever it is you've bought.'

'I haven't bought it yet,' he drawled. 'I may be arrogant but I thought you might actually like to have a say in the house you want to live in.' Eyes on her, he signalled for the bill and then stood up.

He dominated the space around him and she was helplessly drawn towards him, like a moth to a bright light. She couldn't quite understand how it was that he could continue to exercise this powerful effect on her after what he had done, or how common sense and logic hadn't prevailed when it came to stepping back from him. She wondered whether pregnancy hormones had taken over and were controlling all her responses, heightening her emotional state and making her vulnerable to him when she should have been as detached from him as he was from her and getting down to the business of building a friendship for the sake of the child she was carrying.

Outside, his chauffeur was waiting for them, but instead of accompanying them he drove them to his office where they switched cars, and Matias took the wheel.

'Where is this house?' Sophie asked because she had expected something in Chelsea or Mayfair or one of those frighteningly expensive postcodes close to where he had his own apartment.

'I'm going to disappoint you...' he slid his eyes sideways to glance at her and smiled '...by keeping it a surprise. Now, talk to me, *querida*. Don't argue with me. Tell me about that client of yours...'

'Which client?' Because stupidly, even though she had so many defences erected when it came to Matias you could construct a small town behind them, she *still* found it frighteningly easy to talk to him when he turned on that charm of his.

'The vegan with the wart on her face.'

'I didn't think I'd mentioned her to you.'

'When we're not fighting,' Matias murmured softly, 'we're getting along a hell of a lot better than you give us credit for. There's so much more we could be doing, *querida*, instead of making war...'

Sophie only realised that they had been driving for longer than she thought when the crowded streets and houses fell away to open space and parks and they pulled up outside a picture-perfect house shaped like a chocolate box with an extension to one side. Wisteria clambered over the front wall and, set right back from the lane, the front garden was dilapidated and overgrown.

'It needs work,' Matias told her, reaching into the pocket of his jacket, which he had flung in the back seat, and extracting some keys, which he jangled on one finger as he opened his car door. 'And it hasn't been lived in for several months, hence the exuberance of the weeds.'

'I hadn't expected anything like this.' Sophie followed him up to the front door, head swinging left to right as she looked around her. The house stood in its own small plot, which was hedged in on three sides. He opened the door, stood aside and she brushed past him and then stood and stared.

There were rooms to the right and left of the hallway. Lovely square rooms, all perfectly proportioned. A sitting room, a more formal living room, a study, a snug and then along to the kitchen and conservatory, which opened out at the back to a garden that was full of trees and shrubs and plants that had taken advantage of absentee owners and decided to run rampant.

The paint was faded. In the sitting room, the gently flowered wallpaper seemed to speak of a different era.

'The house was owned by an elderly lady who lived

here for most of her life, it would seem,' Matias was murmuring as he led her from room to room. 'She didn't have any children, or perhaps they might have persuaded her that the house was far too big as she got older, but it would seem that she was too attached to it to sell up and leave and as a consequence the latter part of her life was spent in only a handful of rooms. The rest were left in a state of gradual decline. When she died a little over a year ago, it was inherited by a distant relative abroad and the probate took some time, hence it's only just come onto the market.'

She walked from room to room. Her silence spoke volumes. She wasn't bristling; she wasn't complaining. In the matter of the house, he had clearly won hands down.

Matias intended to win hands down in every other area as well.

He was waiting for her in the hallway, leaning against the wall, when she completed her third tour of the house, and he didn't budge as she walked towards him, her eyes still wide as saucers.

'Okay.' Sophie smiled crookedly. 'You win.'

'I know.'

'Don't be arrogant, Matias,' but she was still smiling and she wasn't trying to shuffle more distance between them. The silence stretched until she licked her lips nervously.

But she hadn't taken flight.

'I don't just want to win when it comes to finding a house for…you,' he said gruffly.

'Matias, don't.' But her voice was high and unsteady, and against her will her body was straining with desperate longing towards him, liquid pooling between her legs, the swollen tips of her nipples tightening into sensitive buds.

'Why do you insist on fighting this thing that's still here between us?'

'Because we can't give in to…to lust…'

'So you finally admit it.'

'That doesn't mean anything. It doesn't mean I'm going to do anything about it.' She looked at him and couldn't look away. His dark eyes pinned her to the spot with ruthless efficiency. She couldn't move, couldn't think, could scarcely breathe.

Her head screamed that this was *just not going to do*. She couldn't afford to lose sight of what was sensible but her body was singing from a different song sheet and when he lowered his head to hers, her hands reached out. To push him away? Maybe. Yet they didn't. They curled into his shirt and she melted helplessly as he kissed her, softly and teasingly at first and then with a hunger that matched her own.

His tongue found hers. His hands, on her shoulders, moved to her arms then cupped the full weight of her breasts.

He played with her nipples through her top but then, frustrated, pushed open the buttons and groaned as he felt the naked skin of her chest and then, burrowing beneath the lacy bra, finally got to the silky fullness of her breasts and the ripe protrusion of a nipple.

'You're definitely bigger.' His voice was shaking.

'Matias…'

'Touch me.' He guided her hand to his erection, which was a hard, prominent bulge against the zipper of his trousers.

'We can't make love here!'

Wrenched back to the reality of what she was saying, Matias struggled not to explode in his trousers.
He breathed deeply, cupped the nape of her neck and
drew her to him so that their foreheads were touching.

Her breath was minty fresh, her skin as soft as satin
and he ached for her. 'We talk, Sophie,' he breathed in
a driven undertone. 'Don't tell me we're at one another's throats all of the time. And we want one another.'

Sophie knew what he was saying and she longed to
capitulate but she was only in this place because she
was pregnant. Had she not been, they would be enemies
on opposite sides of the fence. Were it just a question of
her, then would she think about his offer? Maybe. She
could cope if it turned out that she couldn't trust him.
Again. But she couldn't trust him with Eric. Could she?

Confusion tore through her.

'Come back to my place with me,' he urged.

'I won't marry you,' she said weakly.

Matias all but groaned in frustration but he didn't.
Instead, he smoothed his hands over her shoulders and
kissed her very gently, very persuasively on her mouth
and felt her move from hesitation to abandon. He kept
kissing her. He kissed her until she was breathless. He
kissed her until he knew for certain that there was nothing and no one left in her head but him, then he broke
apart and said, in a barely restrained voice,

'Let's go.'

CHAPTER NINE

HER HOUSE.

In her head, to go to Matias's house would have been a complete declaration of defeat. Within the confines of her own four walls, however, she could kid herself that she was still in control, even though she had lost it in his arms and even though *she wanted to carry on losing it*.

If I sleep with him, she thought, then it would be *a conscious decision*. It wouldn't mean that she had lost all control and it certainly didn't mean that she would marry him. She would never trust him again. How could she? She would never jeopardise Eric's privacy because she'd made another mistake, but...

She wanted Matias so badly. He was in her system like a virus and she wanted to be cleared of that virus because it was driving her round the bend.

He reached out to link his fingers lightly through hers in the car. They barely spoke but the electricity between them could have set a forest ablaze. His mobile phone rang several times. He ignored it. Looking at his strong, sharp profile, the lean contours of his beautiful face, Sophie wondered what was going through his head. He didn't love her but he still fancied her. He'd told her that there was no need for her to keep trying to prove to him that she was no gold-digger, but deep down she knew that he would always believe her culpable of trying to get him to sink money into her father's dying company and invest in a man who had turned out to be a thief. He had no idea that Eric existed and so would never understand why she had done what she had, and she could never tell him about her brother because family loyalty was more powerful than anything else.

But whatever the situation, he was right. A fire burned between them and what were they to do about it?

Having never invested in the crazy notion that lust was something that couldn't be tamed, Sophie was realising just how far off the mark she'd been with her orderly, smug little homilies.

It was after four-thirty by the time they made it to her house. Sophie thought it was serendipity that Julie was out on a job, setting up with an assistant they had hired, for a lavish dinner party in Dulwich.

Compared to the glorious setting of the house they had just seen, her two up, two down, squashed in the middle of an uninspiring row of terraced lookalikes, was a shock to the system. She'd vigorously defended her little place but now she felt that she could see it through Matias's eyes. Poky, cramped, unsatisfactory.

She turned to find him looking at her with a veiled expression as he quietly shut the door behind them. Shivers of anticipation raced up and down her spine.

'Empty house?' he asked, walking very slowly towards her, and Sophie nodded.

'Julie's on a job. She won't be back until tomorrow afternoon. Matias… I'm glad about the house… This place would really not have been suitable for a baby. I mean, of course, it would have worked if there were no other option but…'

'Shh.' He placed one finger over her lips and her heart sped up. 'Don't talk.' He was directly in front of her now and he bent his head and kissed her. A long, lingering, gentle kiss that made her weak at the knees. 'Much as I enjoy the sound of you telling me that I was right, there's more, a lot more, I want to enjoy right now.' He cupped the back of her neck and carried on kissing her, taking it long and slow and feeling a kick of satisfaction as her body yielded to his, moulding bit by bit to his hard length until they were pressed together, entwined.

Without warning, he lifted her off her feet and Sophie gasped and clung to him as he made his way up the narrow staircase.

He'd seen enough of her place to know that finding her bedroom wasn't going to require in-depth navigation skills. The place was tiny. He doubted there were more than two bedrooms and he was proved right, finding hers with no trouble at all as it was at the top of the stairs.

Cheerful colours tried to make the most of a space that could barely contain the bed, the chest of drawers and the wardrobe that were crammed into it. Two posters tried to attract the eye away from the view outside of other terraced houses and beyond that a railway line.

He set her down on the bed and she promptly pushed herself up onto her elbows to look at him as he drew the curtains together, shutting out the weak sunlight and plunging the room into subdued tones of grey and sepia.

'It's been too long,' he intoned with a slow, possessive smile that ratcheted up her spiralling excitement.

He was standing with his back to the window and he remained there for a few seconds, just staring at her, before walking towards the bed, ridding himself of clothes on the way.

He was sheer masculine, powerful beauty in motion and he took her breath away.

She was frankly amazed that she had been able to withstand his potent sex appeal for as long as she had, but then today was the first time he had yanked that monster out of the cupboard and forced her to confront it.

She half closed her eyes, watching as, down to his boxers, he stood by the side of the bed and gazed down at her.

Tentatively, she reached out and ran the tips of her fingers across the washboard hardness of his flat stomach.

He was wired for her. His erection was prominent under the boxers, which didn't remain on for longer than necessary.

'I don't have to tell you how much I want this,' Matias said gruffly. 'The evidence is right in front of you.'

Sophie gave a soft little whimper and sat up straighter, angling her body so that she could lick the shaft of his pulsing erection.

She tasted him like someone savouring an exquisite delicacy. Her tongue flicked and touched, her mouth closed over him and she sucked while, with her hand, she enjoyed the familiar feel of his hardness. His taste was an aphrodisiac.

She felt as if somewhere, in the back of her mind, she had stored the memory of the noises he made when she did this, his deep, guttural grunts. His fingers clasped in her hair were familiar. She wanted him so badly she was melting for him and wanted nothing more than to fling off all her clothes so that he could take her.

Reading her mind and knowing that if he didn't watch it, he would come right now, in her mouth, Matias reluctantly separated her from him. When he glanced down, his shaft was slick and wet and he had to clench his fists to control the urge to put her right back there, have her take him across the finishing line with her hands and her mouth.

No. He'd fantasised about this for far too long to blow it on a horny, teenage urge to grab and take.

But hell, he was on fire as he sank onto the mattress so that he could remove her clothes.

She was wearing far too much and he was way too fired up to do justice to the striptease scenario. He needed to get under the layers of fabric as quickly as possible so that he could feel her.

Her clothes hit the deck in record time and she helped, squirming out of her cumbersome bra and wriggling free of the lacy underwear, which, he noted in passing satisfaction, was of the sexy thong variety, a choice of lingerie he knew he had encouraged her to wear.

It was almost a shame that he was so hot and hard because he would have liked to have taken his time teasing her with his tongue through the lace of her underwear.

'Matias…' Sophie fell back against the pillow and arched a little so that her full breasts were pushed out invitingly to him.

He was kneeling over her and, on cue, he took her breasts in his big hands and massaged them gently until his thumbs were grazing her nipples and sending shivers of racing pleasure straight downwards.

She circled him with her hand and played with him, knowing just how fast and firm he liked the rhythmic motion of her hand.

'Matias…what?' he encouraged with a wicked smile and she looked back at him with wry understanding because she knew just what he wanted.

'You know…' she blushed furiously '…what I like…'

'Oh, I know…' He bent to suckle her nipple, drawing it into his mouth and taking his time to lave it with his tongue, circling the aching tip until she was writhing under him.

He knew her so well. It felt as though they had been making love for ever. Knew that she liked him to be just a little rough, to nip her big, pouting nipples until she became even wetter and more restless. He knew what else she loved, and he explored lower down her glorious body, taking time to appreciate all the small changes he had wondered about.

Her breasts were at least a cup size bigger and her nipples were more pronounced in colour, no longer a rosy blush but a deeper hue. Her belly was just a bit more rounded. Having never thought about babies or becoming a father, at least not since the hapless incident a thousand years ago with the ex-girlfriend who had tried it on, he had never looked twice at pregnant women, but this woman, with his baby inside her, was beyond sexy.

Her roundness thrilled him, made him even harder than he already was.

Working his way down her body, he slipped his hand between her legs and played with the soft down between them. Then he slipped his finger into her and she moaned softly and squirmed until his finger was deeper inside her, finding her softness and working a path to the tiny bud that was begging for attention.

He knew that if he dawdled too long there, she would come. She was the most responsive woman he had ever known. So he played with the tingling bud, then stopped, then played with it again, until she was begging him to take her.

'Not just yet,' he whispered. Hands on her waist, he dropped down between her legs and nuzzled, breathing in her honeyed sweetness.

He flicked his tongue along the slit of her womanhood, then began exploring her wetness.

His finger had already teased her and now his tongue did the teasing, until she was moaning and wriggling, pushing him down hard one minute, jerking him up the next, her fingers curled into his hair.

She bucked against his mouth, rising up with jerky movements, and he cupped her buttocks, holding her still and torturing her with the insistent push of his tongue inside her.

'I'm going to come,' she gasped as her body began moving quicker to capture every small sensation of him between her legs. 'I don't want to come like this, Matias… I want to *feel you inside me*.'

Matias rose up. He automatically reached down to find his wallet but then he remembered that there was no need for protection and he dealt her a slashing smile.

'The horse has already bolted…' he grinned '…so no need to do anything about locking the stable door.'

Sophie drowsily returned his smile. Her body was hot and flushed and the waves of pleasure that had almost but not quite taken her over the edge were still there, making her want to wriggle and touch herself.

'You're so hot for me, *querida*...'

'I can't help it,' Sophie half groaned. 'It's a physical thing.'

'Now, now, don't go spoiling the mood. I want to ride you and take you to the outer reaches of the universe.' He prodded her with the blunt head of his shaft and she parted her legs, unable to contain her eagerness to have him deep inside her.

He slid in and the sensation was beyond belief. She was slick and wet and tight and her softness welcomed him in ways that he couldn't define but just knew made him feel better than good.

He wanted her so badly. This was going to have to be fast and hard. He couldn't hang around any longer, he couldn't devote any more time to foreplay or else he risked the unthinkable.

He drove into her, thrusting long and deep, and she wrapped her legs around his waist and, yes, he rode her until she was bucking and crying out with pleasure, until the breathing hitched in her throat. Until, cresting a wave, she came just as he did, with a rush of sensation that flowed over her and around her like a tsunami.

She arched up and stiffened as his powerful body shuddered against her and she panted and rocked beneath him until at last...she was spent.

Matias levered himself off her. It was a downright miracle of circumstance that he now found himself here, with her. The number of *what ifs* between them could have stocked a library.

What if...she hadn't crashed into his car?

What if...he hadn't lived a life hell-bent on revenge?

What if...he hadn't seen fit to weave her into his revenge agenda?

What if…she hadn't spent time under his roof at his place in the Lake District?

What if, what if, what if…?

But here they were, having made the most satisfying love imaginable. In no way, shape or form was he tiring of her. On the contrary, he desired her with an urgency that none of his other relationships had ever had. He felt a possessiveness towards her that defied belief.

He had accepted the shock to his system that impending and unforeseen fatherhood would confer.

He had risen above the challenge of playing a blame game that would get neither of them anywhere.

But had he really believed that this unforeseeable passion and downright *insatiable craving* would form a part of the picture? Was it the evidence of his own virility and the fact that she was carrying his baby that made his feelings towards her so…*ferociously powerful*?

She had stuck to her guns about not marrying him, frustrating his natural urge to get what he wanted. His powerful need to *never* back down until he had what should be his within his grasp had hit a roadblock with her. He refused to contemplate any situation that involved him losing control over his child, and by extension, he told himself, *her*.

Seeing his mother as she recuperated in hospital, as he had now done several times, had only reinforced his determination to take her as his wife.

Thus far, the inevitable meeting between his mother and Sophie had been avoided, but sooner or later his mother would want to meet the woman who was carrying her grandchild and when that time arrived Matias was determined that marriage would be on the cards. There would be no difficult conversation in which his mother would be forced to concede that the grandchild she had always longed for would be a fleeting presence in her life.

'Was that as good for you as it was for me, *querida*?' He shifted onto his side and manoeuvred her so that they were facing one another. He brushed a strand of hair away from her face and then kissed her very gently on her mouth, tracing the outline of her lips with his tongue.

Sophie struggled to think straight. She had done what she had spent weeks resolving not to do. She had climbed back into bed with him and where did that leave the *friendship* angle she had been working so hard at since she had turned down his marriage proposal?

What disturbed and alarmed her was the fact that it had felt *right*.

Because…because…

Because she loved him. Because he'd swept into her life, inappropriate and infuriatingly arrogant, and stolen her heart, and even though he had used her and couldn't be trusted, because who knew whether he would use her again, she still couldn't help but love him. She'd made love to him and it had been as wonderful and as satisfying as walking through the front door of the house you adored and finding safety within its four walls. Which was a joke, of course, but then so were all the stupid assumptions she had made about love being something she would have been able to control. She could no more have controlled what she felt for Matias than she could have controlled the direction of a hurricane.

'Well?' Matias prompted, curving a hand possessively around her waist, challenging her to deny what was glaringly obvious.

'It was nice,' Sophie said faintly, still wrapped in the revelation that had been lurking there, just below the surface, for longer than she cared to think.

'Nice? *Nice?*' Matias was tempted to explode with outrage but ended up bursting out laughing. 'You certainly know how to shoot a man down in flames.'

'Okay.' She blushed. 'It was pretty good.'

'Getting better,' he mused, 'but I still prefer *amazing.*'

'It was amazing.'

'When you showed up at my office,' Matias said softly, 'it was a shock, but I really want this baby, *querida*. You tell me you don't want to marry me. You tell me the ingredients for a successful marriage aren't in place, but we talk. Yes, we fight as well, but *we talk*. And we still have this thing between us. We still want one another passionately. Isn't that glue enough? You say you're not prepared to make sacrifices yet *I* am, because I truly feel that any sacrifice I make for the sake of our child will, in the end, be worth it. Don't we both want what, ultimately, will be best for our baby? Can you deny that? We can't change the past but we can move on from it. We can stop it from altering the course of the future.'

Sophie could feel the pulse in her neck beating, matching the steady beat of her heart, the heart that belonged to him, to a man who would never, *could* never return the favour.

He talked about sacrifices, though, and surely, *surely* he would never use her again? Not when they shared a child? Could she trust him or had the past damaged that irreparably?

'Maybe you're right,' she said, meeting his eyes

steadily. 'Of course I want what's best for our baby. Of course I know that two parents are always going to be better than one.' And maybe, she dared to hope, in time she would trust him enough to confide in him about her brother, despite what had happened between them. Alan had turned away from what he had perceived as a challenge too far in Eric and she had locked herself away after that. Of course, she had never consciously decided that remaining on her own was the preferred option, but how could any relationship ever have blossomed in the bitterness that had grown over the hope and trust she had invested in her ex-boyfriend? Alan had not deserved the faith she had put in him. Compared to Matias, what she'd felt for Alan was a pale shadow of the real thing. But however strong her love, she still couldn't guarantee that Matias, a guy who had been motivated by revenge when he had decided to *cultivate her*, would live up to her expectations.

But they were having a baby together and she *wanted and needed him*.

In due course, he might even jump through all the hoops and prove to be worthy of her trust, but that was something she would never find out unless she gave him a fighting chance.

Matias looked at her and wished that he could see what she was thinking so seriously about. She was staring back at him but her thoughts were somewhere else. Where? Never had the urge been so strong to *know* someone, completely, utterly and inside out. He had never delved into what the women he dated thought about anything. He had wined and dined them and enjoyed them but digging deep hadn't been part of the equation. Sophie made him want to dig deep.

'So…?' he murmured, with a shuttered expression.

'So we don't have to get married…' Sophie breathed in deep and prayed that she was doing the right thing '…but we can live together…' That was called giving him a chance, giving him an opportunity to prove that he could once more be trusted before she opened up that part of her he knew nothing about.

Matias greeted this with a lot more equanimity than he felt. Live together? It wasn't the solution he was after, but it would have to do. For now…

Matias got the call as he was about to leave work.

'I'm sorry.' Sophie was obviously moving in a rush. Her voice was tight and panicked. 'I'm going to have to cancel our dinner date tonight. Something's come up, I'm afraid.'

'What's come up?' Already heading to his jacket, which was slung over the back of the cream sofa that occupied the adjoining mini suite in his glasshouse office, Matias paused, returned to the desk and grabbed the little box containing the diamond bracelet he had ordered three days previously and had collected that day as a surprise for her.

He had taken to surprising her every so often with something little, something he had seen somewhere that had reminded him of her.

Once, it had been an antique book on culinary art in Victorian times, which he had quite accidentally found while walking to his car after a meeting on the South Bank. The bookshop had been tucked away next to a small art gallery and he had paused to glance at the offerings in painted crates on trestle tables outside.

She had smiled when he'd given it to her and that

smile of genuine pleasure had been worth its weight in gold.

Then he had bought her a set of saucepans specially made for the stove in the new house, because he had found one of her house magazines lying on the sofa with the page creased with an advertisement on their lifetime guarantee and special heat-conducting values. Whatever that was supposed to mean.

And again, that had hit the spot.

The diamond bracelet was the most expensive item he had bought thus far and he sincerely hoped that she wouldn't refuse to accept it. She could dig her heels in and be mulishly stubborn about things that were beyond his comprehension and for reasons he found difficult to fathom.

Matias knew that he was shamelessly directing all his energies into getting what he wanted because the longer he was with her, the more unthinkable it was that she might eventually want to cut short their *living together to see how it goes* status and return to the freedom of singledom, free to find her soul mate.

He shoved the box into the inside pocket of his jacket, which he had stuck on without breaking the phone connection.

Her voice, the strained tenor of it, was sending alarm bells ringing in his head. She had been fine when he had seen her the day before. They had met for breakfast because she had gone to help Julie and he had wanted to see her before he headed off to Edinburgh, where he was taking a chance on a small pharmaceutical company that was up for grabs.

'Where are you, *querida*?' he asked, doing his utmost to keep his voice calm and composed.

'Matias, I really have to go. The taxi is going to be here any minute and I have to get a few things together before I leave. In fact…wait…the taxi's here.'

'Taxi? Don't you dare hang up on me in the middle of this conversation, Sophie! What taxi? Why are you taking a taxi somewhere? What's wrong with the car? Is it giving you trouble? And where are you going, anyway?'

'The car is fine. I just thought that, in this instance…'

Her voice faded, as though she had dumped the phone on a table because she needed to do something.

What?

Matias was finding it impossible to hang onto his self-control. She sounded as though she was on the verge of tears and Sophie never cried. She had once told him that when things got tough, and there had been plenty of times in her life when they had, then blubbing never solved anything.

It had been just one more thing he had lodged at the back of his mind, something else that slotted into the complex puzzle that comprised her personality.

And now she was on the verge of tears for reasons she would not identify and she didn't want to talk to him about it. He had done his damnedest to prove to her that she had been right to take a punt on him. He had not batted an eyelid at the very clear nesting instincts that had emerged when she had begun decorating the house. He had also gone light on her creep of a father in the wake of the company takeover, allowing him to salvage some measure of self-respect by not sending him to prison for being trigger-happy with the pension pot, although Carney was much diminished by the end of proceedings, which had afforded Matias a great deal of satisfaction.

He had even deflected an immediate visit to see his mother, because, while she was recovering nicely, much spurred on by news of a grandchild on the way, he had wanted to protect Sophie from the inevitable pressing questions about marriage. The last thing he'd wanted was to have her take fright at his very forthright mother's insistence on tradition and start backing away from the arrangement they had in place.

But even with all of this, it was now perfectly clear that there were parts of her that still bore a lasting resentment because of the way their relationship had originally started.

Why else would she be on the verge of tears and yet not want to tell him why?

'What do you mean by "in this instance"?' he demanded, striding towards the door and heading fast to the bank of lifts.

Most of his employees had already left. The hardcore workaholics barely glanced up as he headed down to the underground car park where his Ferrari was waiting.

'I have to go.'

'Tell me where. Unless it's some kind of big secret?'

'Goodness, Matias!' Hesitation on the other end of the phone. 'Okay, I'm heading to Charing Cross hospital.'

Matias froze by his car, sickened at the thought that something was wrong with her or the baby. 'I will meet you there.'

'No!'

He stilled, unwilling to deal with what her stricken response was saying to him. 'Okay…'

'Matias, I'll see you back at the house. Later. I don't know what time but I'll text or I'll try to. You know what they can be like at hospitals.'

'This is my baby as well, Sophie. I want to be by your side if there's any kind of problem.'

'There's no problem there. Don't worry.'

Naturally, Matias didn't believe her. Her voice was telling a different story. She was frantic with worry but when it came to the crunch, she didn't want him by her side to help her deal with it.

She would show up the following morning and would be bright and cheery and would downplay his concern and they would paper over the unsettling reality that in a time of crisis she would simply not allow him to be there for her.

There was no point driving to the hospital—the parking would be hellish—but Matias was going to be there. He was not going to let her endure anything she might find distressing on her own, and, he grimly acknowledged, it wasn't simply because it was a question of *their* child.

He didn't think twice. His driver was on standby. He would hit the hospital running before she even got there. Playing the long game was at an end. Like it or not, there was going to be a pivotal change in their relationship and if he had to force her hand, then so be it.

Rushing into the hospital after too many hold-ups and traffic jams to count, Sophie raced through the revolving doors and there he was, right in front of her.

He towered, a dark, brooding presence restlessly pacing, hand shoved deep in his trouser pocket. A billionaire out of his comfort zone and yet still managing to dominate his surroundings in a way that brought her to an immediate skidding halt. The cast of his beautiful face was forbidding. People were making sure not to get too close because he emanated all kinds of danger signals that made her tense up.

'Matias…'

Eyes off the entrance for five seconds, her voice brought him swinging round to look at her. 'I'm coming with you,' he said grimly. 'You're not going to push me out this time.'

'I haven't got time to do this right now,' but her heart was beating wildly as she began walking quickly towards the bank of lifts, weaving through the crowds.

'Sophie!' He stopped her, his hand on her arm, and she swung to face him. *'Talk to me.'*

Their eyes tangled and she sighed and said quietly, 'Okay. It's time we had a talk. It's time you knew…'

CHAPTER TEN

MATIAS EXPECTED HER to head straight to the maternity ward. However, she ignored the signs, moving fast towards the lift and punching a floor number while he kept damn close to her, willing her to talk and yet chilled by her remoteness. She barely seemed aware of his presence as she walked quickly up to one of the nurses at a desk and whispered something urgently to her, before, finally, turning around and registering that he was still there.

Matias looked at her carefully, eyes narrowed. They hadn't yet exchanged as much as a sentence. He was a guy who had always made it his duty to keep his finger on the pulse and know what was going on around him, because if you knew the lay of the land you were never in for unpleasant surprises, but right now he didn't have a clue what was going on and he hated that, just as he hated the distance between them.

Was this the point when everything began to fall apart? A sick chill filtered through his veins like poison.

'What's going on?' he asked tightly and Sophie sighed.

'You'll find out soon enough and then we'll need to talk.' She spun round and he followed as she walked straight towards one of the rooms to gently push open the door.

Matias had no idea what to expect and the last thing he was expecting to see was a young man on the bed, obviously sedated because his movements were sluggish as he turned in the direction of the door, but as soon as he saw Sophie he smiled with real love and tenderness.

Matias hovered in complete confusion. He felt like an intruder. He wasn't introduced. He was barely noticed by the man in the bed. He was there to watch, he realised, and so he did for the ten minutes she gently spoke to the boy, holding his hand, squeezing it and whispering in soft, soothing, barely audible tones.

She stroked his forehead and then kissed him before standing up and gazing down at the reclining figure. The boy had closed his eyes and was breathing evenly, already falling into sleep.

She glanced at Matias, nodded as she raised one finger to her lips, and only when they were outside the room did she turn to him.

'You're wondering,' she said without preamble. He was so shockingly beautiful and she loved him so much and yet Sophie felt as though they had now reached a turning point from which there would be no going back. She hadn't considered when the time would be *right* for him to meet Eric. Fear of an eventual negative outcome had held her back but Fate had taken matters into her own hand and now here they were.

'Can you blame me?' Matias responded tersely, raking his fingers through his hair, his whole body restless with unanswered questions.

'We need to talk but I don't think the hospital is quite the right place, Matias.'

Matias was gripped by that chill of apprehension again because there was something final in her voice. 'My place. It'll be quicker than trying to get back to the cottage.' On this one, single matter he could take charge and he did. Within ten minutes they were sitting in the back of his car, heading to his penthouse apartment, to which she had been only a handful of times.

The silence between them was killing him but he instinctively knew that the back seat of a car was not the place to start demanding answers any more than the environs of a hospital would have been.

He glanced at her a couple of times, at her averted profile, but she was mentally a million miles away and he found that incredibly frustrating. He wanted to reach out and yank her back to him. He found that he just couldn't bear the remoteness.

Caught up wondering how she was going to broach the taboo subject she had successfully managed to avoid so far, Sophie was barely aware of the car purring to a stop outside the magnificent Georgian building that housed his state-of-the-art modern penthouse apartment.

It was an eye-wateringly expensive place, now seldom used because he had become so accustomed to spending time at the cottage. They had fallen into a pattern of behaviour and it was only now, when the possibility of it disappearing was on the horizon, that she could really appreciate just how happy she had been.

Even though she knew that he didn't love her, he was perfect in so many ways. He just didn't feel about her the way she felt about him.

The cool, minimalist elegance of his apartment never failed to impress her, although, for her, it was a space she could never have happily lived in.

Now, though, with so much on her mind, she barely noticed the large abstract canvasses, the pale marble flooring, the pale furniture, the subtle, iconic sculptures dotted here and there.

She went directly to the cream leather sofa and sat down, immediately leaning forward in nervous silence and watching as he sat down opposite her, his body language mirroring hers.

'So?' Matias asked, his beautiful eyes shuttered and tension making his voice cooler than intended. 'Are you going to tell me who that guy was?' He saw the way she was struggling to find the right words and he added, tersely, 'An ex-boyfriend?'

'I beg your pardon?'

'Is he an ex-boyfriend, Sophie?' Matias demanded icily. 'The love of your life who may have been involved in an accident? I watched the interaction between the two of you. You love the guy.' Something inside him ripped. 'How long has he been disabled? Motorbike accident?' Every word was wrenched out of him but he had to know the truth.

'I do love him,' Sophie concurred truthfully. 'I've always loved him.'

Matias's jaw clenched as the knot in his stomach tightened. He wasn't going to lose it but he wanted to hit something hard.

'And he wasn't involved in an accident, at least not in the way you mean. Eric has been like that since he was born.'

Matias stilled, eyes keen, every pulse in his body frozen as he tried to grapple with what she was saying.

'Eric is my brother, Matias,' Sophie said quietly.

'Your brother…'

'He lives in a home just outside London, but something spooked him and he had a panic attack and went a little berserk. Hence why he's in hospital. He hurt himself while he was thrashing around. Nothing serious but they couldn't deal with it at the home.'

'You have a brother and you never told me...'

'I have no idea where to begin, Matias. If you just sit and listen, I'll try and make sense. My father only had contact with our family because he was left without a choice. When Eric was born, my mother knew that the only way she would ever be able to afford to take care of him would be with financial help from James. She had a lot of faults but a lack of devotion to Eric wasn't one of them. She made sure James paid for Eric's home, which is very expensive, and when she died it was up to me to make sure he carried on paying. It sounds callous, Matias, but it was the only way.'

'You wanted me to invest in your father's business because you wanted to make sure he could carry on paying for your brother's care.'

Sophie nodded, relieved but not terribly surprised that he had picked it up so quickly. For better or worse, it was a relief to be explaining this to him. If he chose to walk away, then so be it. She would be able to deal with the consequences, even though she knew that she would never be the same again without him in her life.

'I've always managed to put aside a nest egg and I've been dipping into it to cover the costs of Eric's home since James's business went to the wall, but, yes, I encouraged you to think that investing in James would be a good idea, not because I wanted the money for myself, but because I would have done anything, I'm afraid, to make sure my brother is safe and happy.'

'Why didn't you tell me?'

'How could I, Matias?' Sophie tilted her chin at a mutinous angle, defensive and challenging. 'You used me to confirm your suspicions about James and even when you came back into my life, it was because you felt you had no choice.'

'Sophie...'

'No, let me finish!' Her eyes glistened because if the end was coming then she would have to be strong and she didn't feel strong when she was here, looking at him and loving him with every bone in her body. 'I didn't tell you about Eric because there was no way I wanted you to think that you could exact more revenge by going public with what my father had done, shaming him by telling the world that he had fathered a disabled child he had never met and only supported because he had no choice.'

And just like that, Matias knew the depth of her distrust of him. Just like that he saw, in a blinding flash, how much he had hurt her. She had bowed her head and listened to him accuse her of things she had never been guilty of, and she had closed herself off to him. She clearly didn't trust him and she never would.

'I wish you had told me,' he said bleakly.

'How could I?' Sophie returned sadly. 'How could I take the risk that you might have been tempted to involve Eric in your revenge scheme, when the press would have turned it into a story that would have ended up hurting him, destroying both his privacy and his dignity? And also...'

Matias was processing everything she said, knowing that he had no one but himself and his blind drive for vengeance to blame for where he was right now. 'Also?' He looked at her.

'Eric is fragile. When Alan, my ex-boyfriend, walked out of my life, having met him just the once, Eric was heartbroken and felt responsible. I thought Alan was the one for me and I just didn't think that he would walk away because the duty of caretaking Eric was too much.'

'Any creep who would walk away from you because of that was never the one for you,' Matias grated harshly. 'You should count your lucky stars you didn't end up with him.'

'You're right. What I felt for Alan wasn't love. I liked him. I thought he was safe, and safe was good after my mother's experiences with men. But yes, I had a lucky escape. Don't think I don't know that.'

'I was driven by revenge.' Matias breathed in deeply and looked at her with utter gravity. 'It was always there, at the back of my mind. I was always going to be ambitious, I guess. I was always going to be fuelled to make money because I knew what it was like to have none, but I also knew what it was like to know that *I should have*. Your father was to blame and that became the mantra that energised a lot of my decisions. For a while, the chase for financial security became a goal in itself but then, like I told you, my mother fell ill and I discovered those letters. At the point when you entered my life, my desire to even the score with your father was at its height and…you became entangled in that desire. You didn't deserve it.'

Sophie looked at him questioningly, urging him to carry on and weak with relief that he seemed to have taken the situation with her brother in his stride.

'I thought you wanted to push me into investing into someone you knew was on the verge of bankruptcy and probably crooked as well because you wanted to carry on receiving an allowance from him.'

'I understand,' Sophie conceded, 'that you would have thought that because you knew nothing about Eric… You didn't know that there were other reasons for my doing what I did.'

'I saw red,' Matias admitted. 'I felt I'd been used and I reacted accordingly, but the truth was that deep down I knew you weren't that kind of person. *Querida*, you didn't trust me enough to tell me about your brother and I can't begin to tell you how gutted I am by that, even though I know that I have no one but myself to blame. I expected you to wipe away the past as though it had never existed, and I couldn't appreciate that I hurt you way too much for you to find that easy to do.'

This was the first time Matias had ever opened up and she knew from the halting progress of his words that it was something he found difficult, which made her love him even more. He was apologising and it took a big man to do that.

'I never want to hurt you again, my darling. And I will always make sure that your brother is protected and cared for in the way he deserves. Just give me the chance to prove to you how much I love you and how deeply sorry I am for putting you in the position of not thinking you could trust me with the most important secret in your life.'

Sophie's eyes widened and her heart stopped beating before speeding up until she felt it burst through her ribcage.

'Did I just hear you say…?'

'I love you,' Matias told her simply. 'I never thought that I would fall in love. I was never interested in falling in love, but you came along and you got under my skin and before I knew it you had become an indispensable part of my life. When we went our separate ways, it was weird but I felt as though part of me had been ripped away. I didn't understand what that was about, but now I realise you were already beginning to occupy an important position in my life.'

'You never said,' Sophie breathed. 'Why didn't you say?'

'How could I?' Matias smiled wryly at her. He stood up and went to sit on the sofa next to her but he didn't try and pull her towards him, instead choosing to reach out and link her slender fingers through his. He absently played with her ring finger, giving no thought to what that said about the road his subconscious mind was travelling down. 'I was barely aware of it myself. We never expect the things that take us by surprise. Love took me by surprise.'

'As it did me,' Sophie confessed, so happy that she wanted to laugh and cry at the same time. 'When I first met you, I hated you.'

Matias's eyebrows shot up and he shot her a wolf-ish smile. 'Yet you still managed to find me incredibly sexy...'

'Don't be so egotistical, Matias.' But Sophie couldn't resist smiling back at him because he could be incredibly endearing in his puffed-up self-assurance. 'I thought I was going to see Art and instead I was shown into the lion's den.'

'It's a good job you *didn't* see Art,' Matias said drily. 'You would have walked all over him. He would probably have ended up giving *you* a new car and forgetting all about the damage you did to mine. You charmed the socks off him.'

Sophie blushed. 'We would never have met, though…'

'We would have,' Matias asserted. 'Our paths were destined to cross, even if you *did* hate me on sight.'

'Well, you *were* threatening to pull the plug on my business because I'd bumped into your car…'

Matias acknowledged that with a rueful tilt of his head. 'And so the rest is history. But,' he mused thoughtfully, 'I *should* have suspected that the ease with which I became accustomed to the notion of being a father was a pointer as to how I felt about you. If I hadn't been so completely crazy about you, I would have never slipped into marriage proposal mode so seamlessly.'

'And then I turned you down…'

'You did. Repeatedly. You have no idea how much I've wanted to prove to you that you could take a chance on me.'

'And you have no idea how much I've wanted to take that chance, but I was just too scared. I think, to start with, it really was because I was suspicious and unsure as to what you might do if you found out about Eric. My gut told me that I could trust you, despite all the water under the bridge, but my gut had lied once and I dug my heels in and refused to listen to it a second time. And then, later, I was scared to think about how you might react to Eric. Alan had been a dreadful learning curve for me. I'd been hurt and bewildered at the man he turned out to be and Eric had been terribly upset. He doesn't have the wherewithal to cope with upsets like that. Whatever happened, it was very important to me that he not become collateral damage. I could cope with that but he would never be able to.'

'I'm glad I met him,' Matias said seriously. 'Now can we stop talking? Although, there *is* one thing I still have to say…'

'What's that?' Sophie whispered, on cloud nine.

'Will you stop sitting on the fence and marry me?'

'Hmm…' Sophie laughed and pulled him towards her and kissed him long and hard, and then she brushed his nose with hers and grinned. 'Okay. And by that I mean…yes, yes, yes!'

A handful of months later, another trip had been made to the hospital. Sophie's labour had started at three in the morning and had moved quickly so that by the time they made it to the maternity ward baby Luciana had been just about ready to say hello to her doting and very much loved-up parents.

She had been born without fuss at a little after nine the following morning.

'She has your hair.' Sophie had smiled drowsily at Matias, who had been sitting next to her, cradling his seven-pound-eight-ounce, chubby, dark-haired baby daughter.

'And my eyes.' He had grinned and looked lovingly at the woman without whom life meant nothing. His life had gone from grey to Technicolor. Once upon a time, he had seen the accumulation of wealth and power as an end unto itself. He had thought that lessons learnt about love and the vulnerable places it took you were enough to put any sensible guy off the whole Happy Ever After scenario for good. He had sworn that a life controlled was the only life worth living. He'd been wrong. The only life worth living was a life with the woman he adored at his side.

'And let's hope that's where the similarities end,' Sophie had teased, still smiling. 'I don't need someone else in my life who looks bewildered at the prospect of boiling an egg.'

And now, with their beloved baby daughter nearly six months old, they were finally getting married.

Sophie gazed at her reflection in the mirror of the country hotel where she and her various friends, along with Matias's mother, had opted to stay the night.

Rose Rivero was back on her feet and, as she had confided in her daughter-in-law-to-be some time previously, with so much to live for that there was no question of her being ill again any time soon.

'You look stunning,' Julie said and Matias's mother nodded. The three of them were putting the final touches to Sophie's outfit, making sure that every small rosebud on her hairpiece was just right. 'You're having the fairy-tale wedding you've always longed for.'

Sophie laughed and thought back to the journey that had brought her to this point. 'It's not exactly been straightforward,' she murmured truthfully.

'I could have told you that my son is anything but straightforward,' Rose quipped. 'But you've calmed him down and grounded him in ways I could never have imagined possible.'

'You wouldn't say that if you could see him storming through the house looking for his car keys, which he seems to misplace every other day.' Sophie laughed and walked to the door, while the other two followed, to be met by the rest of the bridal party in the reception downstairs, where cars were waiting to take them to the quaint church, perched on a hillside with a spectacular view of the sea beneath.

Never in her wildest dreams had she imagined a life as perfect as this.

She still had an interest in the catering firm and frequently went there to help out, but it was largely left to Julie and her three helpers, who now ran the profitable business with a tight rein. Their beautiful new premises had been up and running for some months and they were even thinking of expanding and opening a restaurant where they would be able to showcase their talent on a larger scale and to a wider audience.

James Carney had avoided the harsh punishment originally planned by a vengeful Matias, but life had changed considerably for him. With the company no longer in his hands, he had been paid off and dispatched down to Cornwall where he would be able to lead a relatively quiet life, without the trappings of glamour that had been gained from his underhand dealings with Tomas Rivero. Occasionally he dropped Sophie an email and occasionally she answered, but she had no affection for the man who had made her mother's life and her own a nightmare of having to beg for handouts and always with the threat that those handouts could stop at any given moment.

Matias was in possession of the company, which his father should have jointly owned, and it was now a thriving concern, another strand in his hugely successful empire.

But it was with Eric where Sophie felt the greatest flush of pleasure, for her brother could not have been made more welcome by Matias and he was developing skills that still continued to amaze her. He was no longer living in his own little world, really only able to communicate with her, his carers and a handful of other patients. Now, he was making strides in communicating with the outside world, without the fear and panic that had previously dogged him, and she could only think that Matias's patience and little innocent Luciana were partly responsible for that progress. And maybe, she occasionally thought, he was intuitive enough to realise that the sister who came to visit him was no longer stressed out. He was safe for ever. He had begun a specially adapted computer course and was showing all sorts of talents hitherto untapped.

Sophie thought of her daughter as she was driven to the church. Luciana would be there, with her nanny, and although the ceremony would mean nothing to her she would enjoy the photos when she got older.

Sophie breathed in deeply as she stepped out of the chauffeur-driven Bentley and then she was in the church, as nervous as a kitten to be marrying the man who meant everything to her.

Matias turned as everyone did, as the music began to play. This was the final piece of the jigsaw. He was marrying the woman he loved and he could not have been prouder.

The breath hitched in his throat as he looked at her walk slowly up the aisle towards him. The cream dress fitted her body like a glove. She had returned to her former weight and all those luscious curves were back, tempting him every single time he looked at her. She was holding a modest bouquet of pale pink flowers and her veil was secured by a tiara of rosebuds that mimicked the flowers in her hand.

She was radiant. She was his. Possessiveness flared inside him, warming him.

He'd never contemplated marriage but now he knew he wouldn't have been complete without it, without her having his ring on her finger. And the wedding could not have been more to his taste. He might be a billionaire, but this simple affair was perfect.

'You look stunning, *querida*,' he murmured, when she was finally standing beside him and before they both turned to the priest.

'So do you.' Sophie gazed up at Matias. He did this to her, even though she saw him daily, even though he was as much a part of her life as the air she breathed. He made her breathing ragged and he made her heart skip a beat.

The special girl in my life, Matias thought with a swell of pride. Well…one of them.

He looked to the back of the church and there was the other one, being cradled by the nanny, fast asleep.

Matias smiled and knew that this was exactly where he was meant to be, and much later, when all the revelry had died down and the last of the guests had departed, he felt it again, that flare of hot possession as he gazed at the woman who was now his wife.

The following morning, they would be off on their honeymoon. Luciana would be there, as would her nanny and his mother.

'Why are you grinning?' Sophie asked, reaching to undo the pearl buttons of the lavender dress she had slipped into after the wedding ceremony had finished.

Sprawled on the four-poster bed in the hotel where they would be spending the night before flying by private jet to one of Matias's villas in Italy, he was a vision of magnificent male splendour. He had undone the buttons of his white shirt and it hung open, exposing a sliver of bronzed, hard chest.

'I'm grinning,' he drawled, 'because not many newly-weds take the groom's mother with them on their honeymoon.' He beckoned her to him with a lazy curl of his finger and watched, incredibly turned on, as she sashayed towards him, ridding herself of her clothes as she got nearer to his prone figure.

By the time she was standing next to the bed, she was wearing only the lacy bra that worked hard to contain her generous breasts and the matching, peach-coloured lacy pants.

Whatever he had to say to her flew through the window because he couldn't resist rolling to his side and then sliding his finger under the lacy pants so that he could press his face against her musky, honeyed wetness, flicking an exploring tongue along the crease of her womanhood and settling to enjoy her for a few moments as she opened her legs a fraction to allow his tongue entry.

Then he lay back and sighed with pure pleasure when, naked, she lay next to him and slipped her hand under his shirt.

'You and Luciana mean the world to her,' Matias said softly, 'and I want to thank you for that, for taking the sadness out of my mother's life and...' he stroked her hair and kissed her gently on her full mouth '... I want to thank you for being my wife. You put the sound and colour into my world and I would be nothing without you.'

Sophie pushed aside his shirt and licked his flat brown nipple until he was groaning and urging her down as he unzipped his trousers.

'I love you so much,' she whispered. 'Now you're going to have to keep quiet, husband of mine, because it's our honeymoon and there are a lot of things I want to do with you before the night is over...'

* * * * *

BOUGHT FOR THE BILLIONAIRE'S REVENGE

CLARE CONNELLY

For Dan, my beloved

PROLOGUE

His car chewed up the miles easily, almost as though the Ferrari sensed his impatience.

He exited the M25, the call he'd received that morning heavy on his mind.

'He's broke, Nik. Not just personally, but his business, too. No more assets to mortgage. Banks are too cautious, anyway. The whole family fortune is going to go down the drain. He's about to lose it all.'

Nikos should have felt overjoyed. There was something about chickens coming home to roost that ought to have brought him amusement. But it hadn't.

Seeing Arthur Kenington suffer had never been his goal.

Using the man's plight to avenge the past, though... *That* idea held infinite appeal.

For six years he'd carried the other man's actions in his chest. Oh, Arthur Kenington wasn't the first elitist snob Nikos had come up against. Being the poorest kid at a prestigious school—'the scholarship boy'—had led to an ever-present sense of being an outsider.

But it had been so much worse with Arthur. After all, the man had paid him to get out of Marnie's life, declaring that Nikos would never be good enough for his precious daughter. Worse, Marnie had listened to her father. She'd dropped him like a hot potato.

Marnie.

Or 'Lady Heiress', as she was known: the beautiful, enigmatic, softly spoken society princess who had, a long time ago, held his heart in her elegant hands. Held it, pummelled it, stabbed it and finally, at her father's behest, rejected it. Thrown it away as though it were an inconsequential item of extremely limited value.

It had hurt like hell at the time, but Nikos had long ago credited it as the fuel that had driven his meteoric rise to the top of the finance world.

A dark smile curved his lips as he navigated the car effortlessly through London's southern boroughs.

The tables had turned; the power was his and he would wield it over Marnie until she realised what a fool she'd been.

He had the power to help her father, to prove his own worth, and finally to hold her heart in his hands and see if he felt like being gentle…or repaying her in kind.

CHAPTER ONE

SHE SHOULDN'T HAVE COME.

The whole way into the city she'd told herself to turn around, go back. It wasn't too late.

But of course it was.

The second Marnie had heard from him the die had been cast. It had fallen into the water of her life, changing stillness to storm within seconds.

Nikos.

Nikos was back.

And he wanted to see her.

The elevator ascended inside the glass building, but it might as well have been plunging her into the depths of hell. A fine bead of perspiration had broken out on her top lip. Marnie didn't wipe it. She hardly even noticed it.

Every cell of her body was focussed on the next half-hour of her life and how she'd get through it.

'I need to see you. It's important.'

His voice hadn't changed at all; his tone still resonated with assuredness. Even at twenty-one, with nothing behind him, Nikos Kyriazis had possessed the same confidence bordering on arrogance that was now his stock in trade. Sure, he had the billions to back it up these days, but even without the dollars in his bank he'd still borne that trademark ability to command.

For the briefest of moments she'd thought of refusing him. So long had passed; what good could come from re-hashing ancient history? Especially when she knew, in the deepest corner of her heart, that she was still so vulnerable to him. So exposed to his appeal.

'It's about your father.'

And the tiny part of Marnie that had wanted to run a mile at the very thought of coming face-to-face with this man again had been silenced instantly.

Her father?

She frowned now, thinking of Arthur Kenington. He'd been different lately. Distracted. He'd lost a little weight, too, and not through any admirable leap into a healthy life-style. She'd become worried, and Nikos's call, completely out of the blue, had underscored those concerns.

The elevator paused, the doors sliding open to allow two men to enter, both dressed in suits. One of them stared at her for a moment too long, in that way people did when they weren't sure exactly where they knew her from. Marnie cleared her throat and looked straight ahead, her wide-set eyes carefully blanked of any emotion. She tried to conceal the embarrassment that always curdled her blood when she realised she'd been recognised.

When the elevator doors swished open to the top floor of the glass and steel monolith at the heart of Canary Wharf, she saw an enormous sign on the wall opposite that pronounced: KYRIAZIS.

Her heart thumped angrily in her chest.

Kyriazis.

Nikos.

'Oh, God,' she whispered under her breath, pausing for a moment to settle her nerves.

The painstakingly developed skill she possessed of hiding her innermost thoughts and feelings from the outside world failed her spectacularly in that moment. Her skin, usually like honey all year round, was pale. Her fingers trembled in a way that wouldn't be stopped.

'Madam? May I help you?'

She blinked, her golden-brown eyes showing turmoil before she suppressed the unwanted emotion. With a smile that sat heavily on her lips, Marnie clicked across the tiled foyer.

More recognition.

'Lady Kenington,' the receptionist said with a small tilt of her head, observing the visitor with undisguised interest from the brown hair with its natural blonde highlights to the symmetrical features set in a dainty face down to the petite frame of this reclusive heiress.

Cold-hearted, the tabloids liked to claim, and to the receptionist there seemed indeed an air of aloofness in the beautiful woman's eyes.

'Yes, hello. I have an appointment with…' There was the smallest hesitation as she steeled herself to say his name aloud to another soul. 'Nikos Kyriazis.'

'Of course.' The receptionist flicked her long red hair over one shoulder and nodded to a banquette of chairs across the room. 'He won't be long. Please, take a seat.'

The anticlimax of the moment might have made Marnie laugh under different circumstances. All morning she'd counted down to this very moment, seeing it as a sort of emotional D-day, and now he was going to keep her waiting?

She moved to the seating area, her lips pursed with disapproval for his lack of punctuality. Behind her there was a spectacular view, framed by a wall of pure glass.

She'd followed his meteoric rise to the top, reading about each success and triumph in the papers alongside the rest of the world. It would have been impossible not to track his astounding emergence onto the world's financial stage. Nikos had built himself into a billionaire with the kind of ease with which most people put on shoes in the morning. Everything he'd touched had turned to gold.

Marnie had contented herself with congratulating him in her dreams. Or reading about him on the internet—except when her heart found it could no longer handle the never-ending assault of images that showed Nikos and *her*. The generic 'Other Woman' he habitually dated. She was always tall, with big breasts, blonde hair and the kind of extroverted confidence that the Marnies of this world could only marvel at.

In a thousand years she'd never be like one of them. Those women with their easy sexuality and relaxed happiness.

As if to emphasise her point, her fingers drifted to the elegant chignon she'd styled her shoulder-length hair into that morning. A few clumps had come loose. She tucked them back into place with care, then replaced her manicured hands in her lap.

Almost twenty minutes later the receptionist crossed the room purposefully. 'Lady Kenington?'

Marnie started, her face lifting expectantly.

'Mr Kyriazis is ready to see you.'

Oh, *was* he? Well, it was about time, she thought crossly as she stood and fell into step behind the other woman.

A pair of frosted glass doors showed a dark, blurred figure that could only be him. The details of his features were not yet visible.

'Lady Kenington, sir,' the receptionist announced.

On the threshold of not just the door but of a moment she'd fantasised about for years, Marnie sucked in a fortifying breath and then, on legs that were trembling lightly, stepped into his palatial office.

Would he be the same?

Would the spark between them still exist?

Or had six years eroded it completely?

'Nikos.'

To her own ears her voice was cool and detached, despite the way her heart was stammering painfully against her ribs. Standing by the windows, he turned to face her at the receptionist's pronouncement, the midafternoon sun casting a pale glow over him that focussed her attention on him as a spotlight might have.

The six years since she'd last seen him had been generous to Nikos. The face she'd loved was much the same, perhaps enhanced by wisdom and the hallmarks of success. Dark eyes, wide-set and rimmed by thick black lashes, a nose that had a bump halfway down from a childhood accident, and a wide mouth set above a chin with a thumbprint-sized cleft. His cheekbones were as pronounced as always, as though the features of his face had been carved from stone at the beginning of time. It was a face that conveyed strength and power—a face that had commanded her love.

He wore his dark hair a little shorter now, but it still brushed his collar at the back and had the luxuriant thickness that had always begged her to run her fingers through it. His dark eyes, so captivating, flashed with an emotion that seemed to Marnie almost mocking.

With pure indolent arrogance he flicked his gaze over her face, then lower, letting it travel slowly across her unimpressive cleavage down to her slim waist. She felt a spike of warmth travel through her abdomen as feelings long ago suppressed slammed against her.

Where his eyes travelled, her skin reacted. She was warm as though he'd touched her, as though he'd glided his fingertips over her body, promising pleasure and satisfaction.

'Marnie.'

Her gut churned. She'd always loved the way he said her name, with the emphasis on the second syllable, like a note from a love song.

The door clicked shut behind her and Marnie had to fight against the instinct to jump like a kitten. Only with the greatest of effort was she able to maintain an impassive expression on her subtly made-up face.

Under normal circumstances Marnie would have done what was expected of her. Even in the most awkward of encounters she could generally muster the basics in small talk. But Nikos was different. *This* was different.

'Well, Nikos?' she said, a tight smile her only concession to social convention. 'You summoned me here. I presume it's not just to stare at me?'

He arched a thick dark brow and her stomach flopped. She'd forgotten just how lethal his looks were in person. And it wasn't just that he was handsome. He was completely vibrant. When he frowned it was as if his whole body echoed the feeling. The same could be said when he smiled or laughed. He was a passionate man who hid nothing. She felt his impatience now, and it burned the little part of her heart that had survived the explosive demise of their relationship.

'Would you like a drink?' His accent was flavoured with cinnamon and pepper: sweet and spicy. Her pulse skittered.

'A drink?' Her lips twisted in an imitation of disapproval. 'At this hour? No. Thank you,' she added as an afterthought.

He shrugged, the bespoke suit straining across his muscled chest. She looked away, heat flashing to the extremities of her limbs. When he began walking towards her, she was powerless to move.

He stopped just a foot or so across the floor, his expression impossible to interpret. His fragrance was an assault on her senses, and the intense masculinity of him was setting her body on fire. Her knees felt as if they might buckle. But although her fingers were fidgeting it was the only betraying gesture of her unease. Her face remained impassive, and her eyes were wide with unspoken challenge.

'You said you needed to speak to me. That it was important.'

'Yes,' he murmured, his gaze once again roaming her face, as though the days, months and years they'd spent separated were a story he could read in it if he looked long enough.

Marnie tried to catalogue the changes that had taken place in her physically in the six years since he'd walked out of Kenington Hall for the last time. Her hair, once long and fair, was shoulder-length and much darker now, with a sort of burnt sugar colour that fell with a fashionable wave to her shoulders. She hadn't worn make-up back then, but now she didn't leave the house without at least a little cosmetic help. That was the wariness she had learned to demonstrate when a scrum of paparazzi was potentially sitting in wait, desperate to capture that next unflattering shot.

'Well?' she asked, her voice a throaty husk.

'What is your rush, *agape mou*?'

She started at the endearment, her fingertips itching as though of their own free will they might slap him. It felt as though a knife had been plunged into her chest.

She flattened the desire to correct him. She needed to stay on point to get through this encounter unscathed. 'You've kept me waiting twenty minutes. I have somewhere else to be after this,' she lied. 'I can't spare much more time. So, whatever you've called me here to say, I suggest you get it over with.'

Again, his brow arched imperiously. His disapproval pleased her in that moment. It eclipsed, all too briefly, other far more seductive thoughts.

'Wherever you've got to be after this, I *suggest* you

cancel it.' He repeated her directive back to her with an insouciant shrug.

'Just as dictatorial as ever,' she said.

His laugh whipped around the room, hitting her hard. 'You used to like that about me, I seem to recall.'

Her heart was racing. She lifted her arms, crossing them over her chest, hoping they might hide the way her body was betraying her. 'I'm definitely not here to walk down memory lane,' she said stiffly.

'You have no idea why you're here.'

She met his gaze, felt flame leaping from one to the other. 'No. You're right. I don't.'

Wishing she'd obeyed her instincts and refused to see him, she began to walk towards the door. Being in the same room as him, feeling the force of his enmity, she knew only that nothing could be important enough to go through this wringer.

Some paths were best unfollowed—their relationship was definitely one of them.

'I don't know why I listened.' She shook her head and her hair loosened a little, dropping a tendril from her temple across her cheek. 'I shouldn't have come.'

He laughed again, following her to the door and pressing the flat of his palm against it. 'Stop.'

She started, and it dawned on him that Marnie was nervous. Her facade was exceptional. Cold, unfeeling, composed. But Marnie was uncertain, too. Her enormous almond-shaped eyes, warm like coffee, flew to his face before she seemed to regain her footing and inject her expression with an air of impatience.

But she *wasn't* impatient. How could she be? The past was claiming her. He was him, and she was her, but they were kids again. Teenagers madly in love, sure of nothing and everything, unable to keep their hands off each other in the passionate way of illicit love affairs.

Sensing her prevarication, he spoke firmly. 'Your father is on the brink of total ruin, and if you don't listen to me he'll be bankrupt within a month.'

She froze, all colour draining from her face. She shook her head slowly from side to side, mumbling something about not being able to believe it, but her mind was shredding through that silly denial. After all, she'd seen for herself the change in him recently. The stress. The anger. The drinking too much. The weight loss. Disturbed sleep. Why hadn't she pushed him harder? Why hadn't she demanded that he or her mother tell her honestly what was going on?

'I have no interest in lying to you,' he said simply. 'Sit down.'

She nodded, her throat thick, as she crossed the room and took a chair at the meeting table. He followed, his eyes not leaving her face as he poured two glasses of water and slid one across the table, before hunkering his large frame into the chair opposite.

His feet brushed hers accidentally beneath the table. The shock of her father's situation had robbed her of her usual control and she jumped at the touch, her whole body resonating before she caught herself in the childish reaction.

And he'd noticed it; the smile of sardonic amusement on his face might have embarrassed her if she hadn't been so completely overcome by concern.

'Dad's…I don't…' She shook her head, resting her hands on the table, trying to make sense of the revelation.

'Your father, like many investors who didn't take adequate precautions, is suffering at the hands of a turbulent market. More fool him.'

He spoke with disrespect and obvious dislike, but Marnie didn't leap to defend Arthur Kenington. At one time she'd been her father's biggest champion, but that, too, had changed over time. Shell shock in the immediate aftermath of Libby's death had translated to the kind of loyalty that didn't allow room for doubt. Her need to keep her family close had made it impossible for her to risk upsetting the only people on earth who understood her grief. She would have done anything to save them further pain, even if that had meant walking away from the man she loved because they'd expressed their bitter disapproval.

Her eyes were cloudy as they settled on his frame. Memories were sharp. She pushed at them angrily, relegating them to the locked box of her mind.

Those memories were of the past. The distant past. She and Nikos were different people now.

'He will lose everything without immediate help. Without money.'

Marnie turned the ring she always wore around her finger—a nervous gesture she'd resorted to without realising. Her face—so beautiful, so ethereally elegant—was crushed, and Nikos felt a hint of pity for her. There was a time when he would have said that causing her pain was anathema to him. A time when he would have leapt in front of a speeding bus to save her life—a time when he had promised to love her for ever, to adore her, to cherish her.

And she'd answered that pledge by telling him he'd never be good enough for her, or words to that effect.

He straightened in the chair, honing in on his resolve.

But Marnie spoke first, her voice quietly insistent. 'Dad has lots of associates. People with money.'

'He needs rather a large sum.'

'He'll find it,' she said with false bravado, unknowingly tilting her gaze down her small ski slope nose.

His smile was almost feral in its confidence. 'A hundred million pounds by the end of the month?'

'A…hundred…' Her feathery lashes closed, muting any visible shock. She was hiding herself from him, wanting to keep her turmoil private and secret.

He didn't challenge her; there was no need.

'And that is just to start,' he confirmed with a small nod. 'But if you want to leave…' He waved a hand towards the door, as though he didn't give a damn what she chose to do.

Marnie toyed with the ring again, her eyes studying its gentle golden crenulations before shifting their focus back to his face. 'So? What's *your* interest in my father's business?'

'His business?' Nikos's laugh was short and sharp. 'I have no interest in that.'

Marnie's eyes knitted together, confusion obvious on her features. Even her hair looked uptight, knotted into that style. Her hands, her nails, her perfectly made-up face: she was the picture of stylish grace, just as her parents had always intended her to be.

'I presume you called me here because you have a plan.' She pinned him with her golden-brown eyes until the sensation overpowered her. 'I wish you'd stop prevaricating and just tell me.'

His smile was not one of happiness. 'You are hardly in a position to issue commands to me.'

Marnie's face lifted to his in surprise. 'That's not what I was doing.' She shook her head timidly from side to side. 'I didn't mean to, anyway. It's just…please. Tell me everything.'

He shrugged. 'Bad decisions. Bad investments. Bad business.' He pressed back further in his chair, the intensity of his fierce gaze sending sharp arrows of awareness and emotion through her blood. 'The why of it doesn't matter.'

'It matters to me.'

He spoke on as though she hadn't. His eyes bored into hers. 'I believe there are not ten people in the world who would find themselves in a financial position to help your father. Even fewer who would have any motivation to do so.'

Marnie bit down on her lower lip, trying desperately to

think of anyone who might have enough liquidity to inject some cash into her father's crumbling empire.

Only one man came to mind, and he was staring at her in a way that was turning her mind to mush.

Unable to sit still for a moment longer, Marnie scraped her chair back and stalked to the window. London vibrated beneath them: a collection of cars and souls all going about their own lives, threading together into one enormous carpet of activity. She felt as if she'd been plucked out of the fibres and placed here instead, in a madhouse.

'Dad's never been your favourite person,' she said softly. 'How do I know you're not making this up for some cruel reason of your own?'

'Your father's demise is not a well-kept secret, *matakia mou*. Anderson told me.'

'Anderson?' The name was like a knife in her gut. She thought of Libby's fiancé with the shock of grief that always accompanied anything to do with her sister. With *Before*.

'We're still in touch,' he said with a shrug, as if that wasn't important.

'He knows about this?' She thought of Anderson Holt's family, the fortune they possessed. Maybe *they* could help? She dismissed the thought instantly. A hundred million pounds—cash—was beyond most people's capabilities. Besides, Arthur Kenington would never let himself be bailed out.

'It is no secret,' Nikos said, misunderstanding her question. 'I imagine the whole city knows the truth of your father's position.'

Her spine stiffened and sorrow for the man who had raised her pushed all thoughts of her late sister's fiancé from her mind. She blinked quickly, denying the sting of tears that was threatening. She was not willing to show such weakness in front of anyone, let alone Nikos.

'He *has* seemed stressed lately,' she conceded awkwardly, keeping her vision focussed on the buzz of activity at street level.

'I can well imagine. The idea of losing his life's work and the legacy of his forebears will be weighing heavily on his conscience. Not to mention his monumental ego.'

She let the barb go by. Her mind was completely absorbed with trying to make sense of this information. 'I don't understand why he wouldn't have said anything.'

'Don't you?' His eyes flashed with anger and resentment as his last conversation with Lord Arthur Kenington came to mind. 'The man prides himself on shielding you from the world. He would do anything to spare you the pain of actually inhabiting reality with the rest of us.'

'You call *this* reality?' she quipped, flicking a disapproving glance around the cavernous glass office decorated with modern art masterpieces and furniture that would have looked at home in a gallery.

A muscle jerked in his cheek and Marnie wished she could pull those words back. Who was *she* to sit in judgement of his success? She didn't know the details, but she knew enough of his childhood to realise that if anyone on earth understood poverty it was Nikos.

'I'm sorry,' she said stiffly, lifting a finger to her temple and rubbing at it. 'None of this is your fault.'

A pang of something a lot like sympathy squeezed in Nikos's gut. Recognising that she could still evoke those emotions in him, he consciously pushed aside any softening towards her.

'No.' He rubbed a hand across his stubbled jaw. 'He stands to lose it all, Marnie. His investments. His reputation. Kenington Hall. He will be a cautionary tale at best, a laughing stock more likely.'

'Don't…' She shivered, thinking of what her parents had already suffered and lost in life. The thought of them enduring yet another tragedy weighed so heavily on her chest she could hardly breathe.

'I would be lying if I said I'm not a little tempted to leave him to his fate. A fate that, as it turns out, is not at all dissimilar to what he predicted for *me*.'

A shiver ran down her spine. 'You're still angry about that?'

His eyes flashed. 'Angry? No. Disgusted? Yes.' He dragged a hand through his hair, as though mentally shaking himself. 'He would spend a lifetime repaying his creditors.'

Nikos was conscious that he was driving a proverbial knife into her. He didn't stop.

'Some of his decisions might even be seen as criminally negligent.'

'Oh, my God, Nikos, *don't*.' She spun to face him; it was like being hit with a sledgehammer.

He ground his teeth, refusing to feel sympathy for her even when her world was shattering. 'It is the truth. Would you prefer I'd said nothing?'

When she spoke her voice was hoarse, momentarily weakened by the strength of her feelings. 'Does this bring you pleasure? Did you bring me here to gloat?'

'To gloat?' His smile was like a wolf's. 'No.'

'Well? Then what *do* you want? Why are you telling me any of this?'

A muscle jerked in his cheek. 'I could alleviate all of your father's problems, you know.'

Hope, a fragile bird, fluttered in her gut. 'Yes?'

'It would not be difficult for me to fix this,' he said with a shrug.

Marnie's head spun at the ease of his declaration. 'Even a hundred million pounds?'

'I am a wealthy man. Do you not read the papers?'

'God, Nikos.' Relief was so palpable that she didn't

even acknowledge the insult. Hope loomed. 'I don't know how to thank you.'

'Delay your gratitude until you have considered the terms.'

'The terms?' Her brows drew together in confusion.

'I have the means to help your father, but not yet the inducement.'

Aware she was parroting, she murmured, 'What inducement?'

The breath burned in her lungs. Her heart was hammering so hard in her chest that she thought it might break free and make a bid for freedom. Tension was a rope, twisting around them. She waited on tenterhooks that seemed to have sharp gnashing teeth.

'You, Marnie.' His dark voice was at its arrogant best. 'As my wife. Marry me and I will help him.'

CHAPTER TWO

SHE'D NEVER UNDERSTOOD how silence could vibrate until that moment. The very air they breathed seemed as if it was alive, crackling and humming around them. His words were little daggers, floating through the atmosphere, jabbing at her heart, her soul, her brain, her mind.

'Marry me and I will help him.'

Only the sound of her heavy breathing perforated the air. For support, she pressed back against the glass window. It was warmed by the sun.

'I don't understand,' she said finally, squeezing her eyes shut. Every fibre of her being instantly rejected the idea.

Or did it?

Briefly, childish fantasies bubbled inside her, spreading the kind of pleasure she'd once revelled in freely.

When she blinked a moment later, Nikos was holding a glass of water just in front of her. She took it and drank gratefully, her throat parched.

'It is not a difficult equation. Marriage to me in exchange for a sum of money that will answer your father's debts.'

'That makes no sense,' she contradicted flatly.

'No?'

'No!'

It seemed like the right reaction. It was an absurd proposal, after all. Wasn't it? She should have felt panicked by the very idea. And perhaps a part of her did. This was the man who had disappeared from her life but never fully from her heart.

But panic and wariness were only tiny components of her emotional tangle. Hope and an intense flare of passionate resonance also filled her.

'Marriage…' Her heart squeezed. Her words were a whisper. 'Marriage…is for people in love. That's not us. How can you be so cavalier about it?'

He took a step closer, curling his fingers around the glass. Instead of taking it from her he kept his hand over hers. Electricity sparked along the length of her arm, shooting blue fire through her body.

'Call it…righting a wrong,' he said darkly, his eyes scanning her face with hard emotion. 'Or repaying a debt.'

Her stomach rolled.

'Your father paid me a considerable sum to get out of your life six years ago.'

Her mouth formed a perfect 'o' and she gasped in surprise. He gathered she hadn't known *that* little piece of information. It didn't make him proud, but he enjoyed seeing her sense of betrayal and outrage before she schooled her features once more. Her mask was excellent, though the more tightly she held on to it the more he wanted to force her to drop it. To shock her, surprise her, make her feel so strongly that she could no longer remain impassive.

He put his thumb-pad over her lower lip, remembering how soft they were to kiss.

'I didn't know.' Her eyes were earnest and it didn't enter his mind to doubt her.

'No.' He shrugged. 'It wasn't necessary, in any event. He obviously didn't realise that you had already conclusively ended things.'

Marnie's heart squeezed. 'I had no choice.'

'Of *course* you had a damned choice.' He controlled his temper with effort. 'You could have told him that you'd fallen in love with me. That no amount of comment about the fact that I didn't live up to his exalted expectations would change how you felt about me. You could have told him to shove his snobbery and his stupidity. You could have fought for what we were—as I would have.'

She sucked in a deep breath. The pain was as fresh in that instant as if it was six years ago. She ached all over. 'You know what we'd been through.' She squeezed her eyes shut. 'What my family had lost. I couldn't hurt him. I had to choose between him and...what I felt for you.'

'And you chose him.' His stare was filled with a startling wave of resentment. 'You switched something in here—' he lifted a finger to her chest, pointing at her heart '—and that was it. It was over.'

She swallowed convulsively. It had been nothing like that. He made it sound easy. As if she'd simply decided to forget Nikos and move on. But she hadn't. She'd agonised over the decision.

She'd tried to explain to her parents that she didn't care that Nikos didn't have money or come from one of the established families they approved of. But arguments had led to the unsupportable—her mother in tears, her father furious and not speaking to Marnie, and the certainty that they just wanted Libby back—perfect Libby—to make good choices and be the daughter they were proud of.

'In any event, the financial...*compensation* for leaving you helped to soften the blow. At first I swore I wouldn't take it. But then...'

He spoke with gravelled inflection, sucking Marnie back to the present.

'I was so angry with you, with him. I took it and I told myself I'd double it—just to prove him wrong. To prove a point.'

Marnie's cheeks were flushed. His hand moved to cup her face. She could have pulled away, but she didn't. 'I think you did more than that.'

His smile was grim. 'Yes.'

So Arthur had given her boyfriend money to get out of her life? A chill ran the length of her spine. It seemed like a step too far. Pressuring her to end it was one thing, but actually forcing Nikos out?

'I'm sorry he got involved like that. It wasn't his place to...to pay you off.'

'Not when you'd already done his bidding,' Nikos responded with a lift of his shoulders. 'Your father forbade you from seeing me and, like a good little Lady Heiress, you jumped when he clicked his fingers.'

'Don't call me that,' she said distractedly, hating the tabloid press's moniker for her.

It wasn't that it was cruelly meant, only that they mistook her natural reserve for something far more grandiose: snobbery. Pretension. Airs and graces. The kind of aristocratic aspirations that Marnie had never fallen in line with despite the value her parents put on them. The values that had been at the root of their disapproval of Nikos.

'So this is revenge?' she murmured, her eyes clashing fiercely with his. Pain lanced through her.

'Yes.'

'A dish best served cold?' She shook her head sadly, dislodging his hand. 'You've waited six years for this.'

'Yes.' He brought his body closer, crushing her with his strong thighs, his broad chest. 'But there will be nothing cold about our marriage.'

Desire lurched through her. The world began to spin wildly off its axis. 'There won't be a marriage,' she said, with a confidence that was completely forged. Already the options were closing in around her. 'And there certainly won't be...what you're...suggesting.'

'What's the matter, *agape mou*? Do you worry that we won't still feel as we did then?'

He ground his hips against her and she groaned as sensations that had long since been relegated to the past flared in her belly. Of their own volition her fingers curled into the fabric of his shirt, the warmth from his chest a balm to her fraught nerves.

'Do you remember how I respected your innocence?' He brought his mouth close to hers, so that his words were a breath on her lips. 'How I told you we should wait until we were married, or at least engaged?'

Shame, desire, misery and despair slid through her like a headless snake, twisting and writhing in her heart. She pulled her lower lip between her teeth and nodded once.

'How, even though I had kissed your body all over, and you had begged me to take you, I insisted that I wanted to wait? Because I thought I loved you and that it mattered.'

He dropped his hands to her hips, holding her still as he pushed against her once more. She tilted her head back as far as she could, the window's glass providing a hard barrier.

'Do you remember how you laughed in my face and told me you'd never marry someone like me?'

Those words! How she'd hated saying them! She'd rehearsed them for days, and when the moment had come only the belief that she was doing the right thing for her family had spurred her on to say them. It was the most difficult thing she'd ever done. Even now, six years later, she wondered at the way she'd been led away from him despite the intensity of her feelings.

'*Do* you?' he demanded, scraping his lips against her neck, sending her pulse rioting out of control.

'Yes!' She groaned as desire and memory weakened her body.

'I have met many people like you in my life—like your father. Snobs who value centuries-old fortune above all else.'

'That isn't me,' she said with quiet determination.

'Of course it is.' He almost laughed. 'You broke up with me because you knew your destiny was to marry someone like you. Somebody that your parents approved of.'

'That's what *they* wanted. I just wanted *you*.'

'Not enough.' He sobered, his mouth a grim slash.

Frustrated, she tried to appeal to the man he'd once been: the man who had known her better than anyone on earth. 'God, Nikos. You *know* what my life was like then. We'd just buried Libby. We were all in mourning. I couldn't upset them like you wanted me to. I *couldn't*. Don't you dare think for a moment it was because I thought you weren't good enough.'

'You thought as your parents wished you to,' he said with coldness, shrugging as though it no longer mattered. 'But they will shortly come to realise there is one thing that carries more sway than birth and breeding. And when you are as broke as your father that is *money*.'

His words fell like bricks against her chest.

'Now you will marry me, and he will have to spend the rest of his life knowing it was *me*—the man he wouldn't have in his house—who was his salvation.'

The sheer fury of his words whipped her like a rope. 'Nikos,' she said, surprised at how calm she could sound in the midst of his stormy declaration. 'He should never have made you feel like that.'

'Your father could have called me every name under the sun for all I cared, *agape*. It was *you* I expected more of.'

She swallowed. Expectations were not new to Marnie. Her parents'. Her sister's. Her own.

'And now you *will* marry me.'

Anticipation formed a cliff's edge and she was tumbling over it, free-falling from a great height. She shook her head, but they both knew it was denial for the sake of it.

'No more waiting,' he intoned darkly, crushing his mouth to hers in a kiss that stole her breath and coloured her soul.

His tongue clashed with hers. It was a kiss of slavish possession, a kiss designed to challenge and disarm. He blew away every defence she had, reminding her that his body had always been able to manipulate hers. A single look had always been enough to make her break out in a cold sweat of need.

'No more waiting.'

'You can't still want me,' she said into his mouth, wrapping her hands around his back. 'You've hardly lived the life of a monk. I would have thought I'd lost all appeal by now.'

'Call it unfinished business,' he responded, breaking the kiss to scrape his lips down her neck, nipping at her shoulder.

She pushed her hips forward, instinctively wanting more. Wanting everything.

Her brain was wrapped in cotton wool, foggy and filled with questions softened by confusion. 'It was six years ago.'

'Yes. And still you're the only woman I have ever believed myself in love with. The only woman I have ever wanted a future with. Once upon a time for love.'

'And now?'

'For…less noble reasons.'

He stepped away, breaking their kiss so easily it made her head spin.

'Your father isn't the only one I intend to prove wrong.'

She narrowed her eyes, her heart racing. 'What does *that* mean?'

His laugh was without humour. 'You said I didn't mean

anything to you. That I had been merely a distraction when you needed to escape grief.'

He brought his face closer to hers once more—so close that she could see the thousands of tiny prisms of light that danced in his eyes.

'You told me you didn't want me.'

'I…' She squeezed her eyes shut. 'I don't remember saying that,' she lied.

'You said it. And I will delight in showing you how wrong you were.'

He stepped away, leaving her cresting a wave of emotion. Striving to sound cool, she said, 'So you've been… what? Pining for me for six years? Give me a break, Nikos. You moved on pretty damned fast, so it's a little disingenuous to be playing the heartbroken ex-lover now.'

'We were never lovers, *agape*.'

Her stomach churned; her cheeks were pink. 'That's not the point I'm making.'

'Whatever point it is you are attempting to make it is irrelevant to me.'

She sucked in an indignant breath but he continued. 'I have not been pining for you. But I *am* an opportunist.' His smile was almost cruel—at least it looked it to Marnie. 'Your father's situation presented me with an opportunity I felt I couldn't resist.'

'Oh, yeah?' she snapped, trying desperately to think of a way out. A way to make him realise how foolhardy this was!

'You will spend every day of our marriage faced with the reality of just how wrong you were.'

Speechless, she fidgeted with her ring, her mind unable to grasp exactly what was going on.

Seemingly he took her silence as a form of agreement. 'A licence can be arranged within fifteen days. I have engaged a wedding planner to oversee the details. Her card is on my desk; take it when you leave.'

She shook her head as the words he was saying tumbled over her. She needed to process what was going on. 'Wait a second. It's too sudden. Too soon.'

He arched a single thick brow. 'Any delay will make it impossible for me to help your father in time.'

'You're saying we have to actually *be* married before you'll help him?'

His lip twisted in a smile of cynical derision. 'It would hardly make sense to prop him up *before* the pleasure of having you… As my wife.'

To Marnie, his slight pause implied that he meant something else altogether. That he wanted to sleep with her before money changed hands. It made her feel instantly dirty, and she shifted away from the window, crossing her arms in an attempt to stem the pain that was perforating her heart.

'Do you think I'd renege on our deal?' she asked, realising only after posing the question that it showed her acquiescence when she hadn't actually intended to agree…*yet*.

'I think you will do whatever pleases you—as you always have done.' His eyes narrowed. 'Forgive me—what is the expression? Having been bitten, I am…?'

'Once bitten, twice shy.' She sucked in an unsteady breath, waiting for relief to calm her lungs. But still they burned painfully. She tried to salvage her pride. 'If I agree to do this, I *will* go through with it.'

'I'm not sure I can put much stock in your assurances,' he said with a shrug. 'I credit you and your father for my scepticism. Were it not for you, perhaps I would have continued to take promises at face value. Now I live and die by contracts.'

'That's fine in business. I'm sure it's wise, in fact. But marriage is different, surely.'

'A *real* marriage,' he conceded, with a tight nod.

'You're saying you don't want ours to be a real marriage?'

His laugh sent a shiver down her spine. 'Oh, in the most important ways it will be.'

'Meaning…?' she challenged—though how could she not understand his intention?

'Meaning, Marnie, that I have no interest in paying a hundred million pounds and tying myself to a woman *purely* for revenge.'

His smile curled her toes.

'There will be other benefits to our marriage.'

Her heart slammed hard in her chest. 'I…' She clamped her mouth shut.

What had she been about to say? That she was still a virgin? That after being so madly in love with him and letting him go she'd found she couldn't feel that same desire for another man? Especially not the men her parents approved of her dating.

'I'm not going to sleep with you just because you appear out of the blue…'

'That is not why you'll sleep with me,' he said.

He spoke with a confidence that infuriated her. But he was right! Despite the passage of time, and the insufferable situation she found herself in, she couldn't deny that the same need was rioting through her now, just as it had in their past.

'This is a deal-breaker,' he said with a shrug. 'These are my terms. Accept them or don't.'

'Wait.' She shook her head and lifted a hand to make him pause for a moment. But she was drowning. Possibilities, questions, wants, needs, doubts were churning around inside her—it was background noise but it was going to suck her under. 'There's so much more to discuss.'

'Such as?' he prompted, crossing his arms over his broad chest.

She tried not to notice the way the fabric strained to reveal his impressive pectoral definition.

'Well, such as…' She darted her tongue out and licked her lower lip. 'Say I went along with this absolutely crazy idea—and I'm not saying I will, because clearly it's madness—where would you see us living?'

'That is also non-negotiable. Greece.'

'Greece?' She was in free fall again. 'Greece, as in… You mean Greece?'

He stared at her for a long moment, his eyes mocking her. 'Athens. My home.'

'But I've always lived *here*. I can't move.'

Their eyes locked; it was a battle of wills and yet when he spoke it was with an easy nonchalance she admired.

'I will be spending a considerable fortune to save your father's reputation. You do not think it's fair that *you* should make some concessions?'

'Marrying you is *not* a c-concession,' she stammered in disbelief. 'It's so much more than that. And the same can be said of moving to a different country.'

'You are *so* sheltered,' he murmured. 'What would you suggest? That we live in London? Within arm's reach of your father? A man I will always despise? No.'

'How can I marry you knowing you feel that way about him?'

His expression was rock-hard. 'You will find a way.' He shrugged. 'While it might be difficult for you, it is the only way to spare him—and your mother—from a considerable fall from grace.'

'So this is how it would be? You'd dictate terms and I'd be expected to fall in with them?'

The air was thick between them. He studied her for a

long moment and she wondered if he wasn't going to answer. Finally, though, he sighed.

'I have no intention of being unreasonable. When you make a fair request I will hear you out. But this is not one of those instances. I live in Greece. My business is primarily controlled from Athens. You still live with your parents, who hate me as much as I do them. You have no business to speak of. It is obvious that we should move.'

'Just like that?' she murmured, shaking her head at his high-handed dictatorial manner even when a small part of her brain could see that he was raising a decent rationale for the suggestion.

'These are my terms,' he said again.

'You're unbelievable,' she replied softly, worrying at her fingers.

She spun her ring some more, trying to think of a way to appease him that didn't involve anything so drastic as this ridiculous marriage. But there was nothing. He had the money. And there was no way he'd help unless she made it worth his while.

'Yes.' He shrugged. 'So?'

'I wouldn't want a big wedding.' She was thinking aloud, really, though to her ears it sounded as though she was going along with his proposal. 'If I had my way it would just be us. No fanfare. No fuss.'

'Hmm…' he murmured with a shake of his head. 'And no one need ever know? No. I want the world to see that you are my wife. You—a woman who once felt I was far beneath her. A woman who declared she'd never marry someone like me. I want your father to have to stand beside us, smiling as though I am all his dreams come true, when we three will know that I am the last man on earth he wants his daughter to marry.'

The way he'd been treated by her and her parents was a nauseating truth. She wished—not for the first time—

that she'd been able to stand up to them. That she'd been wise enough to fight for the relationship that had mattered so much to her.

'Nikos…' She furrowed her brows, searching for words. 'You have to understand why I…why I couldn't be with you. You know how my parents were after Libby…after…'

He studied her face, torn between listening and shutting down this hollow explanation.

'I know I never explained it properly at the time. The way I was always in her shadow. The certainty that I was a poor comparison to her. The absolute blinding fact that they wished again and again that I could be more like her.' She swallowed, an image of her sister clouding her eyes and making her heart ring with nostalgic affection. 'They wanted me to marry someone like Anderson—her fiancé. And I wanted their approval so badly I would have done anything they asked.'

He compressed his lips. 'Yes. I presumed as much at the time.'

He brought his face closer to hers, so she could feel the waves of his resentment.

'You walked away from me and what we were to each other as though I was nothing to you. You can blame your sister, or you can blame your parents, but the only one who made the decision was *you*.'

'I'm trying to explain why…'

'And I'm telling you that it does not matter to me.' His eyes flared. 'You were wrong.'

She had been. In the six years since she'd watched Nikos leave for the last time, his shoulders set, his head held high, she'd never met anyone who excited in her even a tenth of the emotions he had. He alone had been her true love. And she'd burned him in a way that he'd apparently never forgive.

He brought the conversation back to the wedding. 'The guest list will be extensive and the press coverage—'

'Nikos!' Marnie interrupted, her voice strained.

Something in the pale set of her features communicated her distress and he was quiet, watchful.

'Please.' Her throat worked overtime as she tried to relieve her aching mouth. 'I can't do that.'

'You do agree to marry me?'

She nodded. 'But not like that. I… You know how I feel about the media. And, more to the point, how they feel about me.' She flashed a look at him from beneath thick dark lashes. 'I'll marry you. I will. But without all the fuss. Please.'

It was tempting to push her out of her comfort zone. To say that it was a big wedding or none at all. She was staring at him with a look of icy aloofness that had no doubt helped earn her the nickname of Lady Heiress. That look of untouchable elegance bordering on disdain that he understood was her tightly held shield in moments of wrenching panic. That same look he was desperate to dislodge as soon as possible, shaking her into showing her real feelings.

'You don't like the press any more than I do,' she said with measured persistence. 'If you insist on a big wedding we'll both know it's simply to be spiteful to me. And you're not that petty—are you, Nikos?'

He felt his resolve slipping and a grudging admiration for her reasoned argument spread through him. Still, he drawled, 'I'm blackmailing you into my bed and you don't think I'm petty?'

Heat flooded her system, warring with the ice that had coated her heart. 'No, I don't. I think you want me to marry you. What does it matter how we do it?'

She had an excellent point. Besides Marnie there was only one other person he really cared about having at the wedding.

'Fine,' he said, with a nonchalant lift of his shoulders. His eyes glittered with determination. 'So long as your father is there the rest does not greatly matter.'

'It's enormous,' she intoned flatly, rubbing her fingertip over the flattened edges of paper.

Nikos's stare was loaded with emotion. 'It needs to be.' His accent seemed thicker, spicier than it had been the night before. Her gaze flicked to his face, then skidded away again immediately. His face was all angles and planes, unforgiving and unrelenting.

Harsh.

She had never comprehended the full extent of that hardness before. Not in the past, anyway. When she'd loved him as much as the ocean loved the shore. She had felt, then, just like that. As if she would spend the rest of her life rolling inexorably towards him, needing to touch him, to wash over him, to feel him beneath her and around her. She had believed them to be as organically dependent as those two bodies—sea and sand. That without him she would have nowhere to go.

Foolishly, she had thought he felt the same.

But Nikos had moved on quickly, despite his protestations of love, and his bed had been such a hot spot it might as well have had its own listing on TripAdvisor.

'Mind if I have my lawyer check this out?'

He shrugged his shoulders. '*Sígoura.* Certainly. But that may cause a delay to proceedings.'

Her eyes narrowed. 'You mean you might not be able to help Dad in time?'

He sat back in his chair, his body taut, his face unreadable. 'I will not apply for the marriage licence until you have signed the pre-nup.'

A frown formed a little line between her eyes. 'Why not?'

His laugh was a sharp sound in the busy café. A woman

at the table beside them angled her head curiously before going back to her book.

Marnie lowered her voice, not wanting to risk being overheard. She was obliged to lean a little closer. 'Does it matter if I don't sign it in the next week or two? So long as you have it before the wedding...?'

'The minute I apply for our certificate there's a high probability the press will pick up on it. Do you *want* the world to know we were hastily engaged and that the wedding was then cancelled?'

Her cheeks flamed. 'As if the journalists of the world have nothing better to do than search the registry for your name, waiting with bated breath until such time as you see fit to hang up your well-worn bachelor belt,' she muttered.

He arched a single brow, his expression making her feel instantly ridiculous. 'If you believe our wedding won't excite media interest then you're more naive than I recall.'

Yes, she definitely felt childish now. She dragged her lower lip between her teeth, then caught the betraying gesture and mentally shook herself. She was Lady Marnie Kenington, and it was not for Nikos to berate and humiliate her.

'Each of us on our own would create a stir of interest. Marrying one another guarantees press interest.'

'I know.' She nodded. There was no point, after all, in arguing the toss. He was absolutely right. 'But we agreed on a quiet wedding.'

'And I will do my best to arrange this,' he promised.

'Okay.' She nodded again quickly.

His first instinct was to feel impressed by her ability to be reasonable in the face of an argument. But he quickly realised that she wasn't reasonable so much as changeable. That she was deferring to him at the first sign of pressure. Was that how it had been with her parents?

His mouth was a grim line in his face. 'There are four pages you need to sign.'

She expelled a heavy breath and tapped the pen against the side of the table.

Memories, visceral and sharp, twisted his gut. How familiar that tiny gesture was! Flashes of her studying for exams, writing lists, pausing midsentence to capture the next, flashed into his mind. When she'd had a particularly large problem to solve she'd chewed on the end of the pen, waiting for clarity to flood to her from its inky heart.

'Nikos…' She lifted her gaze to him. 'Doesn't this all seem a bit crazy?'

He didn't react.

She huffed out a sigh. 'I don't know you any more. And you definitely don't know me.'

He narrowed his eyes almost imperceptibly. 'I know you perhaps as well as ever.'

She bit on the pen again and shook her head. 'I just don't see why we have to rush this.'

'It is your father's financial situation that puts a time limit on matters.'

'But—'

'No.'

He leaned across the table, pressing his hand on hers. Sparks shimmered in her heart. Angered by her body's ongoing betrayal to his proximity, she worked overtime to conceal the explosive desire. Her glare was dripping with ice.

'This is the only way I will help your father. It's not a negotiation.'

Backed against a wall, she wondered why she didn't feel more angry.

She looked down at the thick pile of papers. 'If you expect me to sign this today then you're going to have to explain it to me.'

'Fine.' He flicked a glance at his gold wristwatch.

'Sorry if I'm taking up too much of your time,' she snapped sarcastically, and for the briefest moment he felt the full force of her emotions—emotions she was so good at guarding. Fear, worry, stress, uncertainty.

But he had no intention of softening towards his fiancée. He nodded curtly, his expression rock-hard. 'The first section deals with our assets. Any assets you bring to the marriage will be quarantined against becoming communal.'

'So I get to keep what's mine?' she interpreted.

'Yes. I have no interest in your money.'

The way he said it, with such vile distaste, made Marnie shiver.

'Fine. Just as I have no interest in yours.'

He arched a brow, his face filled with sardonic amusement. 'You mean, I presume, beyond the hundred million pounds I will be giving your father?'

Her cheeks flamed. 'Yes.' She couldn't meet his eyes because she felt the sting of tears in her own.

'Irrespective of that, you will be entitled to a sum for each year we remain married.'

'I don't want it,' she said through clenched teeth.

'Fine. Give it away. It's not my concern.' He reached forward impatiently and turned several pages until he arrived at the end of that section. 'Sign here.'

Pressing her lips together, she scrawled her name, blinking her eyes furiously.

They were still suspiciously moist when she lifted her face to his. 'Next?'

He appeared not to notice how close her emotions were to the surface. 'The next section deals with the moral obligations of our union. Any infidelity will lead to an immediate termination of the marriage. It will also invalidate the financial agreement, and will necessitate your father returning half of the money I have given him to that date.'

She blinked in confusion. 'You think I'm going to cheat on you?'

His lips compressed with a dark emotion, one she couldn't fathom. 'I could not say with certainty.' His smile was wolfish. 'Though I imagine this makes it considerably less likely.'

She ground her teeth together. 'And what if *you* cheat?'

'Me?' He laughed again, this time with real humour.

'Yeah. You're the one who seems to be constantly auditioning lovers. What happens if you get bored in our marriage and end up in another woman's bed?'

'You will just have to make sure I don't get bored.'

Her breath snagged in her throat. The threat weakened her. Her pulse throbbed painfully in her body. 'When did you get so cynical?'

He narrowed his eyes, stunning her with the heat she felt emanating from him. 'When do you think, *agape mou*?'

She shook her head, hating the implication that she'd somehow caused his character transformation. 'Nikos…'

What did she want to say? She'd already tried to explain about Libby, and the burden she'd felt to please her parents—a burden that had increased monumentally after Libby's death. He didn't care. He'd said as much. She clamped her mouth shut and shook her head. It was futile.

'I have a meeting after this.'

She swallowed, shaking her head to clear the tangle of thoughts. 'Fine.'

'The third section deals with children.'

Her eyes startled to his face. 'Children?' Her heart was jackhammering inside her chest.

He turned several pages but Marnie was too shocked to bother trying to read them. He fixed her with a direct stare. 'It stipulates that we won't have a child for at least five years.'

Fire and ice were flashing within her, making speech

difficult. She blinked her enormous caramel eyes, then shook her head, but still it didn't make sense. 'You want children?'

He shrugged. 'Perhaps. One day. It's hard to imagine right now—and with you.'

'Oh, gee, thanks.' She rolled her eyes in an attempt to hide the way his words had wounded her. 'As if I'm just lining up to be your baby-baker.'

'My…*baby-baker*?' Despite himself, he felt a smile tickle the corner of his lips.

'I can't believe you're actually contracting hypothetical children.'

He arched a brow. 'It makes sense.'

'A baby isn't…' She dropped her gaze. 'A baby isn't *Section Three, Subsection Eleven A.* A baby is a little person. A new life! You have no right to…to…make such arbitrary decisions about something that should be magical and wonderful.'

'A baby between us would *never* be magical and wonderful,' he responded, with such ease that she genuinely believed he hadn't intended to be unkind. 'It is the very last thing I would want. As for it being arbitrary…' He shrugged his broad shoulders with an air of unconcern. 'You seemed perfectly fine making such decisions in the past.'

'Not about a child!'

'You just said you don't want to be my…baby-baker. Have you changed your mind suddenly?' he asked cynically, his eyes drifting over her features with genuine interest.

'No.' She bit down on her lip. The lie—and she recognised it as such—hurt. Images of what their children might look like were hard to shake. Instantly she could see a tiny chubby version of Nikos, with his imperious expression and dark eyes, and her heart seemed to soar at the prospect.

'Our marriage is not one of love. I can think of nothing worse than bringing a child into that situation.'

'But in five years?' she heard herself ask, as if from a long way away.

He shrugged insolently. 'In five years we will either have found a way to live together with a degree of harmony, or we will hate one another and have long since divorced. It gives us time to see what's what. No?'

She nodded jerkily. He was right. She knew he was. But as she signed her name on the bottom of the page she felt as if she was strangling a large part of herself.

'Next?' She forced a tight smile to her lips; her tone was cool.

'A simple confidentiality agreement. Our business is our own. The press has a fascination with you, and I have often thought, despite what you say, that you court their interest.'

'You've got to be kidding me!' she interrupted sharply. 'I go out of my way to stay off their radar.'

'Which in and of itself only heightens their attention and speculation.'

'So I flirt with the press by hiding from them?' She crossed her legs beneath the table. 'That's absurd.'

'You are "Lady Heiress". They call you that because of your behaviour—'

'They call me that,' she interrupted testily, 'because I refuse to engage with them. After Libby died they were everywhere. I was only seventeen, and they followed me around for sport.'

She didn't add how horrible their comparisons to the beautiful Libby had made her feel. How Marnie's far less stunning looks had drawn the press's derision. She had refused to court them in order to create the impression that she didn't care, but each article had eroded a piece of her confidence until only the 'Lady Heiress' construct had remained. Being cold and untouchable, a renowned ice queen, was better than being the less beautiful, less popular, less charismatic sister of Lady Elizabeth Kenington.

He shrugged. 'You will not be of such interest in Greece. Here you are a society princess. There you will be only my wife.'

Why did that prospect make everything inside her sing? Not just the prospect of marrying him, but of escaping it all! The intrusions and invasions. Freedom was a gulf before her.

'Your parents are included in this agreement. They are to believe our wedding is a real one.'

'Oh? I would have thought you'd like to throw the terms of our deal in Dad's face, just to see him suffer,' she couldn't help snapping.

'Perhaps one day.' His smile tilted her world off-balance. 'But that is *my* decision. Not yours.'

She furrowed her brow. 'This agreement doesn't apply to you?'

'No. It is a contract for you. So you understand what is expected of you.'

'That definitely isn't fair.'

He laughed. 'Perhaps not. Do you want to walk away, Marnie?'

The sting of tears was back. She lowered her eyes in an attempt to hide them and shook her head. But when she put her signature to the bottom of the page she added something unexpected.

A single teardrop rolled down her cheek and splashed onto the white paper, unconsciously dotting the 'i'. It was the perfect addition to the deal—almost like a blood promise.

She closed the contract and pushed it across the table.

It was done, then, and there was nothing left to do but marry the man. Except, of course, to break the news to her parents.

CHAPTER THREE

'You can't be serious.' Arthur Kenington's face was a study in apoplexy, from the ruddy cheeks to bloodshot eyes and the spittle forming at the corner of his mouth.

Marnie studied him with a mix of detachment and sadness. Perhaps it was normal to emerge into adulthood with a confusing bundle of feelings towards one's parents. Marnie loved them, of course, but as she sat across from Arthur and Anne in the picture-perfect sunroom of Kenington Hall she couldn't help but feel frustration, too.

She lifted her hand, showing the enormous diamond solitaire that branded her as engaged. Anne's eyes dropped to it; her lips fell at the corners. Just a little. Anne Kenington was far too disciplined with her emotions to react as she wished.

'Since when?' The words were flat. Compressed.

'Be vague on the details.' That had been Nikos's directive when they'd spoken that morning. Had he been checking on her? Worrying she was going to balk at this final hurdle? Did he think the idea of breaking the news to her parents might be too difficult?

'We met up again recently. It all happened very fast.'

'You can certainly say that.' Anne's eyes, so like Libby's had been, except without the warmth and laughter, dropped to Marnie's stomach. 'Is it…?'

'Of course not!' Marnie read between the lines. 'I'm not pregnant. That's not why we're getting married.'

Arthur expelled a loud breath and stood. Despite the fact it was just midday, he moved towards the dumb waiter and loudly removed the top from a decanter of sherry. He poured a stiff measure and cradled it in his long, slim fingers.

'Then why the rush?' Anne pushed, looking from her husband to her daughter and trying desperately to make sense of the announcement that was still hanging in the air.

'Be vague on the details.'

'Why not?' she murmured. 'Neither of us wants a big wedding.' She shrugged her slender shoulders, striving to appear nonchalant even when her heart was pounding at the very idea of marriage to Nikos Kyriazis.

'Darling, it's not how things are *done*,' Anne said with a shake of her head.

Marnie stiffened her spine imperceptibly, squaring her shoulders. 'I appreciate that your preference might be for a big, fancy wedding, but the last thing I want is a couture gown and a photographer from *OK! Magazine* breathing down my back.'

Anne arched one perfectly shaped brow, clasped her hands neatly in her lap. At one time, not that long ago, Marnie might have taken Anne's displeasure as reason enough to abandon her plans. But too much was at stake now. If only her parents knew that the wedding they were so quick to disapprove of was their only hope of avoiding financial ruination!

'You don't like the press. That's fine. But our friends. Your family. Your godmother…!'

'No.' Marnie didn't flinch; her eyes were tethered to her mother's. 'That's not going to happen. Just you and Dad.'

'And Nikos? Which of *his* family will be there?' Anne couldn't quite keep the sneer from her voice.

'As you know, he has no family,' Marnie responded with a quiet dignity. 'Besides me.'

How strange it was to say that, knowing it was the literal truth if not a particularly honest representation of the situation.

'I don't like it,' Arthur interjected, his sherry glass empty now, and his focus on Marnie once more.

Marnie had expected this, and yet still she heard the words with an element of disappointment. 'Why not?' she queried quietly.

'I have never thought he was right for you. I still don't.'

There was nothing inherently offensive in the statement, but it was the reasoning behind it that Marnie took exception to. Six years ago she'd let the implication hang in the air, but now she was older and wiser and significantly less worried about upsetting her parents. 'For what reason, Dad?'

He reached for the sherry once more and Anne Kenington, across from Marnie, stiffened visibly.

'He's just not *right*.'

'That's not a reason.' Marnie's smile was forced.

'Fine. He's different. From you. From us.'

'Because he's Greek?' she asked with an assumption of mock innocence.

'Don't be obtuse,' he snapped.

Anne stood, moving her slender figure across the room towards the large glass doors that opened out onto the rolling green grass of the East Lawn. A large oak broke up the expanse of colour a little way in the distance, casting dark shadows beneath its voluminous branches.

'Is there any point in having this discussion?' she asked wearily.

'Meaning…?' Marnie asked softly.

'Your plans appear to be set in stone,' Anne continued, her pale eyes skimming over the gardens, her face a mask of calm despite the storm Marnie knew to be raging beneath.

Was that the only thing they had in common? Their steadfast commitment to burying any display of emotion? Keeping as much of themselves as possible hidden from prying eyes?

Marnie shifted her gaze back to her father. He looked as if he was about to pop a blood vessel. He was glaring at the sherry decanter, his fingers white around the fine crystal glass.

'One hundred per cent.' Marnie nodded. 'I hope you can put the past behind you and be happy for us.'

Arthur's harsh intake of breath was smothered by Anne's rushed statement. 'You're a grown woman. Who you marry is your choice.' She practically coughed on the statement.

Marnie stood, not sure what else she could add to the conversation. 'Thank you.'

A ridiculous way to end the conversation but, then again, what about the circumstances of this wedding *wasn't* ridiculous?

She slipped from the room, the muted voices of Arthur and Anne chasing her down the long corridors of Kenington Hall. She emerged onto the front steps and breathed in deep. Her cheeks were flushed, her skin warm. She moved deliberately away from the East Lawn, wanting to be far from her parents.

She walked with innate elegance until she reached the edge of the rose gardens. Then she slipped her pumps from her feet and cast one last glance towards the house. She began to move as she'd wanted to since she'd first seen Nikos again. As though the earth had turned to magma and was burning through the soles of her feet. She couldn't stand still; she could no longer be composed and calm.

And so she ran.

She ran as though the ghosts of the past had taken animal form: they were lions and tigers and they were chasing her, making her tremble with fear and terror.

'No daughter of mine is going to throw her life away on a no-hoper like that! You will end it, Marnie, or you will be out of this house faster than you can say inheritance.'

Arthur's hateful declaration was a cheetah, fierce and gnashing its teeth.

'I don't care about money! I love him!'

She sobbed as she remembered her impassioned cry, her belief that if she could only get her parents to understand what a good man Nikos was they would shelve their dislike.

But their dislike hadn't had a lot to do with the man he was so much as the man he *wasn't*.

'He's got no class. He will never make you happy, darling.'

At least Anne had tried to couch her objections gently. But her meaning had been clear. No class. No money. No social prestige.

Even then she'd stood fast. She'd fought for him.

'We've been through enough this year, for God's sake!' Arthur had finally shouted. *'We've already lost one daughter. Are you going to make us lose you, too?'*

Marnie ran until her lungs burned and her eyes stung with the tears the wind held in check. She ran past the lake that she'd fallen into as a child, before she'd learned to love the water and to navigate its murky pull; she ran around the remnants of the tree house where she and Libby had spent several long, sticky summers, pretending they were anywhere but Kenington Hall. She ran to the very edges of the estate, where an apple orchard shielded the property from the curious view of a passer-by.

Finally she came to an abrupt stop beneath a particularly established tree, bracing her palm against the trunk and staring back at the sprawling stone mansion.

Her whole life had been lived within its walls. She'd learned to walk, she'd played hide-and-seek, she'd read book after book, she'd been a princess in a castle. It was her place in the world.

But why hadn't she left when her parents had taken a stand against Nikos? Why hadn't she moved to London like most of her friends?

Because of Libby.

A sob clogged her throat. She swallowed it.

They'd lost Libby. And it had changed them for ever. Maybe they would have been difficult and elitist, anyway. But their grief had made it worse. And it had made Marnie more forgiving.

How could she run away from them and leave them alone after burying one of their daughters?

She groaned now, shaking her head.

So she'd put her life on hold. She'd remained at home, under their roof, managing the gardens, working in her little home office, pretending she didn't resent them for their heavy-handed involvement in a relationship that had been so important to her.

Was this marriage to Nikos a second chance? Might they even fall in love again?

Her heart turned over in her chest as she remembered the exquisite emotions he had evoked in her as a teenager. She had loved him fiercely then—but not enough. Because she'd walked away from him instead of staying and fighting and there was no turning back from that.

Goose bumps danced along her soft skin. 'This is beautiful.'

And it was. The house was nothing like she'd imagined. Set high on a hill on the outskirts of Athens, it was crisp white against a perfect blue sky. Geraniums tumbled out of window boxes, creating the impression that the flowers had sprung to life there and decided to blow happily in the light, balmy breeze. Clumps of lavender stood proud from large ceramic pots and the fragrance of orange blossom and jasmine hung heavy in the air.

'I'll give you a tour tomorrow—introduce you to the household staff.'

'Staff?' That was interesting. 'How many staff?'

He put his hand in the small of her back, propelling her gently towards the front door. 'My housekeeper, Eléni, and her husband, Andréas. Two gardeners...'

'That's good,' she said with a nod.

His laugh was a short, sharp bark. 'Did you think it would be just you and me?'

Of course she had.

He leaned closer, so that she could see the hundred and one colours that danced in his irises.

'Don't worry, *agape mou.*'

The heat of his words fanned her cheek.

'They will give us plenty of space in the beginning. We *are* on our honeymoon, after all.'

Her stomach lurched. Desire was swarming over her body, making her pulse hammer. Moist heat slicked through her. It felt as if she'd been waiting an eternity to be possessed by this man. The time was almost upon them, and anticipation was flicking delicious little sparks over her nerves.

He pushed the front door inwards. A wide tiled corridor led all the way to glass doors that showed the moonlit Aegean Sea in the distance.

'Are you hungry?'

Despite the fact that it was their wedding day, she hadn't eaten more than a piece of wedding cake after the ceremony. A sip of champagne to wash it down and Nikos had whisked her away from the disapprovingly tight smiles of her parents.

Her stomach made a little growl of complaint. 'Apparently,' she said, with an embarrassed smile.

His smile was the closest thing to genuine she'd seen on his face. It instantly offered her a hint of reprieve.

'There is food in the fridge. Come.'

She fell into step behind him, taking in the blur of their surroundings as she walked at his pace. Beautiful modern artwork gave much-needed colour to a palette of all glass and white. The home was obviously new, and it was a testament to minimalist architecture. While beautiful, it was severely lacking in comfortable, homely touches.

The kitchen housed a large stainless steel fridge. He reached in and pulled out a platter overflowing with olives, cheese, bread, tomato and *dolmades*. Another selection of bread was complemented with sliced meats and smoked fish.

'Wine, Mrs Kyriazis?'

The name splintered through her heart. 'I thought I'd keep Kenington,' she said, though in truth she'd barely contemplated the matter.

He poured two glasses of a pale, buttery-coloured wine, his face carefully blank of emotion. 'Did you?'

She shrugged. 'Lots of women do, you know.'

He nodded thoughtfully. 'But you are not "lots of women". You are my wife.'

He said it with such a sense of dark ownership that she was startled. Marnie couldn't have said if it was surprise at being spoken of almost as an object that inspired her sense of caution, or the fact that his passionate statement of intent was flooding her with desire and overarching need. A need that made rational thought completely impossible.

She sipped her wine in an attempt to cool the fire that was ravaging her central nervous system. It didn't work.

She nodded jerkily, at a loss for words.

'I want the world to know it.'

The statement hung between them like a challenge.

Her stare was direct. 'I'm not planning on hiding my identity.'

He reached for a cube of feta and lifted it towards her lips. Surprised, she parted them and he slid the cheese into her mouth, watching with satisfaction as she chewed it.

'No.' His eyes bored into hers, holding her gaze for several long, fraught seconds. 'My wife will bear my name.'

There it was again! That flash of pleasure in her abdomen. A sense of *rightness* at the way he wanted to claim her. To possess her. The desire to subjugate herself completely to his will terrified her. She bucked against it even as she wanted to move to him and offer her submission.

'Will she, now?' she murmured.

'Of course it is not too late to back out of this agreement.' He shrugged. 'Our marriage could be easily dissolved at this point, and I have not yet spoken to your father about his business concerns.'

Something lurched inside her. She stared across at him, needing her wine to banish the kaleidoscope of butterflies that were panicking, beating their wings against the walls of her stomach.

'Are you going to threaten me whenever I don't let you have your way?'

His laugh was without humour. 'That was not a threat, Mrs Kyriazis. It was a summation of our current circumstances.'

'So if I don't take your name you'll divorce me?'

His lips twisted in a wry smile. 'At this point I believe we could simply seek an annulment.'

'You should have put it in that damned pre-nup,' she said with a flick of her lips.

Anger flared inside her and beneath the table she turned the ring on her finger, looking for comfort and relief.

'I would have if I had known you were going to be so irrational about such trivialities.'

'It's not a triviality!' she demurred angrily, tipping more wine into her mouth.

How could she possibly explain her feelings? Explain how essential it was to hold on to at least a part of her identity? How terrified she was that she was married to a man who despised her, who was using her to avenge an ancient rebuff, who was determined not to care for her—a man she had always loved?

'You are my wife.'

'And taking your name is the *only* way to be your wife?' She had to force herself not to yell.

'Not the only way, no.'

His teeth were bared in a smile that sent shivers down her spine. Need spiked in her gut. She wouldn't acknowledge it. She couldn't.

'Fine.' She angled her head away. 'Whatever. I don't care enough to fight about it.'

That bothered him far more than the suggestion she might not take his name. The way she'd rolled over, acquiesced to his wishes at the first sign of conflict. Just like the last time he'd challenged her and she'd almost immediately backed down.

Arthur and Anne had insisted she couldn't be involved with him. Had she argued calmly for a moment and then given up? Given *him* up, and with him their future? Had they invoked her dead sister, knowing that Marnie had never felt she measured up to St Libby? Had they compared him—a poor Greek boy—to Libby's blue-blood fiancé, with his title and his properties? Had she looked from Nikos to Anderson and agreed that, yes, she needed someone like the latter?

'These olives are delicious,' she said quietly, anxious to break the awkward silence that was heavy in the room.

But when she lifted her gaze slowly to his face she saw he was lost in thought, staring out of the kitchen windows at the moonlit garden. It allowed her a moment to study his face and see him properly. He looked tired. No, not *tired*, exactly, she corrected, so much as…what? What *was* the emotion flitting across his face? What did she see in the tightening of his lips and the darkening along his cheekbones? In the knitting of his brow and the small pulsing of that muscle in his jaw?

'Fine.' He blinked and turned to face her. 'I'll show you the house now.'

She nodded out of habit.

It was enormous, and modern throughout. Wide corridors, white walls, beautiful art, elegant lighting…

'It's like a boutique,' she murmured to herself as they finished their tour of the downstairs rooms and took the stairs to the next level.

'This will be our room.' He paused on the threshold, inviting her silently to precede him.

Our room. Did he expect her to argue over their sleeping arrangements? She had no intention of giving him the pleasure.

'It's very nice.' Her almond-shaped eyes skimmed the room, taking in the luxurious appointments almost as an afterthought. King-size bed, bay window with a small seat carved into the nook, plush cream carpet and a door that she imagined led to a wardrobe.

She spun round, surprised to find him standing right behind her. They were so close her arms were brushing his sides.

She stepped back jerkily. 'I'm going to need an office space.'

'An office space?' His laugh was laced with disbelief and it irked her to the extreme.

'Yes. Why do you find that funny?'

'Well, *agape*, offices are generally for *work*.'

'Oh, I see.' She nodded with mocking apology. 'Work like *you* do, I suppose you mean?'

He crossed his arms over his chest, drawing Marnie's attention to the impressive span of musculature.

'Yes, generally.'

Her temper snapped, but she didn't show it. She'd had a lot of practice in keeping her deepest feelings hidden—she could only be grateful for that now.

'I need an office.' She said the words slowly and with crisp enunciation. 'For *my* work.'

'What work?'

Curiosity flared in his gut. Six years had passed and he'd presumed she was still simply Lady Marnie Kenington, daughter of Lord and Lady Kenington, employed only in the swanning about of her estate, the beautifying of herself and the upholding of the family name. It had never occurred to him that she might have done what most people did and found gainful employment. Frankly, he was surprised her parents had approved such a pedestrian pursuit.

'Does it matter? Do you care? Or are you just surprised that I haven't been rocking in a corner over the demise of our relationship since you left?'

Though frustrated by her reticence to speak honestly, he liked seeing the spark that brought colour to her cheeks and impishness to her eyes.

It intrigued him. He far preferred it to the obedient contrition she'd modelled in the kitchen. Instantly he thought of other ways in which he might inspire a similar reaction.

He nodded, concealing his innermost thoughts. 'Fine, have it your way. I do not need to know about your employment if you do not wish to speak of it.' He shrugged, as though the conversation was now boring him. 'I'll have a room made available. Just let my assistant know what you need in terms of infrastructure and he'll see you're set up.'

'*He?* You have a male assistant?'

It was Nikos's turn to act surprised. 'Yes. Bart. He's been with me five years.'

She laughed quietly and shook her head. 'I guess that makes sense. I can imagine you'd run through female secretaries pretty damned fast, given your track record for taking any woman with a pulse to bed.'

'Jealous, *agape*?'

She'd been jealous, all right. For years she'd followed his exploits in the gossip columns. Like watching a train crash, she'd been powerless not to stare at the pictures. They'd come to life in her over-fertile imagination so that she hadn't simply looked at an attractive couple coming out of some hot spot so much as imagined them in bed, or perhaps on the dining table, or the kitchen floor, while *she* lay in her own bed. Alone, untouched, able only to dream of Nikos rather than feel his hands on her body...

'Oh, yes,' she simpered, with an attempt at false sincerity. 'I've spent the last six years *desperately* waiting for you to reappear in my life. I've been missing you and dreaming about you and praying you'd turn up and blackmail me into a loveless marriage. This is pretty much the high point of my life, actually.'

'And we haven't even slept together yet,' he said, in a voice that was honey and dynamite.

Her breath caught in her throat. She spun away from him, her cheeks flushed.

'What is it, *agape*? Suddenly you are shy? It is our wedding night.'

She lifted a hand to her throat and lightly rubbed her skin. 'I... Of course not.' She squared her shoulders.

Hadn't she been dreaming about this for as long as she'd known him?'

'Relax.' His hands on her shoulders were firm. He spun her in the circle of his arms so that they were facing one another, his warmth offering some comfort to her. 'You are shaking like a leaf.'

Tell him the truth!

She fluttered her eyes closed, her lashes dark circles against her pale cheeks.

'You are my wife.' He pressed a finger under her chin, lifting her face to his. His eyes were troubled, tormented. 'Are you...*afraid* of me?'

It was so uncharacteristic of him to show doubt that she raced to reassure him. 'Of course I'm not.' She shook her head, inhaling a deep breath that flooded her system with his spicy scent. 'I'm afraid of *myself*, and of what I want right now.'

He nodded, silently imploring her to continue.

'You hate my father. I think you might even hate me.' She lifted a finger to his lips to stop him from speaking. 'But I don't hate you.' Her eyes were enormous, loaded with fear and desire. 'I don't hate you...'

Her finger, initially placed against his mouth to silence him, dragged slowly across his lower lip. Her eyes followed its progress as if mesmerised.

She knew he was going to kiss her. The intent was in every line of his body. If she'd wanted to she could have stepped away. She could have asked for more time. Instead she lifted herself up on tiptoe, crushing her mouth to his.

In that bittersweet moment all Marnie needed was to right one of the biggest wrongs of her past: she wanted Nikos and, damn it, she was finally going to have him.

To hell with the consequences. They'd be waiting for her afterwards.

CHAPTER FOUR

HER BODY FLASHED like flame when his mouth crushed down on hers with the kind of intensity that spoke of long-held desire. She was powerless to swim against the tide of need: powerless and unwilling.

Her feminine heart was hot and wet, slick with moisture and need. Unfamiliar but instinct-driven urges were controlling her body. Her hands pushed under his shirt, seeking skin and warmth. She traced her fingertips up his hair-roughened chest, splaying her fingers wide. She felt the beating of his heart beneath her touch; it was as frantic as her own.

His body weight pushed her downwards—not to the bed but to the floor, to her knees. He knelt with her, kissing her, his tongue clashing fiercely with hers as his hands pulled through her hair then pushed at her head, holding her against his mouth. She groaned into him, marking their kiss with the desperation that was scrawling a painful tattoo across her being—inking her as his in a way that would never be erased.

He pulled at her as his body pushed at hers until she fell back onto the carpet. His weight on top of her was divine. She curved her hands to his back, digging her nails into his warm skin as she felt the power of his arousal for herself. Hard and firm through their layers of clothing, A bodily ache was spreading through her. She lifted her hips, silently begging him for more. To mark her once and for all.

'Nikos!' She cried his name into the room and he groaned in response. 'Please!' She dug her hands inside his jeans, cupping the naked curve of his arse, pressing him against her and grinding herself intimately against his masculinity.

He laughed throatily. 'You want this, huh?'

He kissed her again—hard, fiercely, possessively—and then roamed his lips lower, encircling one of her erect nipples through the fabric of her dress and her bra. Even with such obstacles in the way the warmth and pressure of his mouth sent sharp arrows of need spiralling within her.

'Yes!' she hissed, arching her back, desperately needing more. 'Please, please...'

'In time.'

He smiled, running his mouth lower, over the fabric of her dress, until he reached the apex of her thighs. He skimmed lower, to the hem of the dress, and finally pushed it upwards, so that only a flimsy scrap of lace stood between him and her most intimate flesh.

Her cheeks were pink, her eyes fevered. Even when he wanted to go quickly he took his time, removing her underpants, sliding them down her soft, smooth legs and discarding them to one side. He let his hands dance patterns along her thighs, revelling in the way she quivered beneath his touch as her body responded instantly to him.

His fingers worshipped at her crease, teasing her, exploring her, aching for her. He was more gentle than he'd known he could be, perhaps afraid that she might regret her decision at any moment. That after years of waiting this was, after all, *not* to be.

Greek words, whispered hoarsely, filled the air. Words that swirled around her, wrapping her in magic and myth.

She didn't have a clue what he was saying, but she loved the sound of his native language.

When he slid a finger into her core she bucked hard, writhing at the intimate touch. Even back then, when they'd been fevered and passionate, he hadn't passed *this* threshold. His invasion was completely, utterly unprecedented.

Sharp, hot barbs of pleasure drove through her body, into her mind, weakening every earthly thought before it could be imagined. He moved slowly, curiously, watching her face as he stroked her sensitive flesh, learning what made her almost incandescent with desire before pulling out of her.

She gasped, the withdrawal of his touch an unbearable pain she could not withstand. But he didn't leave her for long before dropping his lips to her opening. His tongue was warm, but she was more so. Her body was on fire… his mouth seemed to kiss flame into her.

It had been a long time since Marnie had felt anything like this. She was completely unprepared for the insanity that his ministrations would bring. She was digging her nails into the carpet at her sides now, her knees lifted towards the ceiling as her toes curled into the ground and her whole body shook and quivered.

The orgasm was intense. She screamed as it saturated her being in long, luxuriant waves.

Sweat beaded her brow; heat painted her cheeks pink. Her throat, her arms—she was burning up. Her breath was loud in the room as she panted, satiated passion making her lungs work overtime.

Before she could drift down from the clouds that had absorbed her into their heavenly orbit Nikos was straddling her, his arousal pressed against her tingling core.

Marnie stared up at him, and everything in her world was perfect.

He studied her as his hands worked the buttons of his

shirt, and she was powerless to look away. Her tongue darted out, licking her lower lip, moistening it hungrily.

His smile was sexy as sin. She groaned, impatient for more. As he pushed at his shirt her trembling fingers unfastened his belt and pulled it from his jeans. She cast it across the room, wincing apologetically when it hit the wall loudly. He didn't react.

His shirt was unbuttoned, his chest exposed to her greedy eyes, and she stared and she touched and she felt, tracing his muscles, circling his nipples and filling with pride when he sucked in a raspy breath. He rotated his hips, taking back the upper hand, making her weak with the promise of what was to come.

She pushed at his shirt, chasing it down his arms, catching the fingers of one hand as she passed, lifting it to her lips and kissing him. It was a tender moment in the midst of passion. Their eyes locked and the past was all around them, threatening to suck them into the vortex of what had been.

'It might have cost me a small fortune, but finally you are going to be mine.'

His eyes glittered with dark anger, and the moment was swallowed up by cruelty as though it had never been.

Marnie bit down on her lip, trying not to react, trying not to let the pain sour what they were sharing.

She didn't have long to absorb his words, to turn them over in her mind. He shifted his body weight so that he could kick his jeans and boxers off. He was naked. Gloriously, wonderfully naked. She stared at him, her mind disappearing completely at the sight of Nikos Kyriazis. Her husband: the definition of tall, dark and sexy.

She groaned, dropping her hand to her womanhood, her fingers lightly grazing her flesh. His chest heaved as he sucked in a breath, his eyes sparking with hers. He stood over her, incapable of looking anywhere but at her hand and incapable of moving.

Until something snapped—and a desperate need to finally possess her cracked through him.

'You're on the pill.'

It was a statement, not a question. As though it hadn't occurred to him in earnest that she might not be.

Her cheeks flushed pink as she nodded. It had been the first thing she'd done after signing the pre-nuptial agreement. It had been all she could do to prepare for this moment, for him.

'I am safe.'

He straddled her, almost trapping her hand, but she snaked it higher. Tentatively, nervously, as though she had no right, she touched his length. He jerked instantly in her palm. She smiled a feminine, feline smile of innate power.

'You?'

'Me…?' He was long and smooth and so, so hard.

He laughed throatily. 'You've been tested?'

'Oh.' She hadn't been but, having never shared her body with another, she supposed it was the same thing. 'I'm safe, yes.'

He kissed her mouth, squashing her hand, his flesh against her stomach. 'Good. Because I want to feel you, *agape. Really* feel you.'

He jerked out of her grip, bringing his tip to her opening, teasing her with his nearness before pulling away. His hands pushed her dress higher, so that he could lift her breasts out of her bra, rub his palms over her flesh. He pushed the dress roughly over her body, the fabric grazing against her over-sensitised skin, pushed it over her face. She shifted upwards so that he could lift it and toss it. Her bra was next.

She opened her mouth, knowing she didn't want to surprise him with her virginity. She had no sexual experience, but even *she* thought it was somehow not good etiquette to spring that on someone.

But his mouth took hers, making speech impossible, driving rational thought from her brain once more. She tried to cling on to her conviction, to the knowledge that she should speak the truth to Nikos, but it was like chasing a piece of shell in eggwhite.

It slipped out of her mind. Only the physical remained.

His hands were insistent on her breasts, his thumb and forefinger teasing her nipples, rolling them, before his mouth dragged down her throat to take a peach areola into his mouth. His tongue lashed it and she groaned, felt pleasure building to another inevitable crescendo.

Her heart hammered against her ribs, so hard and fast she could hear the pounding of it in her ears.

She lifted her legs, wrapping them around his waist, pulling him closer. He groaned, his stubble-roughened chin like sandpaper on her soft flesh as he moved his mouth to her other breast, delighting it with the same treatment. His tongue lashed her, chasing invisible circles around the erect peak until she could bear it no longer.

'Nikos!' she cried out, tightening her grip around his waist. 'Please, please now...'

He laughed, but it was a sound without humour. 'I thought we'd at least get to bed,' he said ruefully, bringing his tip closer.

There was no fear for Marnie. Despite her innocence, and his impressive size, she knew that this coming together was somehow destined. She had waited a long time for him, and she wasn't about to let something as silly as fear or concern take the shine off the moment.

Still... That explanation she owed him...the warning...

'Nikos, I need to tell you—'

'No.' He pinned her with his gaze as he lifted himself

up on his arms so that he could stare into her eyes. 'No more explanations. No more words. Not now.'

'But—'

'This is not the time for conversation.'

She might have argued with him. After all, she had a strong sense that it was an important thing to share. But before she could say another word he parted her legs, pressing them back onto the carpet, splaying them wide, and thrust into her.

Not gently, nor slowly—why would he?

They were at a fever pitch of desire and he had no reason to suspect that everything they were doing was new and therefore held the potential for pain.

Her eyes squeezed shut as he slammed past the invisible barrier of her innocence, discarding it as swiftly and easily as he had her bra. He swore, the harsh sound jarring her nerves, then swapped to Greek and released a litany of words in his own tongue.

The pain, which had been sharp and searing, was quick to vanish. Like a receding shoreline it disappeared, leaving only the surrender to pleasure in its wake. She moaned as her muscles stretched to welcome him, squeezing his length, gripping him at her core.

He swore again and then shifted, moving gently now, slowly, his eyes on her face, watching for any sign of discomfort. There was none. She began to moan as he stoked her fires. His lips claimed hers, his tongue duelling with hers in time with each delicious thrust until she was about to explode. She curled her toes into the carpet and cried out, the sound muffled by his mouth.

She was incapable of controlling the sensation of release. It burst from her through every pore, every nerve ending. It flew from her body like a bubble being released underwater. It burst, spilling her pleasure across the room in an effervescence of cries and hard breathing.

She arched her back in an ancient step in the dance of sensuality. He gripped her hips, holding her there, his fingers digging into her flesh. He pressed his forehead to hers, their sweat mingling.

He didn't let her catch her breath before he was torturing her anew. Nerve endings already vibrating at an almost unbearable frequency began to quake and quiver. She groaned as another orgasm, bigger and scarier, chased the other away. This time, though, when she cried out into the room, he chased after her, his own voice combining with hers as pleasure saturated their surroundings.

It was a perfect moment.

Marnie caught the pearl of memory—the way he felt, smelled, tasted—and wrapped it deep into the recesses of her mind, knowing she would want to visit this feeling again and again and again.

He lifted up from her, and the absence of his weight was a pain she hadn't been prepared for. He pulled away, removing himself from her heart and standing in one swift movement. He paced away, gloriously naked, and for the briefest moment Marnie thought he was actually going to stalk out of the room without a word!

Incensed, she got to her feet, wincing as muscles that had never been tested began to groan in complaint. The sound of running water heaped fuel onto the fire of her anger. He was actually going to shower straight away? Hell, she had no point of reference, but Marnie would have put money on that being an absolutely hurtful thing to do.

The door she had initially thought was a wardrobe must conceal an *en-suite* bathroom.

The shower was running when she stepped into the tiled room, but Nikos was not behind the glass. He stood, naked, his hands braced on the vanity unit, his head bent. She couldn't see his expression in the mirror, but tension seemed to emanate from his strong frame.

It arrested her in her tracks.

Fear that she'd somehow got something wrong swirled through her.

She cleared her throat, uncertain what she wanted him to say but knowing she needed to hear *something*. Some form of reassurance or kindness.

He lifted his head, his eyes spearing hers in the mirror's reflection. His face was strained, his expression otherwise unreadable. He scanned her face, seeming to shake himself out of his own reverie, then turned to look at her.

'Did I hurt you?'

It was so far from what she'd expected him to say that relief whooshed through her. She shook her head wordlessly.

He held a hand out, inviting her to join him. She placed her smaller hand in his palm, feeling as if it was symbolic of so much more, and took a step closer. A small line had formed between his brows; he was scowling. Thinking. Deep in analysis.

'I did not expect…' he said, shaking his head again.

He tugged her lightly, pulling her to his body. His hands ran the length of her back gently, carefully.

'Here.' He swallowed, his Adam's apple bobbing visibly as he tried to gain a perspective on this turn of events. He guided her into the shower without breaking his contact with her.

He had one of those enormous ceiling shower heads; warm water doused her the minute she stepped in and she made a little yelp of surprise. Her dark hair was plastered to her face. But once she became accustomed to it the feeling of warmth on her skin was beautiful.

She watched as Nikos took a soft sponge from the shelf and poured shower gel on it. His eyes clung to hers.

'I do not understand,' he said finally, bringing the sponge to her shoulders and soaping her slowly.

The shower gel frothed against her skin. It smelled of lime and vanilla.

'I'm sorry,' Marnie said, then wished she could take the words of contrition back. She bit down on her lower lip. 'Not that I think I did anything wrong,' she hastened to correct. 'Only that I probably should have warned you.'

'Warned me?' A smile flicked at the corners of his lips. 'You think this is something for which I needed *warning*?'

'Well…' She huffed, crossing her arms over her chest. 'I don't know.'

Her eyes dropped to the tiled floor, where the soapy water was fleeing the scene, racing towards the drain.

'Not warning,' he said firmly. 'Just…explanation. How is this possible?'

Her cheeks were glowing; she could feel them. 'Well, it's not that difficult. I've just abstained from having sex. Hardly rocket science.'

His laugh was thick and throaty. Desire flickered in her abdomen, surprising her into blinking her eyes up at him. The air around them seemed to be supercharged with awareness.

He sponged across her décolletage, then lower, slowly, torturously circling one already over-sensitive breast.

'Was it a decision you made? To remain a virgin?'

She was on a precipice. The question wasn't a simple one to answer. If she responded with the truth it would reveal so much more of her heart than she wished to show him! What if she were to tell him that she'd never met a man who'd made her feel remotely tempted in the way he had?

Instinctively she shied away from handing him such a degree of power. 'Yes. I made a little pre-nup with myself,' she breathed with a hint of sarcasm.

He transferred the sponge to her other breast, his attention focussed on the small orbs and the erect nipples that were straining for his touch.

'You wanted to sleep with me back then.'

She shrugged. Her heart was pounding, though. Why hadn't she realised that he would hone in on that? 'Any chance we can *not* talk about this?'

He opened his mouth to say something, but then he nodded, a muscle jerking in his cheek. 'I was surprised,' he said simply. 'You've had boyfriends?'

'Of course I have,' she said, thinking of the handful of men she'd gone on dates with. The men her father had approved of. Suitable men who had left her stone-cold.

'Then how...?'

'I thought we weren't talking about this?' she reminded him quietly.

He nodded once more, his frustration obvious despite his acquiescence. 'It's just so unusual. You are twenty-three years old.'

She nodded, but speech was becoming difficult as he moved the sponge lower, dragging soapy suds over her stomach and lower still, to the space between her legs.

The warm water was heaven against her body. She moaned as he dropped the sponge to the ground with a splash and let his palm rub against her womanhood instead. After wondering briefly if she should be ashamed of the certainty that she wanted him again, she discarded the thought, pressing herself lower, begging him with her body not to remove his hand.

He watched as a fever of desire stole through her body. 'You must have been tempted. From what I recall you had a healthy sexual appetite when we were together.'

She gasped as he teased a finger at her entrance, incapable of responding.

'I had imagined you to have slept with several men by now.'

How those thoughts had tortured him!

'Yes, well...' She groaned, lowering her hips, begging

him for more. 'We're not all as libidinous as you.' She pushed the words out from between clamped teeth.

'*You* are,' he said simply, marvelling at how her body was clamping around him.

He dragged his lips along her jaw, nipping the flesh just beneath her ear before taking an earlobe into his mouth and flicking it between his teeth.

She writhed against the tiles and he jerked in immediate response.

'I would take you again already if I weren't worried about hurting you.'

'You won't hurt me,' she promised throatily. Her eyes were enormous as they lifted to his. 'I want you. *Now.*'

He arched a brow, moving his mouth to her breasts. The soap had long since been washed away and they were warm and moist between his lips. The feeling of his lips on her flesh made her jerk.

'Nik!' she cried out, digging her nails into his shoulder.

The name jarred. *No.* Out of nowhere, it infuriated him. A white-hot rage slammed against him—completely inappropriate but impossible to ignore.

Just her simple use of that name—as though she was slipping back into the past and forgetting that they were no longer a couple. Yes, they were married, but resentment had led to that. Anger, and even hatred. Referring to him as she had done when they were together wasn't something he welcomed.

Nik she'd called him back then. Never Nikos. And her lips had always curved into a sweet smile, as though his name was an invocation of secrets and hopes.

But that had all been a lie. She hadn't really cared for him then; she'd just made him believe she had. She'd played the part perfectly. And he'd fallen for it hook, line and sinker. Well, not again.

She had married him, but only for the sake of her father.

Just as she'd broken up with him because of her father. This was a business deal, plain and simple, and just as in business he needed to keep his focus. Her virginity, while interesting, did not change a thing about their arrangement.

He lifted her against the tiles and wrapped her legs around his waist, driving into her as though his life depended on taking her, on being one with her. It was just sex, but Nikos didn't want anything else from Marnie, anyway. And, no matter how great the sex was, he couldn't forget that.

It was up to him to remember just who he'd married. She was cold to the core—except in his bed.

CHAPTER FIVE

MARNIE PADDED DOWN the stairs, her eyes straining a little against the brightness of Greece and the whiteness of his home. It was warm, too, though a breeze shifted through the wide corridor, lifting her Donna Karan dress as she reached the ground floor.

The house was quiet, except for a buzzing noise coming from the direction of the kitchen. Curious, she followed the sound, her tummy making a little groan of anticipation.

She'd slept late.

Then again, she'd been up late, too.

Her cheeks flushed as she remembered making love to Nikos in the shower, and then afterwards, when she'd almost drifted off to sleep, she'd felt his mouth teasing her body, drifting over her breasts, down her abdomen, to torment her one last time.

It had been a fantasy. She could almost believe she'd dreamed the whole thing. Except that she felt a little sore and tender in the light of day.

The sight of her husband in the kitchen made her heart skid to a stop. She swallowed, drinking him in hungrily. Awareness flooded her body. He was dressed in a business shirt, the sleeves rolled up to his elbows, exposing those dark, muscled forearms of his. The shirt sat tucked in at the waist, revealing that honed stomach and firm hips. A burst of adrenalin and desire flared through her.

She bit down on her lower lip in an attempt to stall the smile that was threatening to split her mouth apart.

'Morning,' she murmured, her eyes sparkling with remembered intimacies.

He flicked a gaze to her, then returned his attention to the broadsheet paper that was spread across the bench. 'Coffee?'

Her smile was quick to snap into a small frown. 'Oh… um…yes.'

She wasn't sure he'd heard; he remained perfectly still, his head bent as he read an article. After several long seconds he sipped his own coffee, then placed the mug down and moved to the corner of the kitchen. She'd expected to see a machine, but she saw Nikos had one of those stainless steel coffee pots. He poured a measure for Marnie and she wrinkled her nose, remembering instantly his predilection for coffee so thick it was almost like tar.

'Perhaps I'll have tea instead.'

He shrugged. 'I would be surprised if you find teabags. I don't drink the stuff.' He left the coffee cup on the bench beside her, then topped up his own mug. 'Speak to Eléni about your requirements. She will see the house has whatever you need.'

'Eléni?' Marnie murmured, her voice soft in response to his emotional distance.

'My housekeeper,' he reminded her.

'Right.' She nodded, sipping her coffee and pulling a face at the liquid, claggy against her tongue.

Her eyes lifted to the window, and beyond it to the view. The beach was shimmering in the distance, invitingly cool given the warmth of the day.

'I'm happy to go shopping.' A frown pulled at her brows. She wasn't sure she wanted to leave a housekeeper to run the house completely. 'I suppose we should talk about that, actually.'

He gave no indication that he'd heard her. Whatever he was reading was apparently engrossing. Or he was avoiding her like the plague. But that didn't make sense. Not after what they'd shared the night before.

'Nik?' she murmured, moving to stand right beside him.

There it was again. The word that he hated hearing from her mouth. *Nik.* The name that had given him such pleasure in the past was now like an accusing dagger in his gut. A reminder of what they'd been contrasted with what they were now, of the pain of their history and the resentment that had fuelled this union—all contained in that small, soft sound. *Nik.*

Harsh emotions straightened his spine. He pressed his finger into the page, marking his spot, then lifted his eyes to her face. He skimmed her features thoughtfully, careful not to betray the emotions that the simple shortening of his name evoked.

'I think we should stick with Nikos, don't you?'

The rebuff stung. No, it *killed*. A part of herself withered like a cut flower deprived of water.

She narrowed her eyes, ignoring the tears she could feel heavy in her throat. 'Are you sure you wouldn't prefer Mr Kyriazis?'

A muscle jerked in his jaw but he returned his gaze to the paper and read on for a few moments before closing the pages and turning around, propping his butt against the edge of the kitchen bench. His eyes locked with hers.

'What did you want to speak to me about, Mrs Kyriazis?'

She swallowed, all desire to act the part of his wife for real evaporating in the face of his coldness. Confusion was swirling through her, biting at her confidence bit by bit.

'The housekeeper,' she said finally, knowing the only thing worse than looking overeager was looking like an idiot who couldn't finish a thought. 'I can do some of her stuff.'

He arched a brow, silently imploring her to continue.

'Well,' she said, bitterly regretting embarking on this path. 'I did my own shopping at home. Most of my cooking, too. I also took over the gardens.'

'You? Who can't tell wisteria from jasmine?' he prompted sceptically.

She squared her shoulders. 'That was a long time ago. I love flowers now. Roses especially.'

She was babbling. What was that pervasive feeling of grief? And how could she stem its tide?

'Do you grow roses here? I suppose not. They're more of an English thing, aren't they? But, anyway, you said you have gardeners. In England I...' She tapered off at his complete lack of responsiveness.

'Eléni has been my housekeeper for a long time,' he said finally, his tone as far from encouraging as it was possible to get. 'I am not willing to offend her. She will not want to share her responsibilities.'

Marnie stared at him with rich disbelief. 'Even with your *wife*?'

His smile was not softened by anything like happiness or pleasure. 'My wife has other responsibilities.'

Marnie reached for her coffee. Thick and gloopy or not, it still had the ability to put some fire in her blood. 'What's got into you?' she asked when she'd drunk almost the whole cup. 'You're treating me like...like...'

He waited for her to continue, but when she didn't speak, letting her sentence trail off into nothingness, he prompted, 'Like what?'

He was impatient now. She felt like a recalcitrant child. 'Like you hate me.'

His nostrils flared as he expelled an angry breath. 'Your

words, *agape*, not mine.' He pushed up off the bench. 'I'll be home for dinner.'

'Where are you going?' She stared at him incredulously.

He laughed. 'Well, Marnie, I have to go to *work*. You see, our so-called marriage is really a business deal. You've upheld your end of the bargain spectacularly well so far—even bringing your virginity to the table. Now it is my turn. My assistant's number is on the fridge, should you need me.'

He walked out of the kitchen without so much as a kiss on the cheek.

She stared at his retreating back, gaping like a fish dragged mercilessly from the water. Hurt flashed inside her, but anger was there, too. How could he be so unkind? They were married, and only hours earlier had been as close as two people could be. That had moved things around for her; it had changed the tone of her heart. She wasn't the same woman she'd been the day before, or the week before, or when they'd made this hateful deal.

But for Nikos apparently nothing had changed. *Nothing.*

And he hadn't even told her to call *him* if she needed anything! She was so far down the pecking order that she was supposed to go through his assistant if she needed her own husband for anything.

Well! She'd show him!

She ground her teeth together and wandered over to the newspaper, simply for something to do. The article he'd been reading was an incredibly dry piece on an Italian bank that was restructuring its sub-prime loans.

She flicked out of the finance section and went to international news. Though she generally liked to keep abreast of world events, she looked at the words that morning without comprehension. The black-and-white letters swam like little bugs in her eyes until she gave up in frustration and slammed the paper shut.

She sipped the coffee again, before remembering how disgusting she found it, and then glided across the kitchen floor, pulling the fridge open. The platters from the night before were there; they'd been put back on their shelves. The flavours were reminiscent of childhood family holidays, when the four of them had travelled by yacht around the Med, stopping off at whichever island had taken their fancy, enjoying the local delicacies.

Libby had loved squid. She'd eaten charcoaled tentacles by the dozen. Whereas Marnie had been one for olives, cheese, bread and *dolmades*. Libby had joked about Marnie's metabolism in a way she'd been too young to understand, though now she knew that she'd been unfairly blessed with the ability to eat what she wanted and not see it in her figure.

It was the one small genetic blessing Marnie had in her favour. The rest had gone to Libby. The shimmering blonde hair that had waved down her back, the enormous bright blue eyes, a curving smile that had seemed to dance like the wind on her face, flicking and freshening with each emotion she felt. And Libby had almost always been happy.

Marnie padded across the tiled floor, drawn to the glass doors that framed the view of the ocean. It sparkled in the distance, and she saw with a little sound of pleasure that there was an infinity pool in the foreground. She toyed with the door handle until it clicked open and then slid the glass aside, stepping out onto the paved terrace as though the breeze had dragged her.

She breathed deeply. Salt and pollution were a heady mix for a girl who'd spent much of her time in the English countryside. She grinned, trying to put her situation with Nikos temporarily out of her mind. An almost childlike curiosity was settling around her, and she slipped across the terrace and stood on the edge of pool. The water was turquoise.

Her toe, almost of its own volition, skimmed the surface before diving beneath, taking her foot with it.

Perfection.

Uncaring that her expensive linen dress might get crumpled or wet, and for once not thinking about photographers or what people might think, safe in the knowledge that she was completely alone, Marnie lifted the dress over her head and left it in a roughly folded heap on the tiles.

In only her bra and underpants she slid into the water, making a little moan of delight as it lapped up to her neck. As a child she'd gone swimming often.

She ducked her head underwater, beyond caring that her artfully applied make-up would smudge, and stroked confidently to the far end of the pool. She propped her chin on the edge, studying the bright blue sky, turquoise ocean and faraway buildings for a moment before duck-diving underwater once more and returning to the house side.

It felt good to swim, and she lost count of how many laps she completed. Eventually, though, as she drew to the edge of the pool, her arms a little wobbly, she paused to gain breath.

'You are fast.'

A woman's accented voice reached her and Marnie started a little, her heart racing at the intrusion.

Not knowing exactly what to expect, she spun in the water until her eyes pinned the source of the voice.

A woman was on the terrace, a mop in one hand, a smile on her lined face. She had long hair, going by the voluminous messy bun that was piled on top of her hair, and it was a grey like lead. She wore a dark blue dress that fell to the knees and sensible sandals.

The housekeeper. What had Nikos said her name was? She wished now she'd paid better attention, rather than focussing her mental skills on just what the hell had happened in the hours since they'd made love.

'You swim like a dolphin, no?' the housekeeper said, and when her smile widened, Marnie saw that she was missing a tooth.

'Thank you,' she said, inwardly wincing at how uptight she sounded. She tried to loosen the effect with a smile of her own. 'I'm Marnie.'

'You Mrs Kyriazis.' The housekeeper nodded. 'I know, I know.'

She was tall and wiry and she moved fast, propping the mop against the side of the house before lifting the lid of a cane basket. 'I always keep towels in here. Mr Kyriazis likes his swim after work.'

Dangerous images of Nikos—bare-chested, water trickling over his muscled chest and honed arms—made her insides squeeze with remembered desire. 'Does he?'

'So the towels always are fresh. I can get you one.'

True to her word, she lifted one from the box and placed it on the edge of the pool, beside Marnie's dress. Her hand ran to the item of clothing, lifting it as if on autopilot and draping it over a chair instead.

Marnie was a little shamefaced at the uncharacteristic way she'd discarded it.

'I'm sorry,' she said, her tone stiff. 'Nikos didn't mention your name,' she fibbed.

'I'm Mrs Adona.' She grinned. 'You can call me Eléni, though, like Mr Kyriazis does.'

'Eléni.' Marnie nodded crisply. *That was it.* Curious, she tilted her head to one side, watching as the older woman returned to fetch the mop. 'It's nice to meet you.'

Eléni cackled quietly in response.

'That's funny?' Marnie prompted with a small smile on her face.

Later, she would be mortified to realise that she had big black circles of smudged mascara beneath each eye.

'Oh, it is nice for me to meet you, I was thinking. Nice for him to settle down. In my day men didn't work as hard as him. They had one woman and a simple job. You'll be good for him,' Eléni said, with an optimism that Marnie was loath to dispel.

So she nodded. 'Perhaps.'

Something occurred to her and, spontaneously, she called the woman nearer to the pool.

'Eléni? Nikos is worried that I'll step on your toes if I do the odd bit of grocery shopping or cooking.'

She watched the other woman carefully for any sign of mortification or offence, and instead saw a broad grin.

Spurred on, she continued, 'The thing is, I quite like to cook. And I don't have a lot to do here yet, and shopping kills time. So…well…I hope you won't be upset if you see that happening?'

'Upset?'

Her laugh was contagious and alarming in equal measure. Loud—so loud it seemed almost amplified—it pealed across the courtyard and out towards the sea. Marnie found herself chuckling in response.

Eléni said something in her own language, then rubbed her angled chin as if searching for the words in English. 'I don't know he can like a woman who cooks.'

The sentence was a little disjointed, and the accent was thick, but the meaning came to Marnie loud and clear.

Nikos didn't bring women who cooked to his home.

They had other talents.

And wasn't that just an unpalatable thought?

Well, Marnie would show him.

By the time he returned that night Marnie and Eléni had moved a table onto the tiled terrace and Eléni had set it beautifully. A crisp white cloth fell to the floor, and in its centre she'd placed orange blossoms and red geraniums to create an artful and fragrant arrangement of blooms.

Marnie was just pulling the scallops Mornay from the grill when he arrived. It was difficult to say who was more surprised. Nikos, by the sight of his wife in a black-and-white apron, kitchen glove on one hand, feet bare but for the red toenail polish that was strangely seductive, or Marnie, who took one look at her husband and felt such a surge of emotions that she had to prop her hip on the bench behind her for support.

He placed a black leather bag on the kitchen floor, then crossed his arms. 'I thought we discussed this,' he said finally.

So much for new beginnings.

'*You* discussed it, as I remember.' Her smile was overly saccharine. 'I listened while you told me that I shouldn't get comfortable in your home.'

Her acerbic remark had caught him unawares—that much was obvious.

Choosing not to tackle the bigger issue of her statement, he said thickly, 'I told you—I don't want you upsetting Eléni .'

'Yes, yes…' She moved to the fridge and pulled a bottle of ice-cold champagne from the door. She placed it in his hand and paused right in front of him. 'You also told me that I should save my energy for other wifely duties.'

He had. And he'd enjoyed, in some small part, seeing the way he'd shocked her. But having her say the words back to him switched everything around. A hint of shame whispered across his features.

'Eléni's very happy that you've married someone who enjoys cooking,' she said, with an exaggerated batting of her long, silky lashes. 'I think she finds me surprisingly traditional compared to your usual…*companions*.'

'You've spoken to her?' he said unnecessarily.

'Yes. So you don't need to worry that I've sent her off to cry into her pillows.'

He curled his fingers around the neck of the bottle and unfurled the foiled top, his eyes lingering on his wife's face. Her honey-brown hair was plaited and little tendrils had escaped, curling around her eyes. Her make-up was impeccable, and beneath the apron he could see that she was wearing a simple dress that he was growing impatient to remove.

'You have a smudge on your cheek,' he lied, lifting his thumb to his mouth to wet it before wiping it across her skin. He was rewarded with the sight of her eyes fluttering closed and her full lips parting as she exhaled softly. The same knot of desire that had sat in his gut all day was inside her, too, then.

'I've been busy,' she said softly, her eyes bouncing open and clashing with his. As if consciously slicing through the web that was thick around them, she stepped backwards. 'You open that—thank you.'

A grudging smile lifted half his mouth. 'Yes, Mrs Kyriazis.'

She turned away before he could see the way the name brought an answering smile to her own features.

He popped the top off the bottle, placed the cork on the bench. He reached for two glasses at the same time she did. Their hands connected and she stepped aside quickly. 'You do it. I'll get our starter.'

'Starter?' he murmured, watching as a pink like the sunset dusted her cheekbones.

'Uh-huh. I told you—I like to cook.'

That was new. 'Since when?'

She began to place the scallops in their fan-like shells on a plate, forming a spiral of sorts. 'Some time after we broke up—' she skidded over the words a little awkwardly

'—I discovered it as a hobby. It turns out I love cooking. I've always loved food.'

She reached for a spoon and ran it around the edge of a shell, coating it in the Mornay sauce. She lifted it to his lips and he widened his mouth to taste the sauce. It was as delicious as it smelled.

'Apparently you excel at it.'

'Thank you.' The compliment was a gift. A beautiful gift to cherish in the midst of the turbulent ocean they were stranded in. She lifted the plate and smiled. 'Shall we?'

He turned, two champagne flute stems trapped between the fingers of one hand, the bottle in his other. He began to retreat from the kitchen, but Marnie stalled him.

'Not the dining room,' she said over her shoulder, weaving through the kitchen towards the patio. It was then that Nikos saw that against the backdrop of the setting sun, and the evening sky that sparkled with tiny little diamonds of stardust, a table glowed with candlelight.

Emotions, warm and fierce, surged in his chest. '*You* did this?'

'Eléni helped,' she said honestly, nudging the door with her shoulder.

The night was blissfully warm. She placed the scallops on the table and then stretched behind her back for the ties of the apron.

'Allow me,' he said throatily, settling the drinks onto the table and reaching for her. His fingers worked deftly at the strings but, once they were untied, he kept his hands on her hips. He spun her in the circle of his arms so that he could stare down at her face. In the softness of dusk she was breathtakingly beautiful. But the fragility he sensed in her terrified him.

He wasn't prepared for Marnie's vulnerability. He had no protection against it.

He dropped his hands to his sides and moved to a chair instead. He pulled it from the table, waiting for her to settle herself in the seat. She pushed the apron over her head, not minding that it roughened her hair. She draped it over the timber back of the chair, keeping her eyes on the spectacular view as she sat down.

He glided the chair inwards a little way, his hands resting on her bare shoulders for a moment before he moved to the other side of the table.

At another time, or for another pair, the moment would have been singing with romance. But Marnie knew they didn't qualify for that. And yet the setting was so magical that for a moment she let herself forget the tension and the blackmail, the resentments and regrets.

'Do you remember when we had that picnic in Brighton?'

His eyes skimmed her face, tracing the features he'd stared at that night. It had been only a few weeks before he'd told her he wanted to marry her one day—before she'd told him that would never happen.

'Yes.' He pressed back in his chair. The past was a sharp course he didn't particularly like to contemplate. 'I remember.'

'The sun was a little like this,' she said, obviously not sensing his tone, or perhaps willfully ignoring it.

She watched the glow of the golden orb as its own weight seemed to catch up with it, making it impossible for day to remain any longer. As the sun dipped gratefully towards the sea the sky seemed to serenade it, whispering peach and purple against its outline.

'This is my favourite thing to watch,' she said softly, a self-conscious smile ghosting across her face as she returned her attention to the table.

'Why?'

She lifted a scallop and placed it on her plate, indicating that he should do likewise. But he was fully focussed on his bride.

'I guess I find it somehow reassuring,' she said with a small shrug of her slender shoulders. 'That no matter what happens in a day there'll always be this.'

He arched a brow, finding the sentiment both beautiful and depressing. 'I am more for mornings,' he said after a moment.

'I remember.' She grinned, trying hard to inject their evening with the normality she'd longed for that morning. 'You wake before the sun.'

'I do not need a lot of sleep.'

'Apparently.'

Her cheeks flushed pink as she remembered the previous night—the way he had commanded her body's full attention even when she had been exhausted. And she'd responded to his invitations willingly, rousing herself to join with him, needing him even from behind the veil of exhaustion.

He ate a scallop, though he wasn't particularly hungry. It was divine. A perfect combination of sweetness and salt. He didn't say anything, though, so Marnie continued to wonder if he'd enjoyed it or was simply being polite when he reached for another.

'How was your day?' she asked, after a moment of prickly silence had passed.

He regarded her for a long moment. 'I spoke with your father, if that is your concern.'

Her face slashed with hurt before she concealed it expertly. 'It wasn't,' she responded, shrugging as though he *hadn't* scratched her with the sharp blade of recrimination. 'I was simply making conversation.'

His eyes glowed with the strength of his feelings. Marnie pressed back in her chair, her own appetite waning. She thought of the fish she was baking in a salt crust. What a waste it would be if they couldn't even make it through a few scallops without breaking into war.

'Let us not pretend, Marnie, when there is no one here to benefit from the performance.'

CHAPTER SIX

SHE PLACED HER fork down carefully beside the plate, using the distraction to rally her rioting emotions. His mood and manner were on a knife's edge. She felt the shift in him and wanted to protest. She wanted to address it. But the implacable set of his features thwarted any thought of that.

'I'm not pretending,' she said instead, with a direct stare that cost her a great deal of effort.

'Of course you are.' He was bored now, or at least he seemed it.

'Really? Why? Because I asked about your day?'

His eyes narrowed. 'Because you act as though your primary concern in this marriage is not your father.'

Denying that assertion wasn't an option—at least it wasn't if she wanted to protect herself from seeming motivated by other more personal feelings. What would he say if she told him more than money had motivated her into marrying him? Would he run a mile? Or use her confused feelings to keep her exactly where he had her?

'Well, Nikos,' she said, impressed that she sounded almost condescending, 'given that you used my father's debts to blackmail me into this, are you really so surprised?'

'I made no claim of surprise,' he corrected. 'I intended to point out the futility of your charade.'

'Wow.' She blinked and lifted her champagne, drinking

several large gulps despite the pain of the bubbles erupting against her insides. 'That's spectacularly rude,' she said when she'd settled the glass back on the table.

'Perhaps.' He shrugged insouciantly. 'In any event, your father was both grateful and, I believe, resentful of my offer to help.'

She was startled, her enormous eyes flying to his face. 'You're not saying he turned you down?'

'He has agreed to take the bare minimum from me to stave off foreclosure. That will buy him another month at the most.' A frown crossed his features. 'He is a stubborn man.'

'Remind you of anyone?' she snapped tartly, biting into another scallop.

'I would not be so foolish as to turn away a lifeline if I were in his situation.'

'He's very proud,' she said silkily, and though she'd meant it to be a subtle insult to Nikos it was ridiculous. She'd realised as soon as she'd uttered the words. For there was no man on earth with more pride than Nikos. She'd damaged it six years earlier and he'd moved heaven and earth to make her pay now.

'To a fault.'

'Thank you for speaking to him,' she said quietly.

She meant it. Were it not for Nikos, her father would have no hope. At least he knew now that there was an option. An alternative to bleak bankruptcy and failure.

'It was our deal, remember?'

The deal. The damned deal! She wanted to tear her hair out! But why? One day after their wedding, did she *really* think anything would have shifted? Just because they'd slept together, and her body had begun to vibrate at a frequency that only he could answer, it didn't mean that it was the same for him.

'Nonetheless, you didn't have to do this. Any of it. You

could have left him to suffer and watched from the side-lines.'

He braced his elbows on the table, his eyes pinning her to the chair as though his fingers were curled around her shoulders. 'Where would the fun be in that?'

The air crackled and hummed with the intensity of his statement.

'You find this *fun*?'

His smile was pure sensual seduction. Like warmed chocolate being dripped over her flesh.

'Last night was certainly pleasurable.'

Memories seared her soul. She shifted a little in the chair as her insides slicked with pleasurable anticipation. 'I'm glad you think so,' she murmured, her heart racing like a butterfly trapped against a window.

His smile was pure arrogance. It said that he knew she thought so, too. 'You disagree?'

Damn it. The wedge between a rock and hard place was a little constricting. She dropped her gaze, unable and un-willing to duel with him in a battle she'd never win.

But Nikos wasn't going to let it go. 'You seemed to enjoy yourself...' he pushed, one hand flicking lazily across the tablecloth, trapping her fingers beneath his. He turned her palm skywards and began to trace an in-visible circle across the soft pad of her hand.

'Now who's acting?' Her question was breathy, infused with the hot air in her lungs.

'When it comes to my desire for you there is no neces-sity to lie.'

'Thank heavens for small mercies.' The statement was lacking sass; it fell flat. She cleared her throat and pulled her hand away. 'How much money?'

The change in conversation, and the removal of her hand, confused him momentarily. But not for long. Nikos hadn't built an empire from scratch by being slow on the uptake.

'Why does it matter? Do you want to make sure you haven't overpaid your end of our bargain?'

She made a sound of surprise and shook her head.

'You did offer your virginity. Perhaps you feel anything less than a hundred mill isn't quite fair on you.'

'How *dare* you?' Her voice quivered with the force of her hurt. 'How dare you equate what we did with an amount of money?'

He had gone too far. He realised that, but it was out of Nikos's character to apologise. Instead he came back to the original question, speaking as though he *hadn't* just virtually equated their marriage with prostitution.

'I have helped him enough for now,' he said, his words soft to placate the rage he'd breathed into her. 'He will not go broke, Marnie. I will not allow that to happen.'

She pulled her lower lip between her teeth, her feelings jumping awkwardly from one extreme to the other. Hurt was making her body sag, and her throat was thick with tears that she damned well would *not* let fall. But there was relief and gratitude, too. Because she *did* trust Nikos. Despite all this, all that he'd done, she believed that he would keep her father from destitution.

He lifted another scallop and ate it, then another, and Marnie watched, a frown unconsciously etched across her face.

'Are you going to have any more?' he prompted, reaching for the second-last.

She shook her head. 'I'm fine, thanks.'

He placed his fork down and stared at her. 'Your father has asked us to return to England for his birthday.'

Marnie nodded thoughtfully. 'He doesn't like to do much, but Mum generally twists his arm into a small party.'

His expression was guarded. 'Would you like to travel home again so soon?'

Home.

The word was one syllable that throbbed with an enormous weight of meaning. She reached for the last scallop, despite having just given up her claim to it. She needed to distract herself and to hide her face as she unpacked the impact that single word was having.

Home.

Other than here.

Home.

Not here. Not in *his* home.

She blinked and shook her head a tiny bit, pushing the thoughts away. 'I'd like to see them,' she said cautiously. 'But it *is* soon. I didn't really imagine that we'd go to England again yet.'

Her family complicated matters. What hope did Nikos and she have of forming any kind of relationship with her parents and his antipathy towards them in the foreground?

'You want to refuse?'

She toyed with her ring, turning it round her finger. 'I didn't say that.'

'No. You didn't say anything,' he drawled, the words lightly teasing.

But Marnie was not in the mood to be teased.

'God, Nikos, you're impossible.'

He laughed throatily, the sound doing something strange to her fractured nerves.

'I am honestly asking what you would like. It occurred to me that I would have more success persuading your father to be reasonable if we were to meet in person.'

The tears he'd brought to the surface were closer now, and she had to dig her nails into her palms to stop from weakening and letting her eyes become moist.

Out of habit, she hardened her expression, creating an

air of nonchalance when she tilted her face to his. 'You'd do that?'

His eyes glittered in his handsome face. 'You'd be content if I didn't?'

Damn it. She was being careless. Slowly she shook her head from side to side, her eyes not quite meeting his. 'You told me you'd sort it out. It's the only reason I married you, remember?'

'Good. Honesty is so much better than role-play.'

She cleared her throat and focussed her gaze on the view. What she'd just said hadn't been honesty, but she let it slide. 'Fine. We'll go back for a weekend. In a month.'

And in the back of her mind she really did hope that their difficulties might have been resolved by then. There had been a time when they were so comfortable together. Was it so unlikely to believe they might return to that footing?

She looked at the man opposite, her heart turning over in her chest.

So familiar.

So foreign.

She knew him intimately, and yet she didn't.

He was a stranger, and yet her husband.

The dichotomies kept flowing through her mind, thick and fast.

'You are staring, Mrs Kyriazis, in a way that makes me want to peel that dress from your body and claim you here and now.'

She started, her pulse shearing her skin. 'I was just thinking…' Her voice was thick with the desire he could so easily evoke. 'So much has happened in six years. You're my husband, and at one time I would have said I knew you better than anyone. But I don't know you at all now.'

'You know me,' he responded, standing up swiftly and reaching for her plate.

She watched as he cleared the table, her mind overflowing with questions.

'When we were together, you only had aspirations in finance. How did you do all this so fast?'

He sent her a look of impatience. 'When someone tells you that you will never amount to anything, that you are not worth a damn, it *is* rather motivating.'

Her father's words mortified her. 'He shouldn't have said that.'

'No.' His eyes glittered. 'But that is what you people are like. Do you *really* believe that the blood in your veins is of more value than mine simply because you can trace your lineage back thousands of years and I am not able to do so?'

'Don't do that.' She followed him into the kitchen. 'Don't tar me with the same brush.' A frown drew her brows together. 'I don't really understand why my dad spoke like that to you. He's not—'

'Of course he is,' Nikos interrupted. He tamped down on his temper with effort, stacking the plates neatly into the dishwasher.

He worked with a finesse that made her wonder if he did this simple domestic act often. Though incongruous, it made sense. Nikos hadn't been born with a silver spoon in his mouth. He'd grown up poor. He'd presumably shouldered his fair share of domestic duties for most of his life.

'Whatever you're about to say, make no mistake. He *is*.'

'Anyway…' She made an effort to salvage the situation. 'I understand why you might have felt you had to prove something. But *how* did you do this?'

His eyes skimmed her face. 'In the same way I won a scholarship to Eton and then Cambridge. I worked a thousand times harder than anyone else. I always have. I don't sleep much, *agape*, because I work.'

Admiration soared through her. 'I think you've done something very impressive,' she said quietly.

He propped himself against a bench. 'Your turn. Why did *you* do all this?' He gestured around the kitchen.

Because I missed you. Because I couldn't stop thinking about you.

'It's our honeymoon, isn't it?'

His lips lifted in a half-smile. 'If you say so.'

The rejection hurt, but she didn't show it. 'Why don't you sit down? I'll get the main course.'

He crossed the kitchen so that he stood right in front of her, without touching. Goose bumps littered her exposed flesh.

'I have a better idea.'

She lifted her eyes to his face slowly. Breathing was suddenly difficult. He overwhelmed every single sense in her body. 'Oh?'

'Let's have a break between courses.' His smile was tight. 'I do not usually eat so early.'

'Oh…'

He'd upset her. He squashed the urge to apologise. 'It is a…ritual I have. I swim as soon as I return from the office. I find it rids me of the day.' He reached down and linked his fingers. 'Join me.'

A command or a question?

An order or an invitation?

Whatever the case, she found herself nodding. 'Okay. I'll just go and get changed.'

His laugh was throaty. 'Why?'

Her eyes were wide. She watched as he began slowly to unbutton his shirt until the sides were separated. He pushed it off his arms, then stepped out of his trousers. In just his boxers, he reached over and lifted her hand to his lips.

His kiss breathed butterflies into her veins. She stifled a moan and then pulled at her hand. It was a necessary tool. She felt around for her zip, and when she couldn't immediately catch it he reached behind her and loosened it, sliding it slowly, seductively, teasingly down her spine.

She shivered as his fingers lingered, taunting the flesh at the small of her back. She lifted her gaze to his face again, searching for something there. Kindness? Affection? She saw only lust. Pure and simple.

It was better than nothing.

With a small exhalation she stepped backwards. 'I'll just need a minute.' She took another step backwards to underscore her resolve. 'I'll meet you in there.'

He shrugged indolently and strode across the tiles with that almost feral power that seemed to emanate from his frame. She watched him go, greedily waiting to see him dive into the water. His muscles rippled as he speared through the air then beneath its surface. She held her breath unconsciously until he stood at the other end. His dark hair was slicked to his head like an animal's pelt.

She moved quickly up the stairs and into their bedroom. The sight of her face that had confronted her after swimming earlier that day was hauntingly close to the surface. She didn't want to turn into a panda again. She lathered her hands with soap and washed at her face until every hint of make-up was removed, then changed into a swimsuit with a low-cut vee at the front and delicate beading in the fabric. It was elegant and inviting.

He was swimming laps when she emerged, his strong body pulling powerfully through the water, each bronzed arm worthy of its own sculpture. He was naked. His boxers had been discarded and she could see his whole body as he cut through the water.

She swallowed huskily, her eyes tracing his progress from where she stood at the edge of the pool. A warm breeze drifted past, lifting her hair. She tucked it behind her ears and approached the edge. He turned underwater, his stroke not breaking the surface.

With a smile, she dived in, pulling up beside him. Underwater, their faces were illuminated by the green lights embedded in the side of the pool. He turned to her. Their eyes locked and Marnie almost lost her rhythm, so fierce was the tumble of awareness that accosted her body.

But she quickly regained her focus, racing him to the end and touching the rounded edge of the pool just as he did. She laughed when they both lifted onto their feet, the thrill of adrenalin and the rush of endorphins pumping through her body.

He stared at her with a sense of confusion.

Her laugh.

That beautiful laugh.

It was as if she'd burst through the cracks in his memory, slowly infiltrating him with what she'd once meant to him.

It wasn't only the musical sound, it was her face. Wiped of make-up, radiating happiness, with a little bit of honey in her complexion from the day she'd spent outdoors.

He swallowed and turned to the view, his face unyielding in profile.

'I haven't swum like this in years,' she confided easily, blissfully unaware of the hurricane of feelings that was besieging him.

His smile lacked warmth. He pinned her with eyes that she couldn't read. A sense of loss wiped the smile from her own features and she spun away, kicking to the opposite side of the pool and propping herself against it. The coping was still warm from the day's heat, despite the lateness of the hour and the coldness of his look.

The sense that her husband—the man she'd married and had once loved—despised her, made her heart hurt in her chest. She turned slowly to see him walking through the water towards her, his gaze pinned to hers.

He was going to kiss her. The fine pulse at the base of her throat was hammering wildly in expectation, and yet every sensible thread of her mind was telling her to step backwards and talk to him.

What did it mean that she had such a small understanding of everything that made him tick except his desire for her?

'Nikos,' she said softly, her eyes silently imploring him to help her make sense of it all.

He caught her hips underwater, pulling her the final distance to meet him. Their bodies melded as one. She drew her lip between her teeth, ignoring the warning voice in her mind as she wrapped her arms around his neck. Her fingers teased the wet hair at his nape.

'I know.'

Her breath hitched in her throat. She wasn't alone. This maelstrom of need after six long years was as unsettling for him as it was her.

Good.

For now that would have to be enough.

His kiss was a claim. It was a seal of their union. She kissed him back fiercely, her tongue clashing with his, her body wrapping around his beneath the water. The feeling of his arousal between her legs, straining at the fabric of her swimsuit, with the warmth of the pool water surrounding them was almost too much to bear.

Impatience crested inside her, bubbling out of control.

She made a sound into his mouth as she pushed back a little, her fingers toying with the straps of her swimsuit. They were saturated, and stuck to her body like a second skin; it didn't help that her hands were unsteady.

He had no such difficulty.

With total confidence he slid the straps down her arms,

revealing her breasts. The dusk light bathed her, spreading gold and peach over her flesh. He continued to push the fabric away, and Marnie lifted her legs to make it easier.

Naked in the water with him, she had a blinding sense that she might actually die if they didn't make love. If something were to happen to change his mind she wasn't sure she could recover. Her desperation for him would have terrified her if she'd had any mental space left with which to process it.

He pulled her back towards him, settling her legs around his waist. His eyes showed strain as he paused, his hard cock nestled between her legs without yet invading her womanhood.

'You have not been sore today?'

She shook her head.

'You must tell me…'

Groaning, she repositioned herself, startling him by thrusting down on his length and taking him deep inside her core. Relief spread through her body, weakening and strengthening her in yet another contradictory sensation. He held her hips, his fingers digging into her soft flesh, his lips seeking hers. His tongue was harsh in her mouth, echoing the movements of his body as he made her completely his.

Her orgasm burst over her swiftly; there was no time to prepare.

The entire day had been a kind of torturous foreplay for Marnie. Memories of their night together had tormented her, driving her body to fever pitch, so that the tiniest things—such as the feeling of the apron as she'd wrapped it around her over-sensitised nipples—had almost driven her over the edge.

Nikos watched as she crested the wave, her face a thousand little nerve endings vibrating with pleasure. The answering swelling in his heart was not something he wished to acknowledge.

Telling himself it was simply relief that they'd found themselves to be sexually compatible, he pushed deeper into her, drifting his fingers lower to cup the neat softness of her buttocks. He dragged his lips down her throat, flicking his tongue against the pulse-point that was frantically trying to move blood through her body, then lower still to her breasts. They were lapped by the water, and he had to lift her a little to take one into his mouth. The second he did she cried out, tilting her wet head back into the water so that her hair, no longer braided, fell like a dark curtain.

He moved one hand to tangle in its lengths, holding her head there while he plundered her core in an insatiable rhythm.

His own control was slipping. Her muscles, so moist and tight, were squeezing him as her pleasure spiralled, and when he felt her tremble and knew she was about to crest the wave again he went with her, holding her close, mirroring her movements until they were both panting, drenched in sweat and pool water, satisfaction emanating from every pore.

Their coming together had been as intense as it had essential. But it was just a prelude to the slow exploration he had been distracted by thinking of all day. To the myriad ways he wanted to torment and delight her.

Satiated, Marnie slowly relaxed, her body reassuring her that nothing bad could eventuate when such uncontainable desire abounded.

It was only then that she remembered the fish in the oven. It would be burned to a crisp.

Well, if that was the only casualty of this desire then she could live with it.

In the small hours of the morning, their naked limbs tangled with crisp white sheets, bodies sheened in post-coital perspiration and satisfaction, sleep fogging around the edges of their tableau, Marnie shifted a little, tilting her head to observe her husband.

His eyes were shut, his breathing heavy.

'How can you call this a pretence?' she whispered—to herself more than anything.

Without opening his eyes, he said thickly, 'This is just great sex, Marnie. Do not confuse it with anything more substantive or you will be hurt.'

He rolled over, his broad, muscled back turned to her, his heart apparently closed.

CHAPTER SEVEN

A FORTNIGHT HAD passed and his words were still sharp in her brain, like shards of glass that made her weep blood whenever she ran the fingertip of her mind over them.

'This is just great sex... Do not confuse it with anything more substantive...'

Her coffee-coloured eyes were flecked with gold as they drifted over the view from the window. For her office she'd chosen a room far away from the pool, their bedroom and the kitchen—that was to say far from any of the rooms that distracted her with what Nikos and she had shared there.

It was a small room, but she didn't need a lot of space, and it afforded an outlook of the city, rather than the ocean. In the distance she could see the Acropolis, bathed in early-evening light, and the buildings of the city sprawled almost like a child's model.

Though she took solace and inspiration from the outlook, this was not why she'd chosen this particular spot from which to work. From her seat she could see the curve of Nikos's driveway. The second his car thrummed through the gates she knew. And then she had the maximum time to prepare herself for his arrival, to gather the facade she had perfected around her slender shoulders. A facade that was essential when faced with her husband.

They shared meals and polite conversation. They were

unstintingly civil. But there was a torrent of emotions swirling hatefully beneath all their appropriate conversations. Only when they came together at night did she find an outlet for her rampant emotions. Sex. Passionate, all-consuming sex that explained everything. She was addicted to him. To his body and to the way he made her feel.

Marnie clicked out of her spreadsheet, her mind half-absorbed with the call-list she had for the following day. How grateful she was to have her work! Were it not for the distraction of the behind-the-scenes fundraising she did for the Future Trust she might have exploded already in a scene reminiscent of Vesuvius.

She flicked a glance to the clock above the door. He was late, and nerves that had been stretched tight for two days—since he'd told her about this event—were at breaking point.

For the first time since marrying they were going *out*.

Strange how she hadn't even realised that she'd become a virtual recluse, spending her time almost exclusively within the confines of his home except for brief trips to the markets with Eléni.

Now it was time to meet the world. She was Mrs Kyriazis—billionaire's wife.

What a joke.

Their marriage was little more than revenge and sex, and yet tonight she would play the part of doting newlywed to perfection. If only to show him how little she cared.

She heard his car and rose quickly from her desk. It wasn't that she had intended to be secretive about her work, but Nikos never came into her office. As if that conversation on her first afternoon in Greece had flagged something in his mind and he had subsequently delineated her office as her own space. For all he knew she might be running some kind of international drug ring, she thought with a small smile as she pulled the door shut behind her.

Marnie rarely wore heels, but for the kind of evening Nikos had foreshadowed she knew they'd be a requirement. They did bolster her height nicely, and she felt the picture of elegance when she walked gracefully down the stairs.

She'd spent a long time styling her hair, and her make-up was a masterpiece. Anne Kenington might not have played Cubby House with her children, nor had she read them the books that a nanny had had more time for, but she had insisted both her daughters were drilled in the skills necessary to present themselves as Ladies.

When Marnie emerged into the foyer at the same moment that Nikos entered the house she waited with a small smile on her red lips for him to see her. Pleasant anticipation swirled through her as she waited for the light of attraction to bounce between them.

The second his eyes lifted to her she felt a bolt of something. Not desire. Not happiness. Something else. Something far darker.

His eyes undertook a slow and thorough inspection, but his expression showed only shock. Marnie held her breath as he stared at her, waiting, aching, needing. Wanting him to say something to explain the reaction.

'You look…' He wiped a hand across his eyes and shook his head.

'Yes?' She braved a smile, though her heart was plummeting to the floor.

'Nothing. It doesn't matter.'

He dropped his keys onto the side table and turned away. Only the ragged movement of his chest showed that he was still struggling with a dark tangle of emotions.

'I will be ready as soon as I can. Why do you not have a drink while you wait?'

A frown marred her features for the briefest of moments before she remembered. She didn't *do* that! She didn't betray how easily he could upset her.

'Fine,' she agreed, her smile ice-cold, her pulse hammering. 'Don't be long. You said it starts at eight.'

He didn't acknowledge her rejoinder. Marnie watched with consternation as he took the stairs two at a time, then she turned away and wove her way to the kitchen.

It was another stunning evening. The sun was almost completely out of sight, leaving inky streaks in the sky and a sprinkling of sparkling lights that heralded night's arrival. She flicked the kettle on to brew tea and then thought better of it. She had a feeling something stronger was called for.

She poured a glass of champagne and held it in both hands as she moved to the terrace. The pool was beautiful. The surface, undisturbed by their usual evening activity, had a stillness to it, and it reflected not only the evening sky and the glow of his house but Marnie's figure, too.

She stared down at the watery image of herself, allowing her earlier frown to tug her lips downwards now that she was alone. Why did he disapprove? Though she hated this sort of mix-and-mingle affair, she'd been to enough of them to know the drill. Her dress was the latest word in couture, her shoes were perfect—everything about her was just what people would expect the wife of Nikos Kyriazis to be.

She crouched down, careful to keep the hem of her dress out of the water, and ran her manicured fingertips through its surface, slashing her image so that only swirls of colour remained. Satisfied, she stood and turned towards the house, startled when she saw Nikos just inside the door.

He'd showered and changed into a formal tuxedo, and his dark hair was slicked back from his brow, showing the hauteur of his handsome features, the strength of his bone structure and the determination of his jaw.

A kaleidoscope of butterflies was swirling through her insides, filling her veins with flutters of anticipation. As she stepped closer a hint of his fragrance—that unmistakably masculine scent of spice and citrus—carried to her on the balmy breeze.

The tuxedo was jet-black and might as well have been stitched to his body; it fitted like a second skin, emphasising the breadth of his shoulders and neatness of his waist.

She waited half a beat, giving him an opportunity to redeem the situation. It shouldn't be hard. He simply needed to offer a smile, or compliment her appearance, or ask about her day. She wasn't fussy. Any of the small ways a husband might greet his wife would have sufficed.

But instead Nikos looked at his wristwatch. 'Ready?'

She compressed her lips, the spark of mutiny colouring her complexion for a minute. 'Do I *look* ready?' she asked tartly, swishing past him and clipping across the room.

In the kitchen, she took two big sips of her champagne and then placed the glass down on the marble counter a little more firmly than she'd intended, so that a loud noise cracked through the room.

'Yes,' he said finally, closing the distance between them.

He stared down at her, his eyes flicking across the inches of her face. She didn't back away from him; she didn't let him see that her heart was being shredded by his lack of kindness. With her shoulders squared she walked ahead of him, out of the house and into the warm night air.

He opened the passenger door of the Ferrari for her and Marnie took her seat, careful not to touch him as she slid into the luxurious interior. The moment he sat beside her she was aware of his every single breath and movement. Unconsciously, she felt herself swaying closer to the window on her side, her eyes trained steadfastly on the view beyond the vehicle as they cruised away from his home.

At the bottom of the drive he turned left. Though Marnie was still getting her bearings, she'd ventured to the markets with Eléni enough times to know that he'd turned the car away from the city.

He drove without speaking, and she was glad of that. She needed the time to regain her composure, though she didn't have long. It was only a short distance to their destination: the ocean—and an enormous boat that was sparkling with the power of the thousands of tiny golden fairy lights that zigzagged across its deck. It was moored just off the coast.

'The party's on a boat?' she murmured, shifting to face him.

His eyes stayed trained on the cruise ship. 'As you see.'

She swallowed and bit back on a tart rejoinder. She'd vowed not to argue with him. Even that would show how she'd come to care too greatly. 'Great,' she snapped with acidity. 'I love boats.'

He was out of the car and rounding the side. Marnie pushed the door open and stepped out before he could reach her. After all, she'd opened her own doors all her life; why did that have to change now?

The ramp that led from the shore to the boat looked to have been specially constructed for the event. Though sturdy, it was obviously temporary. They were the only ones on it—though that was hardly surprising given that they were arriving well after the party had started.

'What is this *for*?' she asked as they stepped onto the polished deck.

'My bank throws it every year.'

'*Your* bank?' she clarified, pausing and turning to face him.

'The bank I work with,' he said distractedly. 'I do not own it.'

'I see.'

But from the second they arrived it became blatantly obvious that Nikos enjoyed an almost god-like status with the high and mighty of the institution.

Drinks were brought, food offered and advice sought.

Much of the conversation was in Greek or Italian, which Marnie understood only passably. She stood beside him listening, catching what she could, but her frustration was growing.

What was going on with him? He was acting as though she'd just knifed the tyres of his car or sold the secrets of their marriage to a tabloid. He was furious with her—and for what possible reason? She had done everything right! The clothes she wore, the hair, the make-up—she had put so much effort into being exactly what he needed of her that night. She was the picture-perfect tycoon's wife. And yet that seemed to have angered him.

When the group of men Nikos was deep in conversation with paused for a moment Marnie squeezed his arm. The smile on her face was broad; only Nikos would be able to detect the dark emotions that powered it.

'Excuse me a moment,' she murmured, pulling her hand away from him.

He bent down and whispered in her ear. 'Do you need something?'

'Yes.' She flashed her eyes at him in frustration, then encompassed his companions in her smile, knowing he wouldn't argue in front of them. 'Excuse me.'

She felt his eyes on her as she walked away, and just knowing that he was watching made her walk as though she hadn't a care in the world. Her feet seemed to glide over the deck, despite the crowds that were thick on the ground.

It was a perfect night. Sultry even though it was late in the summer season, and clear. The breeze was warm and soft, providing comfort rather than chill. She wove her way to the edge of the ship, seeking space and solitude. The polite smile on her face and a faraway look in her eyes discouraged conversation, and when she put her back to the crowds and stared out at the view she was all but absenting herself from the festivities.

She stood like that for a long time, enjoying the privacy of her thoughts, until a hand on her shoulder caught her attention.

Expecting to see Nikos, she masked her features with an expression of bland uninterest and turned slowly.

But the man opposite her caused such a flurry of feeling inside of her that tears welled instantly in her eyes.

'Anderson!' She hugged Libby's fiancé, her mind grappling with the question of why he was there even as she acknowledged how thrilled she was to see him. 'Oh! What a surprise.'

'I was hoping you'd be here.' He grinned. 'Nik wasn't sure you'd want to come.'

A frown briefly flashed in her face as she remembered that these two men were still close friends. Anderson was the one who had told Nikos about her father's dire situation, after all.

'Congratulations on the wedding.' He kissed her cheek, then grabbed two glasses of champagne from a passing waiter. 'To happily-ever-after, huh?' He clinked his glass to hers, earning a smile from Marnie.

'Indeed.' She drank the champagne, watching the man who would have become her brother-in-law over the rim of her glass.

'I wish I had been able to come to the wedding,' he said, nudging his hip against the railing and effectively screening them from the other guests.

Marnie studied him thoughtfully. Did he know what a farce their marriage was? 'I would have liked that,' she said finally, earning a laugh from Anderson.

'You sure? You sound ambivalent.'

She laughed, too. 'Sorry. I'm just surprised to see you. I somehow forgot that you and Nikos were close.'

His smile was warm. 'He's my oldest friend.'

Her heart turned over in her chest. She changed the

subject. 'I haven't seen you in a long time. You've been staying away from our house?'

He grimaced. 'I've been meaning to visit. But…'

'But?' she prompted, a smile belying any accusation.

'You know…I feel bad sometimes. Your parents look at me and see only Libby.' His smile was thin. 'I expect you know exactly what *that's* like.'

She sipped her champagne again, and her voice was carefully wiped of feeling when she spoke. 'It's not the same. They look at me and see only my failings as compared to Libby.'

Anderson rubbed a hand over his chin. 'They're wrong to compare the two of you. There's too many differences for it to make sense.'

Colour flashed in Marnie's cheeks. 'Thanks,' she said, with a hint of sarcasm.

'I wasn't being offensive,' he clarified quickly. 'Libby used to laugh and say that you and she were chalk and cheese. But that you were her favourite of all the cheeses in the world.'

Marnie's smile was nostalgic. 'I used to tell her that *she* was cheese and I was chalk. Doesn't that make more sense? She was sweet and more-ish and fair, and I'm a little…thin and brittle.' Her laugh covered a lifetime of insecurity.

'Don't *do* that,' Anderson said with frustration. 'She wouldn't want you to do that. She wasn't vain and she wasn't self-interested and she adored you. I know Arthur and Anne have always made you feel wanting, but that's not a true reflection. You owe it to Libby not to perpetuate that silliness.'

Marnie bit back the comments that were filling her mind. It was all too easy to justify her sense of inferiority, but with Anderson she didn't want to argue. 'I'm glad to see you,' she said finally.

'And I'm thrilled you and Nikos worked everything out. I know he never got over you.'

Marnie's eyes flew to Anderson's, confusion obvious in her features. Was it possible that even Anderson didn't know the true reason for their hasty wedding?

'Don't look so surprised,' Anderson said, sipping his drink. 'He might have played the part of bachelor to perfection but it was always you, Marnie. You're why he did all this.'

She shook her head in silent rejection of the idea, but Anderson continued unchecked. 'One night, not long after you guys broke up, he had far too much of my father's Scotch and told me that he'd earn his fortune and then win you back.'

'I can't imagine Nikos saying that.' But her heart was soaking in the words, buoying itself up with the hope that perhaps he *did* love her; that he *had* missed her.

'Oh, he talked about you all night. How you would only ever be serious about a guy like me. A guy with land and a title. He was determined to prove himself to you before he came back and won you over.' He laughed. 'If you ask me, he went a little far. I mean…a million would have done, right?'

Her smile was lacking warmth. She focussed her gaze on the gentle undulations of the water beneath the boat, her mind absorbing this information. 'It was never about money,' she said gently.

'Oh, I know that. I told him that a thousand times. But he didn't get it.' Anderson drained his champagne. 'Until you see first-hand the uniquely messed-up way Arthur and Anne made you girls feel you can't really understand a thing about you. Right?'

Startled, she spun to face him. Her breath was burning in her lungs and she wasn't sure what to say.

'You think you're the only one who had them in your

head? Libby almost didn't agree to marry me because she knew how *happy* it would make them. She was so sick of living up to their expectations that she said she wanted desperately to do the *wrong* thing—just once.'

'I can't believe it,' Marnie whispered, squeezing her eyes shut as she thought of Libby. 'She was the golden girl, and I never thought that bothered her.'

'It was a big mantle to wear,' he said simply.

Marnie expelled a soft breath and looked away. The breeze drifted some of her hair loose and she absentmindedly reached for it, tucking it back in place. 'I miss her so much,' she said finally.

Anderson was quiet for so long that Marnie wasn't sure he'd even heard her, or that she'd said the words aloud. Then, finally, he nodded and his voice cracked. 'Me, too.'

She wrapped her arms around him spontaneously, knowing that he understood her grief. That even years after losing Libby he stood before her a man as bereft now as he had been then.

From a distance they looked like a couple, he thought. The perfect blue-blooded pair. She with her couture gown and her swan-like neck angled towards Anderson's cheek. Her manicured hand resting on his hip, her flawless arm around his back.

His wife was beautiful, but in this environment, surrounded by Europe's financial elite, she was showcased to perfection—because she was at home. She was completely comfortable, whereas he felt the prestige like a knife in his side.

'If I did not trust you with my life I would be jealous of this little scene.'

Nikos's accented voice sent shivers of sensual awareness down Marnie's spine. She lifted away from Anderson, her eyes suspiciously moist. It caught Nikos's attention instantly. He looked from his wife to his friend, a frown on his face and a chasm in his chest.

'You are upset?'

She rolled her eyes. 'No. This is my happy face.'

He sent her a warning look that was somewhat softened when he reached into his pocket and removed a cloth handkerchief. She took it with genuine surprise at the sweetness of the gesture, dabbing at the corners of her eyes so as not to ruin her eye make-up.

'We were just reminiscing,' Anderson said simply.

Though he was subdued, he appeared to have largely regained control of his emotions.

'Your father was asking for you,' Nikos said to his friend.

'Bertram is here?' Marnie asked, a smile shifting her lips as she thought of the elder statesman. It transformed her face in an expression of such delicate beauty that Nikos had to stifle a sharp intake of breath.

'Yeah.' Anderson extended a hand and shook Nikos's. 'But I suspect your groom just doesn't want me monopolising you any longer.'

He winked at Marnie, obviously intending to make a swift departure.

She put a hand on his forearm to forestall him. 'Are you in Greece much longer? Will you come for dinner?'

'I'd love that,' Anderson said honestly. 'But we fly out tomorrow.'

Marnie's smile was wistful. 'Another time?'

'Sure.' He leaned forward and kissed her cheek, then winked at Nikos.

Alone with her husband, and the hundreds of other partygoers, Marnie felt her air of relaxation disappear. She reached for the railing, gripping it until her knuckles turned white. 'Are you having a good time?' she asked stiffly, her eyes seeking a fixed point on which to focus.

'It is good business for me to be here,' he said, lifting his broad shoulders carelessly.

'I wouldn't have thought your business required this sort of schmoozing.'

'That is true,' he said simply. 'But I do not intend to grow complacent in light of my success.'

She nodded, adding that little soundbite to the dossier of information she'd been building on him: *Nikos: V 2.0.*

This Nikos was determined to prove himself to the world—or was Anderson right? Was it that he wanted to prove himself to *her*? To prove that he deserved her?

No, that couldn't be it.

Had it not been for Arthur's financial ruin, Nikos would never have reappeared in her life.

'He might have played the part of a bachelor to perfection...' Anderson had said, and it had been an enormous understatement. Nikos had dedicated himself to the single life with aplomb. She'd lost count of the number of women he'd been reputed to be dating. And even 'dating' was over-egging it somewhat.

The women never lasted long, but that didn't matter. Each of those women had shared a part of Nikos that Marnie had been denied—a part that she'd denied herself.

Her eyes narrowed as she turned to study her husband. He'd followed her gaze and his eyes were trained on the mainland, giving her a moment to drink in his autocratic profile, the swarthy complexion and beautiful cheekbones that might well have been slashed from stone.

'Do you see that light over there?'

She followed the direction he was pointing in, squinting into the distance. There was a small glow visible in the cliffs near the sea. 'The hut?' she asked.

'Yes. It *is* a hut.' His sneer was not aimed at her; it showed agreement. He pinned her with his gaze; it was hard like gravel. 'That is where I spent the first eight years of my life.'

'Oh!' She resettled her attention on him, curiosity swelling in her chest, for Nikos had never opened up about his childhood even when they'd been madly in love. 'Is it?' She strained to pick out any details, but it was too far away. 'What's it like? Is it part of a town?'

'A town? No. There were four huts when I was growing up.' He gripped the railing tight. 'Two rooms only.'

She didn't want to say anything that might cause him to stop speaking. 'Did you like it?'

'*Like* it?' He lifted his lips in a humourless smile. 'It was a very free childhood.'

'Oh?'

'My father had a trawler. He came out here every day.'

'Squid?'

He nodded. 'Scampi, too.'

'You said you lived there until you were eight. What happened?'

He tilted his head to face her, his expression derisive. 'There was a storm. He died.'

'Nikos!' Sympathy softened her expression, but she saw immediately how unwelcome it was.

He shifted a little, indicating his desire to end the conversation.

'I should have told you he'd be here,' Nikos said only a moment later, surprising her with the lightning-fast change in conversation.

For a moment she didn't comprehend who he was talking about.

'It did not occur to me that Anderson would upset you.'

She drew her brows together in confusion. 'He didn't.'

'The tears in your eyes would suggest otherwise.'

She opened her mouth in an expression of her bemusement. 'This from the man who seems to live to insult me?' The words escaped before she could catch them.

Nikos nodded slowly, as if accepting her charge even

as his words sought to contradict it. 'Hurting you... That is not intentional. It is not what I want.'

She blinked and spun away, turning her body to face the railing. 'I can believe that.' And that hurt so much more! Knowing he could inflict pain without even trying, without even being conscious of her feelings, simply demonstrated how little he thought of her feelings at all.

'Do we have to stay long?' she asked, doing her best to sound unconcerned when emotions were zipping through her.

'No. Let's go. *Now.*'

He trapped her hand in his much bigger palm and led her from the party. Several times people moved to grab his attention, but Nikos apparently had a one-track mind, and it involved getting them off the boat.

At his Ferrari, with the moon cresting high in the sky and the strains of the party muffled by distance, Nikos put his hands on her shoulders and spun her to face him. His eyes seemed to tunnel into the heart of her soul.

'What is it I have done that's insulted you?'

She knew she couldn't deny it; after all, she'd just laid the charge at his feet. She shook her head, yet the words wouldn't climb to her tongue.

'Tell me, *agape*...'

'Nothing. It's fine.' Her eyes didn't meet his.

'Liar!' He groaned, crushing his mouth to hers.

His hands lifted, pulling at the pins that kept her hair in its chignon until they had all dropped to the ground in near-silent protest. He dragged his fingers through her hair, pulling at it and levering her face away.

His eyes bored into hers. 'I was angry with you tonight. I was rude.'

A sob was filling her chest. She wouldn't give in to it. '*Why?* What in the world could you have had to be angry about?'

Was that really her voice? With the exception of a slight tremor, she sounded so cool and in command! How was that possible when her knees were shaking and her heart was pounding?

'This. *You.*' He stepped backwards, as if to shake himself out of the hurricane of feelings. He pulled the door open and stared at her.

Marnie stared back. She wasn't going to let this go just because he appeared to have decided the conversation was at an end.

'*What?*' she demanded, lifting a hand and splaying her fingers against his broad chest. 'What *about* me? What did I do?'

'Do?' His head snapped back as if in silent revulsion. 'You did nothing. You cannot help that this is who you are.'

Her heart was pounding so hard now that it was paining her. 'I don't understand,' she said, with a soft determination that almost completely hid her wounds.

'No? Allow me to clarify. You are Lady Marnie Kenington and you always will be. You are this dress. This party. This perfect face. You are cold and you are exquisitely untouchable. The girl I thought I loved all those years ago never existed, did she?'

CHAPTER EIGHT

FOR THE FIRST time since her arrival in Greece the early morning was drenched by storm. The sky was leaden with weighty clouds, the ocean a turbulent, raging gradient of steel. White caps frothed all the way to the horizon, and the trees that marked the shore arched in the distance, folded almost completely in half.

Marnie, her knees bent under her chin, her eyes focussed on the ravaged horizon, took a measure of consolation from the destruction. Her mind, numb from the exhausting activity of trying to join the dots of what had happened the night before, looked for some kind of comparison in the wasted outlook.

The storm was trashing everything, and yet in time—perhaps even later that day—the clouds would disperse, the sun would shine, and all would look as it once had. Better, perhaps, for the rain had a spectacular way of cleaning things up, didn't it?

Could the same be said for her and Nikos?

Were they in the midst of a storm that would one day clear? Argument by argument, would they wash away their hurts?

She shook her head sadly from side to side, the question that had plagued her at length tormenting her anew.

Why had he married her?

'You are Lady Marnie Kenington and you always will be. The girl I fell in love with all those years ago never existed, did she?'

Had she?

He was right. Marnie had changed so much since then. He seemed to attribute it to her upbringing, to her parents' snobbery. Wasn't it more likely that she'd simply grown up?

She glanced down at her manicured fingernails and the enormous diamond that sparkled on her ring finger.

They were husband and wife, but outside of that, they were strangers. A lump formed in her throat; futility hollowed out her core.

He hadn't come to bed last night. She'd showered and waited for him—hoping, knowing, that their being together would make sense of everything. That when they made love the truth of their hearts was most obvious.

But she had no experience in the matter. Was it as he said? Just great sex? Or was it love? Or memories of love, like fragments of a dream, too hard to catch now in the bright light of reality and daytime?

She scraped her chair back impatiently. The pool was dark today, too, reflecting the sorrow of the skies. Had it been a stormy day like this when Nikos had lost his father? When the ocean had swallowed him up, perhaps as retribution for the fish he'd stolen out of its belly?

He had been silent and brooding on the car trip home, and Marnie had been too absorbed by his statement to try to break through that mood, to get to the heart of what he had meant.

Perhaps this morning they could talk.

She moved towards the kitchen, the thought of a cup of tea offering unparalleled temptation. And froze when she saw him.

It was like a flashback to the morning after they'd first

arrived. Impeccably dressed in a high-end business suit, he had his head bent over the newspaper and a cup to his left, which she knew would be filled with that thick coffee he loved.

'Good morning,' she murmured, her voice croaky from disuse.

He flicked a gaze to her face, studying her for one heartstopping moment before smiling tightly and returning his attention to the paper.

So that was how it was going to be.

Marnie squared her shoulders and tipped up her chin defiantly. 'Did you sleep well?' She walked to the bench, standing directly opposite him.

Without looking up, he responded, 'Fine. And you?'

It was a lie. He hadn't got more than ten minutes altogether.

'Not really,' she said honestly.

He turned the page of the newspaper. Did she imagine that it was with force and irritation? The admission had cost her. It was an offer of peace—an acceptance of their relationship, faults and all.

'Where did you sleep?' she pushed, determined to crack through the facade he'd erected.

'In a guest room.' Still he read the damned newspaper.

Marnie, trying her hardest to forge past the storm, reached down and put her hand over the article. 'Nikos, we need to talk.'

He expelled a sigh and glanced at his watch. 'Do we?'

'You know we do.' She lifted her hand and moved it to his, lacing his fingers with her own. 'This isn't right.'

He moved his hand so that he could lift his coffee cup and drink from it. 'Talk quickly. I have a meeting.'

Hurt lashed her as a whip. 'That's not fair,' she said, with soft steel to her voice. 'You can't keep doing that.'

'Doing what?'

'Making yourself unavailable as soon as things get tough.'

'I relish obstacles. I relish difficult opportunities. But I cannot see the point in discussing anything with you right now.'

'So what you said last night isn't important enough to talk about?'

'What *did* I say?' he asked softly, his eyes roaming her face.

'Don't be fatuous,' she snapped. 'You made it sound like we didn't love each other. Like we didn't know each other.'

His look was one of confusion. 'But we *don't*.'

Denial! The sharpness of it plunged into her heart.

'I meant back then…' She limped the conversation along even when she felt as if she was dying a little.

'I said that the girl I thought I loved never existed,' he said with a shrug. 'That girl would have stood up for what we were. Would have fought to be with me. But you were never that. Seeing you last night, in that dress, you looked so perfect.' Derision lined his face. 'You've become exactly what your parents wanted.'

'You keep *doing* that! You keep making me out to be some kind of construct of theirs.'

'*Aren't* you?'

'Aren't we all?' she challenged. '*You* are a product of your life just as I am of mine. But if you hate me so much why the hell did you insist I marry you? It *has* to be more than revenge against my father'

He closed the paper and drained his coffee cup before placing it neatly on the edge of the sink. The seconds ticked by loudly in the background.

'Why do you think?'

A thousand possibilities clouded her mind, some of them dangling hope and others promising despair. 'I don't know,' she said finally, warily, shaking her head.

'To prove that I could have you.'

She had to brace her hands on the edge of the bench for support.

Her face flashed with such a depth of hurt that Nikos instantly wanted to call the words back. To defuse the situation and make her smile again. To make her laugh in that beautiful, inimitable way she had.

Laughter was a long way from Marnie's mind, though. 'You're serious?' She pressed her lips together, her mind reeling. 'This was just ego? As a seventeen-year-old I rejected you, and you couldn't handle that, could you? And now you've bullied me into this marriage so—what? So you can make me feel like this? So you can berate me and humiliate me…'

He held up a hand to silence her. 'I told you last night—I do not mean to hurt you. I never did.'

'Yeah, *right*.' She swallowed, her throat moving convulsively as she attempted to breathe normally. 'It didn't occur to you that this whole idea would hurt me?'

A muscle jerked in his cheek. 'Are you having regrets?'

'How can I *not* be? You put me in an impossible situation.' She spun away from him, looking out at the storm. She was at a crossroads. She could tell him the truth—that it was impossible to be married to him knowing he would never love her. Or she could remember that she *had* married him. A thousand and one reasons had driven her to it, and they were all still there.

Worse, Marnie stared down the barrel of her future and imagined it without Nikos and she was instantly bereft. Even this shell of a relationship, knowing he would share only a small part of himself with her, was better than nothing.

She'd faced life without him and it had been a sort of half-life. She'd poured all her energy into her work, and she'd dated men that she'd known her parents would approve of, but she hadn't felt truly alive until she'd seen Nikos once more.

Was it better to feel alive and permanently in pain or to be alone and feel nothing?

She turned to face him slowly, her face unknowingly stoic. 'I didn't hope for much from you, Nikos, but I expected at least that you would respect me. And do you know why? Because of who *you* are. Last night you said that the girl you fell in love with never existed. Maybe you feel that—maybe you don't. I don't know. But I have no doubt that I knew *you*. Who you were then. I think I know who you are now, too. And the contempt you are meeting me with is completely unwarranted.'

Her eyes sparked as she spoke the declaration.

'You say you married me to prove that you could have me. Well, I only married *you* to save my father. Did you honestly expect me to do anything less?'

'Not at all.' His voice was gravelly. 'You are excellent at taking direction.'

She sucked in a breath at the cruel remark. 'My parents were right to tell me to break it off with you. Not because you had no money or family prestige, but because you're a jerk.'

It wasn't funny but he laughed—a short, sharp sound of disbelief.

'I'm serious,' she said stiffly. 'I *am* Lady Marnie Kenington. I am the same woman I've always been. You forced me into this marriage and now you're angry with me just for being who I am. *You're* the one who's trying to make me something I'm not.'

Her words were little shards of glass, all the more potent for she was right. He couldn't fault her behaviour as his wife. She'd done and been everything he'd required of her. She hadn't shifted the goalposts—he had.

The realisation only worsened his mood. How could he

explain to her that he never enjoyed being at events like the party they'd attended the night before? That he hated most of the people in attendance, despised their grandiose displays of wealth and their desire to outdo one another. That he hated that entire scene and she was the very epitome of it? That seeing her amongst her own people—people who'd been born to wealth and prestige—made him realise that they'd never see the world the same way?

'You make an excellent point. I knew what I was getting when I suggested this marriage.' He looked at his wife long and hard. She was a woman who projected an image of being cool and untouchable—except with him. A gnawing sense of frustration engulfed him. 'Now, I really *am* late.'

He stalked towards the door, then turned back to face her. She was staring straight ahead with such an attempt at strength and resolve that something inside him twisted painfully.

'Marnie…' *What?* What could he offer her? 'We can make this work. The way we are in bed—'

'Is just great sex,' she reminded him, hating the words even as she spoke them.

But it was more than that. In bed, in his arms, Marnie was as he wanted her to be. Genuine, overflowing with desire and feeling: a real flesh-and-blood woman. Not the fancy ice queen she showed the world.

'Yes. And many marriages are built on less.'

'Great.' She appeared calm and in control, but her strength was crumbling. 'Don't you have a meeting to go to?'

He walked out of the door with a heavy pain in his gut that stayed with him all day.

His mind was shot. He lost concentration, he sent emails to the wrong people, he inverted figures on his spreadsheets.

He gave up on work in the early afternoon.

When he arrived home the place was deserted. He wandered from room to room, pretending he wasn't looking for Marnie, until he heard her voice drifting from the small space she'd claimed as her office.

By silent but mutual agreement he didn't intrude on her there. She generally only utilised it when he was at work, anyway. But curiosity drove him towards the door now, and he lingered for a moment on the threshold.

'We're in stage three of some very promising trials. Yes...'

She paused, and he could imagine the way she'd have that little line between her brows that showed deep concentration.

'That's true. Human trials are still a way off. But every day brings us closer.' Another pause. 'You're a gem, Mrs Finley-Johns. That's really very generous. Thank you.'

Silence filled the room for long enough that Nikos presumed she'd hung up the phone. He pushed the door inwards silently.

Marnie—his wife—was sitting at her desk, her honeyed hair piled into a messy bun, her head bent over a page as she handwrote something. He watched her for a moment and then stepped into the room.

That feeling in his gut didn't dissipate. He'd thought seeing her might do it. That just the sight of her might make everything slide back into place. It didn't.

When she realised she was no longer alone and lifted her gaze to his face he waited impatiently for a smile to burst sunshine through the room and relax his chest. It didn't. If anything, she was impatient, lifting her eyes to the clock above the door.

'Nikos? Is everything okay?' She reached for her phone, rotating it in her hands.

'Why do you ask?'

'It's so early,' she said with a look of confusion. 'You're usually not home for hours.'

He felt as if the ground was slipping beneath him. 'My afternoon was freed up,' he said with a shrug. 'You wanted to speak this morning and I rushed you. I thought we could go out for dinner and talk properly.'

The suggestion had come out of nowhere but as soon as he'd issued the invitation he'd known it was right.

'We did speak this morning.'

Their conversation had chased its way through her mind all day. Like a maze, it had twists and turns, but no matter which path she chased down they all finished in a dead end of despair.

'Not properly.' The words were gruff. He dragged a hand through his hair. 'Let's have dinner and try to be civilised.'

She arched a brow, genuine surprise obvious. 'I'm working.' She bit down on her lip. 'And I don't think anything's served by going out, do you?'

She sounded prim, and inwardly she winced. *You'll always be Lady Marnie Kenington...*

He crossed his arms over his chest, staring down at her. Marnie felt the imbalance in their arrangement and fought an urge to stand, to right it. That would just be symbolic; the true imbalance would remain.

'What is it you are doing? For work?' His smile was an attempt to relax her. To elicit a similar reaction in her. It failed. 'Or is it still a secret?'

'It's not a secret.' She shook her head. 'It never has been. I do behind-the-scenes fundraising for a cancer charity. Specifically leukaemia research.'

It wasn't what he'd expected and that was obvious. He rubbed a hand over his stubbled chin, propping his hip against the doorframe. He was settling in. Marnie swallowed. Her insides were clenching with desire, her mind was sore from trying to figure out what the hell they were doing, and all she could think as she looked at him was how much she wanted him. To hell with everything else.

'Why behind the scenes?'

She blinked, passing her phone from one hand to the other. 'It's more my thing.'

'I would have thought your profile would garner donations…'

'My name does that, too.' She shrugged, placing the phone down on the desk and clasping her hands together in her lap. 'And my contacts.'

He took a step into the office, looking at the computer screen. It had a list of names with donations beside them, tracking various contributions for the last few years.

'You are apparently very effective at this,' he murmured, leaning forward and scrolling down the page.

His body framed hers, trapping her within the circle of his arms. She thought of telling him to stop looking, saying that her work was confidential. But why? Nikos Kyriazis was hardly likely to be indiscreet with the information, and most of her donors released details of their charitable contributions as a way of attracting good publicity.

'Thanks,' she said, allowing herself to extract a small kernel of pleasure from his praise. 'I suppose it's because I feel passionately about it.'

'Yes…' He straightened, but stayed where he was, so that his legs straddled hers. 'How come you have not asked *me* to donate?'

Her smile was a twist of her pink lips. 'You don't think you've donated enough to my cause already?'

That feeling in his gut intensified in a burst of pain. 'This is different.'

She shook her head. 'Not really.' She ran a fingernail over the hem of her skirt, drawing his attention to her smooth, tanned legs.

'Why don't we go for dinner and you can tell me about this? Your charity. Pretend I am a donor you want to win over.'

'But you're not,' she said with a shake of her head. 'And I don't want to ask you to put money into this.'

'It matters so much to you, though,' he pointed out logically. 'Surely you wouldn't turn me down?'

She shrugged, perfecting an air of impatient unconcern. 'If you want to donate, you can. That's your business.'

'Tell me more about it first.'

Marnie bit down on her lip, her eyes drifting to his face. The time she'd spent in an attempt to make sense of their situation had all been a waste, for here was yet another facet of Nikos Kyriazis that wholly renewed the riddle. His ability to set aside their contretemps and the harsh words he'd issued made her head spin.

She nodded finally, expelling a soft sigh. 'Fine. We'll talk at dinner.'

Nikos had dismissed enough people enough times in his life to know that he was being dismissed from her office. Feeling that somewhere in their conversation he'd scored a minor victory, he didn't push it.

CHAPTER NINE

In England, Marnie was used to being recognised. She hated the sensation but she'd come to expect it, so she had long ago given up the idea of eating in glamorous high-profile restaurants without expecting to be photographed and approached by all and sundry.

In Athens it was Nikos who drew the long, speculative glances. Nikos whose name opened doors and inspired attention and curiosity.

Marnie was actually enjoying being an outsider to the sense of celebrity. She'd never craved it, and watching him being fawned over by waitresses and even the manager at the exclusive Athens hot spot from the moment they arrived brought a small smile to her lips now.

He saw it immediately. Of their own volition his eyes dropped to the curve of her pink mouth and fire warmed her belly.

'Yes, Marnie?' he prompted, leaning forward so that a hint of his masculine fragrance teased her nostrils, making her gut clench with unmistakable desire. She tried to ignore it.

She crossed her legs beneath the table and shrugged. 'I was just thinking how nice it is that I'm unknown here.'

'Not unknown,' he said, with a small shake of his head.

'Well, *lesser* known,' she corrected. 'Less relevant. And you're…'

'Yes?' He broke off the query when a waitress appeared with a bottle of ice-cold champagne.

'Compliments of the owner.' She smiled at Nikos, her cleavage exposed as she leaned forward to pour some of the liquid into a long, tapered flute.

'Thank you,' he murmured dismissively. 'You were saying…?'

Marnie waited for the waitress to finish pouring. 'You're who everyone wants to see.' She grinned. 'I'm anonymous and you're hot property.'

His laugh surprised her. It was rich and warm, and reminded her of how long it had been since she'd heard the sound.

'Hot property?' He shook his head. 'I'm glad to hear you think so.'

'You know what I mean.' Colour bloomed in her cheeks. She focussed on the menu. 'What's good here? What do you recommend?'

'It is all excellent.' He shrugged.

She scanned the menu but she was far from hungry. Butterflies had taken up residence in her stomach and their beating wings made it impossible for her to imagine accommodating food into their kaleidoscope.

'What do you suggest?'

His eyes narrowed. 'I can order for you, if you'd like?'

'That won't be necessary.' She shut down his perfectly normal offer, knowing how dire it would be to keep conceding to him.

'As you wish.' He pushed the menu away, his mind apparently made up.

She continued to skim her eyes over the words on the page but they were puddles and blurs.

'How long have you done this work?'

She started, despite the fact his suggestion of dinner had been hung on a desire to learn more about the trust.

'About four years,' she said, reaching for the stem of her champagne flute simply for something to do.

'You didn't go to university?'

She shook her head. 'The timing wasn't right.'

A frown smudged his handsome face. 'In what way?'

Marnie pulled her lower lip between her teeth and Nikos surprised her by reaching over and abruptly swiping his thumb across her mouth, disturbing the gesture.

'Don't think.' He spoke commandingly, his words gravelled. 'You do this too often.'

Her expression was blank. 'I wasn't aware thinking was a crime.'

'It is when you are selecting which words to use to your husband. Just answer my questions directly.'

Marnie gaped, her mouth parted on an exhalation of surprise. 'That hardly seems fair.'

'Why was the timing not right?' He returned to his original question, impatient for an answer.

He was right. She *had* been prevaricating, unconsciously trying to select words that wouldn't apportion blame or imply resentment.

'I wasn't ready to leave home,' she said quietly.

But he understood what she hadn't been willing to say. 'You mean your parents didn't want you to go?' His disapproval was marked, despite the way he spoke quietly.

The waitress reappeared, her smile bright. Was it also inviting? Or was Marnie being paranoid?

She flicked her gaze back to the menu, intent on seeming not to notice the way the waitress lingered a little too close to Nikos as she spoke.

Nikos didn't appreciate the interruption, and his annoyance brought a childish kernel of pleasure to Marnie. She hesitated over ordering for far longer than was necessary, finally selecting scampi followed by chicken, having changed her mind several times.

Nikos glared at her and spoke in Greek, quickly dispensing with the waitress.

'They forbade you from attending university?'

She started, shaking her head softly so that her hair flew around her cheeks. 'Not at all.'

'You wanted to study law. You were passionate about it.'

'Not really.'

He ignored the rejoinder. After all, they'd spent a long time talking about their hopes and dreams. He had not misunderstood her desire to go into law. Nor did he doubt she would have achieved the requisite grades.

'But instead you stayed at home, living with your parents, working for a charity that revolves around your sister's illness,' he murmured, with a directness she hadn't expected.

'Do you think there's something wrong with that?'

'Yes.' He leaned forward and put his hand on hers. 'You are a person, too, Marnie. You are not simply Libby's sister. Nor your parents' daughter. You have your own life to live.'

She compressed her lips and pulled her hand down to her lap. 'You say that even after blackmailing me into this marriage?'

She sipped her champagne but it was too sweet. She didn't want it. She was definitely not in the mood to celebrate. She ran her finger around the rim, staring at the hypnotic, frantic movement of the bubbles as her mind spun over the situation they found themselves in.

'It's not as if I can't move on,' she said quietly, her eyes refusing to meet his. 'But without funds research into leukaemia is slow. It occurred to me that the people most likely to succeed at raising money are probably those who have every reason to passionately pursue it. In ten years—who knows? Maybe girls like Libby won't get sick.'

Finally, she forced herself to lance him with her eyes; they were softened by sorrow.

'It's idealistic, but…'

He surprised her by murmuring, 'Not at all. You are right. Progress does not always happen as you expect it to. Sometimes it is hard-fought, and other times it is over-night, as though a cascade of discoveries slides into place. But without funds neither is likely.'

She nodded, distracted enough by the subject matter to speak naturally. 'I thought I'd do it for a year. As a way of giving back to the trust that was so supportive to us. But it turns out I sort of have a knack for it.'

'I can imagine,' he said. 'Do you regret not studying law?'

It was on the tip of her tongue to deny it, but the truth came to her first. 'Yeah. Sometimes. But that would have been about helping people, too. I'm just helping different people now.'

He let the words sink in and shied away from the in-trinsic guilt they evoked. After all, her propensity to help others was what had made it impossible for her to walk away from his marriage proposal.

'And staying at home instead of finding your own place…?'

Her smile was enigmatic. 'You know… Kenington Hall is enormous. I have my own wing. It's much like living on my own.'

'And your parents are your neighbours?' he murmured, his voice ringing with disbelief.

'Yes.' She nodded. 'But apparently I'm a pretty inatten-tive neighbour,' she said with regret. 'I had no idea about Dad's troubles.'

His desire to comfort her displeased him. 'I imagine he was adept at concealing the truth.'

'Not really.' She shook her head wistfully.

The waitress appeared with their starters, placing them on the table and then disappearing without a word. Marnie wondered if Nikos had commanded her to stop making conversation when he'd switched to speaking Greek earlier.

Nikos watched as Marnie lifted her fork and speared a single scampi. She put it down again almost instantly, and when she looked at him he felt a wave of guilt emanating from her.

'I should have seen the signs.'

'What signs?' he prompted.

'He's been stressed. Angry. He's just not himself.'

Nikos found it hard to find any genuine sympathy for the man, but he realised he didn't like seeing Marnie suffer. *At all.* 'Tell me something…'

She nodded, toying with her fork.

'After your father paid me off, were you angry with him?'

Marnie's eyes flashed with emotion. 'I didn't know about that, remember?'

He waved a hand dismissively through the air. 'Fine. After I left, were you angry with him? With your mother?'

'I…' She shuttered her eyes closed, her dark lashes fanning over her translucent cheek.

'Do not *think*!' He repeated his earlier directive and she grimaced.

'I was furious,' she said, so quietly he had to lean forward to catch the words. 'But they're my parents, and they'd been through so much.' She swallowed. 'My father threatened…' She closed her mouth on the threat she'd been about to repeat. 'My father was devastated by losing Libby.'

'And he threatened you?' Nikos prompted, with a smoothness that spoke of determination.

She thought about lying. But wasn't there so much water under the bridge now?

'They made me choose.'

The anticlimax brought about in him an intense sense

of disappointment. Right when he'd thought he might finally be going to understand just what had led to Marnie pushing him far, far away, she'd gone back to the old lines.

'I mean they *literally* told me they'd disown me if I didn't break it off with you,' she added with a look of grief on her beautiful features.

She was back in the past, her mind far from him in that moment.

'I didn't care when they said they'd disinherit me.' She looked at him—and through him. 'Money meant nothing to me. But they were my link to Libby, and they said they wouldn't have me in their lives so long as I was with you. That I would never be allowed to return to Kenington Hall.' Marnie's voice cracked. 'The house was—is—all I have left of her...'

Marnie woke with a start as the plane pitched a little in one direction. She'd dozed off, despite the fact their flight had been a morning one. She stifled a yawn with the back of her hand, her groggy eyes drifting to her husband's bent head.

He was working.

A smile flicked to her lips with ease, though her stomach churned with a mix of anxiety and an emotion that was so much more confusing.

She didn't have time to attempt to understand it before the plane shuddered and Marnie's panic overtook everything. She dug her fingernails into the armrests, her expression showing distress.

Nikos, attuned to her every move, looked up instantly. 'There is thick cloud-cover over London, that's all.'

She nodded, but her childhood fear of flying was ricocheting through her. Marnie stared out of the window, trying to distract herself with thoughts of her father's birthday weekend—anything to curtail the clear picture she had in her mind of the aeroplane spearing nose-first towards the earth.

Their trip had come round quickly—for Marnie, almost too quickly.

After that one night in Athens when they'd shared dinner she felt as if a new understanding had settled between her and her husband and she wanted to hold on to that, to strengthen the understanding that was building between them. Would a trip back to her parents' unsettle the bridge they'd been building?

They were not a normal couple.

There was no shared love between them—at least not on Nikos's part. Perhaps not on Marnie's part either.

She had spent a great deal of her energy trying to decipher and separate her feelings of lust from love; her feelings of past love from present infatuation. Some days she convinced herself that she'd fallen in love with only the *idea* of Nikos—an idea that bore only a passing resemblance to the ruthless, determined businessman he'd become.

But then he would do something sweet—like bringing her tea in bed when she'd slept late, or calling in the middle of the day to remind her of something small they'd discussed the night before—and her heart would flutter and her soul would know she loved him. Not in a sensible, rational way, but in the way that love sometimes bloomed even when it was not watered or fed.

They barely argued. By tacit agreement each tried to respect the other's limitations. Marnie accepted the dark streak that ran through Nikos—the side of him that was so hell-bent on making her father see how wrong he was to have passed Nikos off as a failure that he'd blackmailed her into marriage. If she thought about it too much it made her queasy, so she pushed it to the recesses of her mind and clung to a sort of blind hope. Maybe one day he wouldn't feel that aching resentment so forcefully?

Their truce was underpinned by a sex life that made her toes curl. He had been right about that. Even if it was all they had to go on it would make their marriage worth staying in. Wouldn't it?

But uncertainty lurked just beyond her acceptance. For they had travelled stormy waters, and weren't there always eyes in storms? The calm that gave a moment's respite before the intensity of the cyclone returned with twice its strength?

Was she in the eye of a storm?

Or was this a lasting peace?

Only time would tell, and Marnie had a lifetime to wait and see.

CHAPTER TEN

THE APPLE WAS as sweetly sun-warmed as those she remembered from childhood. Despite the fact the day was cool, the morning had offered just enough heat to darken the flesh of this one more than the others.

Though it wasn't yet midday, she was tired. They'd been travelling since dawn and the return to Kenington with Nikos by her side had brought with it a sledge-load of emotions.

Juice dribbled down one side of her mouth and she lifted a finger to catch it.

Nikos watched, transfixed.

'I used to love coming down here to the apple orchard...'

'I remember.'

Memories. They were his problem. They were thick in the air around them. Memories of how it had felt then. When he'd been young and in love. He would have plucked a matching apple from another branch and enjoyed its fruity flesh alongside Marnie.

She stopped walking and turned around, her back to the heavily adorned fruit trees. 'I always think this is the best aspect of the house.' She lifted her free hand and framed the building between her forefinger and thumb. Her smile was born of whimsy. 'Until I go to the rose garden or Libby's garden. Then I think *that* view is preferable.'

She crunched into the apple once more.

'Perhaps it is the same from all viewpoints,' he suggested, with a hint of cynicism that was out of place and sounded, even to his own ears, forced.

'Maybe.' She shrugged and began to walk back towards the house.

He resisted the urge to ask her to stay with him where they were a little longer.

'Thank you for coming with me this weekend.'

His laugh was short. 'I presumed my attendance wasn't optional.'

She lifted her face to his. 'I would think almost *everything* is optional for you.'

His smile was without humour—a relic of his twisted laugh. 'Not this.'

She didn't pretend to misunderstand. 'When are you seeing him?'

'We're meeting after lunch.'

Marnie stopped walking, reaching for Nikos's hand. Her fingers curled around his as though they belonged. Familiarity and comfort knotted through her, momentarily putting aside the nausea and anxiety that had besieged her since they'd arrived in London.

'What is it, *agape*?'

A husky question. A promise, too, laced with so many emotions she couldn't translate.

'You know how stubborn he is?'

Nikos's lips curled. 'Yes.'

'I just don't know if he'll let you help. And I'm… I'm scared.'

His eyes held hers, probing her, trying to read her soul. 'Tell me something, Marnie. Why do you care?'

She started, scanning his face. But Nikos wasn't backing off. In fact, he moved closer, welding his body to hers, linking his arms behind her back. His nearness was seductive and distracting.

'Besides the fact he's my father?'

'Blood isn't everything. Your parents don't seem too concerned with your happiness. You're not close to them.'

'Of course I am,' she said with a shake of her head.

He laughed, dismissing her assertion easily. 'You don't speak to them. You don't speak *of* them—except with a sense of obligation and guilt because you survived and Libby died.'

She was startled at his perceptiveness.

'You married a man who saw you only as a means of revenge in order to stave off the financial fate that they deserve.'

'They're my *parents*,' she mumbled, her eyes flicking closed. The pain of his words was washing through her. 'And I'm very grateful to you.'

'Grateful?' He stepped backwards, shaking his head. '*Thee mou.* You offer me *gratitude*? I tell you I see you as a means of revenge and you say thank you?'

She frowned. 'You know what I mean.'

'No, I don't. You have been pushed around by your parents, and by me, and yet you seem to treat us all with civility and thankfulness. I cannot comprehend this.'

She swallowed. 'Do you need to?'

He shook his head. 'No.' He lifted a hand to her cheek and stroked it. 'And I suppose the same could be said for you.'

She pressed a hand to his chest, perhaps intending to put some distance between them, but the warmth of him, the beating of his heart, was mesmerising.

'Do you really believe our marriage comes down to revenge and sex?'

'Our marriage—' He began to speak, the words thick with meaning. He stared into her eyes; he was drowning in them. They were the depths to her soul; the truth to her questions. They mirrored his past, his heart and all his hopes.

They were beautiful eyes. How could people mistake her for being cold-hearted? In her eyes there was always a twisting of emotion and thought, of kindness and concern. Yet he had missed it. He had believed her unfeeling and incapable of true emotion at one point. He'd clung to that; he'd enjoyed believing it of her.

'Yes?'

It was a husk. An invitation for him to say something that would smooth away the pain of their predicament. A contradiction of the fact that he had bought her out of a need to avenge past wrongs.

But they were wrongs he'd carried with him for a long time. Was he willing to let them go? And, if so, what did that mean?

'Marnie?'

The voice was shrill and imperious, cutting across the lawn and breaking through the growing understanding that had been forming between them. He was unwilling to close their conversation, but a cloud instantly seemed to spread across Marnie and she stepped back.

The woman who had pulled a sweet apple from a frothy tree and crunched into it hungrily was gone. Lady Heiress was his companion now—only her eyes showed that Marnie was still in there.

'It doesn't matter,' she said quietly, shifting her gaze to the manor house in the background. 'I'm glad you're going to help him. Only be gentle, Nikos. And…' She turned to face him, hurrying now as Anne Kenington approached them. 'I know you said *you* would decide if you wanted to tell him the truth about our arrangement but…'

It seemed like an age ago that they'd had that conversation, but it had only been a month! Something strange lodged in her mind—a recollection she couldn't quite grab so she pushed it aside.

'But could you not? Not this weekend? I know you hate him, and that it's tempting to throw it in his face. But not now. Please?'

He stared at her without speaking and Marnie continued anxiously.

'I don't think I could forgive that. It would be… It really would be the end of what we used to mean to one another.'

Nikos was perplexed—and something else. Something he couldn't analyse or comprehend. So he spoke honestly. 'I have no intention of telling your father you married me to clear his debts.'

'Don't say that!'

She was visibly stricken, but Anne was almost upon them. Like a consummate professional Marnie blinked and slid her mask into place.

It annoyed him, and he wanted to prise it off again—just for a moment. He was sick and tired of masks and pretence.

'It's the truth,' he replied softly, clinging to that fact for her sake as much as his own.

Did he want her to contradict him? Did he want her to redefine their marriage? How could he expect that of her? A challenge? A gauntlet? One he knew she'd never answer.

'Isn't it?'

Their conversation had left Nikos in a foul mood. The lack of resolution, the constant chasing one another in circles, had given him the feeling that as soon as he began to comprehend a facet of his wife she morphed into something else and slipped out of his grip and downstream from him completely.

Worse was the sense that he was losing his own convictions in the face of hers. To lose one's sister would be hard enough, but to have your parents threaten to cut you completely from their life and support… Even Marnie, who had always seemed to have certainty and strength to her, must have been terrified of what that would mean.

How *dared* they? How had they dared to speak to their own child with such cold disregard?

It was not the ideal mind-set to bring to his meeting with Arthur Kenington. Nor was it the ideal backdrop. This study of Arthur's was familiar, yet different. Since they'd stood here six years earlier many changes had taken place—not least between the two men.

The walls were filled with a collection of books, impressive volumes that had never been thumbed—perhaps carefully selected by an interior designer who had chosen the titles because they would add *gravitas* to a man who was otherwise lacking in it—there was an elegant liquor tray that looked to be well-used, and a family photograph that was framed above Arthur's desk.

Arthur and Anne had barely aged, though Libby and Marnie looked much younger, so the picture must have been taken at least a decade earlier.

Arthur caught Nikos's gaze and grimaced. 'Our last family photo. We used to get them done every year until… we lost her.' He coughed, his slight paunch wobbling a little with the involuntary spasm. 'It didn't make much sense after that.'

Nikos didn't respond. Marnie and Libby stood at the foreground of the photo, Libby's arm wrapped around her sister's shoulders. There was an air of genuine affection between the girls: a sign of true camaraderie. Perhaps it had developed as a result of this environment?

'She was such an angel,' Arthur continued, perhaps misunderstanding Nikos's interest. 'Not a girl in the world like her.'

Nikos felt a possessive protective instinct flash in his gut. Yes, Libby had been lovely. And beautiful in a way that was ordinary and common. Unlike Marnie, with her steely, watchful gaze and determined little chin. Her reserve that made it difficult for her to speak to people unless she really, truly admired them.

'We need to discuss your business,' Nikos said sharply, not wishing to wander down Arthur's Libby-paved Memory Lane a moment longer. 'My information on your situation has me…concerned.'

'And what information is that?'

Nikos leaned forward, bracing his elbows on his thighs. 'It is no secret. You are out of immediate danger, but that is only temporary.'

'I don't believe that.'

'Then you are a fool.' Nikos spoke sharply.

Six years had passed since their last private conversation, and in that time Nikos had become used to having the world obey him. Deference generally met his commands—not dithering indecision.

'Do you want to lose it all, Arthur?'

'Of course I don't. But it won't come to that. Mark my words, there'll be—'

'Nothing.' Nikos eased back in his chair. 'You are overcommitted. There are no more assets left to shore your interests up and the market continues to fluctuate wildly. I am your only chance.'

The silence sparked between them. It was electrified by resentment.

'You're enjoying this, aren't you?'

Nikos didn't pretend to misunderstand; his smile was thin and unknowingly filled with disparagement. 'How I feel isn't relevant,' he said finally.

Strangely, he wasn't enjoying it. He had spent a long time imagining a situation like this. How good it would feel to throw his own success in Arthur Kenington's face. A man who had told him he would never amount to anything! He'd fantasised about it, and he'd done everything he could—even sacrificing his conscience—to achieve this moment.

And he felt nothing. Except, perhaps, a pervasive pity for this man who had let vanity and arrogance get in the way of financial security. His voice was softer when he spoke again, conciliatory.

'You cannot lose your business. Nor this house. It would devastate Marnie.'

'Marnie?' A scoff of surprise. 'She'd recover. This place never meant to her what it did to Libby.'

Nikos's fingers flexed into a fist on his lap, but he kept his face impassive. How was it possible that her own father understood her so little? Did he not see what she didn't say? Didn't he understand that her reticence to express emotions didn't mean that she lacked them?

'It is for Marnie's sake that I offer my assistance, so do not disdain her feelings.'

The statement held a barely contained warning. Nikos, though, knew he had no option *but* to help. It was a promise he had made to Marnie and he would never break it.

Arthur dragged a hand through his hair, his eyes skidding about the room. 'There has to be a way…'

'Yes. There is. *I'm* it. You know I have the money. A single phone call would remove this worry from your life.'

'You have the money?' Arthur spat, his eyes glistening with dark rage. '*You.* A boy I all but dismissed as—' He had the wisdom to cut the sentence off.

'Yes?' Nikos demanded through bared teeth.

'Worthless.' Arthur spat the word with satisfaction.

Nikos stood, his powerful stride taking him to the window. He looked down on Libby's garden and imagined Marnie there. His will strengthened. The papers he'd had couriered to him that morning were heavy in his pocket, begging for attention.

'You were wrong.' He turned, his eyes pinning Arthur where he sat. 'Do you want my help or not?'

A long silence clouded them. Nikos studied his opponent—there was no mistaking the adversarial nature of their relationship in that moment. With no one else to witness their interaction both men had dropped their masks of civility.

'I offer it to you with only one condition.'

Arthur snorted. 'I knew it was too good to be true.'

'Perhaps.' Nikos nodded, knowing for certain now the only way he could make sure Marnie was well-looked-after for the rest of her life. 'But it is your only chance to salvage something of your pride, so I suggest you listen.'

'The gloves are off, eh?' Arthur snapped, but there was weariness in his defiance.

'If the gloves were off you would know about it,' Nikos contradicted. 'The terms of my helping you are to stay between us. Marnie need never know what we have discussed here. Understood?'

Was it any wonder that, hours later, surrounded by formally dressed party guests, Arthur Kenington stayed as far from Nikos as possible? His concessions that afternoon had been hard-fought and potentially confidence-destroying. Evidently he found the idea of celebrating his birthday with his son-in-law impossible to contemplate.

Nikos didn't mind. In fact he barely noticed. Making Arthur eat crow had offered him no satisfaction, and yet he'd thought about the moment for years. How odd that once he'd had the chance to make the man beg for help he'd skated over it and provided assistance on a silver platter instead.

He considered the matter with Arthur closed. He didn't intend to think of it again save for one salient point that would require delicate handling. Would Marnie be angry when she discovered the exact nature of his help? Would she resent what he'd done?

His entire focus shifted to her. He watched her speaking to her parents' friends with the effortless grace that had first captivated his attention. Holding a glass of Scotch cradled in the palm of his hand, he felt the full force of that long-ago afternoon swarm through him.

He had come to Kenington Hall reluctantly. Spending time with Anderson and Libby had tended to leave him feeling like a third wheel, and yet Anderson had been so welcoming to him. He had been the one guy at school who *hadn't* seen Nikos as an outsider, and Nikos had repaid his friendship with unswerving loyalty. So when Anderson had asked Nikos to tag along he'd put aside his own reticence and travelled to the estate of one of England's noble families.

And he'd met Marnie.

She'd been seventeen and utterly breathtaking.

'Don't go near the horses. They're in a foul mood today!'

She had laughed as she'd torn past him, her long hair flowing behind her, the horse moving too quickly to catch more than a passing glimpse. Yet she'd reminded him of a sort of young Boadicea. Beautiful and strong, striking and confident, full of life and vitality.

Had he loved her from that moment? He'd certainly been fascinated.

'Hi.'

Her voice came to him now as if from a long way away. He lifted his head, capturing her in his gaze. But that moment was still around him and before he could question the wisdom of it he smiled at her as though they were back in that time, just Nikos and Marnie, without all the subsequent heartbreak.

She felt the purity of his look and it rang through her,

but she'd been worrying all afternoon and the habit was hard to break. 'Did you speak to him?'

He nodded, his stubborn smile still on his features.

Her hair had caught the sunshine as she'd gone past him that day. It had been like gold. He reached for it now and flicked the ends, bringing his body close to hers. She smelled good. Like apples and desire.

'And...?' Her eyes skimmed his, but her breath was coming fast and hard, making her breasts lift and fall.

'And what?' he prompted, wrapping his arms around her waist.

The band was playing a slow jazz song, the singer crooning gently into the elegant space. The formal dining room was large, and it had been converted into a ballroom for the purpose of tonight. Enormous flower arrangements punctuated the walls at regular intervals.

'Did you...?' She looked around, conscious of their surroundings.

'Yes?' he drawled, though he knew where she was going.

'Did you fix it?'

'Well, I couldn't transfer a hundred million pounds to your father in one afternoon,' he murmured sardonically, 'but, yes, *agape*. He has agreed to accept my help.'

She let out a whoosh of relief and he studied her features thoughtfully.

'You thought he might refuse? Even now?'

She shrugged, her shoulders slim and pale. 'I don't know. Like I said, he's stubborn.'

'You don't need to worry about it any more,' he said gently.

'I know.' She smiled up at him. 'Am I allowed to thank you now?'

'No.' He drew her closer, so that she could feel the strength of his body.

'Why not?'

'My helping him was entirely self-serving. You don't owe me thanks.'

She rested her cheek against his chest, listening to the beating of his strong heart. 'Was he grateful?' she asked instead, changing tack slightly.

His laugh was quiet but she felt it rumble through him.

'He was incensed.'

She grimaced. 'It wouldn't have been easy for him to face you, knowing what a mess his interests are in.'

'No,' Nikos conceded, without feeling the need to point out that Arthur only had himself to blame.

'I don't care.' She looked up at him. 'I'm going to thank you, anyway. How can I not?'

He stared down at her familiar face and the past blurred with the present. 'Fine. Then I can tell you how I wish you to express your gratitude.'

'Yes?' she murmured, her stomach swirling.

'For this night let's not speak about your family. Nor our past. We have spent a month retracing it and I wonder if we'll ever understand one another. Tonight I just want to dance with my wife. To kiss her. To feel her body. To be here with her and not think about the reasons we married. Deal?'

Hope blew open inside her. Surely that spoke of wanting a fresh start—of believing they were worthy of one. She looked at him for a long moment and knew exactly what it was that danced with hope.

Love.

Love for *him*.

Despite everything he'd done to get her into his life, she felt fierce love burst through her. It was not born of gratitude. Nor circumstances. It was the same love she'd always felt for him, only stronger—because it had been scorched by life, loss and disappointment and still it was there.

She stood up on tiptoe and pressed her lips lightly to his. 'Deal.'

The next song was another indistinct jazz tune. The singer's voice was low and husky and they danced slowly, in the middle of the crowd but aware only of each other. Marnie breathed in time with him, her eyes whispering shut, every fibre of her being in sync with her husband. So that when he stopped dancing and dropped his arms to his sides, capturing one of her hands in the process, and began to move towards the large glass doors, Marnie went with him without question.

'Do you know what I was thinking about today?' he asked as they emerged to see the moon casting a silver string from the inky sky above.

'Other than the significant hit your finances are about to take?' she offered with a teasing smile.

'Other than that.' He guided her along the terrace towards a small courtyard he'd seen earlier that day.

'What?'

'I was remembering the first time I met you.'

Marnie's heart was thunder; Nikos was lightning.

'Yes…?' Her voice was a husk.

He moved towards a balustrade, reclining against it with an expression that Marnie couldn't fathom.

'Being back here with you makes it feel like yesterday.'

And yet it wasn't. It was far in the past, with no way of recapturing that time. They could only exist in the moment. What they were now had to sustain them. The past would never be enough.

'I thought we weren't going to talk about our history,' she said with an uncertain smile.

'You're right.'

Marnie closed the distance between them as though a magnetic field was drawing her to him. She stood in front of him, the moon dancing across her face, a small smile on her lips.

'So let's talk about now.' She dared herself to be brave. To look at him with all her hope and want. 'Do you still think that we're just about sex?'

'And revenge,' he murmured, but an answering smile was playing about his lips and it surged her sense of hope higher.

'Of course.' She copied his expression, her look droll. 'Well, if it's meaningless sex you're after, that's fine by me.'

His laugh was warm butter on her frazzled nerves. 'I'm glad to hear it, Mrs Kyriazis.'

His fingers traced the bare skin of her arms and she shivered involuntarily. Anticipation trembled inside her. He caught her hand in his and together they walked. Was he leading her? Or the other way around? Marnie couldn't have said.

They went to the room that had been hers as a child. In the distance, the sounds of merriment could be heard. Wine glasses chinking, music, conversation. But it was all far away from where they were. Their world was their own, their breathing and needs the only noise.

She slipped into the room ahead of him, turning around in time to see him click the door shut and press the ancient lock down. His hands were lifting to his tie, loosening it in one movement so that it hung around his neck, a stunning black contrast to the sharp whiteness of his shirt.

Marnie reached for the zip on her dress, tucked under her arm, but a simple shake of Nikos's head stilled her.

'Let me,' he murmured, stalking towards her with a look she couldn't quite understand.

His face was set in a mask of *something*, and that something made her heart hammer in her chest.

'Let me,' he repeated, though she'd offered no opposition. Was he asking for something else? The air felt heavy with unuttered words, but perhaps they were all inside her.

She swallowed, the fragile column of her neck shifting with the movement. His fingers at her side were gentle, pulling at the zip so that she felt the slow whisper of cool air against her flesh. Goose bumps rioted across her and she drew in a sharp breath as he lowered the dress with a reverence she hadn't imagined possible. Standing before him in just a flimsy pair of knickers and heels, she was trembling—almost as though they were about to make love for the first time.

It was ridiculous. She forced a laugh to break the mood; it didn't work.

'Something amusing?' he queried, sliding his hands beneath the elastic of her underpants and cupping her rear.

It jolted her into a state of hyperawareness. She shook her head but his lips were on hers, stalling any further movement.

It was a slow kiss—a kiss that deepened as his hands roamed her body, a kiss he didn't break even as he removed his hands to strip his own clothes away. He stepped out of his shoes, guiding Marnie towards the bed, all small movements, urgent movements, designed to bring them together as quickly as possible.

They'd kissed in her room before, but they had been different people then. He full of hope and certainty and she so willing to surrender herself to the feelings they shared.

He pushed the past away. It had haunted him long enough.

He was making love to his *wife*—not a figment of his memories. She was a red-blooded woman and she wanted him *now*.

His hands glided over her body, feeling every square inch, paving a way for his mouth to follow. His fingers pulled at her nipples while his lips teased the delicate flesh beneath her breasts, breathing warm air and making her back arch with desperate need. He dragged his mouth higher, running his teeth over her décolletage and then meeting her mouth once more.

There was so much he didn't understand about them—about himself. So much he would say if he knew how to find the words. Instead he kissed her with all the confusion he had become, the contradictions that now filled him.

'Nikos...' She groaned.

Did she understand?

Was this her way of telling him that she, too, was ready to let the past go? To lay those ghosts to rest once and for all?

'Please...'

A soft whisper. A sound of need that he would meet again and again for the rest of his life if he had the opportunity.

He entered her gently but she lifted herself higher, taking him deep and groaning as their bodies were unified once more.

Transfixed, he watched as she rode her first wave, her body quickly adjusting to his possession and welcoming him with giddy delight. He watched her fly high into the peaks of pleasure, so beautiful against this bed from her childhood.

And then he was joining her, his body meeting her questions, taking them, answering them, and cresting with her. Her fingers sought his and laced through them. He lifted their arms above her head, kissing away the pleasure-soaked moans that were becoming louder and more insistent. He absorbed them, but he was an echo chamber for them, for those same cries were deep inside him, too.

He felt her slowly quieten, and her body gradually stopped its fevered trembling so that only the sound of her husky breathing was left. He rolled onto the bed, bringing her with him, cradling her head against his chest. And he stayed like that, holding her, not wanting to speak—finding that he had nothing to say in any event—until her continued silence caused him to realise that she had fallen asleep.

He shifted a little so that he could look at her.

And guilt shot a hole in his heart.

It was Marnie—the Marnie he'd once loved and the Marnie he'd married. How could he think the past didn't matter? The past was a part of them. Her rejection had turned him into who he was. It had happened, but it was over with.

She was *his* Marnie.

His wife, his lover. Just Marnie.

Understanding was chased by bitter recrimination, as though he was waking from the depths of a nightmare.

His eyes slammed shut as acid filled his mouth. Because he'd *forced* her to marry him. He'd taken away any choice in the matter, skilfully applying just the right pressure to ensure she had no way of saying no.

And she'd risen to the challenge. She'd done what he'd asked of her. For her father? Or had there been a part of her that had wanted to see whatever it was they had been through to the bitter end?

The end.

He hadn't thought that far ahead. He lifted his finger and traced a line down her arm. In her sleep she smiled. It was a beautiful smile but it might as well have been a spoken accusation.

What the hell had he done? And why?

He lay there for hours, his mind spinning over the past, his body refusing to move from the closeness of hers. But eventually, somewhere after midnight, he gave up on sleep and shifted from the bed, taking care not to wake her. He dressed in a pair of boxers and a loose shirt before stepping quietly from the bedroom.

The house was in darkness, save for a few lamps placed through the hallway.

In the kitchen, midway through making coffee, he heard a noise and looked towards the door.

Whether Nikos or Anne Kenington was more surprised would have been difficult to say with certainty. Nikos flicked a glance at his wristwatch. Despite the lateness of the hour Anne was still wearing the same dress she'd been in at the party.

'Late night?' he murmured, inserting a pod into the machine.

Anne's smile was tight. 'And for you?'

He shrugged. 'I couldn't sleep.'

Anne expelled a sigh that could only be described as disapproving and moved farther into the kitchen. Closer, Nikos caught the smell of alcohol on her breath and realised her eyes were a little unfocussed.

'You're leaving tomorrow?' she asked.

He nodded. A shorter visit had seemed like a good idea, and nothing he'd seen since arriving had changed his mind. Except Marnie's smile. Out of nowhere he saw her as she'd been in the apple orchard, the sun glinting on her hair, a trickle of sugary fruit juice dribbling down her face, and his gut kicked. If anything, it served as vindication for how he'd handled Arthur's affairs. Her happiness here was no reason to remain longer.

'Such a short trip,' Anne murmured as she walked to the fridge and pulled out a bottle of wine.

Nikos watched as she reached into the cupboard and frowned, running her hands over an empty shelf before reaching lower and pulling out a Royal Doulton teacup. She sloshed Chardonnay into it, then placed the bottle on the bench.

'I'd thought you might be here a few days at least.'

His gaze was narrowed. 'Would you have liked us to stay longer?'

Her eyes met his and for a very brief moment he felt a surge of recognition. He'd adored Libby. She had been different from Marnie, but a beautiful person, and she'd faced her illness with such strength and humour. He saw that same resilience in Anne's eyes—and it surprised him to realise that they must have other similarities, too.

'I suppose not.' She laughed—a brittle sound that made him sad for her.

'Why?' he prompted, pulling his coffee cup from the machine and holding it in one hand.

'You're bad for my husband's blood pressure.'

Nikos laughed with true mirth. 'Am I?'

'He was in quite a mood this afternoon. Some birthday present…'

Curious, Nikos nodded. 'Did he tell you what we discussed?'

Anne's face was pinched. 'He gave me an indication,' she responded with cold civility. 'I suppose you think I should thank you?'

Another moment he'd thought he would relish. He shook his head, though, brushing her words away. 'It was no hardship for me to intervene.'

'I'm surprised you bothered,' she said quietly, imbibing more of her wine.

He shrugged. 'For Marnie…'

He let the rest of the sentence hang in the air, knowing he couldn't speak the bald-faced lie now. After all, it had all been for his own selfish gratification. None of this was really for his wife, was it?

'She loves you,' Anne said, her body so still she might have been carved from stone. 'She always has.'

He heard the words without allowing them to find any

credibility within him. 'She loved me six years ago, when you forced her to end it.'

Anne didn't visibly react. It was as though the past was a ribbon, pulling her backwards. 'She was miserable afterwards. I doubt she ever forgave us.'

It was a strange sense; he was both hot and cold. He didn't want to think of how Marnie had felt. He'd been so furious with her, so concerned with his own hurts, he'd never really given her situation any thought. She'd told him she'd been angry, though. Furious, she'd said. Had her fury matched his? It couldn't have or she would have held their course.

'She moved on,' he said quietly. 'Until recently.'

'But she didn't.'

Anne's eyes were darkened by guilt. She pushed up from the bench and strode a little way across the kitchen, then froze once more—a statue in the room.

'She continued to live and breathe, but that's not the same as moving on. She thought I didn't notice her reading about you in the papers. That I didn't catch her looking at photos of you.' She flicked her head over her shoulder, pinning him with a glance that spoke of true concern. 'She was so careful, but I saw the way she missed you. The way she seemed to wither for a long time. It was almost like losing two daughters.'

Disgust, anger and guilt at the way they had all failed Marnie gnawed through him.

Anne sipped her wine and moved back to her original spot, opposite Nikos. 'We introduced her to some lovely young men—'

'*Suitable* men?' he interjected, with a cynical strength to his words. But Anne's statement was slicing through him. The idea of Marnie having pined for him was one he couldn't contemplate.

'Yes, suitable men. Nice men.' She closed her eyes.

'She never mentioned your name, but I always knew you to be the reason it didn't work out. She never got over you.'

Nikos sipped his coffee but his mind was spinning back over their conversation in his office, when he'd first suggested they marry. She'd been so arctic. So cold!

But wasn't that Marnie's defence mechanism? Wasn't that how she behaved when her emotions were rioting all over the place? And her being a virgin? Was that simply because she'd never found someone who made her body tremble as it did for him? Had she chosen not to get serious with another guy because she still wanted *him*?

'I believed we were doing the right thing.' Anne's smile was tight. 'After Libby, we just wanted Marnie to be safe.'

'You thought I was somehow *unsafe*?' he barked, anger and frustration and impotence to change the past ravaging his temper.

'You *aren't* safe,' she responded sharply. 'The way she feels about you is a recipe for disaster.'

Marnie didn't still love him, did she? How could she after what he'd put her through? She might have loved him a year ago…even two months ago. But the way he'd burst back into her life had been the one thing that must have ruined any love between them.

He closed his eyes briefly.

Anne continued speaking, but she wasn't particularly focussed on her son-in-law. 'You must hate us. I know Marnie did for a long time. But I *love* her, Nikos. Everything I've done has been because I love her.'

'Yet you sought to control her life? You told her you would disinherit her if she didn't leave me?'

Anne winced as though he'd slapped her. 'Yes. Well, Arthur did…' A whisper. A hollow, tormented, grief-soaked admission. 'At the time I told myself that she must have known we were right. She broke up with you. And Marnie knew her own head and heart. If she'd *really* loved you, I told myself, she would have fought harder.'

Nikos felt a familiar sentiment echo within him.

'But she couldn't. We were holding on by a thread and Marnie knew that.'

'And what about Marnie?' he asked with dark anger, though he couldn't have said if it was directed at Anne, Arthur or himself.

'She was *Marnie*,' Anne said finally, drinking more wine with a small shrug. 'Determined to act as though everything was fine even if it was almost killing her.'

Nikos angled his head away, his dark eyes resting on their reflections in the window. Anne appeared smaller there, shrunken. Surprised, he looked at her and realised that the changes had taken place in real time—he just hadn't noticed them. She was smaller, wizened, stressed.

'How could you let her go through this?' he muttered, but his blame and recriminations were focussed on himself.

Anne pinned him with eyes that reminded him once more of Libby. 'Libby was such an easy child—so like me. I just understood her. But with Marnie… She's a puzzle I can't fathom.'

Nikos rubbed a hand across his jaw. 'Marnie is all that is good in the world,' he said finally. 'Often to her own detriment. She wants the best for those she loves, even when it means sacrificing her own happiness.'

Guilt over their marriage was a knife, deep in his gut.

'Yes!' Anne expelled an angry sigh. 'I love that girl, Nikos, but I don't always know *how* to love her. I suppose that sounds tremendously strange to you—she's my child, after all.'

His smile was thin. For Anne's words had lodged deep in his mind and begun to unravel with condemnation and acceptance. He had loved Marnie once, too, but never in the way she'd needed to be loved. His faults were on a par with Anne and Arthur Kenington's.

CHAPTER ELEVEN

MARNIE STOOD UNSTEADILY as the plane pitched yet again, rolled mercilessly by the thick cotton wool clouds that had clogged the entire journey from London to Athens.

Nikos, in the middle of a newspaper article, lifted his gaze curiously. He had been distracted for the entire flight, and he seemed almost to be rousing himself from a long way away now.

'Travel sickness,' she explained, moving quickly away from him towards the back of the plane.

She burst into the toilet, relieved to have made it just a second before losing the entire contents of her stomach. Her brow broke out in sweat and still she heaved, her whole body quivering with the exertion.

She moaned as the taste of metal filled her mouth and finally, spent, straightened. The mirror showed how unwell she'd been: the face that stared back at her was bright red, sweaty, and her eyes were slightly bloodshot in the corners.

She flushed the toilet and ran the cold water, washing her hands and splashing water over her face, enjoying the relief of the ice-cold liquid.

As a child she'd been prone to travel sickness. Even a short journey had brought on a spell of nausea. But it had been a long time since she'd felt it. Years. In fact the last time she'd been sick she'd been ten or eleven.

But what else could it be?

Marnie froze midway through patting her cheeks with a plush hand towel. Mentally she counted back the days to their wedding, her mind moving with an alacrity she wouldn't have thought it capable of a moment ago, while doubled over an aeroplane toilet.

They'd been married just over a month and they'd made love on their wedding night. And since that time a certain something had been glaringly absent.

She'd started the pill in plenty of time for it to have been effective. So what did that mean? Had going on birth control simply changed her normal cycle? Was that it? Or was she pregnant with Nikos's baby? Because what she was feeling felt altogether different, and a little terrifying.

The idea was a tiny seed she couldn't shake. It put roots down through her mind, so that by the time she returned to her seat, looking much more like her normal self, she was almost certain that she was indeed pregnant.

She'd need to do a test to be sure, but there was no room in her mind for doubt.

She barely spoke for the rest of the flight, and she was too caught up in her own imaginings to notice that Nikos was similarly silent. Brooding, even.

Athens was cool but humid when they landed; the clouds that had made their flight so bumpy were thick in the air, making the ground steam.

'I have some business to take care of,' Nikos murmured once they'd disembarked. His Ferrari was waiting on the Tarmac. 'I will need to go straight to my office once we're home.'

Marnie, secretly glad for this reprieve, time to ascertain whether or not she was in fact pregnant, nodded. 'Okay.'

It was all Marnie could do not to tell him of her suspicions as he drove the now familiar roads to his mansion.

But she wouldn't do that. Not until she knew for sure that there was a baby.

It would be a surprise—a shock, really.

But it didn't necessarily follow that it would be a nightmare, did it?

'A baby between us would never be magical and wonderful. It is the very last thing I would want.'

The words circled her mind.

She waited until he'd left, and then for Eléni to arrive, and somehow was casually able to ask for a ride to the markets to pick up some groceries.

The whole way there, making halting chitchat with Eléni, Marnie wondered what it would mean if she was actually, truly pregnant.

She paid for the groceries, stuffing the pregnancy test into her handbag rather than stowing it with the other shopping, and listened to Eléni the whole way home.

Finally she removed herself to her room to find out, once and for all, if her suspicions were right.

The test showed exactly what she had known it would.

Two bright blue lines.

She was pregnant.

With Nikos's baby.

Elation danced deep in her being. She felt its unmistakable warmth zing through her and she treasured it—because she knew that it would not last long. Complications would surely arise soon enough and take away the pleasure she felt.

For it was an incontrovertible truth that no matter what she chose to do she would be a part of Nikos's life for ever. And he of hers.

Where was her despair at that prospect? Her concern?

She looked into her heart and saw nothing—just joy.

Tears ran down her cheeks and for the first time in her

life they were happy tears. Tears that warmed her and blessed her and made her feel as if she wanted to shout her euphoria from the rooftops. It was not a simple joy—there would be complications—but they paled in comparison to the happiness that shone before her.

She needed to tell him—but not on the phone. She would wait until he returned and leave him in no doubt as to how pleased she was with this turn of events. Even though she knew they had broken his cardinal rule...

The minutes of the day seemed to gang up on her, deciding that they'd like to drag their way mutinously towards the hour of Nikos's arrival gleefully slowly rather than with the alacrity she craved.

Just wondering when you'll be home?

She sent the message, her impatience burning through her, fear threatening to take hold of her.

Not for a while. N.

Well, he'd be home eventually, and then she'd just have to put her hope in his hands and pray he didn't crush it.

The first sign that there was a problem was that Nikos didn't drive himself home. A luxurious limousine pulled up out at the front and Marnie, hovering in her office with its view of the driveway, wondered briefly if they had unexpected company.

When Nikos emerged from the back his large frame seemed different. Slightly unsteady. He stood for a moment, a hand braced on the roof of the car, his eyes scanning the front of his house. Why did he look so grim? Had something happened?

Concerned, she moved quickly through the house, reaching the front door at the same time he did. She heard his keys drop to the ground outside and pulled the door inwards, her expression perplexed.

Until she smelled the Scotch and realised that her husband—the father of her tiny, tiny baby—had obviously been drinking. Heavily.

'Nik…?' she said with disbelief, holding the door wide and letting him in.

Marnie had never seen him anything other than in complete control. She was struggling to make sense of what might have happened in the hours since they'd returned from London to lead him to be in this state.

'My wife,' he said, as though it brought him little pleasure.

Confusion thick in her mind, she waited for him to move deeper into the house so she could close the door. 'Have you been out?'

'No,' he muttered. 'I have been in my office.'

Unconsciously, she moved a hand to her stomach. 'Drinking?'

He expelled an angry breath. 'Apparently.'

Marnie nodded, but he still wasn't making sense. The uncharacteristic act jarred with everything she knew about this man. He was a disciplined control freak.

Out of nowhere old jealousies and suspicions erupted. 'Alone?'

His eyes narrowed, but he nodded.

'Why?' she asked finally, putting a hand on his elbow in order to guide him towards the kitchen.

But he pulled away, walking determinedly ahead of her, his physical ability apparently not as affected as she'd first thought.

She walked behind him, and once in the kitchen moved to the fridge. As if on autopilot, she pulled out the ingredients for a toasted cheese sandwich, her eyes flicking to him every few moments. And he stared at her. He stared at her with an intensity that filled her body with fire and flame even as she was laced with confusion and anxiety.

So telling him about the baby wasn't going to happen, she admitted to herself. At least not until the following day, when he might be in a headspace to comprehend what she was saying.

'*Why*, Marnie?' He repeated her question in a tone that was so like the way he'd spoken in the past it made her chest heavy; his words seemed to ring with disdain and dislike.

She tried not to let it fill her heart but it was there. Doubt. Hurt. Aching sadness.

'What's wrong?' she said finally. 'Has something happened?'

He reached into his pocket and pulled out an envelope. 'Your mother believes you've spent the last six years pining for me. That you have loved me this whole time.'

Marnie started, her eyes flying to his involuntarily. Her mouth was dry. 'I…I don't understand why that matters. What my mother says…how I felt. What difference does it make right now to this marriage?'

He spoke slowly, his tone emphatic. 'Did you stay single and celibate because you love me?'

Marnie's heart dropped.

She spun away from him but Nikos raised his voice.

'Damn it, Marnie. You broke up with me. You walked away from us.'

'I know,' she whispered, tears springing to her eyes. The happiness of the last twenty-four hours was being swallowed by old hurts. 'I thought we agreed we wouldn't talk about the past any more?'

He slammed his palm against the benchtop. 'Why didn't you come back? Why didn't you call me when you realised you were still in love with me?'

'You'd moved on,' she said simply. 'And nothing had changed for me.'

'You were so emphatic when you ended it. You convinced me you didn't care for me, that you had never been serious. You completely echoed your father's feelings about me and men of my *upbringing*.' He spat the word like a curse.

She recoiled as though he'd slapped her. 'I *had* to do that! You wouldn't have accepted it unless I made sure you truly believed it was over.' She shook her head and no longer bothered to check the tears that stung her eyes. 'I hated saying those things to you when it was the opposite of how I felt.'

He was not his usual self, but even on a bad day and after a fair measure of Scotch Nikos was better than anyone at debating and reasoning.

He honed his thoughts quickly back to the point at hand. 'You admit you've loved me this whole time?'

Marnie froze, her only movement the rapid rise and fall of her chest as she tried to draw breath into her lungs. She felt that she'd been caught—not in a lie so much as in the truth.

'I would never have done this if I'd known,' he said after a beat of silence had passed—one he took for her acquiescence.

'Done what?' She didn't look at him. Her voice was a whisper into the room.

'This marriage…'

Her heart fell as if from a great height. It was pulverised at her feet, a tangling mass of heaving hopes.

'It was the worst kind of wrong to use you like this.'

She couldn't stifle her sob. 'Is that what you were doing?' She forced herself to look at him—and then wished she hadn't when the intensity of his expression left her short of breath.

He spoke with a cold detachment that was so much worse than the heat of an argument. 'I forced you to marry me. Just as your parents forced you to leave me. I am no better than them. Hell, I consider my crimes to be considerably greater.'

He pushed the back of the envelope open and lifted a piece of paper out. One page. When he handed it to her it was still warm from having been nestled close to his chest all afternoon.

'But at least I can atone for my sins.'

'What's this?' she asked, even as her eyes dropped to the page.

'*Petition for Divorce*' was typed neatly across the top, and as she skimmed lower she saw her name written beside Nikos's. He'd already signed his name. A masculine scrawl of hard intent.

Marnie was still. So still. Briefly she wondered if she might pass out. She felt hot and cold, as she'd done on the flight. She dropped the page and moved backwards until her bottom connected with the bench. She stayed there, glad for the support. Her head was spinning.

'Divorce?'

'I was wrong.' The words were saturated with bleak despair. He was begging her to understand. 'I regret everything I said to you that day in my office. I heard your father was going bankrupt and this idea came to me. I acted on it before I could realise what a stupid mistake it was. I need to undo it.'

She stared at him in shock. 'You can't simply *undo* a marriage. You can't undo what we are!'

'This piece of paper would suggest otherwise,' he said, with a factual determination that left her cold.

'Nikos!' His name was a plea. She looked at the paper. 'Do you want me to leave?'

'I don't want you to stay,' he said thickly. 'Not like this.'

Marnie dropped her head forward. Tears splashed out of her eyes.

'I've had the pre-nuptial agreement voided,' he murmured. 'And you need never worry that your father's finances will be in trouble—'

He thought of the other provisions he'd had enabled, but dismissed the need to discuss them at that point. Actually, he doubted he had the mental wherewithal in that moment to do justice to any of the financial arrangements he'd put in place.

'Listen to me,' she interrupted, her voice unsteady, her tone showing urgency. 'My father has nothing to do with this.'

'He *is* why we married.'

But it was almost a question, a demand for information.

His eyes locked to hers in a way that stole Marnie's breath. It was time to tell him the truth. She didn't believe she'd married for love necessarily, and yet hadn't it always been there? Even when she was furious, wasn't it because she loved him so much and felt so hurt by his actions?

But at that moment her courage was thin on the ground. She tried a different approach, desperately needing to understand what was going on.

'Why don't you tell me what's happened? Last night was fine. Last night was amazing. We danced and spoke as though…as though…we were making progress,' she finished lamely. 'We made love,' she said—an anguished reminder of the beautiful way he'd taken her. It *had* been making love—not just sex, but perfect, intimate love.

'You need to leave me,' he said quietly, taking a step backwards. 'Let me be as clear tonight as you were six years ago, when you ended things the first time. For both our sakes, please leave. Our marriage was a mistake. I should have known better than to even contemplate it.

Now you must go. It is over between us and you should be grateful for that.'

She watched as he strode out of the kitchen in what she considered to be the middle of their argument, and was torn between chasing after him and doing just as he'd said. How easy it would be to numbly pack a suitcase and go— to leave this minefield for the peace of solitude.

Only what followed wouldn't be easy. Leaving him once had hurt like hell and she'd never recovered. And the way she'd felt then was a fraction of what she felt now. She'd lived with him, and beyond that she'd committed her full self to this man and their marriage.

But could she keep trying to make their marriage work if he didn't even *want* the marriage any more? She stared at the piece of paper, anger building brick by brick inside her.

When had her mother and her husband had this *tête-à-tête*? And if Anne knew how badly Marnie had longed for Nikos why hadn't she talked to Marnie about it? Why hadn't she taken back the edict that had led to Marnie ruining her relationship with the only man she'd ever loved?

She caught a scream in her mouth; just a muted sound of frustration erupted into the silent kitchen. She had been pulled in a thousand directions by those she most cared about and now fury was building within her.

She stormed across the room, her feet planted heavily on the tiles, until she reached the sliding glass doors. She pushed them open and went outside. At the pool, she ripped her dress over her head, then leapt in. The water was a balm to her fraught senses and it absorbed the stinging, angry tears that were running freely down her cheeks.

Divorce?

After a month?

When she was pregnant with his baby?

And completely in love with him?

And he loved *her*, didn't he? She was almost sure of it. So why tell her to leave, then? None of it made sense.

But she wasn't going to let history repeat itself. She loved him more than ever before, and that meant staying to fight—not running away.

When Nikos awoke the next morning it was still dark and he was alone in his bed. He sat up, intent on going for his usual run, but a blinding headache shattered his temples.

And then it all came flooding back to him.

His conversation with Anne Kenington… *'I love her. I just don't know* how *to love her.'*

The divorce papers that had seemed like such an inspired idea at his lowest ebb.

Marnie's face as she'd stared at him, tears on her lashes, her slender body shaking as she comprehended his words.

'I want you to go. It is over between us.'

He squeezed his eyes shut, but that only enabled him to remember more clearly. The pain had slammed into her like a wall. Her harsh reaction to his simple solution. His belief that by divorcing her he could erase the barbarism of his behaviour.

He swore loudly and stood, ignoring the blinding pain that spiked in his brain. *Marnie.* Where was she? Had she left?

A cursory inspection of their room showed that her clothes were all in their usual spot. Relief was brief. She hadn't gone anywhere. *Had she?* He moved into their *ensuite* bathroom intent on making himself look slightly more civilised before facing the music.

It smelled of her. Lavender, violets…feminine and sweet. His gut clenched and he swore again.

He showered quickly and wrapped a towel around his waist while brushing his teeth. The toothpaste tube was empty and he tossed it carelessly in the rubbish bin. It missed. When he crouched down to retrieve it, his head complaining the whole time, something unusual caught his eye. A box.

He lifted it out and stared at it in confusion.

A pregnancy test?

That didn't make any sense.

Marnie was on the pill. But it sure as hell wasn't Eléni's. Which meant that somehow, for some reason, Marnie had had reason to believe she might be pregnant. He opened the box but it was empty. Nor was there a test in the trash.

With renewed urgency he pulled on a pair of shorts and shirt and practically ran out of the room and through the house. There were several guest rooms but they were all empty. Fear was building.

What if she *was* pregnant? Would he still be strong enough to let her go? If she chose to divorce him—hell, she might have already signed the damned papers—would he let the divorce proceed?

And what if she stayed with him because of the baby? Could he live with her knowing he'd trapped her—twice—into marriage?

He checked her office. It was empty, neat.

Then his own office—empty.

Finally, he went to the kitchen.

And there she was.

Marnie.

Sitting on the sofa, staring out at the lifting sun, her face pale, her eyes a terrifying maelstrom of feelings and fears.

What could he say to her? What right did he have to explain?

He walked quietly and then crouched in front of her, directly in Marnie's line of sight.

'Have you slept?'

She blinked her eyes at him and then looked away, over

his shoulder, focussing on the colours smudged across the sky. 'I didn't leave.'

A muscle jerked at his temple. 'I'm glad.'

Her eyes flew to his again. Confusion. Hurt. 'Why?'

She reminded him of a wounded animal. He swore under his breath and dragged a hand through his hair. He needed to reassure her. To explain. She deserved at least that much. But his own questions were burning through him.

For a man like Nikos, not knowing what to say or how to negotiate on the terms of his marriage brought with it great frustration. He was used to commanding a room. He had not doubted his ability to bring people to his way of thinking for a very long time.

Business, though, was predictable—easy for a man like Nikos. He would discover what motivated a person and exploit that to gain his own success.

Marnie was motivated by love.

Loyalty.

Affection and faithfulness.

And he didn't want her to be with him for any of those reasons but one.

'You gave me divorce papers last night.' Her eyes had an unexpected strength in them. 'Why?'

He expelled a breath. 'Isn't that obvious?'

'You don't want to be married to me,' she whispered, the words a ghost of sentiment in the large room.

'I don't want you to feel *forced* to stay married to me,' he clarified.

She nodded, her gaze refusing to meet his. If only he *had* pushed her away! She'd ended up falling as much in love with him as ever, and now it was so much worse—for she'd tasted the mind-blowing bliss that came from sharing his bed and his life.

'You were happy to give me an ultimatum at one time. What's changed?'

Did he detect the note of challenge in her voice?

His smile was lacking any true happiness. 'We are married, but you are not my wife.' He stood, his back straight, his shoulders square. 'It turns out you can't really force someone into a marriage.'

'Isn't that what's happened here?'

He shook his head. 'I believed that having you as my wife would make you mine. It doesn't work like that, though.' His expression was bleak for a moment, before hard certainty crossed it. 'You will never be able to forget the way I propositioned you, and nor will I. I look at you and see the man I have become. A man I despise.'

'You have helped my father,' she said quietly. 'I could never hate you after what you've done for him.'

'You have to release us both from this. I can't live with how I've hurt you.'

She nodded, her throat raw from unshed tears. 'You *have* hurt me,' she whispered. 'Just as I hurt you. Does that make us even now?'

He stood up, moving angrily towards the glass doors and staring out. 'You were a teenager. A *grieving* teenager. You hurt my pride and my ego and I left. I should have stayed. It takes courage to stay and fight for what you want. But I didn't like how it felt to be rejected, so I went off like a sulking child.' He thrust his hands in his pockets. 'I didn't deserve you.'

She lifted her feet onto the sofa so she could rest her chin against her knees. 'Fighting would have been pointless. You would have only upset me more than I already was. I truly believed I had no choice but to end it.'

He nodded, thinking of the pregnancy test box he'd discovered. He turned slowly, but pain was a fresh wave crashing over him. She was a contradiction of fragility and strength. Broken but resolved. Determined and disappointed.

He strode to her, a guttural sound of angst tearing from his chest. '*I* have broken whatever we used to be—not you. If you are pregnant I will support you. I will make sure you have everything you and the baby need. But I will not let you use that as a reason to stay with me.'

Shock flashed over Marnie and her skin paled to paper-white. 'The…baby?' She swallowed. 'How did you know?' What was the point in denying it?

'I found the box in our bathroom,' he responded, so close he could touch her, but not allowing himself to do so.

She hadn't bothered to hide it because she'd thought they would have a perfect dinner together, over which she would share with him the happy news. *Happy news!* Well, at least there was still some truth in that. Thoughts of the baby filled her shattered heart with a slight antiseptic against the pain.

'Is it true?' he asked, his words anguished.

Slowly she nodded, pulling her lower lip between her teeth. 'Yes…'

'*Thee mou!*' He groaned, standing and running a hand over his eyes. He seemed to stand there for ever, a heaving man, his whole body showing instant rejection of the idea of their child. Just as he'd said he would.

What had she expected? That he would welcome this news?

'I am so sorry.' He groaned again, dropping his hand and pinning her with the full force of his shocked gaze.

'Sorry?' she repeated, feeling numbed now, so fresh pain wasn't capable of sinking in.

'First I trapped you with blackmail and now you must feel trapped by our baby. But you can leave. You *must* leave. A baby is no reason to continue this farce.'

She sobbed and nodded. 'I know that.'

Neither spoke for a long time. Marnie was trying to imagine a life without Nikos and all she saw was the bleakness that had been her bedfellow for these past six years.

'If I could fix this, I would,' he said.

She nodded again, resting her cheek on her knees. She had chosen to stay and fight, but so far she had done a lot of listening and no actual fighting. She tried to find the strength in her heart, but it was in ruins.

'There is something else you should know.' He spoke with a grim finality to his words. 'I could not find the words to explain last night.'

'Explain what?' she whispered, wondering at the pain in her throat.

'I have bought Kenington Hall and put it in your name.'

She lifted her head sharply, almost giving herself whiplash in the process. Everything else disappeared from her mind. 'You've *what*?'

He expelled a sigh and crouched down on his haunches so that their eyes were level. 'You love the property, and I wanted you to know it to be safe. That no matter what happened to your father, or to our marriage, you would have the security of your family home.'

She let that statement sink in. 'When did you do this?'

'When I met with your father.'

She nodded, but nothing was making sense. 'Were you planning to divorce me even then? Was it to be my consolation prize?' Grief lanced her. 'What did I do wrong? I thought we were making this work…'

'You did nothing wrong, Marnie, except fall in love with an arrogant, selfish bastard like me.' He dropped his head into his hands. 'I didn't buy the house because I wanted to leave you. I bought it because I wanted you to understand that you have options. That you and your family are safe. Even before speaking with your mother I knew I had to give you back your freedom before I could even hope to make amends.'

'I have never considered myself to lack freedom,' she inserted seriously, her eyes sparkling, her mind moving quickly. 'So you *did* want to make this marriage a real one?'

A muscle jerked in his jaw. 'I cannot say if I ever thought of it in those terms.'

He dared to lift a hand and touch her soft hair. Fear at what he was on the brink of losing was all around him—a pit of despair he knew would swallow him if he didn't explain himself better than he was doing now.

'I knew only that I wanted you to look at me with the love you once felt. That I wanted to be able to smile at you with the love that is in *here*.' He tapped his hand against his chest.

Marnie made a sound of disbelief.

'You *should* leave me. You can go and it will not change how I feel about you. Your father is out of debt. Kenington Hall is safe in your hands. And I will be as involved as you allow me to be in our child's life. You must decide what will make you happy.'

Happy? That felt so far away.

She stood up, something snapping inside her. She could no longer sit still as though this were a normal discussion. Her temper flared. She spun round, her hands on her hips, her face showing the full extent of her rage. There was nothing remotely cold about her now. She was all feelings and flame.

'You're such an *idiot*!' she shouted at the top of her lungs. 'I have *always* loved you! Always! Even when I thought I was over you, how could I be? I married you! And—newsflash!—I didn't *have* to! Even to save my father's financial situation. I would only ever have married one man on earth. *You.* Only you.'

She wrapped her arms around herself.

'You were right before, when you said that you should have stayed and fought for what we were. I don't think it would have made a difference, but it's what you *do* when you're in love with someone. You don't bloody walk away. I'm not going to walk away now, because I love you—even when you're almost impossible to comprehend.'

He stared at her, but his expression was blank, as though her words were a problem he had to decode.

'I was furious with you when we got married. *Livid.* What a stupid thing you did, blackmailing me like this! But I still loved you. Every night of this marriage has been like slowly unwrapping a present, piece by piece, getting to find my way back to you—'

'I have pushed you away,' he interrupted, arguing the sense of her statement.

'Yes, you have—but you've also pulled me close. So close that I've been inside your soul. You've let me in. And you *dare* turn up with divorce papers, as though our marriage is a simple contract you can dissolve? You *dare* relegate our love to an agreement that you alone can end?'

Startled by her anger, he stood, wishing to placate her. He put an arm on her shoulder but she jerked away.

'No!' she snapped. 'I'm not finished yet.'

Her eyes held a warning and, fascinated, he was silent.

'You have been hitting me over the head with the fact that I flicked a switch and walked away from you six years ago. I didn't. I didn't flick a switch. I made the worst mistake of my life when I left you, and I'm not going to do it again.' She straightened her shoulders. 'If you want to divorce me—if you don't want me any more—then tell me that. You can make that decision. But don't tell me that leaving you is in my best interests—because I know what life is like without you and there is no life on earth that I want more than *this* life, here—right here with you.'

His breath was ragged, torn from his lungs. 'How can you feel that?' he murmured with a growing sense of wonderment. 'I have been—'

'You have been Nikos.' She cut across him, but softly, kindly, with the compassion that was always so close to her surface. 'Determined, arrogant and good.' She moved closer. 'Do you think either of us really understood what we were doing and why? You wanted to help my family. I believe that was at the heart of everything you did.'

He made a sound and shook his head, but she lifted a finger to his lips.

'Whatever motivated you to blackmail me into this marriage, I will never resent you for it. How can I? I've missed you and now I have you.' She paused, her eyes scanning his. 'I *do* have you, don't I?'

He wrapped his arms around her waist, crushing her to him. 'You have all of me, for all time.' The words were a promise against her cheek. '*All* of me. And you are the best of me.'

She shut her eyes and listened to the pounding of his heart. Her lips twitched in a smile that shone with true happiness.

Gradually Nikos pulled backwards, dropping a hand to her flat stomach. 'A baby was not on our agenda,' he said, as if just comprehending the reality of their situation.

'Apparently the baby had other ideas. I dare say it has a lot of your determination.'

He laughed. 'Let us hope that is balanced by your warmth and kindness.'

'Well, I guess we'll find out in about eight months.'

'And you are truly happy?'

'Nikos!' She laughed shakily. 'When I found out I was pregnant I wanted to shout it from the rooftops. I know it wasn't meant to be part of the plan, but it felt so *right*.'

He frowned, wondering how long she'd shouldered this secret. 'When did you first suspect?'

She smiled. 'Not until we were on the plane back to Greece.'

'And then I told you to leave me.' His face paled with remembered regrets. 'It was for *you*, Marnie. I didn't *want* you to go. You know this to be true?'

She nodded. 'I've never seen you like that.'

His smile was grim. 'I have only ever drunk to excess one other time in my life—the night your father paid me off and I took his money. Then, too, I felt like a shadow of the man I wanted to be.'

'Don't say that,' she murmured, resting her head against his chest. She stood there quietly for a moment. 'My father wouldn't have liked selling you the house...'

He breathed in her sweet fragrance and a sense of deep gratitude filled him. To think that he'd almost pushed her away for good! He would never make that mistake again. Not in his life.

'He...understood the necessity of it,' Nikos said after a moment. '*Agape mou*, I thought I would relish that moment. I had fantasised about seeing your father a broken man. I had dreamed of being in a position to throw my own success and wealth in his face and see him suffer. But at the first opportunity to do so I saw only you. I saw you and discovered that loving you meant loving *all* of you. Even your family. If you married me because you love me then you must understand that I have helped Arthur because I love you. It was not a payment for your marrying me.'

The words filled her with love and certainty—certainty that they were right where they should be. Together.

But she pulled a face of mock consideration. 'Well, it seems to me, then, that you haven't upheld your end of the deal.'

Sensing the amusement in her words, he answered in

kind. 'I suppose you're right. Is there something else I can offer instead?'

She pressed a finger to her chin and pretended to consider it. 'I can think of a few things...'

He surprised her by scooping her up and laying her down on the sofa. His mouth sought hers and he tasted her giddy delight there and answered it.

'Starting with right now?'

'I will expect the payment terms to be over a very long time,' she said, pushing at his shorts.

'Would the rest of our lives do?'

She sighed, her body firing with insatiable need for her husband. 'It just might.'

EPILOGUE

One year later

IT WAS THE ice sculpture that was the final straw.

She shook her head, torn between feeling cross and amused as she tore through the villa in search of her husband.

She found him by the pool, hands on hips, eyes staring out at the ocean. They'd been married for almost a year, and still the sight of him could stop her in her tracks. Her heart hammered roughly against her ribs, beating wildly as she approached him.

'A *swan*?' she said from just behind his shoulder, her expression one of utter disbelief. 'Seriously?'

His grin as he turned around skittled any discontent she had felt over his lavish decorations.

'It's summer,' she pointed out with a shake of her head, but her grumble was somewhat faint-hearted.

'Almost autumn.'

'Almost,' she responded archly. 'And it's as hot as Hades today. That thing's going to be iced water before anyone gets here.'

'So we will drink it!' He laughed. 'How many times does our daughter get christened?' he said, with such impeccable logic that all her objections were silenced.

'You're right.' Marnie smiled up at him, giving in to

temptation and wrapping her arms around his waist. 'And now I have another bone to pick with you.'

'Oh?' he murmured, his lips still pressed to hers.

She straightened, trying to be businesslike. 'The trust just called me to report that a rather sizeable donation has been made in Lulu's name.'

His smile lit the world on fire—starting with Marnie's heart. She was scorched with happiness.

'What else can I give you and our daughter on her christening? You will not let me buy you jewels or clothes… you insist she has all she needs. But this, I think, you *will* let me do.'

Marnie nodded, tears of happiness clogging her throat. 'But it's so much…'

'For a cause that means the world to you—and therefore to me. I still remember what you said to me, *agape mou*. That one day, through your efforts and the efforts of people like you, young girls like Libby might not get sick any more.'

He pressed a finger beneath Marnie's chin, lifting her eyes to meet his. She felt the love and commitment that underscored every decision he made.

'We have our own little girl now. How can you doubt my desire to work with you on this?'

Love coiled inside her. 'Thank you.' Her voice was husky. Emotions were too strong to contain. She lifted up on tiptoe and pressed a kiss to his lips. 'Why did we invite all these people over?'

He kissed her hungrily, his tongue exploring her mouth, his hands holding her tight against his body.

But for only a moment.

Then he lifted himself away, grinning as if he *hadn't* been shaken to the core by their molten hot connection.

'To see my ice sculpture,' he said, and laughed.

She rolled her eyes, but her mind was drifting. 'If only we had an extra hour…'

He grimaced, looking past her shoulder. 'If only we had an extra ten minutes…'

He saw their guests through the glass doors and kissed the top of her head.

'I will make you a promise,' he said in an undertone.

Marnie nodded. 'Oh, yes? I'm all ears, Mr Kyriazis.'

'Not from where I am standing.' He grinned at her, his handsome face a collection of lines and shapes that formed an inimitable image of masculinity.

Playfully, Marnie punched his upper arm. 'I believe you were making me a promise?'

'Soon we will be alone in our home again, and then I will show you just what that dress and you are making me want.'

Her pulse was lurching out of control. She lifted herself up on tiptoe again and kissed his lips, smiling as familiar sensations rocked her to her core.

'You'd better,' she said simply.

He wrapped an arm around her shoulder, pulling her to his side and knowing how right it was that they should be together. Everything in his world seemed to shine with the perfection that Marnie brought to his life.

'Your parents are here,' he murmured, looking down into the villa as Anne and Arthur Kenington made their way through the house.

Marnie took a moment to observe them, staying right where she was. Anne was her usual self—elegant and perfectly neat, despite the fact they'd come straight from the airport. Although a flight in Nikos's jet was hardly an arduous ordeal. Arthur Kenington showed the greatest change. He was dressed casually in a pale polo shirt and a pair of beige chinos. His hair was a little longer, and there were more lines on his face now—lines Marnie chose to believe were formed by happiness.

'Darling, there's a puddle forming in the foyer,' Anne said with pursed lips as she swept onto the terrace.

A breeze lifted past them, drawing with it the tang of the ocean and the sweetness of Libby's rose garden. Marnie inhaled, drawing strength from this reminder of her sister before steeling herself to enjoy the next few hours. Her parents were not perfect, but they were still her parents. And, fortunately for Marnie, despite their meddling and strong opinions she and Nikos had found their way together in the end.

'That would be the ice sculpture.' Marnie winked up at her husband, then moved towards her mother, kissing her cheek. She hugged her dad before returning to Nikos's side. 'Thanks for coming.'

'Of course.' Anne nodded. 'Where is our granddaughter?'

'She's with her uncle.' Marnie grinned. 'Her honorary uncle.'

Anderson emerged at that moment, their chubby dark-haired little girl propped on one hip.

'Nothing honourable about *him*,' Nikos teased, with a genuine smile reserved for their closest friend. 'Unlike you, Lady Heiress.'

She shook her head, her hands extended for the baby Elizabeth. But Lulu only had eyes for her father.

Marnie laughed. 'I see!' She shook her head. 'That's the way it's going to be, huh?'

'It is because I am not often here when she is awake.'

'Sure it is,' Marnie said with another laugh. 'And also because you spoil her silly. That's okay—I'm not offended.'

And she wasn't. How could she be? She had everything she'd ever wanted in life.

It was a beautiful afternoon, filled with happiness and

joy. Finally, though, after the last of the guests had left and Lulu was fast asleep, Marnie went in search of her husband.

She found him on the terrace, his eyes focussed contemplatively on the shimmering moon. It was a cool night now, and Marnie wrapped her arms around herself for warmth.

Nikos noticed—as he did everything about his wife—and shrugged out of his jacket, placing it around her slender shoulders on instinct.

'Here, *agape mou*,' he said, pulling her closer to his warmth.

'Thank you,' she murmured, inhaling his intoxicatingly masculine scent. 'Have I ever told you there was a time when I hated you calling me that?' she asked softly.

'Did you?'

'It just reminded me of what I wanted from you. What I doubted you'd ever feel for me.'

Her eyes pierced his, and for a second those thoughts and feelings were right there before her. Such pain and heartbreak! How had that ever been their story when there was now such love between them? Such joy and trust?

She blinked to clear those dark vestiges of the past.

'Did you doubt, Mrs Kyriazis? Did you really doubt?'

His eyes held hers, and in them she saw the truth that perhaps she'd always held deep in her heart. The incontrovertibility of who they were to one another.

His soft sigh breathed warmth across her temple. 'I called you that, even when we were at odds, because I needed to believe we could be that to one another again. I wanted to feel that I had the right…'

Her smile shifted her features, taking his breath away completely.

'It sounds a little like *you* were the one who doubted we'd find our way here.'

He put an arm around her waist, his fingers feathering

over her hip. 'Not for a second.' His voice was gravelly. 'I could never accept a world without you in it.'

'Even if that meant blackmailing me?' she teased, finding it almost impossible to credit the start of their marriage with the state of it now.

'Even then.' He dropped a kiss against her hair. 'Will you ever forgive me for that?'

'Forgive you? Hmm…' She pretended to think, her eyes full of love and amusement. 'I can think of one way you could make it up to me.'

He smiled softly. 'Your wish is my command. Although in this case I think it is my wish also.'

The stars shone overhead and the rose garden was bathed with magical milky moonlight. Nikos Kyriazis kissed his wife, carrying her into their now quiet home.

And it *was* a home. Not simply a house, as it had been for so long.

Now it was a collection of walls that contained their family's life, that was filled with pictures and love and the kind of warmth he had only ever dreamed possible. It was a home he shared with Marnie and Lulu, just as he shared his heart and his being with them.

A man who had never known love was now overflowing with it, and always would be.

* * * * *

LET'S TALK

Romance

For exclusive extracts, competitions
and special offers, find us online:

MILLS & BOON

MODERN

Power and Passion

Prepare to be swept off your feet by sophisticated, sexy and seductive heroes, in some of the world's most glamourous and romantic locations, where power and passion collide.